First Published Worldwide 2024
Copyright © Luke Smitherd 2024

All rights reserved. No part of this publication may be reproduced, stored in a retrieval system or transmitted, in any form or by any means, without the prior written permission of the author, nor be otherwise circulated in any form of binding or cover other than that in which it is published and without a similar condition being imposed on the purchaser.

All characters in this publication are purely fictitious, and any resemblance to real people, living or dead, is purely coincidental.

Cover image by Mike Godwin

Other Books by Luke Smitherd:

Full-Length Novels:

The Physics of the Dead
The Stone Man: The Stone Man, Book One
The Empty Men: The Stone Man, Book Two
The Stone Giant: The Stone Man, Book Three
March of the Stone Men: The Stone Man, Book Four
In The Darkness
A Head Full of Knives
Weird. Dark.
How To Be a Vigilante: A Diary
Kill Someone
You See The Monster
COMING OCTOBER 2025: *No Days Off*

Novellas:

The Man on Table Ten
Hold On Until Your Fingers Break
My Name Is Mister Grief
He Waits
Do Anything
The Man with All the Answers

For an up to date list of Luke Smitherd's other books, YouTube clips, his podcast, and to sign up for the Spam-Free Book Release Mailing List, visit
www.lukesmitherd.com

Dedication:
For Erika

At some point, when you create yourself to make it, you're going to have to either let that creation go and take a chance on being loved or hated for who you really are. Or you're gonna have to kill who you really are and fall into your grave grasping onto a character that you never were.

—Jim Carrey

"Don't get me wrong; who you are inside is everything. The guy who built a house for his family from scratch did it because of who he was inside. Every bad thing you've ever done has started with a bad impulse, some thought ricocheting around inside your skull until you had to act on it. And every good thing you've done is the same—'who you are inside' is the metaphorical dirt from which your fruit grows. But here's what everyone needs to know, and what many can't accept: 'You' are nothing but the fruit. Nobody cares about your dirt. 'Who you are inside' is meaningless aside from what it produces for other people."

—David Wong

"Nothing worth having comes without some sort of fight. Got to kick at the darkness until it bleeds daylight."

—Bruce Cockburn

Reviewer Acknowledgements:

At the time of writing, the following people wrote a nice Amazon or Audible review of **The Stone Giant**. Thank you very, very much. I'm only using the names you put on your reviews, as these will be ones you're happy to have associated with my work (I hope). In no order they are:

Simon Haine, Lauren Bradley, C. Murphy, Stuart Mitchell, Katie Lucas, Alcoblog, Chunderjack, Joanne McCarthy, R. G, CrystalCatz, Kate, Chris Wells, Reader, Mark B, Mr R A Samson, Steve Blencowe, Angie Hackett, Dave T, Book Thief, Katy Costello, Bo, Mr. R. K. Sharp, Kate L., Wayne, Amazon Customer, Robin S, Peter T., Sharon McLachlan, Brian J. Poole, Kenwynman, Eduardo, Phil Eldredge, PR Exeter, Stu, Bex, Gill K, Kia, Rob Pomroy, Phillip Kirton, Lawrence A, Andy, Ang Wallis, Nix, Fayre, Janb, Joolz, Becky, Lauren Pollock, Karsten Thuen, T. H. Flowers, Mag Arnold Pritz, Bsm, Julie Blaskie, Jennit, Kevin The Wonder Horse, Kelly Rickard, 9wt, Lauren Wells, Katrina, Don, Edward B, L. Bailey Humphries, William Baur, George Taylor, Bernie, J O'Quin, JC, Todd Riedel, ABitterScreenWriter, Bnbboy, AI, Bobby, Adam De Jesus, YC, BigOrangeDave, Weez, Scott, Bluelesley, J. Molineaux, Julja, JennyB, SJG< Apocalypto, Mat F, M. Rawson, JoTowns, Kemo, Rachel, Swanbrod, Large Crane, Samantha Liggins, Lmiller, Rott1, Vonbonbon, EmmaJane, Modama, Stephen, Mrs. Snaylor, Ms M Rees, Agentwindowmearl, Ryan Pascall, Steve, Phil A., Anne, Lewis, Neil, R. John, Mike D, David Sharp, Robert Jenkinson, Katof9tails, Ged Byrne, Toni, Nick Gierus, David Close, AJR, D, Johnny, Max, Andrew R. Culbertson, Charles Washington, Jas P, Derrick, James, Mary Beth Jost, Beth Swope, Tina Hansen, LoriA, KendallRN, Eric Comalander, G. Parlee, Chris, Charmaine Drinnon, Dalton, Alydf7, Cynthia, Patrick Leigh, and Tanya M. Corder.

If you asked for a Smithereen title, check out the list after the afterword to see yours!

The Stone Man: Book Four

March of the Stone Men

By Luke Smitherd

The Stone Man Recap

✷✷✷

Andy Pointer, a disillusioned reporter, witnesses the sudden appearance of a colossal **Stone Man** in Coventry City Centre. As it wreaks havoc, anyone who touches it collapses, uttering a strange stream of letters. Andy, drawn by the Stone Man's path of destruction, tracks it across the city but loses it when he faints on a bridge. His apartment is destroyed in the chaos.

Andy spends the night with an old friend, experiencing a seizure and a vision of a blonde-haired man. He realises his connection to the Stone Man might be stronger due to his proximity at its arrival. The next day, using a map, Andy discovers the Stone Man is heading to Sheffield and decides to follow it, using a motorbike. Along the way, he meets **Paul Winter**, a man who shares similar visions and insights. They join forces and, with Paul's help, trace the Stone Man to the home of a man named **Patrick Marshall**.

Patrick, overwhelmed with dread, attacks them but is subdued. They plan to use him to end the destruction, but his condition worsens. The military, led by **Brigadier Straub**, agrees to let Andy and Paul stay involved. As the Stone Man arrives, Andy realises that the letters babbled by the victims are a genetic code. The Stone Man harvests part of Patrick's spine and vanishes.

Andy is then groomed to be the public face of the government's version of events, while Paul returns to a troubled personal life, haunted by Patrick's gruesome death. Andy revels in his newfound fame and wealth, but his success feels increasingly hollow. His hedonistic lifestyle contrasts sharply with Paul's deteriorating mental state. Despite their continued communication, the two men drift apart as Andy's fame grows and Paul's life collapses.

When the Stone Man reappears in the UK, Andy is summoned back. He is reunited with Paul, who is now traumatised but determined to help. They work together to identify the Stone Man's new Targets. This time, they face even more severe challenges, including two new Stone Men—known as Blue Stone Men—that have arrived alongside the original. As they attempt to locate and protect the new Targets, the military coordinates a frantic effort to minimise damage. They discover that if a Target dies before the Stone Man reaches them, the pursuing Stone Man will return to its point of origin, complicating their mission further.

Their search leads them to **Henry Williams**, an elderly former soldier. Henry faces his impending doom with remarkable bravery and composure, which deeply impacts Andy. However, their mission faces further setbacks as they are cut off from their Target by the Stone Men. They realise that one of the Blue Stone Men has vanished, and it becomes clear that the Target—**Theresa Pettifer**, a mother driven to madness—has already killed her child to spare it from a worse fate. This discovery confirms that if a Target dies, the Stone Man will retreat.

In the aftermath, Andy and Paul return to their homes. Andy buys a house in the now-deserted Coventry and isolates himself, drinking heavily and succumbing to paranoia.

He becomes increasingly convinced that he is a Target. As he desperately tries to connect with the Stone Man's signal, he comes to terms with his impending fate. He contacts Paul, who also decides to end his life. They exchange emotional goodbyes, both feeling a sense of guilt for their roles in the tragedy.

Andy records an audio diary, detailing his realisation that the Stone Men's arrivals are not invasions but a breeding programme, with each harvest creating more Stone Men. As Andy prepares to end his life, the news confirms his theory—seven Stone Men have arrived, each a result of previous harvests.

Paul drives out towards the Ladybower Reservoir in Sheffield and sits in a field, phone turned off. He can't bring himself to do the deed … and then an idea occurs to him. Hardly daring to hope, he calls Straub, and she tells him that her new team of Hunters nearly had him tracked down. She tells him of Andy's suicide; Paul's friend has leapt to his death from his hotel window, dying a hero. Paul lays out his plan and Straub considers it; she takes a moment to express her disappointment in Paul's cowardice.

The military arrive and hurriedly landscape the area overnight, erecting a large hangar. The next day Paul waits inside it, seated in the passenger seat of a Jeep. The Stone Man approaches and Paul's plan begins: **an endless game of cat and mouse**, constantly keeping him one step ahead of the Stone Man, giving the military time to study it.

Fast forward three years and Paul now spends his days inside a specially designed cabin on wheels, wondering if his plan might have been more of a curse than a salvation after all. He has discovered that the Stone Men haven't returned since his plan was in place; he wonders if this means he will spend the rest of his life in the cabin.

Paul stares out of the cabin's window, watching the Stone Man continuing its endless pursuit ...

The Empty Men Recap

***

Five years have passed since the Third Arrival.

During that time the British government has revealed its weapon—the **Chisel**—which ministers claim can destroy Stone Men. In a press announcement, it's admitted that a Stone Man had been held in captivity, but was destroyed on the first test fire of the device.

Maria Constance, a woman who suffered a miscarriage after the stress of both a close encounter with the original Stone Man during the First Arrival and a vision of Patrick Marshall (the Stone Man's first Target), returns to the UK after years in self-imposed European exile. After her traumatic experiences led to the collapse of her marriage, her growing terror of the Stone Men returning meant she could no longer stay in the UK. Now she's back for her mother's funeral. The timing couldn't be worse: Maria is on a beach on the south coast just in time to witness the beginning of the *Fourth* Arrival. Ghostly, intangible figures begin to appear all around the country, and the media dubs them **The Empty Men**.

Maria's attempts to flee the country prove fruitless as planes departing the UK crash for unknown reasons, and passengers on cross-channel ferries to Europe jump inexplicably over the vessels' sides. Maria is stranded. She visits her former sister-in-law, **Ruth**, who confesses that she also had visions during the first three Arrivals. When the Empty Men reach Ruth's home, Maria watches helplessly as one of them kills Ruth. The Empty Man then turns towards Maria, who discovers that, under great stress, she can somehow mentally hide herself from its lethal influence.

Meanwhile **Eric Hatton**, Stone conspiracy theorist and brother of **Theresa Pettifer** (one of the victims of the Stone Men during the first three Arrivals, along with her infant son **Aaron Pettifer**), is drawn to another Stone Sensitive person in the ruins of Coventry: an old homeless man called **Harry Regis**. The pair observe the appearance of an enormous Stone-like structure that they nickname **The Prism**. Many of Coventry's remaining inhabitants fall into a zombie-like trance, walking towards the Prism and becoming aggressive if approached. Soldiers from the now partially flattened **Ground Zero** building attempt to move them on; the scene becomes violent, and Eric takes a graze from a bullet in the crossfire. Eric and Harry dub these people the **Shufflers**, and can find no indication of why they're behaving this way. A transparent wall of energy emanates from the Prism and disappears over the horizon, killing everyone in its path . . . except Eric, Harry and the Shufflers. The energy fills the air above them, seeming to surround the city.

The Shufflers prevent Eric from getting into the remains of the Ground Zero building for answers, so the pair depart for Harry's nearby stash of supplies and first aid. While Harry stitches Eric's wounded shoulder, Eric confesses he has recordings of interviews from a facility at the **Ladybower Reservoir** in Sheffield. The voice on the recordings is a civilian volunteer named **Linda Wyken**, a woman who appears to have low-level **Stone Sensitivity**, who talks about her experiences of Paul Winter. Paul has been assisting the military with their experiments, acting as a powerful kind of Stone battery who can boost the abilities of Stone Sensitives. She also talks about a woman called **Sophie Warrender**, a very high-level Stone Sensitive. Eric and Harry sleep, but are woken by a vision of a bright light. They follow their Stone instincts until they find the source: an impenetrable swirling, golden bubble in a squatter's apartment overlooking Ground Zero. Trapped inside it is a young woman, **Jenny Drewett**. Along the way they meet **John Bates**, a man who claims to have gone out to where the wall of energy—the **Barrier**—ends, just outside of the city, forming a now-impassable wall. John carelessly touches Jenny's bubble and is immediately vaporised. Eric realises that he can influence the bubble and tries to free Jenny. With great effort, he wills a small hole in it but can do no more than that. The hole snaps shut, perfectly slicing off Eric's hand and cauterising his wrist. Eric experiences no pain but passes out in shock.

Maria, fleeing a solid wall of Empty Men, is rescued by a woman on a motorcycle, and the pair escape. The woman reveals herself to be **Linda Wyken**, she of Eric's stolen tape recordings, and tells Maria she is heading for **Project Orobouros** at the Ladybower Reservoir. She believes that if anyone can help, they will be there. She also tells Maria that the Chisel is a lie, knowledge she gained from her time at the project; the reason the Stone Man is no longer in the possession of the government is because Paul Winter—the Stone Man's last Target, used as bait for his pursuer for the last five years—

seemingly died, something that sends the Stone Men back to their point of origin.

From Jenny's apartment, Eric and Harry watch as the Prism seems to summon the Shufflers into it, devouring them in the process as it absorbs them into itself. The path now clear, Eric and Harry enter what's left of the Ground Zero building, where Eric retrieves a box full of papers marked with names. It appears to be some kind of census, listing everyone in the UK under five categories: **CROW, TIN, LION, GALE,** and **DIGGS**. They also come across two dead, multi-limbed creatures. Before they can investigate further, they are drawn outside by the sudden appearance of hundreds of Empty Men at Ground Zero. An Empty Man attacks Harry.

At Project Orobouros, Maria meets Paul Winter, who is very much alive and says he wants to take Maria's hand so that he can 'boost' her. She is brought to a room full of what the people at the project call **the Sleepers**. These people are all the GALE level Stone Sensitives that the government have on their books, all gathered together and put into comas the moment the latest Arrival began. All of them are dead, confirmed to have been recently killed by the Empty Men. The head scientist at the Project, **Doctor Holbrooks**, believes Maria's abilities could be useful in turning the tide against the Empty Men. Paul begins the boost, and Maria has an ecstatic experience, receiving a vision of the entire country and a sense of her own raw power. The process is interrupted, however, incomplete, and now the Empty Men—seemingly drawn to the energy generated by Paul and Maria's interaction—have arrived at Project Orobouros. Fleeing for a helicopter, along with Project soldiers **Binley**, **Fletchamstead** and **Edgwick**, as well as an unnamed man that Paul seems to know, they are surrounded by Empty Men. In a Hail Mary move, Paul tries to boost Maria again and this time the process completes. Not only does she effortlessly hide the group, she is also drawn to an energy signal from Coventry.

Eric hears Maria's voice in his head and begs her to save Harry. She does so, remotely hiding Harry from the influence of the Empty Man engulfing him, and then tells Eric to head to the military's fallback position, a base on the **Isle of Skye**. Her signal fades in Eric's mind; Maria has collapsed, unconscious.

At Project Orobouros, Maria receives medical attention as Paul and the unnamed man take in the scene; the unnamed man is revealed to be Andy Pointer, somehow still alive.

In Coventry, Eric watches as Empty Men from around the country pour into the walls of the Prism, sinking into its surface much like the Shufflers before them. The Prism begins to shake, crumbling the remains of the Ground

Zero building and flattening everything within. It then begins to send out a protrusion, one that deposits a pale, semi-transparent humanoid figure into the former Millennium Place.

It is a newborn Stone Man. Armed only with a pistol and a sledgehammer, Eric and Harry approach it . . .

The Stone Giant Recap

***

Eric and Harry launch an assault on the Pale Stone Man but their efforts are futile. Desperate for help, Eric attempts to reach out to Maria telepathically but receives no response. The Pale Stone Man then enters the St. Joseph building and steps through Jenny's protective bubble, consuming her and turning blood red before beginning to grow into the **Stone Giant.** It vanishes, reappearing by the Prism, a process that took months during previous Arrivals, signalling a significant change. Eric and Harry decide to head to the Isle of Skye in Jenny's car, bringing along the box of documents from Ground Zero. Before they can leave, the Horns sound from the Prism, heralding the re-emergence of the **original six Blue Stone Men.**

Eric and Harry reach the Barrier around Coventry, encountering a crowd and a military blockade on the opposite side. Harry's nausea worsens, and Eric grows anxious about the **Quarry Response**, a phenomenon linked to the Stone Men. Eric demands to speak to Brigadier Straub after failing to open the Barrier. Straub, acknowledging the possible onset of the Quarry Response in Harry, urges Eric to kill his friend, explaining the horrifying truth of the Stone Men's process of harvesting their victims to create more Stone Men. Straub **lies**, telling Eric that his sister Theresa was executed by the military (concealing the fact that she was taken to her pursuing Stone Man by the government to end its path of destruction as soon as possible). Eric uses the Barrier to communicate with Maria, who reveals that the Caeterus are searching and that she had to choose between hiding Eric or Harry, ultimately choosing to protect Eric. As Eric warns the crowd, the Barrier rockets away, killing everyone instantly, leaving Eric to return to Harry's bubble where he finds his friend lucid.

In flashback we see Straub offer Andy the choice to be put into a **coma** as an experiment to fool the Stone Men into thinking he had died. It works, and after Andy is revived, he spends several years at Project Orobouros working with Stone Sensitive volunteers in secret, as the government is unsure what the **Caeterus**—the name the government gives to the force behind the Stone Men—know through Paul. Straub and Dr. Holbrooks introduce **Carl Baker** to Andy, a powerful Stone Sensitive. Andy and Carl work together to try to communicate with the Stone Man, but Carl dies, causing a breach in their circuit and revealing Andy's survival to Paul, prompting an emotional reunion.

In the present day, Holbrooks is frantic and paranoid as he treats Maria in the helicopter on the way to the Isle of Skye, suspecting Paul and Andy of ulterior motives. Tensions rise as Holbrooks pulls a gun to stop the others from waking Maria, fearing the Caeterus' influence. Chaos erupts when Linda is shot, and as the helicopter is hit by the expanding Barrier, it crashes from low altitude into the loch below.

In flashback to a year prior, Andy and Paul discuss the challenges they face, including Carl Baker's autopsy results. When Straub and Holbrooks bring Sophie Warrender, a volunteer even more powerful than Carl Baker. Andy feels an immediate connection with Sophie during a joint mental session with the Stone Man. They explore each other's memories, unable to help themselves, as they discover hidden depths within the Stone Man. Their connection is deep but fraught with tension, as Sophie is angry at Andy's distraction from their mission.

Andy proposes getting physically closer to the Stone Man to potentially access its Core, saying they need to be out on the hangar floor. Despite the risk to his life, Paul agrees to participate. As they get physically closer, Andy dives deeper into the Stone Man, finding a weak spot and causing internal collapse. The effort leaves Paul and Sophie severely weakened, but Andy manages to shut down the Stone Man's internal commands, halting its progress as it advances on Paul's stricken cabin. **They've stopped the Stone Man.**

In the present day, Eric's attempts to break Harry out of his bubble fail. The Blue Stone Man arrives and begins to Harvest Harry, Harry's bubble opening in the process. Eric shoots a grieving Harry to end his suffering but this does not stop the Blue from completing its grisly task. Eric continues his journey, determined to keep his promise to Harry and reach the Isle of Skye. He hears the threads of the Caeterus more clearly as he drives, sensing something important nearby. He stops at a farmhouse, discovering **Esther** and her son **Aiden,** who is trapped inside a bubble. Eric resolves to help them, adding new companions to his journey.

Elsewhere, we meet **Colin Renwick**, a helicopter pilot with a phobia of blood who experiences a nightmare scenario when the Barrier bursts through his hotel. Surviving the chaos, he resolves to reach his helicopter and get to his children.

One year earlier, Andy and Sophie, now monitored by ankle tags, contemplate the nature of the Stone Man as they watch its stationary form being moved. Their discussion is interrupted by the arrival of **the Crawlers**, the living versions of the creatures Eric will later encounter, dead, at Ground Zero. Their Arrival has been triggered by the Stone Man's distress signal. Amid the ensuing chaos, Andy seizes an opportunity to save Paul and escape the Project, but they are intercepted by Straub, who reveals the **Permutatio Protocol**: to fly the dormant Stone Man to the most isolated spot on earth. Andy's attempt to leave with Sophie ends in tragedy: as the dormant Stone Man is flown away from Paul, its weakened connection to Paul severs, causing a **Detonation.** The blast hits a mentally injured Sophie and renders her comatose. Andy is devastated but is again refused permission to leave the Project and to take Sophie with him. Andy remains, spending every waking minute by Sophie's bedside.

Andy awakens on the shores of Loch Alshe, having been dragged there by Edgwick. Linda is near death, and the group is devastated. As Andy grapples with his grief, he flashes back to the day Sophie died.

In the flashback, we see the Empty Men wreaking havoc at the Project, slaughtering the Sleepers who had been placed in comas. The coma plan, though unsuccessful, was to hide the Sleepers from the Empty Men in the same way Andy's coma had protected him.

Andy is suffocated in Sophie's room by an Empty Man, but just as he is about to succumb, Sophie's consciousness awakens. With her last breath, she uses her Watchmaker abilities to hide Andy and save him, dying in the process.

In the present, Andy and the team try to remotely enter a Blue Stone Man. They cannot, and their subsequent attempt to access the red Stone Giant ends painfully.

At the farmhouse Eric uses Aiden's bubble to access **Stone Space,** spotting thousands of Targets around the country. He manages to communicate with the pilot Colin. Eric convinces Colin to pick him up in his helicopter, and Eric and Aiden attempt to contact Maria, but Eric is spotted in Stone Space by the Stone powers that be. He has the Quarry Response and begins to be surrounded by a grimy silver bubble. Esther uses Aiden's bubble to communicate with Maria, and together they save Eric's life.

On the road to Skye, Paul, Andy, and Maria reach the **Skye Bridge** between the mainland and the Isle itself. To their great dismay they find their path is blocked by the Barrier, but Straub, standing on the other side of the Barrier, tells them that Eric is on his way and may be able to open it once boosted by Paul. Colin drops Eric off, and he finally meets Maria and the others. Straub then reveals the truth to him, and the **plan**: the Detonation back at the Project a year ago caused the helicopter transporting the Stone Man to crash on the Isle of Skye. It has lain dormant ever since, bleeding energy. The Arrival of the Empty Men caused the government to trigger their emergency protocol, namely filling the impact crater left by the Stone Man with lead.

The Empty Men, Straub explains, have purged all the other GALE people on the list —the ones who could potentially access the inner systems of a Stone Man—and only one remains: Andy. Straub plans to use Paul, Andy & Maria's abilities to drive the damaged and weakened Stone Man to Coventry, smash the Prism, and destroy the Barrier by doing so.

But first, they have to wake the Stone Man.

Foreword

***

This novel concludes the story arc that began with The Empty Men. There is no *To Be Continued* at the end of this book.

Prologue

***

Nathan hadn't brought a weapon with him.

He'd thought about doing so—he hadn't got this far without erring on the side of caution, and to a fault—but actual weaponry seemed like overkill here. He just wanted to talk.

Yeah right, he thought. *Just like that, comme ci comme ca, you're easy either way, answers or no? I don't think so, buddy.* Having knocked, Nathan waited, listening for sounds of movement from the other side of the door. He silently sent up a prayer that the resident was home. He could always come back tomorrow—he would keep coming back until they were here—but it had been a long, long road to get this far. He re-rehearsed his opener in his head:

Hi. I'm thinking about buying number six and wanted to introduce myself. I'm Nathan—

No. Richard. You're going with *Richard.*

I'm Richard. Your neighbours said we should meet, us both being ex-pats.

Technically, he was too young to fit the current cultural understanding of a true British ex-pat—the phrase now meant something radically different—but he didn't look it. His Dad always joked they should change their last name to *Rough.* For use as an 'in' though, the term should work. The wind blew slightly, whispering of the colder days that would soon be coming. Nathan shivered. He glanced nervously up and down the quiet country lane that led along the small, well-spaced row of thatched-roof cottages. These buildings alone constituted about ten percent of the houses in the tiny village. Behind him, a vast expanse of fields—their soil recently picked bare by the final harvest of the year—rolled towards the horizon the view broken up by spartan fences and threadbare hedges. Agriculture was one of the main industries in the Pas de Calais and soon this village, sleepy even for the region, would be comatose.

"Hold on," a woman's voice called from inside the house.

English.

Easy, Nathan told himself.

"Ugh, I can't find my keys," the woman called. "Do you want to come round the back? Just open the gate."

"Okay," Nathan called, hurrying around to the side of the picturesque building and opening the high gate that shrieked quietly on its rusted metal hinges. A narrow passageway lay before him, leading to the rear yard that seemed to extend for quite some way behind the property. Nathan could see a line of washing blowing with the wind, kicking up a chorus line of tracksuit bottoms, blouses, and towels as the weather continued to turn. Not far from here, Nathan knew, the waves in the English Channel would be lifting too; the sky was darkening quickly, and a storm was coming in.

There was no side entrance to the building, so Nathan continued around to the back of the cottage. A small, paved area sat behind the house, a work bench sitting in its centre. A half-carved log lay in the bench's clamp, a frozen shape beginning to emerge from its wood. It looked like a table or mantlepiece ornament, perhaps; a rough-hewn human outline, a body pushing against some sort of large ball. In this particular piece only a third of the boulder was presented, slowly tapering out into fragments like a half-reconstructed Death Star. It took Nathan a moment to identify the small sculpture's subject, those endless public schooldays finally making themselves useful: Sisyphus, that tragic victim of the gods. Here he was presented in a frozen moment of unbearable, eternal weariness as he stood, spent, his chest pressed against what was supposed to be his boulder; the endless burden that he must push uselessly uphill only to have it roll back to the bottom of the gradient each time.

"It's a work in progress," the woman's voice said behind Nathan, startling him. He spun round, surprised by the voice; he'd been caught momentarily by the look on Sisyphus' unfinished face. He noticed that the back door was still closed. She'd come around from the front of the house then, following him along the alleyway, standing now in its entrance. "How can I help you?" the woman said. She was wearing a handkerchief on her head, her grey hair tied back underneath it. Her body was covered in overalls. Unlike Nathan, she looked older than her years—Nathan knew her actual age, of course—but he supposed that was to be expected. Her lined face was smiling.

For a moment, Nathan couldn't speak.

She was the absolute last thing he'd expected and now he couldn't believe what he was seeing. He was too stunned to think, to cover—

Keep it fucking together, NOW, he told himself. *You had a cover story, use it—*

"Hi," Nathan said, breaking into a smile and stepping forward, managing to keep the amazed shake out of his voice. "I'm considering buying number six a few doors down, I'm Richard." The set of lies sounded genuine, his voice holding steady. He could riff for a moment while he got himself back together. "They told me another Brit was living here, so obviously I had to come and say hello." The woman looked surprised as she shook Nathan's offered hand.

"Pascal and Edith are selling?" she asked.

"Thinking about it," Nathan said, forcing a shrug. "It's not even officially on the market yet, but we have a mutual friend, and I was thinking of moving out of Calais and into the countryside, so …" He shrugged again. Too much shrugging, too antsy. *Calm the fuck down.* "Thought I'd have a look, and I fancied the drive."

"Sneaky sods," the woman muttered good-naturedly. "They kept that secret. Did you like—wait, sorry." She scowled at herself. "I'm Claire. Most rude of me. Not used to having company. Would you like to come in for some tea? Kettle's already boiling, in fact."

"That's very kind, yes I would," Nathan replied, noting the name as he smiled down at her; she wasn't very tall, and Nathan was. The woman turned, heading towards the back door, walking with a barely detectable limp. Nathan followed, keeping his cool as best he could. The lead he'd followed here had given him little more than an address, but to find *this*—

"I think it's going to throw it down in a minute," she said. "Take a seat in the living room, I'll take the washing in."

"Oh, I'll help you—"

"Young man," she said, "I wouldn't put you through the distress of handling an ageing stranger's unmentionables." The woman opened the cottage's rear door and stepped back, gesturing into the dark house beyond. "Through the kitchen, living room is your first door on the left. Do you take sugar?"

"Oh, no, thank you," he said, heading inside. Immediately inside the doorway was a small utility room that smelled of laundry detergent. A tiny speaker played away to itself from a shelf in the corner. Nathan couldn't remember the song's name; even for a relatively young man his long-term memory seemed worse every year. He headed into a small lounge that was surprisingly modern compared to the building's exterior. New-looking carpet, sophisticated lighting, an expensive-looking blood-red sofa and armchair with a shockingly wide flatscreen TV adorning the right-hand wall. Nathan sat in the armchair. Despite its remarkable comfort, the tension in his body didn't dissipate.

He nearly didn't come here, nearly missed the fucking *motherlode*—

Just. Keep. It. Together. You'll figure out—

After a moment he heard her boots on the entrance tiles followed by the sound of the back door closing ... and being locked. Her footsteps moved down the hallway. Shortly after that Nathan heard kitchen cupboards opening and closed, followed by the delicate clink of porcelain.

"I'll be sorry to see Pascal and Edith go, Richard," she called. "I always liked them, even if we weren't close. Philip, my late husband, used to play boule with Pascal. He was better friends with them than me."

"Yes," Nathan called back, standing—his nervous energy forced it—and moving to look at the pictures on the mantelpiece. All three of them were of a male and female couple, one of whom was clearly a younger version of his current host. In each image, both subjects held wine or beer glasses, seated at different tables laden with different foods in different places. "They, uh, they mentioned Philip, spoke very well of him."

"I'm not surprised," she called. "Good people, good people."

There was silence, or at least no sound that he could hear over the low-level music—who *was* that singer, he knew that old song—and then the footsteps were heading back down the hallway. Nathan darted back to the armchair, sitting down and crossing his legs. "Apologies for the music choice," her quickly approaching voice said from outside the room. "It's a playlist they update each week, some I like, some I don't. But listen, you're going to see something in a moment that will startle you. Please don't worry, yes? It's just a precaution, I promise."

" ... what?"

Nathan froze, but already she was entering the room. She had taken off her headscarf. The hair was still tied back, long and almost universally grey, but that wasn't the factor that seized his gaze.

The woman held a snub-nosed pistol in her right hand.

"I've never particularly been a fan of Ed Sheeran," she said.

Her face was blank. Nathan's turned white.

"Wait—"

"Relax," the woman added quickly, holding up her free hand. "Please. Like I said: it's a precaution."

Nathan remained frozen. She sounded relaxed. Surely she wouldn't fire—

"I'm pretty certain that I know who you are," she said, "and why you're here. But you look a lot different from your pictures, so I need to check first."

Different from his pictures? How did she know that he'd— "You lost the beard, and I assume you're wearing contacts. Smart, but not smart enough to avoid the obvious giveaways. There is no Pascal and Edith, and I certainly never discussed my husband with any of my other neighbours. He died before I came here, but UK birth and death records were an utter mess after you-know-what happened. You wouldn't know for sure when he passed, or if it was due to the … well." She hefted the gun, showing it to him. "All the same, I've never believed in taking unnecessary risks. You're *Nathan*, yes?"

Nathan's pulse raced in his ears. He hadn't expected this in his worst imaginings of what might happen if something went wrong. His mouth twitched uselessly, flapping open and closed as he tried to form words. An excuse, a lie—

There was no point.

"I'm sorry," he blurted. "I'm sorry I lied, I didn't know what I'd find here so I'd planned to play it safe, I didn't expect to find *you*—"

"It's alright," she said. "ID first, please. your wallet over here. Almost certainly unnecessary, but I do things by the book."

Nathan fished his wallet free and tossed it to the woman's feet, sweat beginning to soak the back of his neck. She bent, keeping one eye on him all the while.

"How do you—" he began, and then it hit him. His eyes widened. The woman smiled as she picked up the wallet, seeing the realisation land.

"There it is," she said.

"*You're* Diggle132," he said. "*You* gave me the lead. You were on the forum—"

The woman nodded as she thumbed Nathan's driver's licence up and out of its leather slot.

"Nathan Matterface," she read, "currently of Madrid. I appreciate the effort with your travel. You've come quite a way to see me."

"Y-yes."

"And you know who I am."

"You-you're former Brigadier Laura Straub," Nathan said, his voice audibly shaking. "You were head of a top-secret government operation known as *Project Orobouros* and a key operative in the formation and execution of protocols *Kindness* and *Goodnight*. Wife to—sorry, widow to—"

"Yes, that's enough," Straub said quickly, tossing the wallet back to him. "Very well." She lowered the weapon. Nathan didn't relax. "I'm very sorry about the gun, especially as I technically invited you here. Protocol, yes, but I know how frightening they are to people who aren't used to them. I'm sure you understand the necessity, though; that there are people who would disagree—in the strongest possible terms—with the decisions I've made in my career. People who lost a lot because of those decisions. I've always anticipated that one of them might show up with ill intent. Yes?"

"Y-yes. I'm not one of—"

"Mm." She sat in the chair opposite, woman and furniture both lightly groaning. "It isn't a huge worry; I think a treason charge is a more likely issue in my future than my being assassinated. I knew what I was doing when I signed the NDAs. My living here is one of those rare cases where that which is prudent dovetails nicely with what I bloody well *want:* to be left alone."

The only sound in the room was the music quietly trilling away.

"What did you think you'd find here, Nathan?"

Nathan moistened his lips, already bone-dry from panic.

"You know what you said."

"I never said. I *hinted.* And you listened."

"How could I not?"

Diggle132 had known a lot about Nathan. Their emails had been so detailed about Nathan's life—things that no-one could have known without somehow having full access to Nathan's digital existence—that Nathan had to believe he was dealing with someone with access to even more. Someone with contacts. *Real* contacts.

"So, do you really have … " Nathan trailed off. He felt stupid asking. "… a recording, then?"

Straub's face stayed blank.

"I think I contacted the right person, Nathan," she said. "I've followed your career very closely in the last few years. You care. You're honest. The pieces you've written for *thevisitors.com* were thorough, and—most importantly, to me—non-sensational. Un-corrupted. I needed—I *need*—a rational voice that I could contact through non-conventional means, and that I could trust. A voice respected just enough to be heard by the upper echelons. I don't have connections to the right people in the right media." She shrugged. "Tell me your story, please. Face to face, in your actual voice. It's been a long time since I spoke to a reporter with an honest soul." She snorted bitterly. "Even if they didn't know that about themselves."

Her face was impossible to read. *Just tell her,* Nathan thought.

"... me—my parents and I," he said. "We survived the ... Barrier spreading." He couldn't bring himself to use the now-ubiquitous term for it: the *New Holocaust*.

"So, they were Stone Sensitive?"

"No," Nathan said. "We just weren't in the country when it happened. We were on a family holiday. Not to Spain, that's just where I live now." He looked at his hands, feeling slightly unreal. He was saying this to *Laura Straub*, in *her house*. "We moved to the continent. We'd had a very, very close-knit extended family in the UK. Now all of them were gone. My parents... they never got over it. My Dad couldn't handle it and, he, uh..."

Nathan trailed off, holding up a finger, wincing.

"I'm sorry to hear that."

"Mum was lost without him," Nathan said. "She started drinking again—she'd kicked it before—and never stopped. After that ...." He shrugged, wiping his eyes quickly. *Get it together,* he tried to tell himself. *Shift things back to her.* "We were from Sheffield, originally," Nathan said, thinking quickly as he watched Straub's face. She had to know where he was going with this. "You ... you knew a man from Sheffield, didn't you?"

Straub's eyes narrowed, but the smile crept back onto her face a little.

"Why *yes*," she said, sarcastically. "You say the name."

"Paul Winter."

"Very good," she said, looking mildly impressed. "Pointer, I would have expected. Winter would be considerably harder to know about."

"How about Maria Constance?"

Straub's face briefly fell... but only for a moment.

"That ... that I didn't expect at all," she said. "You really do know the inside details, then. That's one of the other reasons I picked you. You remind me a lot of—"

"Eric Hatton?"

This time Straub's poker face held.

"The last few communication transcripts," Nathan continued, becoming excited now. "Taken from shortly before the anomaly expanded nationwide—as intermittent and garbled as those communications were—have you being summoned to Coventry to talk to one Eric Hatton. He must have been important to get you to drop everything in the middle of an Arrival? Comms were so badly affected by the anomaly that not a lot of other info got through. But I can't find him on the database you compiled either, so I've no idea what bracket he was in. Who was he?" Straub didn't reply. Nathan sat up a little straighter. "When you flew to the Isle of Skye, you managed to get Maria Constance's name through to your people there to try and find out anything they could. Who was *she*? She wasn't on the handful of Project Orobouros materials I've seen."

Again, Straub's face didn't even twitch.

"I just want to *know*," Nathan said, suddenly earnest, adding: "They took everything."

"There's another reason I picked you," Straub said. Nathan suddenly wanted to scream *why are you picking anyone at all, Brigadier? Why now? Why after all these years? What* else *do you know?*

"I'm guessing," he said, trying not to roll his eyes in frustration, "it's that I've been through the Barnstaple Sequence? Here." He produced his phone, found the PDF image, and expanded it onscreen until the bottom paragraph of the official letter was clear: *We consider Mr Matterface secure to the best of all possible telling.*

The Barnstaple Sequence was totally voluntary. It had been approved and offered by Saoirse—the French-American-Irish coalition—for anyone that wanted it. The international waiting list had been immediate and immense. Even now it took six months to a year to actually be seen and then complete the sequence of testing, followed by six-weeks-of-once-a-week psychological assessments. "It was almost certainly pointless as my parents weren't Stone Sensitive," Nathan said, "but I wanted it fully confirmed: I'm definitely not Stone Sensitive either, all official. You can tell me anything and it'll be kept *Kayfabe.*"

He raised his eyebrows here, letting Straub know he knew. *Kayfabe*, the term the Saoirse spooks used for the overriding theory of knowledge containment: that the Caeterus might know what Stone Sensitives know. Stone Sensitives might be connected to the Caeterus in ways we don't understand. Best to keep it need-to-know. Keep it *Kayfabe.*

"Very well," Straub said, before seeming to hesitate. "Nathan ... I feel duty-bound to add: "The truth won't give you closure, you know. Answers, maybe. But trust me. Closure is very, very hard to come by with anything regarding... *them,* as you say."

Nathan didn't have a clear response to that, the same way he'd never had a response to his wife every time she'd said the same thing, right up until she left him. He needed to know, all the same. He'd needed to know for *years.*

"I understand," he said eventually. "Everyone knows Andrew Pointer's name, of course, from the First Arrivals," he said. "But Paul Winter. Eric

Hatton. Maria Constance. Toby *Edgwick*," Nathan added, putting extra emphasis on Edgwick's surname. He wanted Straub to know he knew this too. It felt childish, yet earned. He'd lost a lot to hold this information; he could allow himself to relish using it. "Their names are never mentioned by anyone. Operation Hail Mary was classified, even if the general outcome is known. Are those people all still alive?" Nathan said, beginning to rock gently back and forth, running his hands through his hair. "The, the Empty Men, they killed all the people on GALE somehow, the ones you collected to try and protect—"

"You've seen the List, then?"

"Yes. And I think you're not telling me the *main* reason why you want to go public now," he said. "People have heard the rumours about what Soairse are planning. The media are calling them conspiracy theories, but no-one buys that. You don't. And you don't want those theories to play out."

"Then tell me," Straub said, "why would going public change that?"

"Because maybe you think the uproar will stop those plans being carried out?" Nathan asked. "Or at least delay them?"

Nathan had already heard that Straub had a great poker face.

"What I *think*," Straub eventually said, "is that perhaps I should have done this sooner." She suddenly picked up the gun and left the room, that slight limp in her gait making her list to the left a little. Nathan didn't move, confused, listening as he heard rummaging sounds outside the room. A moment later Straub reappeared, a sad, soft smile on her face. Her right fist still held something small and black, but it was no longer the gun. The weapon's handle was sticking out of her pocket.

"Once upon a time," she said, "Eric Hatton would have given his right hand to hear the kind of thing you're about to hear. Although it ended up being his left, as it happens. I ended up gaining great respect for ..." She scowled. "Going bloody soft in my old age. That's annoying."

"How well did you know him?" Nathan asked. "All of them?"

"Constance and Hatton hardly at all. Edgwick rather well. Pointer and Winter, intimately."

"Were you friends?"

"I told Andy once that we weren't," she said. "I've always regretted that since. Here." She held out the object to him, and Nathan took it.

It was an MP3 player.

"That," Straub said, "is one of only two recordings of Andy Pointer's second and final journal."

She returned to the sofa, reached over its arm, and produced a set of headphones and a copy of Cosmo. Nathan's goggling eyes moved from the player to Straub and back. "Operation Hail Mary," she said, "in Andy Pointer's words, from start to finish."

Nathan's hand began to shake like he was holding a Dead Man's Switch.

"*Are you serious?*" he whispered. "How did you even *get* this?"

"I'll tell you afterwards," she said. "There's a lot there. You won't get through it all today."

"Oh," Nathan said. "You're ... letting me take it?"

Straub barked out a short, harsh laugh.

"Good *heavens*, no!" she said. "If you want to listen to it, you listen to it here. The windows and the door are all locked. You can get through as much as you can until this evening—I'll make us dinner—and then I'll take it off you before you stay the night. Tomorrow you can listen to it on the way to the ceremony. You can be my escort."

"You *are* serious."

"Yes."

She put the headphones on her head. Nathan continued to stare dumbly at the player. Now the moment was here, he could barely bring himself to press play. Why was he so nervous?

"Why the headphones?" he asked. Straub took them off, looking annoyed.

"What?" she said.

"The headphones—"

"Noise cancellers."

"... why?"

Straub's face darkened.

"I need to keep an eye on you, but I really don't like to listen to that," she said, nodding at the MP3 player. Nathan's thumb hovered over the play button, and yet, to his amazement, he found himself hesitating. Straub couldn't be right; closure was surely here. There would be *something*. That was all he needed, he was sure. To his surprise he saw that Straub was staring at the device in his hand. Her expression was grave, seeming to see something darker than the player's black surface. Then she shook her head. "I'd really get a move on, if I were you," she said. "Time's ticking. If there's one thing I've learned with *anything* Stone related, it's best to get things moving as quickly as possible." She smirked, her face grey in the murky pre-storm light that was bleeding in through the window. "Of course," Brigadier Straub said, "getting things moving is always the hardest part."

March of the Stone Men

Nathan pressed play.

*＊＊

Part One

WAKE THE STONE MAN

Chapter One

Andy at the End

***

Hi.

    … shit.

    Wait. I'm starting again.

***

Okay.

    … you know, really, for the sake of tradition, this should be recorded on an actual Dictaphone. Technology has moved on considerably in the years since the First Arrival—hell, a Dictaphone was probably old fashioned even then—and this phone has a ridiculous five hundred gigabytes of internal memory. They might be useless now for actual communication, but they can record. I'll do some tonight and tomorrow. Maybe the day after that. That should be enough. I want this to be told privately, not overheard by current company. This is personal, even if said current company was with me during the events I'm about to discuss.

    So: hello. I wonder who you are, if in fact anyone actually hears this recording. How did you find this? Is it secret? Does everyone know about it? Did you hear the last recording from way back when? Hello to you if you did. Perhaps you're some spook—if there are any left alive—listening to this one back-to-back with the other at some more settled point in the future? Things are certainly a *long* way from that right now. I only have time to get a little bit of it down on tape. Why bother, you might ask, knowing it might never be heard? Because it might be. Someone needs to make a record of this, as we're the only ones going through it.

    The final push into Coventry begins very soon.

Either way: nice to be talking to you again. One thing *I* can't believe—that I'm recording a potentially final message again. The last time I found myself recording my story this way, I was doomed for certain. This time, my—our—doom is only *extremely likely*.

Heh. That's progress, at least.

I don't know what the others are doing at this moment, other than processing what's just happened. I'm sitting away from them right now. In another time, this wouldn't be the most pleasant space to record; cars would be speeding past. It would be noisy. None of that now. Nice and quiet, meaning I have nothing to distract from the fact that—

...

Fuck. Okay. We just—

They—

... one of our group just died. That's what happened.

That's why I'm recording this *now*. In case any more of us die. More specifically, me. I might not get a chance after this—

Fuck's sake. Fuck's *sake*. I think I've changed so goddamn much, but then find I can't go two minutes without avoiding reality. One of my friends has just *died before my eyes* and I'm moving on already, how is that—

Because I have to get on with the job, that's why. That's what we did, all of us. Back when we'd reached the Isle of Skye—or at least the edge of the Barrier there—and our old, ever-delightful-and-charming friend Brigadier Laura Straub informed us that the entire United Kingdom—save for two thousand or so survivors out of nearly seventy million—was dead. We got on with things after that, didn't we?

One country down. Rest of the world surely next. Time to step up, right? No other choice.

Be honest, Andy.

We were able to get on with things without collapsing on the spot and staying there because none of us had anyone else to grieve for. Until now, at least.

... *Christ.*

...

Get it together. I'll start from when we reached the Barrier, I guess. Where we met up with Straub ... a couple of days ago? Hard to keep track when you haven't been sleeping—

... wait. This will take a *long* time. Maybe I should—

I'm still ... yeah. I have to go. I'll record this later. If I—yeah, later.

***

Okay. I just listened back to all that. A lot of time has passed since I recorded it.

This time I'm going to start and I'm going to try not to stop until most of it's told, because I don't ever want to—

Okay. The Isle of Skye. The project. I want to start with what Eric did.

He'd only turned up about thirty minutes earlier and I had no idea who the hell he was. The others I of *course* knew; Edgwick, our military man from around the Project. Maria, I knew more than I'd initially liked to, but being in a circuit—even for the little while we'd been in one together—will do that to you. Paul … well.

Eric knew who *I* was, but I guess that's not surprising (I was *really* fucking famous once). But I knew nothing of him.

After what he did, I realised—we all did—that Eric was someone special.

***

Chapter Two

Eric Feels the Noise, Silver and Black, and More Empty Promises

***

Eric had only just rocked up, apparently having managed to psychically hook up with some helicopter pilot that had carried him all the way to the edge of the country from the West Midlands (to that man, by the way: thank you. Even if he apparently tapped out of the fight after that to go look after his kids. I get that, but... end of the world and all that? You couldn't leave them with a fucking iPad and some microwave meals?)

Eric stood before the Barrier in a t-shirt and coat that seemed far too large for him—having picked them up from somewhere on the way here perhaps—squinting a little in the glare from Straub's floodlights as the very last of the day's light disappeared from the sky. In front of Eric—in front of all of us—lay the slowly turning and churning Barrier, touching down at our mainland end of the Skye bridge, it's murky, dim light difficult to watch for too long. About two feet beyond it stood Straub and her crew of scientists and grunts, her generator-powered floodlights set up on their side. Eric, like the rest of us, had just learned of the death of almost everyone in the United Kingdom. To say that we were all in some kind of quiet shock would be an understatement, but for once, the Brigadier looked it. Her husband, I knew, had just been killed by the Barrier, him not being on the Stone spectrum. Yet here she was, doing her duty, waiting patiently with her team.

Eric was either about to give slim hope to the human race, or to let us know that we were out of options.

Eric had just finished telling us a potted version of everything that had happened to him, at Straub's request. She'd wanted us all to be briefed. He'd told us about his friend Harry Regis, and about Jenny Drewett being absorbed by the Pale Stone Man. Eric then took off the backpack that he'd been carrying on his right shoulder—he said that his left had been injured and attended to recently—and Paul was preparing to boost him as Maria, Edgwick and myself sat on the ground nearby. Eric's job right now was to be boosted, then to try to open the impossible Barrier that kept us from both the outside world and the resting place of Caementum, the original Stone Man. It lay dormant and buried in a pit full of lead at the military facility called the Chisel, a base that had grown out of the hastily fabricated "chemical spill" dreamed up to conceal the Stone Man's crash-landing there.

"Okay, Eric," Paul said. "Which hand do you want to—oh." He reddened. "Sorry."

"Don't worry about it," Eric said quietly, holding out his remaining hand.

"Sorry," Paul repeated. "You ready?"

"I think so."

"It's quick," Maria said softly, looking up at Eric through the curls of black, frizzy hair surrounding her hung head. She hadn't said much during Straub's surprisingly thorough briefing to Eric. Maria looked the most tired, and I wasn't surprised. If it wasn't for her keeping us hidden through low-level but constant mental effort, the Stone Giant back at the Prism in Coventry would have put all of us inside those terrible, unbreakable bubbles. The strain was starting to show; Maria's bravery and determination hummed in her thread like powerful wattage but there was also a tension there, like an addict quitting cigarettes. "Don't worry. I even enjoyed it when I did mine. Up to a point." She folded her arms quickly, hiding her recently-reset digits under her armpit. Paul had unintentionally broken those fingers during Maria's boosting.

Eric glanced over at the bulky form of Edgwick.

"Don't ask me," Edgwick said. "I'm so TIN that, even when I was boosted, it barely did anything. Never had any strong Stone Phenomena in the first place."

We were starting to work, focus being desperately hurled into anything other than the terrible knowledge that was simply too big to grasp.

Everyone in the country. Everyone.

"Winter," Straub said. Behind her, the bridge stretched away into the darkness that lay between us and Skye. Below us, the sea continued to endlessly churn and crash against the supports of the Skye Bridge, the air thick with the smell of sea salt. "Please. Expediency."

Opening the Barrier was a big ask for Eric—hell, the process of being boosted alone was no joke in itself—but not as big as the one that lay before myself and the others. Now we had someone of Maria's power level in-circuit, we were to wake the Stone Man and communicate with it. If we somehow managed to carry out *that* impossible task we were then to get it under our control, make it crawl out of a lead grave, and then walk it all the way to Coventry. Once there, we were to use the Stone Man to smash what Eric called the Prism, thus destroying both the Barrier and the Stone Men's ability to carry out their Harvests at such terrifying speed. To stand a chance of doing all this, I needed to be *Dispensatori* more than ever, a name that was now so much more than my codename around Project Orobouros. Open the Barrier, then save the world.

Frankly, I was more than happy for Eric to take his sweet time getting the bastard open.

"On three," Paul said, extending his hand. Eric's eyes fell onto me again. I'd seen the furtive, darting glances that he kept stealing my way. I'd seen those before in the eyes of certain civilian volunteers at Project Orobouros; the Stone Conspiracy types who'd won their own personal lottery by getting on the inside. Andy Pointer was, to them, *Andy Pointer.*

Ahh ... I can be honest with you. I got a kick out of that. Couldn't help it.

"You were screaming," Eric suddenly said to Paul, wagging his finger in recognition. "The day of the Big Power Cut, when I got a vision of you in my head. Was that this—what you're about to do to me—happening to you? I am about to be screaming?"

"No," Paul replied. "That wasn't a Boosting, that was something else, a one-off. Can I explain that to you later?"

"... yeah."

Eric's good hand clamped over Paul's.

Both men's bodies stiffened as if a thousand volts had just been fired through their central nervous systems. Eric's jaw locked up. His eyes rolled over white, eyelids flickering as he made light choking sounds in the back of his throat.

"That's normal?" Maria gasped. "That's what it looks like from the outside? They're okay?"

"Yeah," I said. I didn't want her to panic. Maria, Paul and I had consciously shared a headspace, and it had bonded us on some immediate level. I cared about her. But she and I had a rocky start, and I was still figuring her out.

We watched Paul closely. The smaller-than-he-used-to-be-but-still-big man was bent double, eyes screwed shut, teeth gritted and making a noise like a cat trying to hack up a hairball. Then their hands fell apart, Paul gasping and dropping forwards onto one knee as Eric, eyes wild, tried to stay upright. His left stump pressed onto his aching hand, free now from Paul's steel paw.

"Easy," I said, getting up quickly and holding Eric's tall but wiry body steady. "You're back, you're back, just take a second."

"Painkillers," he breathed, bending at the waist. "That set my shoulder wound off. My bag." I looked to where he'd left it earlier, lying right by the Barrier.

"And I'm fine, by the way," Paul said, upright now. I started and he held up a hand. "I'm kidding." He smiled, but it vanished almost immediately, old habits dying in the face of the current situation. "I saw something. I got a vision of a kid—"

"Aiden," Eric said. "Andy—Mister Pointer, would you mind getting the—"

"The painkillers, sorry, of course. Andy, call me Andy—"

"Andy. Eric." It was pointless as Straub had introduced us, but we of course hadn't shaken hands—Paul had to go first, just in case—and first names didn't quite seem right until now. I offered my hand to him for a proper introduction. He went to take it, getting his breath back, but hesitated.

"It's okay," I told him. "It's just with Paul. And maybe a light shock the first time you touch a Stone Sensitive, but you've done that now." Eric's face fell a little; he had, I knew, already touched another Stone Sensitive: Harry, harvested by one of the six Blue Stone Men now walking the country. Used by the Stone Giant and the Prism to create two more Blues that now stood, dormant and waiting, alongside the Stone Giant at Ground Zero.

Eric shook my hand and then nodded to the others one by one.

"Toby," Edgwick said, introducing himself, but Eric looked away quickly.

"Who's Aiden?" I asked.

"The boy I found just outside of Coventry," Eric said. "He's trapped inside a bubble. I have to get him out." He blinked. "Wait; does that mean he's next? If I saw him, does that mean he's next?"

No-one spoke.

"We might have time," Maria said quickly. "Especially if he's a way off from Coventry. And the one that's ... after him; it might be one of the ones that haven't started moving yet, one of the three by the Prism—"

"Mr Hatton," Straub said, "the plan I've laid out is our only chance of stopping the Stone Men; I can tell you now, there are at least another twenty surviving Stone Sensitive children on the List we have. They need you to do this—"

"Yes, yes," Eric said, eyes now locked on the Barrier with a simpleton's stare.

Of course, I thought. *He's seeing it with boosted eyes.*

"What ..." Eric took a step forward on still-shaky legs. "It's even more complicated than ..." His next words were likely to determine the fate of the world. *He might say he can't do it.* Everyone waited.

"It looks different?" Straub asked.

"... no." Eric cocked his head. "But I can feel the way it ..." He stopped right at the Barrier's edge, it's surface deadly and ugly and beautiful all at once. He turned on the spot, then to Maria. "Can you hear them?"

"No," she said. "I'm using up a lot of my mental bandwidth or whatever by running protective interference, but I couldn't hear anything before either."

"I could before, after the Barrier expanded," Eric said. "It's like this screechy, metal noise. I was hearing it all the time. But not like this."

"How did you not go crazy?" I asked. On a handful of occasions, Paul and I heard that sound. They had been more than enough.

"It's not normally that loud, unless I want it to be," Eric said, head down now, eyes closed. "And I get snippets where I understand it here and there. But now there are ... hmm." He let out a noise that was half-chuckle, half-astonishment. "Wow. There are different frequencies. Some are really busy ... some I can barely hear at all, like they're not really being used. Or like ... automated...? I can't explain—"

"What are they saying?" the Brigadier asked, gesturing to a member of her team standing nearby, who rushed forward, holding a recording device in Eric's direction from the other side of the Barrier.

"Nothing of substance, I think," Eric said, brow furrowed. "Not even in the busy threads, if that makes sense. Just like they're constantly pinging one another to keep the communication there, or something? But the busy threads see, *really* busy—"

A horrible, creeping realisation seemed to spread across his face. He turned to me. *No,* I thought. *It cannot fucking be.*

"They're looking for you," he said.

To my shame, I took a step backwards. Paul's hand found my back.

"I've got you, boss," he said. "Maria too. Good lad. Don't worry."

"I know," I muttered, reddening. "Fucking *hell.*"

"Yeah."

I straightened up. *Dispensatori,* shit. The Cacterus—the British army's codename for the entities behind the Stone Men—were looking for me? Fine. I'd do my best to give them something to worry about if they found me. I tried to put fear behind me.

"Okay. Let's—"

"Mr *Hatton*," Straub said, an unfamiliar imploring tone in her voice. Eric blinked, coming back from the louder, newer sounds that only he could hear. "The Barrier. *Can you open it?*"

"I don't know," Eric said, and turned to the Barrier. The wind stirred my damp and chilly clothes—a gift from our low-speed, low-altitude crash landing in Loch Alshe—and I shivered. At least if Eric pulled this off, I thought, we might get fresh army fatigues at the Chisel base. It then struck me how ridiculous it was that I was worrying about cold, wet clothes when everyone in the country was—

Hm. Even now. Even now, I still can't—

One second.

***

I'm back.

Eric. Holding up a hand at the Barrier. Straub moved in front of him on the other side, but Eric shook his head.

"I don't know what happens here," he said. "If it blows outwards or something and touches you, Brigadier, you're gone." Straub sidestepped right.

"Does it feel the same now?" she asked as the very tips of Eric's fingers pressed against the smooth-yet-tumbling dirty silver surface, his hand a standing spider. "To physically touch?"

"Yes and no," Eric muttered. "It's ... not finished yet. Still h*ardening*," he said, his voice light with wonder. "Like a newborn grub or insect, you know? The way they have to dry in the sun. And ... yeah. I think its structure is different to the bubbles."

"How so?"

Eric continued to look at the barrier with an expression of detached wonder.

"The bubbles," he said. "I've seen Stone Men walk through them and then the bubbles just disappear afterwards. They're designed to be temporary. This one ... even if I can open it now ... I think it's going to get harder and harder to *keep* open." He trailed his fingers across the Barrier's surface. "I think this one is trying to become permanent."

"What if we smash the Prism first?" I asked.

Eric blinked.

"Well ... how should I know?" he asked.

"Can you open this one *now*, at least?" Straub asked, frustrated.

March of the Stone Men

Eric squinted at his hand where it rested upon the Barrier. He began to tremble.

"Yes," he said, and pushed his fingers into the Barrier's surface all the way up to the first knuckle.

A short fizzing noise filled the air and then died as ripples of solid light spread outwards from Eric's fingers. They cast outwards for a few feet before fading into nothing. Eric's body continued to shake, eyes wide, mouth closed, breath snorting heavily from his nostrils.

"Oh my God," Maria whispered. Eric was *doing* it.

"His fingers," Straub said. "Eric, your *fingers are sticking out the other side.* Can you put the rest of your hand through?"

Eric's arm moved forward slightly, then stopped, as if he were meeting with considerable resistance. It looked bizarre; the Barrier may have been hitherto impenetrable but it was physically thin, thin as a shallow puddle. Eric tensed and tried again. His hand only moved a few millimetres before he screwed up his face and *pushed*. Now his hand moved through the Barrier all the way up to the wrist, and Eric's shaking worsened as he let out a little gasp. "*It's fighting me,*" he spat.

It was. Something was happening to the light around Eric's hand. It was darkening, thickening, pouring more layers onto itself to keep Eric out.

"What can we do to help, Eric—" Straub began, before quickly stepping back as the Barrier around Eric began to fizz once more, louder now.

"Maria," Eric hissed, ignoring Straub as he looked at our Watchmaker. "They'll feel this—"

"I know, I'm ... taking care of it ..." Maria said, sitting down suddenly. Paul stepped forward but she waved him away. "Eric, watch Eric," she said, and closed her eyes.

"Does it hurt?" I asked Eric uselessly. There was nothing I could do to help. "Can you ... can you take it?"

"Think so, I think—" Eric began, and then let out a moan as he pushed harder, first getting his arm in to the forearm, then the elbow.

"You're *doing it!*" I yelled. I couldn't believe this was working, even as the light around Eric's arm turned from dark silver to dull grey and the Barrier's surface seemed to turn into heavy, slowly running treacle. It was weighing onto Eric, trying to *flatten* this intruder out. Whatever the Barrier was, it had defences, but Eric was pushing on.

"You're nearly there!" Edgwick barked. "*Oose! Oose!* Come on! *Oose!* You have it!"

Eric paused, took a pained breath, and then pushed in up to his shoulder, hesitating as his face grew near to the Barrier. His next push, I saw, would take his eyes inside that thickening grey swirl. Parts of it now were darkening to black. The fizzing became a swarm all around us and the light on Straub's side of the Barrier suddenly spat violently outwards. It wasn't much, perhaps akin to the spark of an arcing live wire, but it was something. Would the Barrier begin to react more violently to this infraction?

"Everyone back," Straub said to her team members standing nearby, boffins and soldiers alike. Eric was trembling heavily. His breathing was laboured, spittle beginning to spray from his lips. No-one spoke. Eric was leading this. Then he ducked his head, took a breath as if he were about to disappear underwater, and groaned with clenched jaws as he pushed sideways into the Barrier, his hip and right leg and then his head getting under and into its now-oozing, blackening light. Now one side of his face was with us and the other with Straub. Even as the Barrier oozed it didn't overrun, didn't slop down and drip into his eyes and mouth. It continued to thicken around his outline. Eric's half in-and-out mouth could breathe, each squinting eye could see.

"*Shit,*" Maria grunted, seeming to sense something as she screwed up her face. Everyone looked her way, but her hand shot up. "*It's fine,* I have it. I just need a moment." She breathed out. "I have it. It's okay. *Eric.* Carry on. You're doing it."

"*Ah,*" Eric hissed. "*Ah.*" His body was now curled inwards slightly on itself, either due to the seeming weight of the Barrier or from the stress of his exertions. Through the Barrier's darkening surface I could see Eric's right knee knocking inwards towards his left. "Okay. Okay. *Ah.* Okay." I thought he was steeling himself, but then as I understood the situation I realised that Eric was having the same revelation.

We hadn't thought about the next step; we'd been so desperate to find out whether Eric could push through the Barrier that we hadn't thought about the main issue. We didn't need Eric to get through it.

We needed him to make it so *we* could get through it.

"Hold ... " Eric stammered. "Hold ..."

"Can you—" I began.

"*Hold on. Wait.*"

Eric began to scream.

The outside-world side of the Barrier spat its frustration again, the spray carrying a few feet this time. Nothing landed on the Skye bridge's tarmac surface; the crackling force seemed to dissipate into nothing as soon as it left the Barrier's main body, but no-one cared as we were all watching Eric. He was dragging his right arm *back through the Barrier,* stopping once it was half-in and half-out of the thin electric waterfall that pressed into the profile of his body. His arm was bent as he pulled it back in, his elbow by his hip.

"Bassssssstardddd…"

Eric began to twist at the waist like a man throwing a punch in slow motion and pushed his arm up and forwards. His fingers were held out straight, forming a blade, and he cut them through the skin of the Barrier. His eyes were screwed tight now as his arm began to form the shape of a crippled Nazi salute. His body was shaking like a shitting dog, but as he continued the motion I saw it was working. The fizzing sound was so loud now that it was like standing next to a PA system blasting out white noise. All around Eric's body the Barrier had turned a transparent black now, but our man had done his job.

Below the bridge of his arm, an archway had formed.

It would be tight, but we could squeeze through. Eric opened his eyes and let out a gasp, staring disbelievingly down at the clear space beneath his arm. Then he gave the smallest nod of his head, the movement compressed by the Barrier's weight. "Okay," he said. "Holding it … is easier. Go. Go *now.* I can hold this. I can hold it for a while, but it's only going to get harder. Literally. You have to be quick, get back quick. Maria—"

"Yes, yes," Maria said, already standing and moving towards the Barrier. "I can keep you hidden—"

"Wait," Paul said, but Maria was already bending and moving through the archway without hesitation. Even though doing so was easy for Maria's small frame, my heart still froze as she ducked and passed under Eric's arm, but already she was through and on the other side in one piece.

"It's fine, come on," Maria said breathlessly, spinning around to face us. She was pale but energised. She looked up at the sky, unfiltered out there by the Barrier's churning surface. "*God,*" she said breathless. "It looks so different."

"Sounds … different," Eric muttered, eyes still fixed on the floor. "Left ear, inside, can hear them. Right ear … just the wind and the … sea."

"Quickly," Straub said, "the rest of you."

I was the next closest. I drew near to Eric and dropped down to all fours, looking at the concrete on the other side of the archway. I didn't think it would snap shut—Eric had it—but I decided to leap quickly through the gap like a pouncing leopard all the same. That was the intention, at least; the motion was more like a pouncing sloth. My right knee banged painfully against the ground and I landed on my side. I rolled over, wincing and taking Maria's offered hand to help me up. I got to my feet, fake-chuckling.

"Messy," I said, and looked to where Edgwick was commando-crawling through the gap—clearly the right technique—with Paul preparing to follow. His crossing was slower than Edgwick's, and I can't lie; the few seconds it took him to pass under Eric's arm seemed like five agonising minutes. I focused on my breathing, trying to keep it steady ... and couldn't. What was this? And it was worsening fast. Was I about to have a panic attack? I looked at the literal threshold I'd just crossed and understood: the first part of the plan had worked, and now I was expected to be the leader, the hero even. The idea was suddenly laughable. I *knew* who I was, my nature. I'd heard the sentence over and over again in the therapy sessions at the Project: *behaviour is negotiable, temperament isn't.*

My temperament was ... not heroic. If we were to die, it would almost certainly be because I couldn't truly be what they needed me to be.

Then behave otherwise, I thought, *at least for now.* Everyone *is counting on you—*

That settled me a little, but I still quietly placed a little privacy blockade on my thread within our circuit to stop the others noticing such strong thoughts. Paul had now crossed over to our side and was getting to his feet, looking at me quizzically.

"You just do something?" he asked. "On your thread?"

I noticed Straub cross to Edgwick to shake his hand. The pair of them began to talk quietly as Paul waited for an answer from me.

"Yeah, just a little block," I said, trying to keep my face casual as I thought up a lie. "I don't want you two to be affected by what I'm thinking about the country. All the people."

Paul and Maria exchanged a glance.

"Ok, buddy," Paul said to me. I felt his and Maria's threads become a little quieter in my head. They had put blocks on too. I put my hands in my pockets to hide their shaking.

"Mister Hatton," Straub said, turning away from Edgwick, "you've done an amazing job. You can step out, now, everyone is through. I want you to step back *inside* the Barrier, in case opening it from this side is somehow—"

"Can't."

The only sound was the harsh crackle of the Barrier's continuing protests.

"You can't move?" Straub asked.

"It's not as bad when I'm ... standing still like this," Eric said, unable to lift his head and talking to the concrete at his feet. "But I don't know if I can ... open this again. It's getting ... " He didn't finish the sentence.

"This creates a problem," Straub said, putting her hand to her forehead.

"What?" I asked.

"We can't fly near the Barrier as it's too risky," Straub said. "It played havoc with our systems when we flew near to it after it appeared, that's only become worse the longer it's been here, although apparently that only seems to apply to flight *outside* the Barrier, judging on Eric's journey here." A scowl flashed across her face. "We'd *planned* to take you, providing you can wake and control Caementum," Straub said, "along the coastline via high-speed sea transport before having you cut back inland once we were aligned with Coventry. Travelling under the Barrier and taking the roads will likely be problematic due to all the—" Her face twitched for a moment as she abandoned the sentence. *All the dead cars.* "Problematic," she repeated instead. "You're sure the Barrier's hardening, Eric?"

"*Certain.*"

"Dammit!" Straub snapped. "Looks like you're all driving or walking to Coventry. We knew we wouldn't be able to fly over the Barrier to keep visual track of you. But I didn't think that journey would be from here—" She stopped herself, watching Maria as she moved to Eric and crouched down so his lowered head could see her.

"Does it hurt?" Maria asked.

"Yeah," he said. "It hurts a lot. But I can hold it. Get moving. Please be quick."

Eric didn't look as if he *could* hold it. I was worried about him, but I was also worried that we wouldn't be able to get back inside.

Get back inside? I thought. *You're* out. *You really want to go back* in?

But I was Dispensatori, and so I would fucking have to.

Great.

"Thank you, Eric," I said, but I meant it. "Okay, let's get to the Housing."

"The Housing?" Maria asked. "I thought we had to get to the Chisel?"

"You do," Straub said, "the Housing is the part of the Chisel where Caementum is currently contained. We'll drive you to the other end of the bridge and then we'll airlift you to the Housing once we're clear of the Barrier."

"We're taking another helicopter?" Maria asked, her face darkening.

"It'll be quicker," Straub said. "The drive all the way there may be very short but a chopper will be faster still; every minute counts for Hatton, and I don't know how long it will take to wake the Stone Man, if at all. We've never been able to do it."

"The boy," Eric hissed, looking suddenly angry, as if dealing with Straub right now was the last thing he wanted. There was history here. "Aiden. Make sure they get to him. I promised. Maria?"

"Yes."

"You'll be able to find him. Won't you. And when the Stone Men walk through the bubbles, they disappear."

The implication hung in the air.

"*We'll* be able to find him," Maria said, "and *you'll* get him out. We're going to be quick, I promise."

She was promising that we'd wake up the fucking Stone Man and make it walk?

"Some of my team will stay here with you, Hatton," Straub said, then hesitated, seeing Eric bowed and surrounded by blackened tar that hung heavily upon him. I saw it too and told myself that I *would not* fail him. Sophie had said I was made of iron and didn't know it.

But where was that iron now, when Eric needed it?

"If it gets too much," Straub said, "they can give you an adrenalin shot. Something to help you if you need it. Hold on. We're coming back."

The ocean crashed against the supports of the concrete bridge, the timing of its roar sounding like an immediate retort of sarcastic laughter.

"Piss off and... do it then, *Brigadier*," Eric grunted.

We turned away and left Eric there.

***

Chapter Three

The Broken Engine, Down in the Darkness, and A Taste for the Theatrical

***

We stepped down from the helicopter with, on my part at least, no small sense of relief; Maria too, that much was clear. She'd spent the entirety of the extremely short flight with her eyes closed, her head lowered, and her arms wrapped around herself. She didn't make any fuss. She simply rode it out. My view from the chopper window showed the grey concrete of the Skye Bridge quickly being replaced by that of the Chisel's landing pad. Not too far away, separated from the rest of the facility by concrete fencing, lay the thirty-feet-wide expanse of lead referred to on-base as *the Housing.*

The fence was a mix of wide, high, and solid panels that slotted into upright girders; no chain link here. The only way you could see inside was from either viewing the feed from the array of cameras pointing into the Housing itself or from stepping through the access gate. The latter was rattling open now, the armed and shell-shocked looking guards allowing us through. Those men and women would almost certainly have had family on the mainland. Now, unless they were extremely lucky, those families would be gone.

The Housing was not so large that it would cause interest from any aircraft that may pass overhead. This was not by design—the government had no part in deciding how wide the crater left by the dying-and-leaking Stone Man's impact would be, falling to earth as it had. As we stepped inside the circumference of the metal fencing, the floodlights came on. All the cabling running around this part of the facility stood out in dark relief due to its triple thick insulation. This had been entirely necessary at the time of installation, preventing the system from being shorted out by the energy emitted by Caementum's still-leaking form. It was potentially unnecessary now, lead having been poured and set the moment the Fifth Arrival began, but before then all efforts to mechanically drag the pre-lead-burial Stone Man from its resting place had proved useless. Nothing Straub's people did to the circuitry could stop any winching cable, hook, or even—somehow—rope from shorting out the devices they were attached to the moment physical contact was made with the Stone Man. Raising it by hand had proved equally useless; the theory was that Caementum had entered some kind of default anchoring mode while in this current state, similar to the one it had employed during the very beginning of the First Arrival, making itself impossible to lift.

I was glad of the floodlighting. I can't lie; I did not want to be waking the Stone Man—if we could—in darkness. The expanse of lead before us was like a frozen pond from some industrial hell. In its depths, monsters swam.

"It's *in* there," Maria said pointlessly, but then I saw her face, pale even in the bright yellow of the Housing's floodlights. She was terrified.

"You can feel it?" Straub asked quickly. "It's awake?"

"No," Maria said. "It doesn't know anything." Know? It wasn't a word I associated with the Stone Men. *Know* implied thought, and I didn't like that at all. Male and female soldiers—in full military fatigues here rather than the polo shirt uniform of Project Orobouros, this was openly an army base after all—brought piles of folded clothes, pairs of boots, and several large backpacks for Paul, Maria and me.

"Get changed," Straub said. "You can't be wet and cold for what we're about to do. Mental relaxation will be important. Apologies for the fit, Maria, we had to guess at your size. You'll all also be taking these packs with you, and Eric's too when you set off. You have provisions, tents, maps, distress flares, some tablets with the List on them, just in case."

"Weaponry?" Edgwick asked. The question made sense. Who knew how the survivors under the Barrier would react?

"Of course," Straub said. "You'll be taking Caludon's rifle but the others will also be getting sidearms. You will, of course, brief them on how to use them safely."

"We're taking guns?" Maria asked.

"Yes."

"... okay. Good idea, I guess."

Her eyes were fixed firmly on the lead. She looked scared out of her mind, and it wasn't from the thought of guns.

"Maria," I began, but as she looked my way a psychic fist wearing a set of brass memories punched me square in the brain. It was so strong that even Maria's in-thread block couldn't stop it.

I'm trapped on a bus full of terrified children. It's coming. It looked right at me—

Then it was gone, and the lights of the Housing filled my eyes. I let out an audible gasp as I came back.

"Sorry," Maria said. "I didn't mean to do that."

Our new outfits were military fatigues too—camo trousers and jacket—along with undershirts, underwear, and socks. I looked around for somewhere private to change but then suddenly Maria was undressing right in front of us, stripping off with her eyes still locked on the lead below her, all terrified business. I turned away quickly, only to get an eyeful of Paul's bare and sagging backside.

"The boots, Maria," I heard Straub say. "Do they fit?"

"Yes, thank you."

"Good. They're important."

Of course they were. We had to get to Coventry from *Skye*.

I finished dressing and squinted a glance at Paul. He was dressed too, staring at the lead. He'd spent years being endlessly pursued by this thing, Caementum slowly draining him and nearly catching him right before we'd stopped it cold. I knew what he was thinking.

What if we started it again and couldn't control it?

I concentrated and sent the thought down Paul's thread; anything I said to Paul in-circuit would have a lot more impact than anything spoken aloud.

If we can wake it up, I told him, *we can stop it again if we have to. Maria is a powerhouse. More than my Sophie. We have backup now like we've never had before.*

Paul's thread settled a little, and then his reply came:

Okay. Thank you.

"Ready?" Straub asked us. I glanced at the frightened faces of my circuit. Their expression was mirrored in everyone there, I realised, even Straub. Paul and Maria nodded, Paul shifting awkwardly, Maria holding herself. Then the sight of the Housing vanished and I was in the darkness of our circuit again, our own seemingly endless void. Maria was keeping us hidden from the wider circuit of the Stone Giant, or the Prism, or the Caeterus, and it was silent inside Stone Space. The only things visible nearby were our ethereal threads. Were they a literal connection to Paul and Maria? Or simply our mind's own interpretation of however our circuit worked? No-one knew. I could feel the distant edge of their emotional states. To share their fear with them remotely, safely, my goodness ... this was understanding.

But we had work to do, always, always, always.

I took a moment to try and send my mind down through the solid lead underfoot, trying to peer below like a nervous swimmer looking into the depths for sharks. Unlike Maria, I couldn't feel exactly where the Stone Man lay, but I knew it was there. Every hair on my body had been standing on end the moment I stepped out onto that lead, even if I'd tried to hide it from the others. This current silence in Stone Space was, I understood, the last piece of relative calm before the storm.

Maria had never tried this before, and Paul and I were the ones who would teach her. I turned to her thread.

Maria?

She was suddenly close to me, so bright and powerful in the darkness that I recoiled a little and felt Paul do the same.

Yes.

Jesus!

She was ablaze.

Her fear was turning into adrenaline, lighting her up in a way we had not yet seen, and as we quickly grew accustomed to her strangely soothing fire—her heat comforting like a roaring hearth on an icy night—I realised Maria was noticing me examining her.

What's wrong, her thread asked.

Nothing. You're just ... intense.

Does it hurt you?

No, no.

If this was what was currently going on inside Maria, then despite her shattered-looking outside appearance, I thought we might still have some gas in our collective tank. We *were* going to wake the Stone Man, and it seemed that—without speaking aloud—we had started.

Maria, I asked. *Can you take us down there? I can't feel it.*

Her thread twanged sharply at the thought of going down into the lead to be with the Stone Man.

Yes, she said.

I need you to channel Paul to me, I told Maria. *He's going to give me the juice, but you're going to have to keep us together. Paul—*

Paul's thread suddenly pulsed silently and whatever power of which he was the steward—the battery—flowed along his thread into me. If Maria's power was bright like a fire, Paul's was a river, as constant and implacable as the Stone Men themselves. I passed Paul's energy on to Maria to shape, reform, and pass back into me as something I could use. Paul the river, Maria the turbine, and me... what was I?

You're Dispensatori, I thought, *remember?*

"Have you started?"

That was Straub out in the physical world. I opened my body's eyes, the floodlight-lit Housing harsh and cold compared to Stone Space.

"*Yes,*" I snapped quickly, closing my eyes again and *literally* dropping back into Stone Space as I found Maria was already doing as I'd asked, sinking our minds down through the lead towards Caementum. Maria's thread sang and I felt her perception of the Stone Man's location hit me like a gentle shockwave. I couldn't 'see' it in my mind, but as Maria took us lower I began to feel the Stone Man's shape. Despite everything, that was exhilarating. In our visits to the Chisel over the last year Paul, myself, and any remaining volunteers had only ever managed to vaguely get a sense of its presence. With Maria—our Watchmaker—powerfully laying the cogs of our circuit into place, it was like we now had functioning sonar, tracing the shape of the thing in the darkness.

There.

The Stone Man lay almost flat in its thick lead cocoon.

Its head was slightly higher than its feet, one arm bent around its back, but we'd been describing its situation all wrong. We'd said it was *dormant*, even if it was leaking energy, but getting a taste the amount of raw, indescribable power here meant the word *dormant* was even more inaccurate than we'd thought. Whatever form I had in Stone Space began to prickle as we moved into the corona of the Stone Man's damaged, bleeding energy. This was not the same as the times back at the Project, when the threads of the Stone Man and the Caeterus themselves were running tautly back and forth, alive with vicious power. To stop the Stone Man we'd had to throw a mental wrench into a gap in its already-failing internal clockwork, but in doing so we had critically broken it. Its threads were still here, emanating outwards from the centre of its body. But now they lay loose, their connection severed, tightropes cut at one end.

Now we would have to repair the monster.

Okay, I told my circuit. *I'm going in.*

Neither agreement or dissent came. I dived in.

I bounced straight out.

What happened, Maria asked.

Uh ... Maria, I need you to kind of—

I couldn't explain it. I didn't have the words. All I know is that I thought to Maria what I needed, she gave it to me, and then suddenly we were shooting forward and inside the painful rush of information that was the Stone Man's upper levels. It was instantly familiar and completely new at the same time.

The explosion of raw and broken data that I remembered to be system commands detonated into my consciousness, only now they were freely powering around inside a network that was failing to contain them. There was no order in here at all, only force. It came at me from all sides. It was as if, before, the internal workings of the Stone Man were like an aging plumbing system, one that channeled water safely all *around* me, contained within pipes and walls. Yes, they had been starting to leak then, but were still just about managing to do the job. Then I'd managed to smash up parts of the creaky system, and the torrent of built-up pressure had been unleashed. Since then, clearly, it had been trying to burst in all directions with nowhere to actually go; it was now, in fact, washing me away—

Maria caught me, but it was a struggle.

I have him, Maria said. *Paul—*

Yes—

I felt Paul strain. It worked. Maria's exertions lessened.

Are you stable, she asked me.

None of us were.

Yeah, I told her.

No, you're not. Take a second.

The inside of the Stone Man, dark as it was, had been a rush the first time, but with Maria involved the experience was now almost at the point of physical pain. We waited, getting our bearings; panic, I realised, was making this worse.

She's right. Be still.

We did. Our awareness of the flood slowly reduced to a comparatively weaker powerwash.

I marveled at our surroundings.

Back at Project Orobouros, Paul, Sophie and I had spent the entirety of our extremely brief time inside Caementum trying to avoid the defensive threads of the Caeterus as they tried to snap closed around us. Now the space was dormant—and with the visual clarity Maria brought—we could take it in, and I was stunned by how different it looked.

The Stone Space inside the Stone Man had previously been a blackness. Now there was a single colour: a distant, dull, familiar greyish brown. It pulsed brighter—if brightness can be used to describe such drab impossibility—in various places, the way distant lightning will pop behind a sky filled with clouds. I felt my friends register the sight: Paul's shock at the unexpected difference, Maria's at being inside the Stone Man at all.

Are you okay, I asked her. *This is probably all pretty shocking—*

There's no time for that shit, Maria snapped. *Eric needs us. What do we do now?*

Your move man, Paul said. *Let's go, Dispensatori.*

I winced at the name.

Okay.

During our last failed attempt to communicate with the Stone Man I'd glimpsed something far down below in its depths, something at its absolute deepest point that I'd perceived as a cage or box of some kind. It had been heavily protected by the Stone Man's internal systems, which had to mean it was important; a central processor? A mind? That felt correct, but we didn't know for sure. If my Sophie hadn't hidden us from the Caeterus' threads back then—as I'd tried unsuccessfully to retrieve said box—we would have been lost. My thinking now was that—if Maria could help get me deeper than Sophie could—accessing that box might hold the key to waking the Stone Man, perhaps even controlling it.

I tried to get a sense of the box, looking below and hoping that Maria's presence would make it easy, but access to those lower levels now seemed to be blocked by something akin to ballast doors on a sea vessel. Perhaps an automated process, triggered by the emergency of the Stone Man being stopped? Either way, we couldn't reach the box.

Now what, Maria asked. *How did you do it before? How did you stop it?*

Stopping it hadn't even been the point of the mission that day; we'd been trying to talk to it. It was only when it went so very badly wrong that I'd been forced to act out of desperation, trying to stop Caementum from walking to—and taking the spine of—the fallen Paul back at Project Orobouros, helpless in the crashed cabin—

You got inside its insides and smashed them, Maria said, interrupting my thoughts. *Didn't you?*

I knew she hadn't pulled that information from my memories. Maria had received a huge information dump from me regarding all things Sophie when

Maria and I were in-circuit and comforting the dying Linda. But she was right: I'd found a damaged opening, a small, worn-open tear that I'd ripped even further agape, allowing access to the data stream flowing around the Stone Man's body. My Stone Space mind had leapt through it and into the Stone Man's *real* insides, becoming a human spanner in the works, twisting and tearing and interrupting the chain. That particular hatchet job meant the tsunami of data was leaking chaotically into the whole system now, presumably flowing out of whatever chink in the internal armour I'd found and worsened—

I had it. The flow. For once, I would have to go with it.

Listen, I told the others. *We have to find the hole, fix it, stop the leak. Maria, keep me attached to you both, okay?*

But if you find it, she asked, *and mend it, then how can you stop the Stone Man from—*

I let the flood take me without answering and before they could protest.

My consciousness was filled with the roar of data around me as I let myself be washed away, hurtling blindly around Stone Space as I bled through its veins. It was like riding inside a waterslide from hell, one made of noise and barbed passageways that ripped at my form. I cried out, aware of Paul and Maria's threads pulled tighter than ever as our connection threatened to snap, feeling my circuit working hard to keep me a part of them. If they failed, perhaps I would be lost forever in here—

There. Something rushed by, far too quickly, just like before. I did another excruciating lap, trying to hear what Paul and Maria were telling me but failing, all my efforts focused on finding that—

There it was again, screaming past me—the leak, the hole—but it was gone, passing by like a bullet train. I thought I had the timing now, racing round the inside of Caementum's ethereal veins like a loosened blood clot, and the third time I shot by it I was ready. I bore down at the right moment, digging the claws of my mind into that snag in the system and gripping tight. Suddenly the roar of data became agony.

Fuck!!

Andy you have it, what's there—

Then the pain became dull, and as Maria's words stopped, I knew that she was salving me somehow. The effort had taken her instantly beyond speech, but Paul picked up the slack.

That's it, he said, *you need to—to—to—*

I didn't know either. I clung frantically to the edges of this rip inside our otherwise impervious erstwhile ally, the pain lessened but my 'grip' fading. Worse, the edges of whatever hole I had previously torn were slowly giving way. Soon it would be unfixable, with nowhere to grip at all, its edges giving way each time I flew around the system and clutched a desperate mental fistful.

Close it!

Paul was right. I felt for the other side of what I perceived to be a hole—or what my mind perceived as one—even as the stream of data hit me like the blast from a riot hose. Then I had the other edge, my consciousness bridging the gap. The pressure of the Stone Man's power made me feel like a button sewn onto a volcanic eruption, but then Paul's power and Maria's awareness moved through me. Our circuit worked.

Cogs of understanding fell into place in my mind.

It suddenly made total sense. Whatever this space was, it was all energy. The Stone Man's *body* was held together by energy, *made* of energy, that strange Stone substance like an impossible cellular ... battery? Structure? It couldn't be truly solid after all; how else could it control its mass like that? But if it had begun to fracture over the years, beginning to leak—

Ideas pinged between us, trying to turn the visualisation of that hole closing into a reality, but the commands on our threads kept flickering out of each other's mental grasp; timing was required, we couldn't get the *close* impulse to catch as a group command, but then we could, and suddenly I was moving this edge *this* way, and this edge *that* way, and we could have the data act like coagulating blood forming a clot—

The edges began to seal together. The incredible pressure began to drop.

Oh my God, Paul's thread gasped.

The hole became smaller, smaller . and closed altogether. At first the seal felt thin, like the skin of an overstretched balloon, but it quickly thickened. We were *doing* it. The battering data continued on its way around the Stone Man's insides, but rapidly began to lessen; the flow was returning into the deeper internal systems now that the exit point was sealed shut. The inside of the Stone Man began to fall strangely still, but still not the same as it had been at the Project. What was different?

The *out*side.

As the shut-down Stone Man had been helicoptered away from the Project—the Permutatio Protocol having been triggered by the arrival of the Crawlers—its weakened connection to Paul had snapped and its energy had detonated into the world. Ever since then it had been bleeding outwards, it was leaking *from the Stone Man's outsides as well somehow—*

Maria, I said. *The outside of The Stone Man!*

What? What should I do?

What should she do?

Cover the outside of it! Like you cover us when you hide us!

Why? Hold on, hold on—

I felt her go away.

Then I heard her scream.

Maria! Maria, what happened?

I'm here, she said, but I could feel the strain in her thread, hear how far away her voice was. *This fucking ... thing! It's falling apart! There's a leak on the outside, not like a hole either. It's like, it's like its whole body is leaking everywhere. But I have it, I'm covering it—*

She was. The chaos of this internal Stone Space was lessening. We had sealed up the breaks.

Are you okay, I asked her. *Will you be able to keep it contained all the way to Coventry?*

It's getting easier already. Despite the strain in her voice, I believed her. Maria was strong. If anyone could do it, she could. *Just get on with it,* she said. *Please. Let's get this thing up and out.*

But we waited: Maria, breathing heavily in my mind. Paul, tense. All three of us waiting to see what would happen now we'd shored up Caementum's body inside and out.

It feels so weak, Paul said. He was right. Even at the Project, where the Stone Man had already begun to gently bleed out, its inner Stone Space—while its body was active—had felt so much stronger than this. If we got the bastard moving, it might be running on fumes. *Maybe the Detonation back in the day dumped most of its energy out?*

The what? Maria began, but then we all felt the space around us shift.

Something's happening—

This was a new pressure change; a sense of the space below us expanding, opening. The remaining loose data stream inside the creature was disappearing down into the depths; the ballast doors were slowly beginning to open.

The Stone Man was coming back online.

And the box down below. Whether it was the Stone Man's brain or not, it was at least some kind of core part of the system—

Suddenly, I couldn't feel my circuit. Paul's thread gone, Maria's thread gone. I was in nothing but darkness, alone and immobile. I couldn't scream. I didn't have a voice. I still had threads, but now there were a great many of them, far more than the two I thought I had, but they were cut and useless, searching around for—

—ndy! Andy!

Then I was back in my circuit, in Caementum's Stone Space with Paul and Maria attached to me, and I realised that I had just flashed into the Stone Man *from inside the Stone Man.* What the hell did that mean?

Holy fucking shit—

What happened?

I think—I think I was just inside its sight. I couldn't feel you two at all—

I understood what was happening.

It's awake. The fucker's awake!

Paul's terror. Maria's terror, the threads of our circuit suddenly trembling and weak.

Maria, Paul screamed. *Keep it together!*

I saw movement. The Stone Man's internal threads were beginning to raise. Searching. Calling.

Maria! Shut that shit down right now!

The threads of our circuit coughed and shook as Maria dragged herself back into the game.

Done!

The internal threads slowly fell away but then the rumbling began. Caementum was trying to move, the rumbling growing heavier, deeper, emanating from all sides.

Time to go to work Andy, Paul babbled. *TIME TO GO TO WORK ANDY—*

I didn't know what to do.

I checked; the ballast doors below—whatever was blocking the lower levels and keeping that mysterious cage or core out of reach—were still opening but weren't open enough for us to pass through. They were moving maddeningly slowly; Caementum would soon be fully awake with our physical bodies —*Paul's* physical body, its previous Target—standing right on top of it. Our best guess of how to take control of the Stone Man—now that its insides were healed—was to access that cage, that box in the depths, but there was no time to try and reach it. We had to get our physical bodies out of the Housing, off the Isle of Skye even, to get some space and plan our next—

Paul and Maria's threads disappeared once more. I had unintentionally flashed into the Stone Man's sight again; *unintentionally* was the only way it had ever been done, but it had never been like this. I could *feel* the Stone Man's broken threads hanging loose from myself. They felt as if they were mine ... yet I was not in control. *But we didn't get the box,* I thought, *didn't get the Core. Do I not even need it then? Can I control the Stone Man if I'm in its sight with* this *level of connection*—

But of course all I could see was blackness; the Stone Man was surrounded by lead. The threads I felt hanging from the Stone Man were not those of my circuit. Isolated in this other section—the Stone Man's eyes, or maybe even its thinking centre or *something* if the Core wasn't its brain after all—I was without Maria and Paul, and that meant control would almost certainly not be possible. I felt for my friends, failed, and then—with a piece of mental gymnastics that I can only equate to looking at a Magic Eye picture, to be looking and not looking at the same time—I found them once more, so distant I could barely catch them.

Help me!

I couldn't see them or hear them, but they helped all the same, and not in a way I expected. Something clicked and I felt another, new-yet-distant connection drop into uncertain place.

I felt myself grow into an arm. Then another.

Our connection to the circuit with the Stone Man—our *system*—might be loose, held together by the mental equivalent of string and glue, but with Paul and Maria's help the darkness around me began to take shape.

I grew into a leg. Then the other. A torso. All of it brimming with power.

I heard that all-too-familiar rhythm, and for once it brought a terrible thrill instead of fear. Andy began to go away. The sensation was both horrifying and blissful at the same time. I was in the moment, in my body—another body—in a manner unimagined during the countless hours of meditation classes at the Project. The idea of being quietly present in my body, my breath, had seemed nigh-impossible, but eventually I'd learned to be so for longer and longer stretches of time. Those moments had been deeply peaceful.

But this ... this was *all body*

I wasn't inside the Stone Man.

I *was* the Stone Man.

Then Paul yelled at me, and I suddenly wasn't.

It's moving! Are you doing this?!

My attention snapped to, understanding what had happened. I had become lost, the lines of awareness overwhelmed and blurred as I sat in the driving seat. There wasn't time to learn how to stay fully one with the Stone body and remain Andy at the same time. I could feel those now-distant-but-connected limbs beginning to move, and not because I told them to. This was no rumbling pre-amble; the Stone Man was already in gear, the arms pushing, clawing as they began to grasp for the surface above. A distant thought penetrated my mind—*lead, this thing is carving its way through solid lead*—but that was forgotten as now Maria was screaming, her distant voice penetrating down her thread to my place in the Stone Man's driving seat:

Andy! Answer him!

I was still only a passenger. I tried to brace what I felt to be my distant arms, trying to affect the Stone Man's leaden upward swim, but it wasn't even close to being enough. I tried harder, but the second my efforts merged me more intimately with those limbs, Andy went away again and all I became was an intention to move. The sense of peace, of release—

ANDY!!

I snapped to, horrified. It was impossible. Any effort to control it meant losing myself. I tried to keep my fear hidden from the other two, but my thoughts could never be quicker than my instincts; my terror had already shot out along the threads of my currently distant circuit.

We had woken the Stone Man, we were standing on top of it, and now we couldn't stop it.

I don't have control inside here yet! We have to get out of the Housing before—

My fear bounced back into me, amplified by that of my friends, which rebounded out once more along our threads; suddenly we were in a feedback loop of emotional impulses that could only be called blind panic.

Just like that, we were done for.

I've thought about that moment often since.

In Stone Space, not only was Maria at her functional best, it was as if she'd somehow left most—not all, but most—of her trauma in her physical body. It really does remember, you know. Paul and I seemed to carry all our baggage in and out of Stone Space, but Maria seemed to float into that void like a balloon suddenly freed from its moorings. I think if, in that moment, she hadn't had the wherewithal to break us free of that feedback loop, it would have crushed us. *Everyone* in our group would have died that evening.

Taking us—out—

Then we were gasping and blinking beneath a different void, this one the jet black of the night sky above the floodlights blasting into our eyes. The lead floor beneath us was shaking; the soldiers shifted nervously on their feet, watching us, understanding that we were clearly not the ones in control of the rumbling metal below. Heavy, metallic popping and cracking sounds began to rend their way through the crisp night air, masking any sound from the nearby sea.

I heard Straub yelling first.

"Pointer! What's happening?"

I ignored her as Maria grabbed my shoulder, beckoning Paul closer as the noise around us grew; the concrete fence panels were beginning to groan as they moved.

"Take—"

The lead below us broke open, the floor shearing apart into five or six larger segments. Thick, deep cuts snaked instantly across the width of the Housing, causing everyone to stumble. *"Back up!"* Maria yelled, meaning the three of us, but all the soldiers and scientists present—including Straub and Edgwick—did as she said.

"It's coming up!" I yelled to the Brigadier. *"Back your men out of here!"*

"Are you in control?" Straub shouted back.

"No!"

Straub whitened.

"Move!" I yelled. *"Just fucking move!"*

"Fall back!" Straub called to her men. Edgwick hesitated, as if wanting to help us, but how could he? Straub turned to us. *"Get out of there you three!"*

"We can't!" I barked. *"We have to stay close!"* The data from testing at Project Orobouros told us that the threshold for flashing into the Stone Man was around one hundred feet. Now, backed up so that we were no longer physically standing on top of the rising Stone Man, I could already feel that—if I wanted to get truly inside the thing once more, to feel those limbs again—then that distance needed to be even shorter.

"Take a breath Andy!" Maria yelled over the sound of rending metal. *"You have to get back in there and stay calm! I can't help if you panic! Both of you!"* She turned to Paul. *"You have to keep it together!"*

"Sorry!" Paul yelled, nodding quickly. *"I'm okay, I'm okay!"*

"Right!" I said, clenching my fists. *"Let's—"*

Three pair of eyes widened as we felt it, looking just in time to see the first protrusion punch through the cracks in the lead. It shook the ground so violently that Maria and I fell to the floor, our vantage point now perfect to see that the protrusion was indeed the lipstick-shaped tip of the Stone Man's hand. The other punched up a few feet away and the floor beneath us progressed from cracking to crumbling; a horrible circle of darkness appeared in the lead around the tips of the Stone Man's hands and then collapsed in upon itself, sinking slightly down to form a concave dip that was already breaking into smaller pieces that rose and undulated sharply as the lead's captive slowly worked its way free. Caementum was moving, of course, in the same way it always had: implacable, inexorable, unstoppable.

The Stone Man's head came into view. Its shoulders followed immediately afterward, rising free without any pause for recovery or restraint. They moved back and forth as the Stone Man rose, swaying with an awful kind of shimmying movement that suddenly reminded me of a cobra's hood, its motion almost rhythmic—

Rhythm.

I just had time to hear that terrible staccato bass note in my head and caught Paul's white expression before I was gone again, flashing into the Stone Man's eyes, its limbs, even if I were simply a helpless passenger within them. Now its head was clear of the lead I had true sight as well as sensation; I saw my friends standing either side of my human body, dragging it backwards, still upright under its own power but with its wide-eyed head tipped to the sky. My body's arms were tight by its sides and its hands were clenched as Maria yelled something I couldn't hear over the all-consuming sound of that rhythm pounding in my Stone head. I looked at Paul and felt the connection, the objective within reach, and my human perception responded with an eagerness—

I saw Maria slap Paul across the face, hard, and as he blinked in shock Maria grabbed him by the back of his head with her free hand. She closed her eyes and then the sound of that awful rhythm instantly became background noise, blasted into silence by the now-amplified chaos of the outside world. What they were hearing, I was hearing. Maria's outside voice:

"Now stay fucking focused!" Her attention turned to me: "Andy, can you see us!? Can you see us!?"

I could ... and I understood what Maria had done now she had Paul's terror in check. She'd lined up the circuit from the outside in; through the sight of the Stone Man, thrown into incredible clarity through the conduit of Maria, *I could now see the energy of our threads flowing from the two of them*. Paul, surrounded by slowly pulsing cloud-like waves of dark, rich, drake's head green, trails of it leaking from his body to where it mingled with Maria's sparking, fizzing yellow, lighting up the space around her as if she were on fire.

I could see what they were made of. It was the most beautiful thing I have ever seen.

It radiated out of their bodies, moving in lines through the air to either side of my vision and meeting my consciousness where it lay inside the Stone Man.

I also saw my own energy, surrounding my body.

It's always looked the same since then. The same every time I saw myself and our circuit through Caementum's sight, my own energy always framed, of course, by my friends' glorious threads where they pass through my human body. I don't know why the colour of my energy is the way it is, especially compared to theirs; I can only hope that it was due to my connection to Caementum. I tell myself that's the reason.

The aura surrounding my body was a low, dull, and all-too familiar greyish-brown.

The Stone Man's viewpoint now looked as if it were clear of the warped and broken lead, having crawled free and onto a more solid part of the surface. It was straightening to its full, impressive height. In a moment it would be walking. I saw Paul's aura *pop* an instant before his terror hit me in the driving seat, snaking down his thread like a lightning bolt. The force of it snapped me out of Stone Space entirely and back into my own body, gasping in air. I saw Caementum standing on top of a creaking, crumbling mound on the Isle of Skye.

It had risen, and it let us know.

I truly wish that, in that moment, I could have stayed inside the Stone Man for a few seconds longer. I've wondered ever since if I would have noticed something go through it just before it gave off that low, booming bass note and turned the air around us to ice. Whether I would have picked up on some conscious thought, gleaned some sort of insight as to what the purpose of those audible and physical blasts were. The wind certainly whipped up and blew grit into our eyes. Whatever that bass note's actual purpose, something in it shorted out most of the floodlights surrounding the fence. The Stone Man stood tall, motionless for a moment, and suddenly thrown into terrifying silhouette by the few remaining floodlights behind it.

If I didn't know better, you see, I could have sworn the son of a bitch had a taste for the theatrical.

***

March of the Stone Men

Chapter Four

Getting a Grip, A Deeper Dive, and the Wrong Cavalry Arrives

***

I didn't know what to do next. Dispensatori was out of ideas.

Fear began to whip around our circuit again, amplifying through my friends' energy and threads—

Threads. Broken threads.

"It's cut off from the wider Stone Circuit!" I yelled. *"Its external threads are broken! They're hanging loose!"*

Before either of them could respond the Stone Man began to walk, crossing the ruined lead. It was heading straight towards Paul.

"It's threads!" I screamed. *"Fuck the Core, you can feel its threads, right?"*

"Yes!"

"Ye ... yes," Paul breathed. We were backing away from the Stone Man now, out of the Housing—

"Pointer!"

That was Straub and Edgwick yelling together, standing in the entrance and flanked by two other soldiers to our left.

In our blind terror, we'd backed up the wrong way.

There was no gap in the concrete fence behind us, and the Stone Man was closing.

"Hook us up to its threads!" I yelled to Maria. *"Make it part of our circuit! Attach its threads to our—fuck it—"*

I sent everything they needed to know down our threads. Understanding shot back the other way; Paul reluctant, Maria determined, but already I could feel Maria moving our energy out like a net. The Stone Man walked into it and suddenly we felt something snag as our circuit connected to its threads.

I began to scream.

My skin burned, the connection ablaze, but my friends remained unaffected. Of course they weren't; I was the pilot, the focal point of the circuit, the little LED light that comes on to say *hey, this is working*. But this was killing me. The Stone Man's threads, hooked up to our own, were now wildly alive, silvery and bright. The ones that still hung loose from the Stone Man were hard to detect now by comparison, dull and diminished. Should I grab them too? No, even the ones I held were too much. They *hurt*.

Our circuit was burning out. Paul was supplying power, but the Stone Man still had power of its own, and the two together—

Paul, I told him in-circuit, unable to speak aloud. *Turn power down—quick—*

The fire quickly became a mere tingling and I felt more alive than I had in my entire life. It sounds like a contradiction: our circuit, aware, transmitting emotion and thought and memory. Yet this new section of circuit was utterly...

Hmm. I don't want to say 'cold' because ... the power.

Oh God, the power.

Andy, Maria's thread said. *The Stone Man, it's still coming!*

It was. Could this new connection be used to stop it?

Fall, I thought.

The Stone Man stumbled. It dropped to one knee, leaving a crater in the ruined lead beneath it.

"Ah!"

That was Paul, barking in amazement. The Stone Man's body lightly twitched as if trying to rise, but never got its knee off the floor. Instead, it continued to convulse lightly on the spot, the way paused people would on old VHS cassette tape movies.

No one moved. No one spoke. I could feel the amazement burning from the human threads of our circuit, the unspoken question of *how did you do that* held back by fear of breaking the spell. I didn't have an answer either. I could feel the threads of the Stone Man running through *my* body's skin, lighting me up. Was this what Maria felt back at Project Orobouros when she'd saved us from the Empty Men, this sensation of raw power that felt like coming home, my entire body saying *yes, this is what I am for?*

The Stone Man stopped twitching. Its left shoulder jerked briefly downwards and then it quickly rose, becoming upright, facing Paul once more.

Andy!

Startled willpower flew away down my thread. The Stone Man paused, that twitching recommencing. The two sides of its internal battle were clear on the surface; my command to stay in place, and its own programming—or instinct—to harvest Paul's spine fighting against it. Perhaps, had it been at full power, it wouldn't have been a battle at all.

"Andy ..." Maria whispered aloud. "Oh my God, Andy ..."

"Wait," I said, holding up a hand. "Paul, turn the juice back up just a little. Just a *little*."

Paul didn't speak, but the tingling in my skin became a sunburn. It was bearable, and more importantly, the Stone Man's twitching ceased.

"Holy shit," Paul gasped, dropping to a knee of his own now, his hand going to his mouth. Maria suddenly hugged me. I felt wetness on my shoulder from her fresh tears of happiness. I was in a state of shock as I dumbly wrapped my arms around her in return, looking over her shoulder at our ominous, stationary ... ally?

Weapon?

"Pointer!" Straub yelled, and I nearly didn't recognise her voice. She sounded delighted. "All of you! This is incredible!" Edgwick stood with his hands on his head, fists clutching at his red hair in amazement. Maria released me and threw her head back, bellowing at the sky.

"Yes!" She spun to face the Stone Man, her tears now running freely as she moved from delight to release. She raised both middle fingers and jabbed them forwards. *"Fuck! YOU!"* Then she dropped down, clutching Paul to her. He buried his face in her shoulder, embracing her back. I stood there awkwardly, watching. This wasn't just their trauma.

The Caeterus had killed everyone. They'd killed everyone in the country—

Nope. We had to be done with that. I *am* done with that. I have to be. I must be.

I turned, swaying, to look at Straub over in the entranceway.

"Andy," she said, using my first name. "Your eyes." Scared, I yanked my phone from my pocket and turned the camera to selfie mode.

The whites of my eyes were almost completely gone, shot through with blood.

My pupils were fully dilated but I looked alert to the point of insanity. I *felt* it.

"I'm ... I'm okay," I said, my voice hoarse. "Guys," I said to Paul and Maria, waving their worries away as they also noticed my eyes. "I'm fine. Look, I think we have this thing under control, but we're still standing right in front of it ..."

"Yeah, yes," Paul said, releasing Maria and standing before grabbing me up in a brief bear hug. *"Good fucking work man,"* he whispered in my ear. *"Bloody hell, good work."*

"All of us," before adding in a mumble: *"We* did it." I felt cheesy saying it, but it had to be said. We moved behind the Stone Man. Outside of Stone Space I didn't have the same my-limbs-its-limbs connection to its body, but I already felt I was starting to get feedback from the thing. I'd only had a few minutes of exerting outside control, too. Would that connection increase?

"The Core," Maria sniffed. I didn't need to ask how she knew the term; she'd been in-circuit with me. "Can you get to it now?"

A good question. Maybe the opening into the depths of the Stone Man would be fully exposed by now.

"We've only just established the thinnest point of control," I said. "I think it's too soon to worry about going for the Core at the same time as learning to *keep* that control." But then what *is* the next step, I wondered. Do we try to make it walk—

The Stone Man stood and took a crunching step forward.

We were behind it, at least, which was undoubtedly a good thing. If we'd been standing in front of it, Paul would have actually shat himself.

"Jesus!" he yelled, and his distraction meant that the sensation in my skin dropped back to a mere tingle. The Stone Man began to twitch once more, trying to regain control.

"No!" I yelled, grabbing at his arm. *"Keep the power at the same level—"*

"Sorry!" The sunburn feeling came back as Paul refocused. The twitching stopped. "Did you do that?" he asked.

"Well, I mean I wondered if we *could* make it walk, and then—"

"You've got to be careful," Maria said quietly, as if I was doing it on purpose or something. Then her face briefly twisted.

"What was that?" Paul asked.

"I'm okay," she said.

"It didn't look okay," Paul said.

"I'm keeping all the energy contained, Paul," Maria said quickly. "That thing's skin is, contrary to everything it does, paper thin. Or at least it is *now*, and in terms of energy. Dealing with that is hard work. Let's just get it out of here. Eric needs us to get it back through the Barrier."

"Right," I said, wondering how the hell we'd get it through the small hole Eric had made. Perhaps the Stone Man would be able to just walk through the Barrier?

"You're ready for this now?" Maria asked Paul. "You're going to have to get used to being next to this thing, you know."

"... I know."

"Okay. Take us out, Andy."

Just like that, I thought. *Sure.* I mentally tightened my grip on the Stone Man's threads.

"I won't let it get you, Paul," I said.

"Well ... it looks like, if you don't keep an eye on it..."

The Stone Man took another crunching step. All of us jumped again.

"*That was you, right?*" Paul barked.

"Yes," I said, as Caementum took five steps and then began to turn, heading the wrong way; its weight swayed too far over in that direction, and it crashed to the floor like a falling anvil.

"Paul, give me a little extra juice, just a little—"

The Stone Man sat upright, twitching, before rising to a standing position. I tried to picture it walking in my mind, a slow steady gait like the one I had seen for countless hours back at the Project. It took two steps forward and then froze mid-stride.

A klaxon-esque noise began to emanate from it. One I'd heard before; a high, reedy sound, even if it was a little different this time. The noise seemed to *creak,* as if the creature's joints were giving way, but then it quickly became louder. The air around us turned into an icy fist, gripping our bodies.

"What's it doing?" Maria asked. The fact the sound was shredded now, more *broken,* had almost stopped me from recognising it. *You should know, Maria,* I thought, *you've seen my memories.* I glanced at Straub, and the terror on her exhausted and ashen face told me she recognised it too.

She'd heard this too, the day my Sophie died. The day the Stone Man had been stopped, and it had summoned—

I tried to feel around in Stone Space for some kind of off switch.

"Make it stop," Paul said, barely audible over the noise, and then the sound suddenly cut off by itself. The temperature returned to normal. There was silence under the black sky and floodlights, but my ears were filled with the sound of my heartbeat.

"What was it doing?" Maria repeated.

"Not now," I said, trying to focus but panicking. The Stone Man's threads felt slippery and I was fumbling them, the creature's shoulders turning slowly now, beginning to face towards Paul.

I found the threads. Gripped them. Told the Stone Man *STOP*, and it did.

Five steps, I told it.

Bam. Bam. Bam ... Bam-Bam.

The Stone Man stopped, rocking on the spot. The steps had been messy, baby deer-like, and in the wrong direction to the Housing exit, but it had done what I'd said. Now.

Left. Right.

Bam. Bam.

Left. Right. Left. Right.

I realised that panic had made us stupid, we didn't need the fucking exit anyway, this was *the Stone Man,* it made its own exits—

Bam. Bam. Bam. Bam.

"You're doing it," Paul breathed, and his thread sang of belief, of confidence, and any other time I would have repeated *we're doing it together* but now all I wanted to say was *shut up, we're all about to die if I can't stay focused, we have to get away from here* now—

The air pressure all around us dropped.

I instantly lost control again and the Stone Man crunched back down to one knee.

"Pointer!" Straub barked, but her helpless-sounding voice was lost under the deafening fizzing noise that began to ring around the Housing. This was too much even for her. There was the screech and clang of a segment of fencing being slammed instantaneously into the ground. The fizzing was so loud and close that Paul leapt sideways, and to make the moment even more bizarre, the fencing was flattened without—for a split second—anything visible in place to show what had crushed it.

Then the reality dropped into place.

It was as if they had been there all along, hidden, and were now suddenly visible. Huge; staggeringly so at such close quarters, their legs drawn in under themselves, pulled tight like the wings of sleeping birds on a wire. Maria screamed, realising what was here, seeing the impossibility of this new Arrival occurring mere feet away.

The fizzing noise stopped, and the cause now lay before us, a dark pair of immense and terrifying visitors.

The Crawlers had arrived.

They stood motionless, just as their brethren had upon their initial Arrival at the Project. Their immense boulder-like ... heads? Torsos? Whatever the correct word was, the central, mushroom-cap-like bulk of the Crawlers stood upon their many curled-under legs, their bizarre but monstrous bodies composed of a grey (and very familiar) stone-looking substance. For now, they stood at around eight feet tall. When they awoke, I knew, they would straighten and rise another three before going about their unstoppable, destructive business. The sudden appearance of such towering, solid bulk was difficult to comprehend even now, after all I had witnessed up to this point.

Maria opened her mouth to scream again and I instinctively pulled her to me, slapping my hand over her mouth as if she would wake them. She immediately slapped herself free, writhing like a trapped cat.

"Get off, get *off!*" she said. "We have to *go*, before they—before they—"

Kill us? Almost certainly, but I knew the reason Maria was stumbling; no-one knew what the Crawlers' exact purpose was.

The breaking of the connection between Paul and Caementum at the Project had triggered the blast of energy I'd originally referred to as an EMP. The term was incorrect—it had caused the helicopter transporting Caementum to crash, but it certainly hadn't fried all the electrical systems the way an EMP would—so we started calling it the *Detonation*. In the short period before that event, they had seemed to search for Caementum around the Project Orobouros hillside, destroying wind turbines and brutally murdering anyone that had come close. But they'd been killed, or at least shut down by the Detonation or whatever you wanted to call it, before they'd reached their assumed objective.

The Stone Man summoned them then, as it had now. Whatever their purpose was, it couldn't be good.

STAY, I told the Stone Man, hoping it would work. I just needed a fucking second to think.

"The dead Crawlers!" I yelled to Straub, thinking of how they had eventually been moved at Ground Zero for further (fruitless) testing. "Are these them..."

It was a pointless question. The Barrier had tanked our comms. Straub would have no way of knowing if these were the original two, somehow transported from the ruins of the Ground Zero facility to the Isle of Skye. Plus, these *felt* new. Fresh. Terrifyingly powerful, silently crackling with energy. I immediately tried to flash into them and, just like before, it was even easier than with Caementum ... even if, just like before, there was nothing in there but blackness and silence. Ruthless efficiency. These Stone enforcers seemed to be built for speed, after all.

"We think they're backup," Paul said to Maria. "What you just heard coming from ..." He glanced sideways at the kneeling Stone Man, "... was some kind of distress signal."

"What these things did," Maria said, "to the soldiers at the Project, the ones that got close." She looked at me, and for a moment I saw something terrible in her eyes. Defeat. "They're going to wake up and do it to us, aren't they?"

"Maybe not," I said, "if you can hide us from them. Do you think you can?"

I felt Maria's thread send something towards the dormant Crawlers, searching.

"I don't know," she said. "I don't think I'll know until they wake up. Hell, Andy, I'm already covering Caementum as well as us now." She was. The threads of the Caeterus or the eye of the Stone Giant would be all around us by now otherwise. But could she hide the Stone Man under the Barrier? "What will the Crawlers do if I can't hide Caementum?"

"Best guess," Paul murmured, "was that they were either here to collect the Right Honorable Gentleman—they have enough limbs for that— and take it home, maybe to stop us doing exactly what we're doing now. That, or they're the repair team. We didn't get to find out."

"Pointer," Straub said. "The plan is the same. Move."

This situation had gone from difficult to impossible and of course fucking Dispensatori had to solve it. I looked at my circuit as they stared dumbly from the Stone Man to the Crawlers and my frustration rose. I sent a little goosing down their threads, feeling a grim sense of satisfaction when they jumped a little.

"Sorry," Paul said quickly.

"Yeah, we're here, we're here," Maria added.

"Right," I said, not knowing how to handle the sudden resolution. "… sorry." I turned back to the Brigadier. "We can't outrun those things. You know how fast they are."

"You have time," Edgwick said, his voice earnest. "They didn't wake up immediately last time. If its anything like then, you'll have about, what, half an hour was it? An hour?"

"We'd have to walk from here to *Coventry* before they wake up," I said. "There's no way we get there first, and even if we do, we don't know if—"

"We do not," Straub said, raising a shaking hand to cut me off, "have any other option—"

"The Core," I snapped. "It's got to be worth a quick check now the Crawlers are here. Racing them won't work."

"Agreed," Straub said. "I'm going back in. Stay here and keep an eye out."

"Do it," Paul said.

March of the Stone Men

I reinforced my previous command of Stay—I didn't know how much lasting power such commands had—and moved back inside the greyish brown of the Stone Man's internal space. The was a weak pulsing light in there now that its internal systems were back in their correct places, even if they were fighting against our control. Leaking and shored up everywhere as the Stone Man may be, it was still the most unstoppable weapon in the history of human armament.

The ballast doors were open down below! I could even see a glimpse of the Core in the depths of the Stone Man's lower level, down in that black maw where even the greyish brown light fell dark. I thought it would be easy now to get down there, but I needed more juice. I called down my circuit's threads to my friends outside.

Paul—

Paul sent the energy, Maria focused it into me, and then I was in front of the Core.

Its size was as remarkable as the sudden increase in pressure all around me. As the weight of the depth crushed in on me like a crowd, I tried to focus, see the edges of the thing, and understood that I had to move away to see it fully. It appeared to be—in the manner that my mind perceived it, at least—the size of a house. I hung before it in the cloudy darkness, suspended at its mid-point as if it were holding me up for inspection. It was bulky and made of straight lines. Its shape appeared uneven, one edge longer than the other. It formed almost a kind of lower-case q, if the bottom tip of the letter were joined back up to the protusion at the top. If there's a name for that shape, I don't know what it is.

Maybe you do. Are you someone smart, getting to hear this? I don't know how you came to be listening to it, after all. I think I know what I intend to do with this recording once it's done, but there could still be other people that hear it. I wonder what's happening with you now, wherever you—wherever *we*—are with all this. I wonder—

Sorry. The Core. I was in front of the Core.

Its shape was filled with that same greyish brown light that danced faintly in the distance; there was just a little more *of* it inside the object, a little extra poured into this enormous shape. Here it was solid, unmoving; the effect was like trying to make out a single cube of ice placed before a distant glacier.

The pressure around me was making it difficult to catch my breath, and I panicked before remembering I didn't *need* to breathe in here, understanding that this was a trick of the mind. Whatever pressure I was feeling wouldn't kill me—wouldn't crush my mind or whatever—but it was intense. I didn't know how long I could stay down here and function properly.

Are you okay?

They'd come inside. Okay. I thought we'd know if any Stone stuff happened outside.

I'm okay, Maria. Can you two see this?

Just about, Paul said. *You're so far away.*

Can you come down here?

A pause. I felt them try.

No.

Okay.

What the fuck was I supposed to do with this thing?

We had no time. The Crawlers were here. I began to reach out to the Core, sending my mind towards it, *into* it, the Core filling my vision until I could see nothing else.

Let him do it, I heard Paul say from far above.

Then—without sound or sensation of impact—I simply couldn't move any further forward. Was I touching it? If so, there was no give, no heat, no cold, just impenetrability. I began to circle the Core, moving slowly, travel down here feeling heavy and difficult. There was no join, no doorway anywhere around it. *Was* it a mind? All I had were guesses.

I can't get in, I told the others.

Can you move it up here?

It was a ridiculous question. The thing was enormous ... but since when did the laws of physics apply in Stone Space?

I'll try.

I swam underneath it, a minnow moving below a Blue Whale, and then moved back up until its unyielding solidity stopped any further progress. I was braced against it, even though the idea felt stupid.

Okay, I said, *try bringing me back u—*

There was a sudden and dramatic reduction in pressure and then shock shot into me from Paul and Maria's threads as they hung in the upper levels of the Stone Man's inner space. They were both amazed by the immense object suddenly appearing before them and by the fact that *it had worked.*

We had brought the Core back up from the depths.

I could see its edges a little easier up here, the lighter backdrop throwing it's darker colouring into sharper relief.

Jesus, Paul said, but there was no time for amazement. The Crawlers were here.

Help me, I said.

How?

I don't know, I said. *Help me to—to—feel for—just spread out, okay?* I felt Paul and Maria's minds move to opposite sides of the immense, uneven shape. *Try to get me in there, I guess. Open it up or something. Focus.*

There was a sensation of electricity and then the internal Stone Space of Caementum became clearer, sharper ... but that was it. There was no more time for this. We had the Core, that was something, but it couldn't help us now.

Everyone out.

I flashed out of the Stone Man's depths, coming back to my body and seeing the Crawlers with my human sight. I turned to Paul and Maria, seeing the same helpless feeling reflected in their eyes. I understood with an awful heaviness that it was my job to make them believe in a plan of escape that I knew was doomed. What could I say?

"Maybe if we get to the Barrier before they wake up," I said quietly. "Maybe ... they can't cross it?"

It was weak. But then I thought maybe it wasn't. I saw Paul thinking the same thing as he considered the Crawlers.

"They *are* made of a similar-looking substance," he said, squinting. "But it's not the *same*. They've always looked slightly different."

Eric had told us the Stone Men could walk through the individual bubbles, but he'd also told us that the Barrier was different to them. And, furthermore, if the Stone Men were made of a different substance to the Crawlers –

"Then maybe they really can't get through?" Maria asked, looking between myself and Paul. She was shaking, but her steel was coming through once again, drawn out by hope like an infection from a wound.

"We have the Stone Man's Core," I said, turning to Straub. "Maybe the Barrier will buy us some time on the other side to figure out a way to open it."

Straub nodded to Edgwick, who spoke into his radio. At this distance from the Barrier we appeared to have some functioning comms.

"Shoreham," he said, "Prep for immediate air transport. What do we have on inbound?" He listened.

"Inbound?" I asked. Edgwick nodded and lowered the radio.

"Warships," he said. He was sweating. "And the news isn't good. As far we can glean from Pallister, they're still some time away, and our international allies are reluctant to bring their vessels close to the Barrier at this point. Not that it would make any difference."

"Mm," Straub grunted. "Pointer. We're going to try to sling Caementum beneath a chopper and fly it back to Eric; you three can ride inside the aircraft."

The memory flashed from me to my circuit, unbidden: the Stone Man, walking during the first Arrival, four military helicopters attempting to lift it via a net and being unable to do so. Holbrooks and co. had their theories on how the Stone Men could manipulate their mass. How would that come into play now? We could barely make the thing walk.

The Stone Man continued to twitch.

Stand, I told it.

It did. All of us flinched.

We'd have to stop doing that.

***

Chapter Five

Flatbed Indeed, The Slowest Race in the World, and an A for E-Effort

***

"I don't think this is going to work either."

That was Maria, behind me. As we walked back from the Housing a field medic had done a quick and superior fixit job on her broken fingers, replacing Edgwick's makeshift splint. Those re-set fingers were now covering her mouth a little as she muttered quietly to Paul. I didn't like that; it felt as if I were the one pushing this idea, the one in charge, and those two were somehow co-conspirators.

The helicopter hadn't been able to lift the Stone Man, as expected.

Everyone had seen the footage from the First Arrival: four Apache helicopters, struggling to lift a net with the Stone Man walking across the centre, the choppers unable to lift the creature off the grassy field's surface. The same result happened here, albeit with only one chopper. But it hadn't been about weight the first time. The Stone Man hadn't left footprint craters in the soil, and certainly not those of anywhere near the depth that kind of Apache-resisting weight would have produced. So surely it wasn't about weight now?

Put it this way, one of Straub's team told me *Electromagnetic force, gravitational force, strong force, weak force: the four fundamental forces of particle physics. We can control these to an extent, or better said, we can take advantage of some of the forces better than others. For example, augmenting the amount and motion of positive and negative charge in a system gives us electricity. But ... as we understand it, there is no opposite charge for* mass. *If there were, we could manipulate gravity and control it the same way we do electricity. But in electricity there is attraction and repulsion. Why is there only positive mass, right? So, what if the Stone Men understand how to manipulate* all *four fundamental forces in certain situations, and to a certain extent? You know?*

I didn't know, at all.

So, I asked, *how does any of that knowledge help me make it lighter?*

Not necessarily lighter, they said. *Weren't you listening?*

I walked away then. Time was against us, and this wasn't helping.

"I never thought this was going to work, either," I snapped at Maria, "so shall we not bother trying?"

We were onto Plan B now.

A tread-plate ramp had been hastily lined up behind a flatbed truck, its cab decked out in camouflage paint. I'd seen the vehicle many times on-base, usually ferrying around things like forklift trucks and heavy machinery. It was parked in the middle of the thin central road. This tarmac strip ran along the outside of the impressive single building that made up the Chisel's remote base. Here, against the darkness above us, there wasn't much light compared to the Housing; a mere three or four portable floodlights that provided illumination for the whole avenue. The truck was currently surrounded by a cluster of roughly thirty soldiers and maybe ten civilian-dress scientist types; surely everyone still on-base. They all looked pale and shocked, either by seeing the Stone Man walk up-close or from the knowledge that everyone they loved on the mainland was—with almost total certainty, given that less than 0.003 percent of the country's population was left alive under the Barrier—dead.

The plan was—if Caementum was somehow automatically resisting being lifted—to try and get Caementum to walk up the metal ramp and onto the truck's bed.

In the short time we'd been driving the Stone Man, we'd already got it moving a little more efficiently. Caementum could now take as many as ten steps before it crashed to the floor or began to turn in the wrong direction; it was currently lying where it had most recently fallen. Dealing with my circuit was proving difficult as well; Paul's and Maria's PTSD seemed to peak with their proximity to the Stone Man, a screeching duet singing down their threads. Receiving it was like a terrible itch I couldn't scratch. I tried to soothe it, soothe *them.* I couldn't.

"Let's just get it on there," Maria snapped back, reddening.

Stand, I told it.

Nothing happened.

"Guys. Please. Focus."

They tried. My—our—circuit's threads hummed and now the Stone Man moved. Its responses were definitely becoming quicker. It sat up and stood smoothly, a surprisingly graceful movement that was totally at odds with everything else we'd tried to get it to do.

"How do you get it to stand like that?" Maria asked.

"That's just it," I said, "I'm not making it do that. I think I'm somehow triggering some kind of pre-programmed *stand* message. I suppose it wants to stand as that would mean it can go after ... ah, *fuck*. Sorry mate."

"Don't worry about it," Paul said, but *he* looked very worried.

I looked at the ramp and guessed at the distance. Four steps to reach it, maybe four more to get up and onto the centre of the truck's bed. Not far, but controlling the Stone Man wasn't always as simple as saying *do this* and watching the results. It was better, I found, to tell the Stone Man what to do and then focus on its movements as it carried out the command, like a parent holding a walking toddler upright by its hands as it learned to walk. But the fucker already *knew* how to walk! It was as if, by preventing its objective of tearing Paul's spine from its body, any access to pre-programmed motor functions was denied. And the Crawlers would soon awaken—

A message came from Maria's thread:

How about you focus too, eh?

Maria's eyebrows were raised, her head cocked sideways. I smirked despite myself, and she actually returned it, a little.

Eight steps, I told the creature.

The Stone Man lurched forward like a drugged bull lumbering out of a rodeo chute. The tarmac of the Chisel's central road cracked with each thudding step.

THUD. THUD. THUD. THUD.

The Stone Man raised its foot to step up onto the ramp, and on cue I closed my eyes and visualised. I felt the other two send the same concept, the same pre-agreed vision that would be our attempt to try and trigger the Stone Man's mass (or counter-force, or whatever the hell) controlling powers: Caementum, hollow and filled with helium, so light now that any one of us could lift it with ease, effortlessly stepping up the ramp and into the truck.

Lighter than air—

BANG. BANG. BANG.

I opened my eyes as I heard the cacophonous screeching of the Stone Man's feet flattening the tread plate, seeing the Stone Man's body causing the back end of the flatbed to concertina in on itself. I sent the command *STOP* but I was too quick; the Stone Man stopped and pitched straight forwards. It crashed through the rest of the truck's bed, wrenching the attached end free from the cab and see-sawing upwards as it sheared free of its steel moorings. Everyone ducked as fragments of metal sprayed through the air like steel buckshot.

"It can't be that heavy!" Maria gasped.

"It's not just about weight as we understand it, remember?" I said. "It's not calibrated properly, either. Maybe its over-correcting as it moves off the earth or something. The ramp, the flat bed are elevated ..."

"Fine," Straub said. "Walk it as best you can. Hatton is waiting."

"Drops?" Maria asked. "He's in trouble? Has word come back?"

"I'd just get moving if I were you," Straub said, but her tone wasn't unkind.

The Stone Man lay twitching, face down, wedged half inside the crushed truck's bed.

Stand.

Nothing happened.

"Paul?"

"Ready."

"Maria?"

She closed her eyes. I felt the constant tension in her thread flicker for a second.

"Try it now," she said.

Stand.

With another smooth, automatic movement, Caementum rose from the wreckage, the metal screeching once more as it yielded to an unstoppable force from another world. Beside me, Paul grunted.

"You okay?" I asked.

"Yeah. I mean ... I'm powering that thing right now, you know."

"You are?"

"Why do you sound so surprised?"

"It might have only been fumes left in there by Stone Man standards, but I suppose it still felt pretty damn powerful. So you're still the main battery then?"

"Maybe not the main," he said. "But I'm providing a lot of it. You can't feel that?"

"I guess." I'd assumed that the constant baseline strain coming down Paul's thread was stress. Maria caught my eye and waved me away.

"I'm fine," she said. "Really. Keeping Caementum sealed and hidden—and us hidden too—is just a lot." *Turn,* I told the Stone Man. It did, tearing a circle in the crushed bed around it. Was its twitching a little less rapid? I thought it might be. "And I'm not sure," Maria continued, "that I'm going to able to keep it hidden if we get back under the Barrier. He's kind of a beacon to *their* circuit, wouldn't you say? And I'm working at capacity already." She sighed wearily. "I keep thinking about that moment, the one right before we left Ladybower. That was so glorious. I had this moment of …" She held up a tightly clenched fist. "And now …" She trailed off. I saw it then, her longing. Maria wanted to return to that feeling, and very badly, an addict already.

"I get it," I said.

"Is that selfish?" she asked, surprising me. "You'd understand this better than anyone."

I didn't know what to say. I watched the Stone Man slowly completing its circle and an idea hit me.

Step forward.

I sent the command early; the Stone Man could have turned completely around and walked back out through the hole it had made in the truck's bed without causing any further damage. Sending the command when I did made the Stone Man kick through more of the truck's bed to free itself. Tread plate steel flew before it like tissue paper; scrappy, screeching metal birds taking to the air. I felt a moment of strange delight.

"See?" I told Maria, forcing a smile. "Those thoughts aren't selfish at all."

No friendly smirk came back this time. I immediately remembered Eric, and how much he was counting on us to get this thing back to him quickly.

"Okay," I said quickly, uncertain. I thought I'd nailed that. "Let's, uh, focus. I'm going to try and do twenty steps. Let's see how we do."

"Okay."

Threads thrummed, and the Stone Man walked.

We actually got to forty steps before it fell to the ground. Eric was running out of time.

***

For every minute that passed, for every stumble or flat-out fall that put the Stone Man on the deck, the tension in my back and shoulders rose another degree.

Not just from the frustration, but the self-recrimination. If we lost concentration? Or became too nervy? Or maybe Paul or Maria did something as simple as *coughing* and that meant their efforts weren't at maximum for the briefest of moments? *Bam,* Caementum took another nosedive. Behind us, the remaining soldiers from the Chisel followed pointlessly; three Jeeps filled with soldiers with the rest of the infantry following on foot. Our packs were in the vehicles to help preserve our strength. Straub and Edgwick walked a few feet behind us. I'd been told repeatedly that the vehicles were in fact Range Rovers, but I just couldn't get my head around referring to the vehicles the *British army* used as the same thing that a footballer's wife uses to drive her French Bulldog to the groomers. All three of us had declined seats in the transports. We were moving at half of regular walking pace anyway, and Maria's response put it perfectly:

"If I'm sitting down, my mind is more likely to wander. I want to walk."

The light from the moon and stars was obscured by the halogen headlights from the Jeeps that lit our way. The Stone Man, walking in front of us, cast a long shadow that reached the edge of the light's circle. High above us, two helicopters followed noisily. One was carrying visible armaments.

We hadn't bickered for a while either, to my great relief. The focus we currently needed meant that communication was at a minimum, and Paul and Maria were working *hard.* Both of their foreheads were covered in a thin film of perspiration. I had the easy part, it seemed, at least in terms of physical strain. I didn't know how I could help. The best I could do was come up with a game:

"Okay, fifty-three steps. That's the record. Let's see if we can get to fifty-four, yeah?"

That was a mistake. The implication was damning and disheartening. Here we were counting double digit steps when we had to walk all the way to Coventry? We couldn't walk the length of a high street without falling over, let alone smash the Prism. We were to somehow swing a punch that could level a Stone building? Yes, we were constantly improving, but we would have to do way, *way* better than this.

Even so, I did catch myself marvelling at Caementum's lurching, uneven gait. I can admit it: I couldn't escape the occasional feeling that *I was making it do that.* I was the one in remote control, but any satisfaction I might have experienced from that—anything that reminded me of the way I used to feel about being Dispensatori—was tempered by the *other* reason for my ever-growing tension.

The Crawlers.

It had to have been at least an hour since they arrived. Of course, we had no definite idea of how long they would take to wake up, or if they even would wake up at all. The radios of Straub and co. did indeed seem to work intermittently this far away from the Barrier, and as we'd walked the first half of this staggering, stumbling journey back to Eric, I'd asked for regular updates from the Housing. Were the Crawlers active? Not yet. But the closer we drew to the edge of the Barrier, the worse the radio signal became, until eventually they died completely. This was worrying; the range of effect hadn't been this wide before. Was this because the Barrier was hardening, as Eric had suggested?

What would that mean for Eric if it fully hardened with him inside it? This interference meant that, of course, we'd been unable to get radio or phone updates about Eric's current state. Any word we'd received had been from personnel in Jeeps (or Chelsea Tractors, if you insist) occasionally ferrying details up to us from the Barrier's edge.

The last message had been simple but worrying: Eric had stopped talking. He was upright but unresponsive.

After that, when any of us asked Straub for details, she only said:

"Concentrate on the mission."

Eventually we were approaching the Skye bridge. We wouldn't be able to see Eric until we had crested its long, gentle rise, and at our current pace that wouldn't be for several minutes. No-one was talking, but there were plenty of sounds: the rumbling of the Jeeps' tyres, the dull thuds of the soldiers' boots biting into the tarmac, the steadily growing sound of the waves. Above all of it, the heavy, heavy pounding of Caementum's feet. Our weapon. Our *best shot*.

The Stone Man fell over again.

"That was sixty three steps ..." Paul said, straightening up, wincing and putting his hands to the small of his back.

We weren't even off the Isle of Skye yet.

***

We crested the rise of the bridge. The edge of the Barrier—and Eric—lay before us, far in the distance.

If it wasn't for the floodlights that Straub's people had set up on our side of the Barrier, we wouldn't be able to make him out. There were no streetlights on the bridge nor the road leading up to it. Eric would have been a tiny, shadowy lump at best from this distance. As it was, he looked ghostly, lit harshly by the portable glare.

It was obvious that he was in trouble.

His stance was much lower now, his legs still straight-ish but his back bent much further. The Barrier immediately around him was now as jet black as the sky above, absorbing a lot of the floodlight. The rest of the Barrier remained mostly transparent, stretching up and across and out and away from our colleague. A handful of personnel were clustered close to him. All of them facing up the bridge towards us, their backs to Eric, their hands limp by their sides. For a moment I was reminded of the Shufflers back in Coventry, and then I realised: they were seeing the Stone Man walk. They were seeing that the plan had worked. They had a sliver of hope, and a mountain of awe.

"We're coming!" Maria yelled. "Eric! We're nearly with you! It worked!"

Eric didn't even twitch in response.

"He might not be able to hear you," I said. I meant it. Eric was a long way away, and the sound of the sea and the wind coming off it were almost certainly carrying her words away.

"Hundred and seventy-two," Paul grunted. "Hundred and seventy-three..."

"Okay," I said, "quick, let's keep this—"

"He's in trouble," Maria said, squinting at Eric.

Some of the personnel had suddenly rushed over to Eric, looking as if they were talking to him, but Eric's head didn't even come up. His body jolted. I felt my anxiety reflected in my circuit's threads.

Out of the corner of my eye, I saw the Stone Man twitch.

"He is," I said quickly, "but we need to make sure we keep—"

"Paul, you have to try to help him," Maria said, ignoring me. "Can you do something from here?"

"*Guys—*" They weren't concentrating. The Stone Man was beginning to turn. I hadn't told it to.

"*Paul!*" I yelled, pushing him backwards and away from the Stone Man as it began to move towards him. "*Focus!*"

Terror seized Paul's features and his thread became wild, energy slicing into me.

Maria, with me—

I tried to force her to use her control, to send one cohesive thought:

Turn back—

It didn't work. The Stone Man took a step towards Paul. My own terror spiked. I managed to send another command, this time to my own circuit:

FUCKING HELP ME—

Our timing was off again. The threads twitched and bucked out of alignment, and Caementum continued towards Paul, who backed away like Ebeneezer Scrooge presented with Marley's ghost, his face a death mask. Our flapping threads were briefly aligned and we bit down as one. The circuit became tight. I threw the command at the Stone Man again.

TURN—

It jolted as if it had been poked in the back. It then began a slow, lurching turn back towards the Barrier, almost literally dragging its feet as, once again, it attempted to resist what we were telling it to do.

"For *fuck's sake, Paul!*" I yelled in frustration. "You of all people! *You!*" Paul didn't speak. He just watched the Stone Man walk, his hand on his rapidly heaving chest. "And you!" I yelled at Maria. "You're supposed to be keeping all this *smooth!*" It wasn't fair, but all the frustration was spilling out of me like a backed up septic tank. "We can't lose control like that! It's *up and running!* Warmed up! Did you feel how hard it was to get control back just now?"

But Maria wasn't even looking at me.

"Will you—" I began, but Maria cut me off.

"*Shh,*" she hissed, still squinting at Eric. My head nearly exploded with rage, but then again saw the distant Eric twitch violently. He still hadn't raised his head or looked as if he were responding to the personnel with him on the bridge. "Paul," she said. "Please. Try and send him something."

"We need to get our rhythm back first," he breathed. "I can't risk it until my bloody heart calms down. We might lose it again."

"Okay," Maria said, "But let me know as soon as you can, please." At our current snail's pace, Eric looked to be at least … six minutes' walk away? Seven? "Sorry again, Andy. But please don't swear at me. I won't have that."

"Sorry," I said, meaning it. I'd just felt the full force of Paul and Maria's fear of the Stone Man, of *this exact* Stone Man. And I was frightened of not being up to the job? I had nothing to complain about. Ahead of us, Eric twitched harder and one of his knees buckled briefly. That was too violent to be fatigue. "Something *is* happening—"

A horrible thought hit me.

"Eric said that he could hear what the Caeterus were saying, right?"

"He said he sometimes got the gist of it," Maria said, "or the tone. Andy, what—"

I felt her reach the same conclusion. Paul too.

"Eric knows," I said, feeling my fingers and toes suddenly go cold. "He can hear them talking about—" I spun to face Straub, seated in the front of the nearest Jeep. "Radio the Housing—" I began, but stopped. The signal on the Housing end would be okay, but ours was too close to the Barrier—

Muffled, distant pops began to float towards us on the breeze.

Gunfire. I saw Straub recognise the sound.

The Crawlers were awake.

"Oh my God," Paul breathed.

"Pointer, Winter, Constance," Straub said sharply. Some of her hair had come loose under her beret and was blowing gently in her face. "*Listen to me. You can get there before they arrive—*"

I was seeing it again: the soldiers dying on the hill at Project Orobouros, pulped into a thick red jelly beneath the machine-gun tattoo of the Crawlers' thunderous feet.

"We won't make it," I said, feeling something drain out of me.

"They were …" Paul stammered. "They were so *fast*…"

"You might still have time," she said, her voice changing into something beyond calm. This, I saw, was why she held her rank. "You have a few minutes before they're here. If you can move, and keep moving, the three of you can do it." It was a lie. We all knew a few minutes wouldn't be enough. The fingers of Maria's shaking hand dug into my bicep. Her eyes were wet, staring.

"Come … come on," she said. "*Dispensatori.* Th-this is *it*."

I tried to feel a surge of belief but it didn't come; terror has a wonderful way of tearing back the layers of our self-deceit. In this instance it vaporised the block on my thread, and in that moment all the shields of therapy and meditation and affirmation were ripped away from me.

I froze. In the moment of action, God help me, I froze. The terrified, shivering and defenceless little boy I truly was, truly *am*, was exposed to my circuit.

Maria recoiled slightly, shocked. Of course she was.

Then she stepped forward.

Something else came down her thread, something that matched, in energy, the physical act she performed: she put her arms around me, held me tight.

All thought stopped at her double embrace. My eyes saw the Stone Man stumble again, but my thread felt the other two take up the slack for a moment, holding it, giving me time. What was happening? I felt Paul's arms encircle me too, standing by my side, and I heard his shaking voice in my head:

And you really were, he said, *going to jump out of that window—*

Tears suddenly burst out of me and ran in rivulets down my face—what the *fuck* was happening—as I felt the Stone Man's threads become crisper, clearer. I looked at Paul and Maria, their faces filling my vision, and I saw that they were crying too.

We were all going to die. But we knew we were going to die trying, and we were going to die together.

I tried to respond.

Let's—fucking WALK—

Electricity fired around our circuit.

We physically separated, watching Caementum straighten ahead of us, its gait becoming steady, constant. Behind us, the distant gunfire suddenly stopped. We knew why, and it wasn't because the Crawlers had been dealt with. Thinking about that wasn't going to help. The wind off the sea caught Maria's hair, blowing it out sideways and making her suddenly look like a goddamn Valkyrie as she straightened her back and strode forward. Paul's shaking hand found the back of my neck.

"Fucking COME ON!" he barked, leaning into the wind and slapping at my neck.

"*Let's have you! Let's have you!*" I yelled, echoing the sentiment, and as I bore down on the Stone Man's threads, I looked down the rise and along the road to Eric. How many steps between us? It didn't matter. I tightened up my connection to the Stone Man as firmly as I could—

Then I suddenly couldn't see the Stone Man anymore.

In fact, I was a little closer to Eric than I had been a moment ago. What the hell was—

I was back inside the driving seat. I was back in the Stone Man's eyes. I'd flashed too far in, swept up in the emotion of the moment, going all the way out of the other side of control and before I knew it, I felt my *other* limbs moving again, feeling their strength.

I had to get out before I lost awareness of where Andy Pointer ended and the Stone Man began, but my resistance was collapsing like a breaking wave. The fear, the joy, all of it was being washed away by a sense of all-pervading peace ... and power.

My God.

Andy—

Walking. I was walking, the motion of *walking*, effortless, steady.

Automatic.

This was how it felt—

Andy, it's slipping away again!

Then I was back in my body, back in the wind and noise and feeling Paul and Maria shaking me. I halted the Stone Man in front of us and its twitching began immediately.

"I've got it!" I gasped, grabbing at both of their shoulders. "I felt it, *I've got it!*"

"Got what!?" Paul said over the sound of Straub's yelled questions and commands to her soldiers.

"Another piece of the autopilot," I said, grabbing Maria's hand, then Paul's. I didn't know if I needed to or not, but it felt right. "Just now, it felt like *this,* Maria, I need you to copy it or something, look, it felt like—" I tried to recall the feeling as best I could. It wasn't as simple as just remembering walking because that was *human* walking; the gait was the same and the body was roughly the same shape, but the pitch was different, the connections, the rhythm, the sensation. Ever since my toddler-self learned to be upwardly mobile I'd spent the rest of my life walking without thinking, my body and brain handling external cues and feedback without conscious thought. We'd been trying to walk the Stone Man the exact same way and finding ourselves unable to understand why it wasn't working; the cues were wrong, the feedback wrong, all of it wrong for what we'd previously spend a lifetime learning and doing.

That moment inside the Stone Man just now had been brief but feeling it walking automatically without my interference—walking automatically as our loss of control had begun—had been a blessing. It had given me a clear *sample* of that physical sensation of alien locomotion, one much clearer now my connection to the Stone Man had grown. I sent the memory to Maria.

"Did you get that? Can you feel it in your body, the way I felt it just now?"

Maria blinked at me, her blown hair partially concealing her face.

"Yes," she said, shocked. "That was—

"*Do you know hip-hop music?*" I barked.

Her face screwed up in confusion, but neither of them said anything stupid like *now isn't the time to be making requests.* They were smart enough to know I was asking for a good reason.

"Yes, I mean a little," Maria said.

"You know how a DJ samples a few bars from an existing song and loops it on repeat?"

I saw her get it.

"Good!" I shouted, almost laughing in my mania. There was that taste of hope in the air again. God, it was maddening. "Okay: loop the memory. Feed it back to me, and keep it coming. You can move the energy around better than any of us, and you know we can move memories. Boilerplate that shit and give it to me on repeat. It's another cog to put into place, Watchmaker."

"Okay," Maria said, looking excited. "Okay!"

The Stone Man's twitches were becoming violent again. We would lose it any second.

"Paul, Maria's going to be doing a *lot* at once, so you power her up." My hands were shaking again, but now it was pure adrenaline. I was a goddamn emotional yo-yo.

But what else was new?

I realised the pair of them were just staring at me without responding. I hadn't seen anyone look at me that way before. "What?!" I snapped. "What are you waiting for, let's fucking *go!*"

"Yes, yes," Maria said, with a funny, giddy smile on her face, slapping at Paul's shoulder, who shook his head in a strange way.

"*Thank*you, Jesus," I said, copying Paul by shaking *my* head. I wasn't letting him be the only one to do it, even if I didn't know what Paul was actually shaking his head at. People are just fucking weird.

I felt a distant surge of power from Paul and already Maria was sending the memory back to me, refined. It was the strangest sensation, having a memory forcibly put back into your head; especially one that ended in an almost artificial cut off so it could instantaneously loop back to the start. Even my own original version of the memory *wasn't as clear as the one coming from Maria.* Madness. But it was the feedback I needed, the blueprint; the Stone Man's threads felt a touch more familiar in my mind, as if my vocabulary had just expanded into a language they spoke.

Walk.

The Stone Man moved forward once more, but now its gait was ... perfect. That was the only word for it, because now it was carrying out the movement all by itself. Yes, I was still simply keeping it on the tracks, but now it felt less like a balancing act; now the Stone Man's engine was steady and consistent, and all I had to do was steer without worrying about keeping it upright.

Now it felt like driving.

"*Yes!*" Maria bellowed joyfully. "*Ha-haaaa!*" I nearly chastised her for losing concentration, but I realised that the Stone Man was continuing apace regardless. It was *really* working. Instead, I reached out and pulled her to me. She returned the motion, throwing her wiry arms around my waist and pulling me up onto my tiptoes. *"It's working!"*

The memory sample in my head ended and looped back to the start. As it did, I saw Caementum give the slightest stagger before correcting itself again. The loop we'd created wasn't perfect, its ending coming off the 'beat' and imperfectly returning to the start like a mix by an amateur DJ. One of the many party Americans I'd met during my time in New York had referred to that effect perfectly: *sounds like sneakers in a tumble dryer.* Even so, it worked.

The Stone Man walked.

"That'll do, that'll do!" Paul said as we fell into step behind the Stone Man.

"What did you do?" Straub yelled. "That's ... that's *incredible!*"

"We're coming, Eric!" Maria yelled, wiping fresh beads of sweat from her forehead. *"We've got it, we're coming!"*

We were. The Stone Man was moving at double our previous speed, striding proudly forward, and I could not believe that this was a sight at which I took immense delight. Its head was high, its movements fluid—this bringer of death, this harbinger of doom—and I watched it and felt that hope ... along with a strange and slightly concerning sense of pride.

The loop reset, the Stone Man stumbled, but it continued as Eric grew larger in our sight. We were what, maybe three minutes' walk away from him now at this speed? Where were the Crawlers? *We might make it.* I looked back along the bridge. We had travelled down to the bottom of its long, steady rise now, and so the far end—and the shore of Skye—was hidden by the bridge's slope. The ocean crashed below us, the idling engines of the Jeeps rumbled behind us, and the helicopters blades droned above us, the faster pounding of the Stone Man's feet shaking the ground with each step.

"Eyes ahead, Andy," Straub called. "There's no point in looking back!" I ignored her. I could feel the Stone Man from here; I could look away from it for a moment, at least. A Jeep—one that had hung back on the Skye side of the bridge—suddenly crested the rise behind us and screeched to a halt on top of the tarmac hill. It sounded its horn in a long blast.

The message was clear, but unnecessary; not only could I feel the Crawler's growing presence through my connection to Stone Space, but their rapid approach was becoming clear in the realm of the physical. The rhythm of the Stone Man's steps in the tarmac was now being underscored by a distant tattoo, a dim rumble that trickled through the bridge's surface to our feet. It was like standing near the track at a horse race.

They were *galloping* after us.

"*Keep going,*" Straub snapped, "just keep going!"

Fresh terror in the threads, but if we could stay present, if I could keep the circuit focused on the movement, acknowledging the fear and letting it pass over us—*thoughts like passing traffic,* the meditation classes used to say, *you just watch them, let them go*—then we could keep the Stone Man in locomotion.

The loop, I told them, *focus on the loop, nothing else matters.*

But we were full of adrenaline, and staying calm was impossible. I saw Straub mutter something to Edgwick and then turn to fall into pace with the Jeep driving slowly behind us. She talked to the soldier in the driver's seat: a white guy about my age, who stared blankly at the Brigadier for a moment before nodding in a strange, zombie-like way.

Then he stopped the Jeep.

He got out and saluted Straub. She responded by offering the soldier her hand. He looked down at it, pale-faced, then took it, shook it, and released it before straightening and saluting once more. Now Straub returned the gesture. The soldier then moved around the Jeep, calling to the other men in the cluster of vehicles behind his. They got out and huddled around him. Straub and Edgwick moved to the back of the nearest vehicle and pulled out the five backpacks. Five, I wondered? One would be for Eric—should he survive what he was going through—but the fifth? As she handed three of the packs to Edgwick, I realised who the extra pack was for. Edgwick was Stone Sensitive; he could safely cross the gap in the Barrier, and Straub would want a military person with us. Straub talked quietly with him and Edgwick nodded solemnly as if he had been expecting this. Did he have family? There was no salute this time. Instead Edgwick and Straub, arms full, carried the packs over to us—Straub struggling a little with the weight of two packs, but managing it—and handed them to us. We pulled them on as we continued to walk after the Stone Man, feeling numb, the message in Straub's actions clear. She fell into step with us, Edgwick carrying Eric's pack.

"What's happening?" Paul asked her.

"We're going to blow the bridge behind you, so you need to make as much progress as you can towards *that* end before—"

"You're going to blow it?" I cried. "What if the whole thing collapses—"

"We know where to hit it," she said, her voice shaking, "to minimise that chance."

"But what if—"

"*It's that or they catch you,*" she said quickly, gritting her teeth. "The fact that transport is already signalling us tells me just how fast they're moving. They're too fast, and they will get you." Maria's hand went to her mouth but came away quickly. Behind Straub, the soldiers were doing something with their hands, gesturing towards one another, facing inwards in a circle. They then straightened, exchanging glances; three of them now looked as pale as their comrade had a moment ago. They all saluted one another, and then several of the terrified-looking men headed to the Jeeps. "Look at me," Straub said, suddenly grabbing my face painfully tight, and angling it down to hers. "Get to the Barrier. Get to Eric. Get to Coventry. Smash the Prism. Right?"

"You're coming too?" Paul asked Edgwick.

"Yes," Edgwick said, and gave no further comment.

"Where are they going?" Maria asked, watching the three Jeeps quickly turn and speed back along the bridge. Straub looked at Maria and I saw something in Straub's face I had never before witnessed; a thin smile born out of madness. A warrior feeling her death approaching and turning her terror into a thrill.

Then she turned and spoke into the darkness behind her, watching the Jeeps.

"They're going to try to buy you some time."

The remaining soldiers watched the Jeeps go for a moment, and then began to jog after them. A few of the soldiers briefly turned to look back at Edgwick, who nodded and threw them up a sharp salute. They returned it, then called and waved to the soldiers and other personnel down at the Barrier with Eric. Then they turned back to chase after the Jeeps. The Barrier crew, soldiers and scientists alike, reluctantly began to head in our direction, breaking into a run. Soon they reached and passed us, giving the Stone Man a wide berth as they did so. One of the scientist-looking types caught my eye just before he and the others became shadows disappearing back over the bridge; he looked to be in his mid-fifties. My circuit looked at one another, speechless. "I'm going with them," Straub said. "If any of us survive, we'll want to be on *that* side of the bridge. We have supplies on the base, and I don't know how long rescue might be or if any of the inbound vessels will come that close to the Barrier. Getting stuck on the mainland end with nothing but an energy wall for sustenance would not be good, and we can't be any help there."

The talk of supplies made sense ... but they would have to get past the Crawlers first. Maybe they would live if they didn't interfere with the visitors? Or did Straub expect even the non-soldiers to help 'buy us some time' too, with all of humanity at stake?

"We're on our own now?" I asked her, the words coming out as *werronnarurnow* because my jaw was held tight in Straub's hand.

"You knew you were going to be," Straub said, her eyes shining in the floodlights' reflected glare. "Good luck, Dispensatori. All of you." Then she released my face and turned away without another word, breaking into a sprint. "*At the double!*" she barked, catching up to the others as they all charged back up the hill that was the Skye Bridge. Straub raised a hand as she ran, signalling to the two choppers hovering in the far distance. The military truly did not trust the Barrier. One of the choppers began to turn as Edgwick fell into backwards-looking step with us.

Something streaked out of the sky above us with a deafening roar, and my circuit jumped. The armed chopper above had just launched a missile at something on the other end of the bridge, but not *at* the bridge yet; it looked like the target was too far away for that, maybe just beyond the bridge's Skye end. Almost immediately after the launch, the explosion came. It cast the hump of the bridge's rise into darker silhouette as an orange glow bloomed into brief, chaotic life behind it, overpowering even the distant floodlights.

"Tha—" I began, but then the chopper released a volley of missiles in rapid succession, screaming out of the racks slung underneath its belly. They slammed to earth milliseconds later, and from our vantage point it briefly looked as if the gates of hell had been opened up on the shores of Skye. Certainly, there were monsters there now. Gunfire began again, much closer, and there were muffled shouts. Why wasn't the helicopter firing again? Why weren't there more gunships here?

The answer came to me quickly: the Chisel was a research station overseeing a lead-buried, dormant asset, not a weapons cache. Most of our fleet would either be docked and dead under the Barrier or overseas, too far away to be here in time, and even those close enough to potentially help were under orders not to come near the Barrier—

Then I realised that the chopper had stopped firing because it needed enough missiles left to blow the bridge behind us.

I looked beyond the proudly striding Stone Man to the Barrier, to Eric. We were maybe two minutes away from him now. Edgwick was peering through small binoculars; he saw me looking and handed them over. Through them I could see how red Eric was in the face, his forehead thick and swollen with blood. How much had the Barrier hardened? What had it done to him?

A shrill scream came from the other side of the bridge—audible even over the gunfire—and then quickly cut off. An immense crash was quickly followed by an explosive wrenching sound, and I spun back just in time to see a dark flash of something large flying through the air off the right-hand side of the bridge, followed by a soft *smack* as that large something hit the water below. It had to be one of the Jeeps, flung like a toy through the roadside barrier. In the distance, the armed chopper was turning to face the bridge. The other helicopter suddenly banked and flew out of sight beyond the bridge's rise. To help survivors? The civilians that got past?

"Get alongside the Stone Man!" Edgwick shouted to us over the extremely close-sounding rattle of machine guns. "Or ahead of it, not walking behind it! They're going to shoot the bridge, we need to be further up the road than this!"

The gunfire stopped as a series of brutal thumps—faster even than the sound of the machine guns' previous discharges—thrummed through the floor beneath us. All sound from the other side of the bridge stopped.

Bang.

I saw the shadow of another Jeep soaring out over the right-hand side of the bridge. There was a pause, and then—

Bang.

The third Jeep flew up and over the hill of the bridge, crashing down to the tarmac behind us in a shower of shrapnel and sparks. It slid to an ear-splitting, screeching halt.

"*What are they waiting for?*" Maria suddenly yelled. "*Blow the fucking bridge—*"

Her words were cut off by the roar of the chopper unloading the last of its missiles.

The bottom of the bridge's hill was vaporised behind us. It burst upwards in a cloud of grey rubble and smoke that dropped sharply out of sight through the freshly-created hole into the unseen sea below. It was hard to truly know from here, but the new gap was *big*, maybe the width of three buses laid end to end. A horrible, heavy scrabbling sound began to rattle from the other side of the bridge, matching the rumbling that we'd felt through the floor.

"Keep it together," Edgwick said quietly.

The scrabbling noise became a rapid drumming.

"They're here," Maria said.

The Crawlers crested the rise of the bridge.

They really were *fast*.

In seconds they were up and over it, completely alien not just in their appearance but in their movements; they pursued with the speed of scent hounds, travelling at perhaps 20 miles per hour, but *scuttling* like spiders or crabs. Their immense bulk hurtled forwards with the grace of gazelles as their myriad legs worked and pumped at incredible but nauseating speed. They were deeply unpleasant to watch in motion. I only had a moment to comprehend just how quickly they were moving before they were already halfway down the rise and *coming after us*. The chopper above us suddenly unleashed a deafening volley of bullets into them, a torn metallic scream that filled the air with madness; of course, the hail of ammo was completely ineffective, and after a few seconds the helicopter's twin minigun turrets whirred empty. My heartbeat filled my neck as I turned to look back down the bridge towards Eric; the edge of the Barrier was still perhaps a minute away. Eric, a lone, catatonic-looking figure, stooped like Atlas with the weight—or rather, the *fate*, in this case—of the world on his back. I looked back at the Crawlers; at their current speed, they had to only be about a minute away from us too, if that. Would the gap in the bridge be wide enough to stop them? Holy shit, it was going to be so close, and if they could somehow leap across, the Barrier was no guarantee at all—

I felt our terror bounce around our threads, mingling and growing in a fatal echo chamber, and I realised what was happening.

No! Don't be afraid! We can make it!

But that was lost as terror turned to panic. The threads of the Stone Man became slack and all three of us tried to snatch them back, but it was too much, a heavy-handed overcorrection, our attention divided between the killing machines racing towards us and keeping the Stone Man locked into auto-walk. We should have gone back to the sample loop, keeping it running, but in our amplified panic, we couldn't.

The Stone Man stumbled, took a lurching step sideways, and crashed to the floor.

The drumming of the Crawlers' feet sounded like the charge of an army of berserkers as all three of us grasped at nothing, the threads of the Stone Man now intangible in our fear.

Get off! I told the others. *Let me do it!*

I looked back; the Crawlers were thundering up to the gap in the bridge—

Don't look at them, Paul said, *look at the fucking* Stone Man!

I did, but those terrible scuttling thuds and my heartbeat were roaring in my ears.

FUCKING GET UP, I told it.

I couldn't feel the Stone Man, could barely feel my circuit—

The rumbling abruptly stopped. I turned back to look.

The Crawlers had reached the far edge of the gap and stopped. One of them stretched a leg forward, testing the air, assessing. They shifted slightly, twitching back and forth a little. One of them began to move left and right, pacing.

"Holy shit," I muttered. "It worked, look, look at them—"

The Crawlers suddenly crouched down. There was a mild change in the air pressure around us. It began to feel thicker, heavier.

"Feels like they're building up ..." Paul said. Maria pointed a finger

"They're going to jump it," she said, as the Stone Man twitched sharply on the floor and began to rise.

"*Are you doing that?*" Paul yelled, jumping back. "*Andy, are you—*"

"No," I whispered. In our fear, we had lost control completely.

The Stone Man rose.

"Get it back," Maria hissed, backing up. "Come on, both of you, focus, *focus!*"

I slapped myself across the face, hard, and then I was seeing the Barrier, and hearing an altogether different rhythm. There was an unspeakable urge within me, and then my sight was turning towards Paul—

I came back to my body and saw the Stone Man turning smoothly and effortlessly as it began to stride towards my friend.

"*Run, Paul!*" I yelled at him. "*We can't get it under control in time, just run for the—*"

Wait. Run for the Barrier?

That was *exactly* what he had to do.

I grabbed Paul and yanked him sideways, taking him around the approaching Stone Man. I saw the understanding in Maria's face.

"*Yes—*" she gasped.

"Run for the Barrier, Paul!" I screamed at him, but his feet were stumbling as I dragged him towards the Barrier, his terrified gaze locked onto the Stone Man as it strode within six feet of him, *coming for him,* his worst nightmare made manifest. I opened my hand and smashed him as hard as I could across the face, and his eyes blinked and found mine as the pressure in the air around us continued to increase. "The Stone Man will follow you, and *that's what we want*, you can outrun it in a sprint, easy! Get under the Barrier, Edgwick you go with him, we can figure out how to—"

The air pressure suddenly released in a silent gasp, and I looked back in time to see the Crawlers lurch forward with incredible force, taking to the air and crunching down onto our side of the bridge with a slamming weight that shook the ground enough to stagger us all. They nearly didn't make it, their back legs—for one brief sliver of hope—scrabbling for purchase on the ruined edge of the gap. Then they had their footing and suddenly shot forward, immediately moving at pace towards us.

"*Fucking run!*" I yelled, shoving Paul forwards. Now he ran, and as I beckoned frantically to Maria the four of us broke into a sprint along the bridge towards the Barrier.. At this speed we were perhaps ten or twenty seconds away from Eric.

That was too far. We weren't going to make it.

I saw and felt Crawlers' thunderous approach and knew that, even if we somehow *did* make it, they would get to the Stone Man before it reached the Barrier and all would be lost. All I could think to do was to keep running, wheezing as Edgwick, Paul and Maria ran ahead of me, fitter than I was, even Paul was now, I was slow, too damn slow, and the Barrier looked—

—closer?

Then I heard Eric screaming. I saw what he was doing.

The lower half of Eric's face was a crimson mask, the blood vessels in his nose finally having ruptured. The liquid ran from his nostrils as he walked forward, bent at the waist, chin up, arms raised ... and moving the Barrier out with him, a bulging, swirling, Eric-shaped protrusion that was slowly surging forward to greet us. As Eric pushed, stretching the Barrier further, he was creating a kind of extended tunnel, the darkness around him became light again, or at least light*er*; a halo of that greyish light emanated around him at about a one-foot radius. Already it was trying to darken again but Eric kept moving, the Barrier stretching and thinning around him like old chewing gum being pulled. The veins in his forehead stood out like ropes, his beetroot-red face contorted in a scream that told us that the effort was killing him. He tried to take another step. Couldn't.

"*We can make it! We can make it!*" Maria screamed, looking back at me, but when she saw the sight behind me her face told me all I needed to know.

"*Help him Paul!*" I yelled, pointing at Eric and barely finding the breath to speak. "*You don't need to focus on anything else now, help him!*" Paul didn't even turn around but I felt something from his thread and Eric suddenly straightened up, his eyes completely bloodshot and far away as he blinked dumbly at what was behind us. He screwed his eyes shut and let forth another guttural scream.

Eric began to run.

He moved towards us, a staggering, heavy-footed, head-down-and-gasping gallop that was using everything he had left. Within seconds we reached each other, Eric still coated in that grey-and-already-getting-greyer-water-swirl. He stopped abruptly, swaying so heavily on the spot that I thought he would fall, but he stayed upright, setting his shaking feet wide and then reaching out his right arm, unable to speak. But there was no hole now—

Eric's fist came out at around chest height, first making the coating Barrier tentpole outwards around his arm, and then slowly form a wall of light that reached both to the floor and back to the main body of the Barrier itself. Clenching his fist, Eric's heavily-sweating brow furrowed as the webbing began to thin, thin … and then disappear completely. There was now a fresh hole in this newly-created extended section of Barrier, a gap that hung underneath Eric's arm. It began at the side of Eric's torso and ended at his fist, the edge running in a twitching, spasming line of ugly light from his knuckles to the ground.

"*Now,*" he gasped, "*now … never—*"

Edgwick reached the hole first, throwing his rifle and Eric's backpack through then stepping back to allow Maria passage first. This was no act of chivalry; Edgwick was on an escort mission. Even the much shorter Maria had to fling herself to her knees to get through the gap under Eric's outstretched arm, keeping her splinted hand slightly up and scrabbing with her good hand across the tarmac. She immediately jumped to her feet on the other side, staggering backwards to watch Paul as he followed. It's with no small amount of shame that I confess I dropped down, put my shoulder to Paul's buttocks, and shoved him through ahead of me in my haste to get through the hole. For one horrible moment I found myself stuck before realising that my backpack was catching on Eric's arm, trapped, and then I dropped down and Maria was pulling at my arms as Edgwick pushed me from behind. Then I was through, falling flat onto my face. Paul hauled me up, and as I looked beyond Edgwick as he clambered through after me, I now saw how close the Crawlers were to the Stone Man. Eric had closed the gap but the Crawlers would be upon

Caementum in seconds, dwarfing even the Stone Man with their size as they grew larger and larger behind it.

Paul lunged forwards, putting his hands on Eric's back, and a bolt of feedback shot around our circuit, giving us a taste of what he had just done to the man in the Barrier.

The pair of them screamed as one. Eric again began to run forwards once more as Edgwick pushed.

Maria and I ran close beside them, seeing the tears of effort running from Eric's eyes and mingling with the blood covering the bottom half of his face as, the Stone Man growing in our sight, we drew closer, closer. On this side, I could see how much Eric was a part of the Barrier now, the entirety of his bent-at-the-waist torso and face wedged into that substance, the rest of him clear in the air behind it. I saw Paul falter as we came within a few feet of his pursuer, understanding that he was racing towards his own death.

"To Eric's side, stand in front of the gap Paul!" I yelled, and Paul complied; the Stone Man would need to pass by Eric to get to Paul without flattening the younger man. We needed to give it the right direction to aim at. The Stone Man shifted its angle of approach slightly, heading towards Paul, who began to step backwards. It was mere steps away from the protruded Barrier's edge, but the Crawlers were only a few seconds behind it, barrelling their scrambling way after their asset. The thundering in the ground was madness.

"It's here Eric!" I yelled, wanting to encourage, but Eric was beyond hearing. "The Stone Man's here!" And it was... but I realised that there was no way it was going to fit through Eric's gap. It was too tall, and we didn't have the control yet to make it crawl. Maybe it could pass through the Barrier, I thought, but my mind hissed back:

Then maybe the Crawlers can too—

Fuck that, I thought, but the hole needed to be bigger

"Think *up!*" I yelled at Eric, grabbing him around one of his upper legs and trying to lift. I couldn't grab his waist, he was too wedged into the Barrier for me to get purchase. "Edgwick! His other leg! The gap isn't high enough!" I tried to lift him and couldn't. It wasn't Eric's weight—he was tall but skinny— but the incredible force of the Barrier. Now Eric had taken that horrible light as far out as he had, it was beginning to blacken again all around his head and shoulders, starting to obscure his face from sight. Edgwick grabbed Eric's other upper leg and we strained together, managing to lift him, dragging the stretching point of resistance that was Eric upwards, raising the end of this

Eric-made Barrier tunnel with him. I looked back; this new height of the tunnel's ceiling was mirrored all the way back to the main body of the Barrier. Fizzing and crackling sounds filled the air as the tunnel—and the hole—extended higher just at the moment the Stone Man reached it.

Still not high enough, though; even with Edgwick and I holding Eric aloft, his arm was only at around six or seven feet. The Stone Man's head hit the top edge of the hole, pushed *into* it for a moment like moving against soft rubber, and then its whole body rebounded gently, taking a step back. The movement was casual, as if there weren't two thundering monsters from nightmare mere feet behind it.

"Higher! Hold him higher!"

We did. But it wasn't quite—

Eric's body stiffened, tensed, and then he let out a fresh scream as his spine straightened, his body reaching its full height. The hole—the tunnel roof—was tall enough. The Stone Man casually strolled through.

But all we could see beyond the Barrier now were the Crawlers, and they filled the world.

"Get him out!" I yelled at Edgwick, and we yanked Eric backwards and down. He popped free surprisingly easily, as if the Barrier were all too glad to be rid of him, but as he slumped into mine and Edgwick's arms his weight was dead and his eyes were closed. The blackening, hardening part of the Barrier that he had left behind briefly carried an impression of his body, like the clear plastic of an action figure's packaging with the figure removed. The next second the hole Eric had made snapped shut with an ugly *crack* sound, sounding like the pop from the world's largest piece of bubble wrap, and the blackened part of the Barrier's extended surface began to wash back to its normal opacity. But that wasn't the only thing was that was beginning to return to its original state. This Barrier-tunnel that Eric had dragged out of the main Barrier body was now slowly retracting. All of us, Stone Man and humans alike, were still standing inside it, and the Barrier's main edge was now many feet behind us. "Move!" I called, and Maria broke into a run, snatching up Edgwick's pack and rifle with a grunt. She staggered after Paul, who was already sprinting to stay ahead of the Stone Man. Edgwick and I got our shoulders under the lifeless Eric's armpits and carried him as we ran headlong, the Barrier tunnel pulsing all around us now as it returned to its default position. The Stone Man had moved past us in its steady pursuit of Paul, but now we accelerated past it as we hustled along. Would the walking

Stone Man be back inside the main Barrier by the time the tunnel retracted all the way home?

Eric opened his eyes, gasped, and then let out a grunt of heavy air from his lungs—*UGH!*—as his remaining fist, his whole body, suddenly clenched. I heard the Crawlers' cacophonous approach grind to a halt and, even as I huffed and grunted with Eric's weight, I looked back. The retracting tunnel had frozen. So had the Crawlers.

They didn't seem to have had any choice; they were partway wedged inside the Barrier's retracting edge. Their back legs outside, their many legs on the inside still scrabbling forwards but coated in a glaze of the Barrier's disgusting, swirling light; it was as if they had instantaneously dropped into ultra-slow motion, their movement suddenly becoming like dying insects swimming through amber. Their full-speed impact with the extended part of the Barrier's surface had happened so suddenly that the pair of them were almost clambering over each other in their semi-frozen state. The Stone Man walked on, oblivious.

The thought hit me:

They'd made it, and they were starting to come through—

"Look at them," Maria said, trying to slow her breath. She'd stopped a few feet ahead of us. I looked for Paul; he was a long way up the road but had now stopped to catch his breath, eyeballing the following Stone Man from a safe distance. I realised that the protrusion that Eric had made hadn't actually stopped retracting; it had simply slowed greatly. We watched as it retracted all the way back to its original starting point, the struggling Crawlers being dragged along with it all the way; would they pass through now that the Barrier was reformed correctly? We backed away, horrified. There was no point in running if they did. It would be like trying to outrun a motorbike. The Stone Man passed by us, following Paul, but we continued to watch the Crawlers. After a few seconds the monsters still hadn't made it any further forward; their legs continued to weakly scrabble, caught. Edgwick and I lowered Eric to a seated position, holding him up.

"Can you hear me?" I asked him.

"*Gfff,*" he slurred.

"Can they get through?" I asked, frantic. "You, you caught them? You said the Barrier was trying to become permanent—Eric?"

Eric frowned for a moment, his eyes still closed. He tried the same word again, and this time it was clear:

"*Go.*"

He twitched violently a few times. Then he became totally limp in our arms.

"Eric? Eric!"

He had given everything.

"What's wrong with him?!" Maria asked. I couldn't respond, even as Edgwick laid Eric's body down, uselessly checking his pulse. He then moved around Eric, avoiding my gaze as he began to compress Eric's chest, Edgwick's solemn face confirming my fears. Edgwick would have enough battlefield experience to know what could be done for a fallen comrade outside of a medical facility. But my knowledge was Stone related, and I could feel Maria's thread beginning to understand it too as she felt for Eric's Stone frequency. "What's—what's wrong—" she repeated, trying to deny the truth.

"Let him ... work," I mumbled, not knowing what to say. Anguish flowed down Maria's thread and she lunged forward, barging Edgwick's token efforts aside and squatting down, tears streaming from her face as she fruitlessly took over compressing Eric's chest. I caught Edgwick's eye now—should we stop her?—and he gently shook his head no. He was right. Later, she would need to be able to tell herself that she'd done all she could.

"*Come on!*" she sobbed. I looked away, feeling as if I'd been slugged in the back of the head. I'd spent enough time around dead or dying Stone Sensitives to know when it was over. When their energy was spent, and that horrible emptiness was all that remained.

Eric Hatton was dead.

"No, *no no no, ohhh no...*"

Maria had only known Eric briefly, but he was still one of us, and we had only just lost Linda. Against all the odds and evidence to the contrary, we had survived. The Crawlers were somehow caught, but at the cost of another member of our group, one who had died to save us because...

The *because* was another prison sentence. I let it in.

Because we couldn't keep our shit together.

I dealt with it the only way I knew how, despite the hours and hours of therapy at the Project. I got on with things. I moved to Maria, putting my hand on her back, but she shook me off.

"You!" Maria snapped at Edgwick, still pumping Eric's chest. "Take over, you're stronger, do it *properly*! *Save him!*"

I put my hand on Maria's back again.

"We have to go," I said. "Paul needs us. We have to try and get the Stone Man back under control."

"He-he used up everything," she said. "He saved us—"

"He did." I looked at the Crawlers, still swimming their legs through the air. Wait, were they further through? Were they still coming? Or was I imagining it? "Maria... we have to leave him. The Crawlers ... I'm not sure—"

"Is it his heart?"

"What?"

"*His heart has stopped, right?*"

"It's not just that," I said. I felt dizzy. "It's all of—"

"*Where the fuck is Paul?*" Maria shrieked, spinning to look back along the road. We couldn't see Paul for the Stone Man, but—no, there he was, sat at the side of the road and catching his breath. He was just visible in the dark thanks to the last, faint edge of the floodlights' glare, still standing on our side of the Barrier. Paul was watching us, sitting perhaps about one hundred feet ahead of his steadfast pursuer. "*Paul! PAUL!*" I saw Paul straighten up, stand. "*Get here! Paul!*"

"Maria—"

"*Paul is a battery! He's a* battery, *Andy! He's—*"

She suddenly screwed her eyes and fists and the idea shot out around our circuit wordlessly. I staggered backwards with the force of it, seeing Paul stumble too in the distance ... and then break into an all-out run, giving the Stone Man a wide berth as he did so.

It might work, I thought. *Not just a battery; a source of everything that Eric used up—*

"Holy shit, Paul!" I screamed. "*Come on! Faster, faster!*" I jabbed a finger at Edgwick. "She's right, keep doing the compressions!"

"Pointer ... I'm sorry, but I've seen—"

"Do it!"

Edgwick, a smart man, understood that something special was going on. He stopped protesting and went back to work with gusto.

"This is some Stone ... Stone shit, right?" He grunted, pushing. I didn't even know if there was any point to Edgwick's efforts, but screw it, now Paul was reaching us, pushing between Maria and I. Maria's hands were in her hair, both of us hopping from foot to foot as Paul slid to the ground next to Eric. Edgwick jumped aside to make room, Paul's hands finding Eric's chest as he looked back up the road to the Stone Man in the distance, checking. His endless pursuer completed its turn and began to walk back up the road towards Paul, who looked down at Eric, closed his eyes, froze for a moment, arms straight ... then pushed.

Body and Stone-mind together.

Push.

Maria and I both jolted, the force of it feeling not as if it had come down our threads, but through the ground and into our feet, Paul's first thrust of energy pushing through Eric's body and into the earth.

Push.

The second one was even harder, so much so it hurt.

Push.

"Uh!" Maria gasped. Even Edgwick flinched a little. The power involved to make that happen—

PUSH.

If that couldn't restart a heart, then nothing could.

Eric's body bucked suddenly on the floor.

"*There!*" Maria yelled. "*You see that?*"

PUSH.

"Arrrrrr—"

Eric opened his eyes and his body jerked sideways, fighting for breath, painful and ragged wheezes that sounded as if his lungs were full of rust. "*Ahh, ahh—*"

I let out an involuntary sob as Maria grabbed at my shoulders. I simply could not believe it. Edgwick hustled in, trying to put Eric in the recovery position, but Paul shook his head, keeping his hands on Eric's back.

"Not yet," Paul said quietly, glancing back down the road again. The Stone Man was about 20 seconds away and closing. "I'm still keeping him going. Give it a second and it'll be all him. Let it run for a minute."

"You can restart hearts?" Edgwick said, falling onto his backside and running his hands through his red hair.

"I don't know," Paul said, eyes still on the Stone Man. "Maybe only Stone Sensitives. Maybe because of the way he'd burnt himself out using his gift, or I caught in time, I certainly wouldn't want to bank on it in—"

"*What happened?*"

Eric's voice was hoarse, torn up by the guttural screaming he'd let forth during his exertions. Maria was right; he'd given *everything*.

He'd actually done it.

"Okay," Paul said. "That's ticking away by itself." He took his hands away and stood, Edgwick hustling in and moving Eric into the recovery position. Paul walked away quickly without another word, taking an even longer path around the approaching Stone Man. It of course slowly turned, following Paul's new trajectory.

"Eric, can you hear me?" Maria said, wiping her eyes.

"You saved us, Eric," I forced out, and even though I wanted him to know he had my respect, giving it still somehow took effort. This was progress; not so long ago, I would have kept my mouth shut. "That was … amazing."

It was, and this had been an indescribable win. We had all been as good as dead—Eric *had* been dead—and yet here we all were. Sure, there was the not-inconsiderable issue of the now fully out-of-control Stone Man, and we would have to get it back under somehow. There was also the not-negligible fact that we had to walk the length of the country without being killed by the indestructible death machines that would come after us if Maria couldn't keep us hidden. *And* there was the ultimate dice roll of whether we could even smash the Prism at the other end.

But right now, we'd beaten the odds.

We hadn't known if we could wake the Stone Man. We hadn't known if we could control it. We hadn't known if we'd be able to escape the Crawlers, which, for now at the very least, it seemed we had.

We'd won all of those battles.

Now we just had to win all the others.

✼✼✼

Part Two

MARCH OF THE STONE MEN

Chapter Six

A Promise Is Kept, The Group Regroup, Empathy Squared, and Sight Versus Sound

***

"Everything hurts," Eric said. He'd been lucid for a few minutes now, eyes open, and blinking with a bloodshot redness that matched my own. "Vision's blurry."

"It … took a lot out of you," I said, glancing at Maria. She shook her head quickly. No, we wouldn't tell him. A few feet away from us the Crawlers' limbs continued to work. They didn't seem to be getting any further through. "Eric, did you do something there? When the Crawlers started to come through?"

"… the what?"

Eric tried to sit up and Edgwick put a gentle hand on his shoulder to restrain him. Eric slapped Edgwick's hand away with surprising force.

"Get off," he grunted, sitting up.

"I don't think that's a good idea," I said, but Eric was already upright at the waist, blinking around himself in the dark. He looked at the Crawlers and nodded.

"Yeah," he said. "I did that."

"You caught them?"

"Yeah." Eric winced and put his hand to his head.

"Hold on," Edgwick said, producing what looked like a mini Maglite and shining it into Eric's eyes. "Look at the light, Eric … ok, pupils are good. We'll see how you're doing in a minute and maybe we can give you some painkillers."

"Need my antibiotics," Eric muttered. "For shoulder wound. In the bag I brought." Edgwick went to grab the bag Eric had left by the Barrier earlier, giving the protruding legs of the Crawlers a wide birth. "Remember how I said … Barrier was still setting?" Eric said. "Hardening?"

"Yes."

"I tried to speed it up. At least on that little piece of the Barrier's surface."

"So you could slow it down then?" Maria asked. "Maybe so much that you could open it again?" She looked towards Paul, watching as he continued to jog away from the Stone Man.

"No," Eric said, taking the antibiotics from Edgwick along with some water from our supplies. "At least not any time soon, and by then I think this whole thing will be set as hard as … well." He flapped his hand in the direction of the Stone Man, and then sipped at his water. "Once upon a time, I would have committed almost any crime—apart from murder or something—to be up close with it, with any one of those things. Now I've been within touching distance of three of them. I couldn't wish harder to be done with them if I tried."

"Three different ones?" I asked.

"Yeah. Including that one just now."

That was, upon reflection, more than I had. Paul, too.

Don't worry, a cruel part of my mind whispered. *Soon, there will be plenty of them to go around. You've seen how the projections, how the numbers compound: after just fifteen Arrivals, we would have fourteen point three million Stone Men. After twenty Arrivals, half of the world's population has been wiped out. And thanks to the good ol' Prism, the time between Harvesting and reappearance had been reduced from a matter of months to a matter of hours—*

Eric suddenly stood up.

"Woah, woah," Edgwick said, putting a hand on Eric again, but once more Eric slapped him away.

"Stop fucking touching me," Eric said angrily. What was his problem? Instead of retaliating in kind, Edgwick—the bigger man in the literal sense—just held up his hands.

"Your funeral, buddy," he said, stepping backwards as Eric swayed gently on his feet.

"Be careful, Eric," Maria said. "You just, uh, you had, uh … you just collapsed."

"It's okay," Eric said, cocking his head. "I feel … alright. I have a headache and my shoulder is still sore, but it was sore this morning and I expect it still will be tonight." Maria, Edgwick and I all exchanged a glance. How was this possible? Eric's hand touched the bottom of his face, found the sticky blood there. "What the hell …" he said, and then cocked his head again. He frowned, looked at the Crawlers stuck in the Barrier, then at the spatter of his leaked blood on the ground where he had fallen.

"Did I die?"

"Your heart stopped," Edgwick said. "We couldn't start it. Then Paul did."

Edgwick looked down the road for Paul. We couldn't see him anymore. He'd moved too far away into the darkness.

"*Shit* …" Eric breathed. Then he nodded at the Crawlers. "And I've seen those before. The Crawlers, if we're calling them that. Dead ones. In the Ground Zero building."

"Eric, are you sure you're—"

"I'm fine," he said tersely. "Can we just stop with the questions for a minute? I need a second."

The sound of Paul's feet slapping upon the road began to come back towards us. We couldn't see the Stone Man anymore—presumably Paul had turned back once it was around a hundred feet from us—but we could just about hear the distant returning thuds of its feet. Shortly, he reached us.

"Jesus, Eric, how are you—" he began, but Maria put a hand on his shoulder. Paul took the hint. "Thank you, man. You saved us all."

"You're welcome," Eric said, but he looked miserable. "To fight another day, eh?"

"… yeah," Paul said. "Yeah, something like that. But listen: I can't do this running back and forth all day." He forced a nervous laugh, but his haunted eyes kept looking back down the road into the darkness beyond. "We failed there, team. Badly."

"Are you kidding?" I asked. "That was the most unlikely series of wins possible!"

"But we completely lost it when the pressure was on. Me more than anyone, not pointing fingers. We've lost full control now. How are we going to get it back the way we had it?"

"We couldn't get it back under control before," Marla said, "because we were panicking. Let's get some miles under our feet and get calm again. Try and get the Stone Man back under once we're not pumped full of adrenaline? I know it's hard for you Paul, but we need you to just keep ahead of it. Just for the next twenty minutes or something while we get our heads in the game."

"Why don't you just let it follow you all the way to Coventry?" Eric asked. "Wouldn't that be easier?"

"Because we've got between now and the time we get there," Paul said, still looking back down the road, "to master the thing. Not just so we can smash the Prism, but in case we need to deal with any … obstacles."

I didn't even want to think about that. Eric, talking with the freedom afforded to the temporarily delirious, looked at the Crawlers.

"Looks like some *obstacles* might be coming sooner rather than later, don't you think?"

"But they're stuck? Aren't they?" I asked. The Crawlers still didn't look like they'd made any forward progress at all, despite their continuing movement.

"Oh," Eric said, looking surprised. "You mean *you* can't tell, then? Andy Pointer?"

"Can't tell what?"

"Hmm," Eric said, not listening. "Maybe it's 'cos I'm, you know." He waved his hand at Paul. "Since you boosted me. In tune with this shit. No, they're on their way through for sure. It's only a matter of time until they get free."

This news delighted no-one.

"But you hardened the—"

"Yeah, but they're still working their way through. Very slowly, but …" He squinted at the Crawlers. "I don't know if it was just me, you know. I think they might have struggled anyway. They look like they're made of different stuff, don't you think?" I thought he might be right. Caementum had seemed to bounce off the hardening Barrier, after all.

"How long until they're on the inside?" I asked

"I can't say," Eric said.

I felt cold, then realised it *was* cold. We needed to get moving, get warm.

"Then Straub's plan," I said, "is our best bet, for now—"

Eric let out a grunt, backing up a step, his head twitching left and right as if he were listening.

"They know," he said, his brow furrowed. "They know you're back under here. I can't tell what they're saying exactly but the noise has changed. They're looking in this direction. I don't know if they can see you, but … you don't want to be here, I think."

But if they know where we came through, I thought, *then they could start sending Stone Men in this direction*—

"Maria?" I asked, "are you hiding us?"

"It's a lot harder now," she said. "Under here, with the Stone Man so intimately connected to Paul … it's *much* harder."

"I can feel you working," I said. "But listen: is it worth the risk of checking remotely where all the Stone Men are? It might not even be possible if you're—"

"Give her a moment, Andy," Paul said. "Come on. She already said she was at capacity."

"Well, they know where we are right now anyway, and it could be very useful—"

"It's alright," Maria said, sighing heavily. "He's right. I can do it once, and it's worth a try—"

"No," Eric said, but Maria was already closing her eyes.

"It's alright," she repeated, frowning with the effort as she began to concentrate. "They're…" She gave a gentle, startled sound. "It's just so hard to see while I'm—they're moving out from Coventry—"

"Stop *now*," Eric said, taking a staggering lunge forward to grip Maria's shoulders. She opened her eyes, startled. "I'm sorry," Eric said quickly, "but you need to put *all* energy into hiding *right now*, okay? *Now!*" Maria stared at him, confused, but only a second. She closed her eyes and breathed out … and as she did so I noticed an unpleasant, retreating creeping sensation in the air that I hadn't even realised was upon us. Then it was gone. I felt my shoulders loosen.

"Jesus," Edgwick said. "Sneaky, sneaky … what the hell…"

"Got it," Maria said, her eyes still closed. "We're off the radar. Right, Eric?"

"Yeah," he said, cocking his head again. "That was close."

"What was that?" Edgwick asked him.

"You can't do that again," Eric said to Maria, releasing her shoulders, his wide bloodshot eyes making him look like a ghoul. "You can't look into the signal, even for a second. *They nearly had us*. The moment you started looking I heard the signal go crazy, like they were …" His head twitched. "Didn't you have a near miss before, Maria? When I was at Aiden's house and you saved me from the bubble?"

"Yes, but, with all due respect … so what?"

"I think it learned. It was trying to be sneaky this time. The big one, the Giant. It's clever. Or the Prism is, and the Giant is channelling it, or … just don't do that again, okay?"

I hadn't expected Maria, our ace in the hole, to be this hobbled. We knew she would have her hands full, but I thought maybe occasional, brief trips into the visual of the Stone Circuit would be okay. Now such a thing would in fact be incredibly dangerous. The fog of war had just unequivocally fallen upon us.

"Fuck, Eric," I said. "*Fuck*—"

Eric did that thing again with his head.

"Give me a second," he said. He paused, eyes closed, then scowled. "*Dammit.*" Then he opened his eyes, looking astonished. I realised that he'd gone straight to the Barrier after being boosted. He hadn't had a chance to experiment with his gift. Eric put his hand to his mouth in amazement, leaving a smear in the drying blood there. We really had to get the poor bastard a wash. "I can't actually *see* where they are, but I can … hear it? It's like … radar or something." He turned to me. "I think I can *hear* where they are."

"Okay," Maria said, a funny expression on her face. Was something wrong? I went to check her thread to find out, but stopped myself, feeling that her block was still in place. Boundaries. I had to observe them here or our entire circuit would fall apart. I turned to Eric instead.

"Won't they sense you when you use your gift?" I asked. "The way they sense Maria?"

"Not yet, I think," Eric said. "Not while she's hiding us at least, but even so … it's like I can feel when they start to pay attention. It feels …" He listened again. "Like I'm crawling through the undergrowth to avoid detection. If I do it slowly and carefully, I'm okay. Ugh, but the *sound*." He shook his head before looking at Edgwick with a gaze of distaste. What was Eric's problem with the military man? "What's the route you're planning on taking?"

He was asking Edgwick? I'd assumed until that moment that I was the one in charge, surely?

"Originally," Edgwick said, "the plan was to head through Glasgow and between Liverpool and Manchester. But, if you're right and those things—" Here he pointed a finger at the slowly writhing Crawlers. "—can eventually get through, we need to figure out some kind of rapid transit to stay ahead of them. They're much faster than we are. The A roads will be physically longer, but they'll be less congested with dead cars than the motorways. We should be able to head south faster along them, but if all the Blues figure out where we are and start to close in, it'll be about the timing—"

"That's not why I'm asking," Eric said, letting out a heavy sigh before muttering to himself: "Huh. Guess I made my fuckin' mind up. Shit." I didn't understand, but then Eric looked at me. "It's about the *kid*. Remember? I said he's trapped." Why was he talking to just me? "I promised him, Andy. *Gah,* why do I keep making stupid promises?" *How should I know*, I thought. *I don't even know you.* "We have to stop on the way," Eric said. "Aiden, the boy, he's in in a bubble, in this farmhouse near the M6. I can get him out. I can take us there."

"I'm not sure we should be making any diversions," I said, "Let's get the job done first and then we can—"

"Guys," Paul said. The sounds of the Stone Man's footsteps were growing louder. All of us turned to watch it as it slowly emerged from the darkness. "It's still drawing from me," Paul muttered. "I can feel it. It might be walking on its own but it's still helping itself to my, you know. My juice, my *kishkas*."

"Let's get moving over that way," Edgwick said, watching the Stone Man approach and pointing us away to its right. Paul eagerly led the way as we moved around it, Eric dragging his feet a little and wincing as he pulled on his new backpack. Edgwick had decanted the contents of Eric's previous pack into the larger government-issue one. "I'm *okay*," Eric said, seeing my expression. "Everything hurts, but I can take it. I'll carry my own pack." This man had been clinically dead a few minutes ago? The Stone Man turned as we passed it, Paul briefly breaking into a light jog to get further ahead.

"We're freeing the kid," Eric said as we walked. "Or at least, I am. I have to."

"We can discuss that," I said, as kindly as I could. "The thing is, once we're close to Coventry, we might really need you to make sure we can get past—"

"Then you all come with me," Eric said, "because either way, I'm going."

"I know how important this is to you, Eric," Maria said, "but I think we only get one try at this, and a diversion is a risk. If I'm reduced, then we need your ears to help us time it—"

"*It isn't out of our way*," Eric said. "And it isn't a risk. What if they harvest the kid and we have even more Stone Men to deal with as a result?"

"If he's that close to Coventry," Edgwick said, looking straight ahead, "then we won't get there in time anyway, Eric. They're already on the move—"

"The Stone Men are very efficient," Eric interrupted, "but their planning stinks. You have no idea how much I researched these things. They never targeted their victims based on proximity. One of the Second Arrival Targets was in *Edinburgh* for Christs' sake—"

"How do you know that?" Edgwick asked, but Eric just continued speaking.

"—and we know that there would have been any number of Targets between here and there. I've seen the fucking List. So we don't *know* if the kid will be next—"

"If he's under a bubble," Edgwick said, "he's already targeted."

The upper half of Eric's face turned reddened to match the crimson mask under his nose. It was such an obvious fact for him to miss.

"Maybe he's being targeted for the new ones," Eric said quietly, a wheedling tone in his voice now. "The ones that aren't ready yet, aren't walking yet. There might be time. And I *promised*."

His voice broke on the last word, and Eric suddenly screwed up his fist and put it to his temple.

"I can *hear* one of them," he whispered. "One of the Targets." All of us (except Paul) stopped walking. "I can hear his, his Quarry Response. He's… he's…" He staggered backward a step.

"Come out, Eric," Maria said, following him.

"You can't let this happen to Aiden," Eric said, "you *can't,* listen to them—"

His hand shot out and grabbed Maria's wrist. She didn't have time to pull away before the sensation transferred from Eric. It shot into her and then out along our circuit with the physical force of a taser. I staggered as I heard Paul cry out a few feet away. Suddenly I had that old familiar feeling, the one that said *doom was coming and you must hide, hide, you are exposed, you are EXPOSED—*

Smack.

I heard the sound as I gasped for air, the sensation vanishing, and saw Eric staggering backwards, holding his jaw. Edgwick's meaty fist had collided with Eric's face, breaking his grip on Maria's arm and freeing us.

"*Breathe,* soldier," Edgwick was saying, his voice surprisingly kind. "You're hysterical." Eric opened his mouth to cuss Edgwick out, but one look at Maria's pale face made him hold up his hand and stump.

"I'm so sorry, I'm sorry, I didn't mean to—"

"It's alright, it's okay," Maria said, but her voice was shaking. Behind her, a few feet away, Paul was walking backwards, the expression on his trembling face clear even at a distance—*what the fuck are you* doing—but he was still watching the Stone Man. I didn't think what Eric had done was *okay* at all; what if he'd somehow just exposed us all? But we needed everyone to calm down. Eric's eyes moved between myself and Maria, clearly horrified at the circuit feedback he'd received from us all.

"You … why did that …" he said.

"It's PTSD," Maria said, and I was amazed at the direct confession. "All of us. Andy. Paul. Me. And you have it too," she added, stepping towards Eric. "Don't you?"

He frowned and looked down.

"Aiden's house is on the *way*," he repeated. "We have to try."

"Yes," I said, feeling my face continue to tremble. Trying to be present wasn't helping; the *present* situation was fucking awful, after all. "We'll try." I didn't mean it one fucking bit. "Look: stay with us at least until we have Caementum under control again. Then we can figure out a way to try and get you to the kid's bubble more quickly. How's that?"

"Okay," Eric said, sounding grateful for the concession. "But what are you guys gonna do when you need to sleep?"

"We'll get a car or something, like Edgwick said, even if we have to drive it slowly for now while the Stone Man walks. But we'll figure that out later, let's just *walk*, please. And I really need some quiet for a minute. I'm sorry."

Paul was now some distance away from us, backing up the road ahead of the Stone Man. It occurred to me then how, since we woke the Stone Man, it hadn't put him inside an old-school barrier the same as Patrick Marshall and the others. Again, I realised: Maria. The Stone Man may have had Paul in visual range, but whatever force it would have used to pin him in place didn't seem to be an option anymore.

A quickly growing sound came from behind us.

I spun around to look at the trapped—*were* they trapped—slowly wriggling Crawlers. The noise wasn't coming from them; a distant movement in the night sky above the ruined bridge answered the mystery. It was an approaching chopper. The aircraft halted a healthy distance from the Barrier, a tiny hovering shape. What fresh, happy horseshit was this now?

Oh please, I thought, *let it be her. I don't know why I care so much. Just let it be her.*

"You did it," a voice said over the aircraft's loudspeaker. It was so far away that even the aircraft's powerful PA system—perhaps used for crowd control in the past—could barely be heard.

It was Straub. I slapped a hand to my mouth.

"Good God," she said, "*I—wuh—*" She broke off. The *wuh* was the only time I had ever heard Straub let out any kind of shocked grunt. This had to be due to her seeing the Crawlers, clawing at nothing where they sat half-wedged in the Barrier. "Keep—*keep going*," Straub said. *"We have survivors on our side, Edgwick. Some of us made it."* The big soldier heard this and lowered his head, breathing out. *"I wish we could track you all the way to Coventry but flying close—"* There was a crackle as Straub broke off for a moment, perhaps talking to the pilot. *"We see five of you. Raise your arms if you're all okay."* We did. "That's good," Straub said. "*Don't take any risks, stick to the plan. Good luck, everyone—*" There was a pause. The helicopter's blades whirred in the night.

"Everyone is counting on you. Godspeed. And thank you." We waited for a moment, and the helicopter continued to hover before we understood that Straub, all business, was done.

But she was alive, goddamn her. *We* were.

"That was totally doomed," I said, looking around at the others. I sounded strong—and I didn't feel it—but I was trying. "All that had no right to work. But it did. When we're out there and it looks like we're fucked ... remember that." It was cheesy. It was lame. "I mean, I don't know. I'm just, I'm just saying. That was something. I think it's important." No-one said anything, but I could feel Maria's thread—even Paul's, I knew he could hear me—respond positively. That was also something.

"Thanks, Andy," Eric said, head down.

"Thank *you*," I said, and nearly patted him on the shoulder. I didn't. "Okay. Let's go."

If that was a speech, it had gone over well. Maybe I *could* do this.

Silence fell as we made our way out along the road from the Skye Bridge and into the mainland. We needed it. Routes, options, everything else could wait for now. My shakes were beginning to subside, the sight—or rather, the sound—of Straub alive having a calming effect. We walked towards the wall of blackness that waited for us just beyond the last of the floodlight's halogen glare, reaching out to swallow us all, and to my surprise the idea was soothing. I could be lost in it for a while. Paul led the way, the Stone Man of course just behind him, the rest of us walking behind the hunter and the hunted.

Then Maria ruined it.

"Straub said," Maria said, "that we had tablets with copies of the List on them. Right?"

"Yes," Edgwick said. "Why?"

"Mm," Maria muttered. "Just checking."

"You want to look at it?" I asked, moving behind her to open her backpack if she wanted.

"No," she said quickly. "It's okay."

"You want to look someone up?" Ahead of me, Paul shot me the stare he used when I was being tactless. I couldn't understand why he would do it now, and then I did, but it was too late—

"Just ... well, Marcus," Maria said. "He's someone I—well, I guess he's my ex. *Is* my ex. I just wondered, is all."

I didn't want to talk but I had to say *something* in response.

"You didn't get on?"

Paul's stare intensified.

"Oh, no, no, quite the opposite," Maria said. "We lost ... doesn't matter. We never got over some stuff from the First Arrival." I thought I knew what it was they had lost. Miscarriages had occurred in a lot of pregnant Stone Sensitives that had been near an active Stone Man.

"Uh ... sorry to hear that, Maria," I tried.

"That's okay. It didn't go well last time I saw him, anyway—" She shook her head quickly, reddening. "I'm talking too much, sorry. Ignore me. We can't afford that kind of indulgence right now anyway, too emotional. I'm sure we all want to look people we know up on the List." I was quietly shocked, both because the idea hadn't occurred to me, and that I didn't know who I would look up anyway. What did Paul think? "Change the subject, change the subject," Maria said, even as I thought *no, let's just be quiet instead.* "How do you already know Brigadier Straub, Eric?" she asked.

"Met her a while back," Eric said, walking with his head down. "Second Arrival."

"How?" Maria asked. Eric grunted, the sound bitter.

"My sister," he said, "was Theresa Pettifer." He jerked his head at the marching Stone Man. "The Stone Men targeted her. The army killed her to make her Stone Man go home; Straub wouldn't admit it at the time, but I got her to finally confess it today. After seeing what happened to Harry... I dunno. I guess I'm glad. Theresa avoided a terrible death."

Maria nodded sagely—of course she knew the name, it had been all over the papers—and Edgwick was busily and noisily fishing the map out of his pack and hadn't seemed to have heard Eric's response.

I certainly had. My skin was suddenly burning as my head had snapped up instinctively, my reaction too fast to stop, but I at least had the wherewithal to look straight ahead and not at Eric. I saw Paul glance trying to catch my eye without Eric seeing.

We'd both noticed something familiar in Eric's energy when he arrived, but we couldn't have known *this*. Why hadn't Straub told us? There hadn't been a lot of time in all the chaos at the Barrier, but sweet Jesus. It was Theresa Pettifer's Quarry Response-induced smothering of her own child that would eventually give humanity vital information—the discovery that the early killing of their Targets sent a pursuing Stone Man home—but that information of course hadn't been known in time to help her.

Theresa Pettifer had not been spared a terrible death. Theresa Pettifer had been taken to her Stone Man to be Harvested. *Was* Harvested. Straub had clearly lied to Eric about that.

And it had been Paul and I that had led Straub and the army right to Theresa Pettifer.

"I'm really sorry to hear that, Eric—Andy?" Maria said, drawing close to me. "You okay?"

"Yeah," I muttered, watching Paul's head quickly turn away once more. We would have to discuss this later. "Like I said, I just need to think."

The Stone Man dictated our pace. For now, we just had to walk, together. The darkness met us, wrapped itself around us, and we moved forward into the night.

...

Sorry. Excuse the flowery language there. I was just caught for a moment. The thought of all of us together like that, walking.

We—

Hold on a second.

... I need to get some water. My throat's dry.

Actually, I need to stop and eat. I've been doing this for hours and I need to take a break. There's some chicken kiev in the freezer and the idea of a proper meal is wonderful. I know I won't get this all done today, but I'm going to do as much as I can and then try to do the rest tomorrow. Excuse me.

✱✱✱

Chapter Seven

The Wanderers, the Batting Cage, The Lawnmower Theory, and Emergency Plans Are Made

***

Right. Eaten, watered, had a piss. Let's go.

Other than the moment Maria asked if someone could get her painkillers from her pack—to take the edge off the ache in her broken and set fingers—there had been silence for about an hour until Paul broke it.

"Oh," he muttered quietly, before looking around himself in confusion.

"What is it?" I asked.

"Never mind," he said, "Every now and then I'll be thinking and I'll get a memory connected to whatever I'm thinking about. Then I realise it's not mine. It's one of Linda's."

"Yeah," Maria said. "Yeah, me too."

"Uh-huh," I agreed. It had happened a few times with me, but I'd kept it to myself. Linda being in-circuit with us when she'd passed had left us with a part of her.

"Who's Linda?" Eric asked.

"Linda Wyken," Paul said. "She was a volunteer from—"

"*Jesus,*" Eric whispered, surprised. "Yeah, I know who she is. I heard her government interview tape. I had a few of them."

"How did you get those?" Edgwick asked.

"That's my business, thanks," Eric said. "So where is she?"

"She died," Paul and Linda said, both answering at once.

"Sorry," Eric said, looking awkward. "She sounded like a nice person."

"She was," I said, wanting to add something even though I barely knew the woman … and yet somehow knowing her. I wondered if her memories would keep popping up in me or if they would fade away.

The darkness above had faded from jet black to include a startling array of stars as we moved away from the floodlights at the bridge; the lack of street lighting in this remote setting meant seeing an incredible canopy above us. Even the ugly filter of the Barrier between us and the heavens couldn't spoil the view. The moon was clear in a relatively cloudless sky, and the low hills around us on the silent road gave the whole setting a beautiful eeriness, capped off by the constant beat of the Stone Man's walking feet. The sight of random, stationary cars dotted here and there became more and more frequent as we moved farther inland. We moved past isolated houses and random roadside businesses: a car dealership, a florist. We broke a window to get into the latter so Eric could wash the dried blood from his face, and it was many minutes before we walked beyond the range of the building's blaring burglar alarm. Eric had turned down the opportunity to change into the uniform from his pack. As we walked, Edgwick insisted on demonstrating the safety switch on our pistols and how to sight the weapon correctly. *I was given an order,* he reminded us. The guns seemed pointless to me; if their purpose was to deal with any problematic humans, we had a fucking Stone Man with us. Who was going to give us any shit? That said, I noticed that Eric was now the only one of us—other than Edgwick—who was actually wearing his pistol in its holster.

Eventually we spotted the distant glow of streetlights. A town was approaching, lying beyond the dual carriageway that sat nestled between two banks of high, sloping grassy hills.

I could have asked Edgwick which one—though everyone had a map each, Edgwick would be the best reader of them—but at that point I didn't care. All we had to do, all I wanted to do, was walk, but answering the already-asked question of sleep would soon become urgent. Part of the solution would be getting a vehicle or two and driving them at walking pace; the roads were clear enough here to easily navigate around any cars of the dead. But every car we passed was filled with the crusted remains of their thoroughly burst and previously intact inhabitants. All the burst cars had their keys in the ignition, so there was no scarcity of selection, none of us could bite that particular bullet yet; there had been too much death, *was* too much death. Our minds were still too rattled to keep a circuit going while also clambering inside a car filled with desiccated remains. When we reached the town, we could surely find an empty parked car outside a house then go inside and find their keys? In any case, finding a solution would mean conversation. None of us wanted that now, especially Paul and me.

Talking might mean discussion of Eric's sister and her death.

After a while, Maria broke the silence.

"Think you could try now?" She was addressing myself and Paul together. I looked her way, seeing her face in the dark for the first time in an hour, and saw it wasn't just a need for calm that had kept her silent. She looked saddened beyond anything any of us were feeling. I didn't think her concern was family as I thought she had none, or at least no more significant family than Paul or I. It had to be thoughts of Marcus. Of course, I diverted.

"Paul?"

He turned back to face me. *Fuck,* I thought. If Maria looked saddened, Paul looked exhausted. We *had* to figure out transport.

"Yep."

"You ready to give it another try?"

"I've been ready for a while," he said, his voice weary. "I'm not going to get any more relaxed with the Right Honourable Gentleman in hunting mode. I just wanted to make sure you two were ready."

"Okay." All of us turned to walk backwards so we could look at the following Stone Man, seeing it walking about sixty feet behind Paul. As I felt tentatively for those ethereal threads, I was surprised how easy it now was to find them. When we were in a blind panic, doing so had been like trying to catch a butterfly in a darkened room. Now it seemed as if they were just sitting there, waiting to be picked up.

"So how do you do it," Eric asked, "if it's not Stone Sight?"

"Kind of like a puppet," Paul said. "It's complicated."

"Paul, Maria," I said. "Give me ... the juice," I said, not knowing how else to end the sentence. Paul obliged quickly, keen, his thread alive before Maria's. The energy seemed to move straight through me, through the Stone Man, and out into the night sky—an uncapped oil well—before Maria's hand came into play to shape it, channel it. The threads of the Stone Man became a clearer suggestion of controlling cables, and the memory of the walking sample loop sharpened in my mind under Maria's guidance. The Stone Man's threads briefly became violent, almost yanking their way out of my mental grip, but I understood that this was resistance and held them fast. I began to send the command *walk*—to make the Stone Man do so at my instruction only—but then the threads jolted again and as the Stone Man stumbled, I recognised it as the little correction the Stone Man went through each time the sample loop repeated.

We were already back in control of the monster, the loop established. It had been so effortless, so automatic, that I hadn't even noticed. This was *teamwork*.

Stop.

The Stone Man stopped. It was twitching again—reluctant—but it had stopped. Beside me, Paul let out a moaning sigh and put his hands on his knees.

"Nice one, folks" he said. "Nice one. Wow."

"That's it?" Maria asked. "That easy?"

"This is *much* easier now," I said. "I can't believe—"

"Let's get behind it," Paul said quickly, straightening and jogging the short distance between us and Caementum and moving past it. stopping perhaps forty feet to its rear. "Set it going," Paul said, his thread surging gently, encouraging me. I obliged, and Maria, Eric, Edgwick moved aside to let the Stone Man walk through our midst and away from Paul. "Please," Paul said, his immense relief clear to all. "Let's not let that *last* little misstep happen again, okay?"

"It won't," Maria said, smiling gently, but at that moment a woman's scream tore through the night air.

All of us jumped; I immediately tried to tighten my grip on the Stone Man's threads, but it wasn't necessary. Being startled, it seemed, didn't have much effect on our control now we had started from a better point of equilibrium. The Stone Man kept on walking, its loop trucking it along.

Two people were standing in the near distance, frozen.

The shorter of the two—the woman who had screamed—had her arms wrapped around her companion's waist, a taller man who was bending down to protectively place his arms around his partner's shoulders.

They had seen the Stone Man walking.

"It's okay!" Edgwick bellowed, holding up his arms. "Don't worry! Just walk around it, come to us! It won't hurt you!" The couple just looked at each other, confused. "Walk over here!" Edgwick called, walking over to the road's hard shoulder, far from the Stone Man. "Walk along the outside! We'll meet you halfway!" The couple glanced at each other again, talking, and then began to make their uncertain way to the roadside to meet us.

"Do we take them with us?" Paul muttered.

"No," Edgwick quietly replied. I was glad he said so; it saved me being the bad guy. I waited for Maria to protest, but to my surprise, she didn't. The newcomers drew closer: an elderly couple, walking towards us and holding trembling hands. They were dressed in what appeared to be light hiking gear, but both their age and clothing were hard to make out more accurately due to the spray of dried and congealed remains covering them both. They stared at the Stone Man as it passed, a familiar expression on their faces, that mix of raw wonder and horror.

"What's it doing?" the woman asked. She had a little turned-up nose like a pug and the facial expression of an abandoned child. "Where's it going?" She looked Edgwick up and down. "You're army?" she asked him. She took in the rest of us. "Are you all army?"

"It's alright," Edgwick said softly, moving his rifle strap around his shoulder so that the barrel was firmly behind him. "Yes, we're all with the army. These are civilian contractors." I heard Eric give an almost-inaudible scoff. "We're investigating what's happening."

"What *is* happening?" the woman asked. "*And where is that thing going?*" She gestured at the Stone Man, and as she looked away Edgwick briefly caught my eye and gave an almost infinitesimal gesture with his head; the Stone Man was moving further and further away. Soon it would be approaching the one hundred feet range. We would have to start moving in a few seconds. The woman's partner rested his hand on her shoulder reassuringly. He was a tall, thin-looking man with a bird-like air, but his back was straight, his posture strong. I was glad they were together.

"We don't know," Edgwick lied, to a degree, and I understood why. The military had kept Paul's continued existence a secret for the same reason: anything Stone Sensitives might know, might get back to the Stone Men. Maria may have been hiding us, but she wasn't hiding these two, or anything *they* might know. "That's why we're following it. Are you hurt? Do you need anything?"

"We're okay," the man said, his voice high and reedy. "We were on our way to see our son and grandchildren. We were in a cab, neither of us drive "

"Is my son alive?" the woman suddenly blurted. "Do you know? The driver *exploded*." Her face shook and the man held her tightly, shaking too. "That thing, that thing," she repeated, pointing at the Barrier churning endlessly above us. "It rushed through the cab and killed the driver and we crashed. We hit another car. If we'd have been going fast, we'd be dead too. What is it? What is that thing in the sky?"

"We don't fully know," Edgwick said, starting to walk slowly around the couple. Their heads followed him, their eyes still in shock, so much so that they didn't seem to realise that we were leaving. "Is your son adopted?"

"What?" the woman asked.

"No," the man said, confused.

"Then he almost certainly wasn't killed by it," Edgwick said. "If you're going to your son, keep going. Take the first available car you can find."

"He's alive?" the woman breathed, her hands going to her mouth. "Are you sure?"

"Almost certainly," Edgwick repeated. "If he's the child of two Stone Sensitive parents. Go to him." He was right; Holbrooks himself had said so. Their son would not only be Stone Sensitive but would most likely be DIGGS.

"Oh my God..." the woman breathed, hugging her partner.

"The Crawlers," Maria muttered, "should we tell them—"

Edgwick waved a hip-height hand at her.

"If you see or hear anything coming," Edgwick said, pointing at the Stone Man, "that looks like it's made of the same stuff as *that*, then stay to the side of the road and let them pass. It won't be coming for you."

Paul suddenly made a *huff* sound and strode towards the old couple.

His hand was outstretched.

"Here," he said, "I might be able to help you a little."

Maria grabbed his arm. The old couple watched, confused. Maria's grip on Paul's arm tightened as I heard her voice in her thread.

You can't boost them, she told him. *They'll be more likely to pop up on the Stone Men's radar and I won't be able to hide them if you do. Do you want to see them inside bubbles?*

But they might be able to help us, Paul said in-circuit. *We don't know what their gifts are.*

That was true.

"Edgwick," I said. "Get me a tablet, please." I stepped up to the couple as Edgwick fished his tablet out of his pack. "Hi. What are your names?" I was sure Edgwick would hear the question and understand.

"Sandra Cliff," the woman said. "This is Howard, my husband."

"Nice to meet you," I said, forcing a smile and giving Edgwick time to work. "I'm Andy. This is Eric, Maria, Paul, and..." I trailed off.

"Toby," Edgwick reminded me, not looking up from the tablet he now held.

"Are you warm enough?" I asked them, further filling for time.

"Yes," Sandra said. "It's a winter coat, but Andy, what do we *do*?"

I saw Edgwick look up.

"Both TIN," he said. Linda's level. The risk of boosting them was, most likely, far greater than any benefit to the mission their abilities might bring. "We have to go *now*. Caementum is at ninety feet."

"How do you know?" I asked, surprised at Edgwick's accuracy.

"Former sniper," he said, shrugging. "I have an eye for these things. Trust me."

"You're leaving?" Howard asked, finally noticing our movements.

"We have to," Edgwick said, and as Howard began to follow, leading Sandra by the shoulders, the soldier held up a hand.

"*No*," he said firmly. "It's not safe this way. When you get to your son, get as far north as you can. As far away from the Midlands as possible. Do you understand? *Continue north.*"

"Can we get out?" Howard asked. "Can we get out of the country?"

"Not yet," Edgwick said. "I'm sorry, we have to go."

The couple stared at us, open mouthed.

"Do you have water?" Maria asked.

"No," Sandra said in a small voice.

"Take mine—" Maria began, stepping forward.

"*No*," Edgwick repeated firmly, so much so that Maria stopped in her tracks. "There's a florist's shop up the way that we broke into," he said to Sandra, "if you stick to the road. We broke in. It has a sink."

But Eric was marching back up to the couple and fishing in his pack. He produced his water bottle and gave it to them.

"Here," he said kindly. He turned and walked back after the Stone Man, passing Edgwick without a glance. The soldier sighed.

"That's going to get old quick," he muttered, before raising a hand of farewell to the stunned-looking couple. "Good luck," he said, before heading after Eric. I did the same, turning away from the couple and leaving them in the midst of this new, empty and ruined world. I didn't look back.

"You know this is a war zone," Edgwick said quietly as I fell into step behind him. "Right? We can't be giving away supplies on a mission."

"Don't look at me," I said. "I was with you."

"Mm."

"We can't help everyone," I said. "That's obvious. I mean, we're trying to save the bloody *world*, aren't we?"

"Well, we won't meet many more people. Even between here and Coventry. Less than 0.003 percent of seventy million left. The odds of even meeting them were incredibly slim. But we must prioritise ourselves if we want any chance of saving everyone under the Barrier, let alone the rest of—"

"Why are you telling me this?" I asked him. "I don't disagree with you."

Edgwick eyed Eric's back. The young man was now at the front of our group, Maria and Paul walking behind Edgwick and I.

"Yeah," Edgwick grunted. "Sorry. You're right. The kid is just pissing me off." The kid? How old was Edgwick? I thought he was about my age, and Eric didn't look *that* much younger than me. Perhaps Edgwick's beard was making his age hard to ascertain. "He was a hero back there at the Barrier," Edgwick said. "I don't understand why he's being such a little bitch right now."

"Didn't you hear him earlier?" I asked. "About his sister?"

"No." Edgwick hadn't. He'd been getting the map out of his pack.

"She was *Theresa Pettifer.*"

Edgwick blew air out between his teeth.

"*Ohhhhh* shit," he said. "Okay."

"How do you *think* he feels about the military?" I asked him. "About Straub? Even if Eric thinks his sister was neutralised and never met a Stone Man?"

Edgwick nodded.

"Even so, Jesus," he said, looking at me. "I don't think *I'm* the one who should be taking that particular flack, do *you?*"

I reddened. I glanced behind me to Paul and Maria, both trudging along, their gaze upon the floor. Behind them, the country road was already empty. The couple had rounded the bend and disappeared from view.

"Let's just start thinking about transportation," I told him.

***

"So right now," Eric asked, "you're controlling it? You can make it stop and go and all that?"

"Yeah," I replied, trying to sound relaxed.

We were now walking through the village of Kirkton, a place that was, as far as I could see from the main road, hardly a village at all; a few ancient looking buildings dotted along the road at lengthy intervals, nestled at the foot of low hills. None of them, annoyingly—now we'd had some time to get our heads together—had cars parked outside, their owners perhaps having headed to be with loved ones when the Barrier arrived. We passed a Toyota Prius that had flattened itself against a roadside drystone wall, its driver's sudden bursting having the car on a collision course. Such things perfectly summed up the fate of the country, but we were moving beyond the horror of that, at least for now. We had to. I thought of holocaust survivors. Nine million of their people dead, and they had *learned to deal*, to use the modern parlance. The numbers here were far greater, though; was there a ceiling on a person's ability to comprehend atrocity?

I was walking only a few feet behind the Stone Man, more comfortable than I'd previously felt at such close range, and trying to avoid conversation with Eric. Theresa Pettifer's fucking *brother*. To be clear, I had nothing at all against him—he had saved my life, after all—but of course he caught up and started walking alongside me. It turned out that Eric Hatton was quite the Andy Pointer nerd.

"How do you tell it what to do?" he asked, eager. "Is it like a mind to Stone muscle connection, like when you think about opening your own hand?"

"No," I said, thinking about announcing it was time to start searching for car keys in any houses we passed. I needed this conversation to end, but now an old, nasty voice spoke up in my head:

Oh, now, *you care,* it said. *Never cared too much about Theresa Pettifer before though, did you? You even got the sex of her baby wrong.* Eric said *Aaron was the baby's name, a boy. You thought Theresa's kid was a girl for years. You cared so little that you didn't even follow the news properly, never followed up with Straub.*

I couldn't, no. Not after Patrick and Henry. Any more was just too much. And unlike the other two, I hadn't had a *conversation* with Theresa. She had been a distant, screaming person I had seen dragged from her home, and that somehow hadn't had the same connection. *Or you were simply too busy thinking about yourself,* the voice said, and fell silent. Ahead of us, the Stone Man stumbled a little as the pre-programmed loop went back to the beginning.

"What was that?" Eric asked. "Am I distracting you? Sorry."

"No, you didn't."

"Sorry," Eric repeated. "I'll be honest, it's kind of hard to believe I'm talking to Andy Pointer. I hope that doesn't make you uncomfortable. I have, let's just say I used to have a *lot* of questions about what was going on behind the scenes—well, I still do really, even if it all seems a bit stupid now—but once upon a time I would have given anything to be able to talk to you."

"Heh," I said awkwardly, trying to sound amused, but Eric just smiled sadly.

"Look man, don't worry," he said. "I'm sure that stuff is the last thing you want to talk about, I get it. I just, well, if I seem a little bit odd when I talk to you, it's just that it hits me every now and then that *holy shit, I'm talking to Andy Pointer,* you know? And I'm also babbling to try and keep my mind off the kid." He shook his head.

"That's okay, you don't seem odd when you talk at all," I said, eager to get off any mention of the past. It also didn't hurt to feel some of the old respect. "I'm sure it's strange meeting someone famous who you know a lot about."

"I thought you were *dead,*" Eric said.

"That does make two of us, you know," I said, and Eric chuckled a little. "But do me a favour?" I asked.

Eric's eyebrows went up.

"Okay?"

"Let up on Edgwick a bit, will you?"

Eyebrows straight back down.

"What do you mean?"

"I've noticed you're being a little... terse, shall we say?"

"Hm. I will if he stops with the *attitude.*"

What attitude, I thought.

"I think we're all more than a little tense," I said diplomatically, "and Edgwick is simply behaving how he's been trained, that's all. It probably comes off as a bit harsh. But we need to keep things smooth here. You know? Greases the Stone wheels, as it were." I tapped the side of my head.

Eric sighed.

"Yeah," he said. "Okay, I will. Sorry. Military types and me, with my sister, it just—"

"I get it, I get it."

"Hey," Eric said quietly. "I'm sorry about what happened earlier. Sharing how the Target felt. I was just freaking out because of the kid, Aiden—"

"That's okay," I said, and I meant it. "Given that you probably saved our lives, what's a near-panic attack between friends, right?"

"Thanks," Eric said, smiling a little, and it briefly lit up his darkened face. He might have been sulking around Edgwick, but I thought Eric was alright.

Then I remembered that I'd sent armed men to kill his sister. I had to get things off the personal.

"You hearing anything from *them* right now?" I asked.

"Since Paul boosted me, it's harder to *not* hear them, even if most of it is just noise. They are looking for us though, definitely. I think they know we have the Stone Man, or that we *did* at least, until Maria got the whole team hidden. When they get interested in something, trust me, I'll make a fuss. It spikes like feedback going off in my head." He chuckled darkly.

"I used to worry about my hearing all the time, being a musician. Were you much of a gig man, Andy?"

"Not really," I said. Eric waited for me to elaborate. "So, uh, you asked how I control it," I said, quickly changing the subject. "We have it on a sort of autopilot loop for walking, the same command on repeat... actually, you ever used a petrol lawnmower?"

"Yes."

"It's sort of like that," I told him. "It'll just keep moving forward by itself once it's switched on, so all I have to do is direct it."

"So, what about more complicated things? Like, what do you do if they send the other Stone Men after us?"

"They won't be able to find us."

"For now. What if they find a way? Or if the Crawlers get through and catch up to us. What will you do?"

"We'll have to fight them," Maria said, speaking up from behind us.

The thought was chilling; fight the Crawlers? Fight the *Stone Men?*

"Nice idea," I scoffed. "I don't know if you've noticed, but we could barely get Chuckles here to walk in a straight line under our control. Unless we find it also has some kind of karate autopilot subroutine, we're going to be out of luck."

Maria shrugged, unfazed.

"Then we need to learn," she said. "Eric's right. We need to understand more complicated movements. We were getting better fast until we lost control; maybe we're even better now. Stop him a second."

What Maria was saying made sense, but to practice meant to acknowledge the possibility of combat. I obliged all the same; the command flew out of me and the Stone Man halted in the middle of the street, twitching on the spot.

Come on, coward, I thought. *She's right. And if you keep resisting everything, this whole thing is only going to be harder than it needs to be.*

Eric watched, looking uncertain. Paul and Edgwick stopped walking.

"I think that once we get a few practice tries in here," Maria said, "this will be something we can repeat as we walk. Get our eye in."

"Practice?" Edgwick asked.

"Yes," Maria said. "Andy? Move its arm."

"In what way?"

"Just—" She impatiently raised her arm and flapped it down to her side again.

I felt her thread firing, ready to be off.

"Paul?"

"Eh? Oh."

Paul's thread came alive too. I tried to find the correct command.

Arm.

Nothing happened. I concentrated, picturing Caementum's limb moving in my mind, and tried again.

Arm up.

The Stone Man's arm came slowly up and out, but forwards. It stayed there in a kind of half-baked Nazi salute.

"Well, that's problematic," Paul said.

Arm down.

The arm came back to the Stone Man's side. I glanced at Eric, who looked impressed and gave me a thumbs up. Yeah, I liked the guy.

"Now do the other one," Maria said, a harder audience. "Do it faster." I pictured the other arm, pictured it flapping up and down the way Maria's had.

Arm.

The Stone Man twitched, froze for a moment, then—after that brief delay—responded, its arm slowly coming out sideways like a bird's wing and then returning to its starting position. Not as fast as I wanted, but faster than before. The speed of the improvements we were making with this thing—no doubt down to Maria's influence—was amazing. Two attempts and we'd already sped things up by at least fifty percent. One of the neurologists at the Project had once told me a phrase: *neurons that fire together, wire together.* It meant pathways in the brain formed and solidified through repetition, but there wasn't a brain in human history that could fire and wire the way our circuit could.

"The other side again," Maria said, her eyes locked on the Stone Man's arms. "See if you can do it faster still."

How about an attaboy, I thought petulantly—yeah, I have it in spades, but at least I can admit it, how about you?—but did as I was told. This time the Stone Man's arm shot up and down at the right speed. Maria actually clapped her hands in approval, forgetting her bandaged fingers and wincing at the impact, but didn't stop smiling.

"Excellent!"

Finally, I thought.

"Bloody hell," Paul said. "See how quickly that improved?"

"I did," I said. It was clear what we were all thinking: if we could do *this*, then another piece of hope had been stacked onto our slowly growing pile. How big that pile looked compared to the Prism remained to be seen, but still.

"This is promising," Edgwick said.

"Hold on," Maria said, spotting something jutting out of the doorway of an approaching roadside cottage. She ran ahead of us, snatched the object free, and ran back. She was now in possession of a rolled up newspaper and a light in her eyes that had been missing for some time. She hurried over to Edgwick, eager. "Hold this," she said, removing the front page and thrusting the rest of the periodical into his hands.

"Of course," Edgwick said, raising his eyebrows, but Maria was already scrunching the front page into a ball.

"Okay," she said. She'd finished screwing up the front page and had walked around to the front of the Stone Man. "Ready?" I began to ask what she wanted to do, but Maria was already showing me the paper ball she'd shaped.

"Might be a tall order," I said, getting it.

"Maybe," she said, but the fire in her eyes was bright. "Let's find out. We're going to be pretty shit in a fight if all we can do is flap our arms like a Stone Penguin." She caught herself. "*Its* arms. You know what I mean. Let's go."

Eric, Edgwick and Paul moved around to the front of the Stone Man to get a better view. Paul, of course, remained off to the monster's side, never wanting to be in front of a Stone Man by choice.

"Go," I said.

Maria threw the ball of newspaper at the Stone Man.

It was the most pathetic throw I've ever seen in my life.

The paper ball fell weakly onto the floor several feet in front of the Stone Man with a *smeck* sound. Fortunately for me, everyone's eyes were on the abject failure rolling on the floor before them. No-one seemed to notice that Caementum's arm had flicked uselessly up and down, moving about two seconds late if the throw had been good.

The men shuffled awkwardly on the spot. Maria hurried over to pick up the ball.

"I'd hate to say anything about stereotypes—" Paul began, but Maria cut him off.

"*My friend Kristie* had the fastest rounders pitch in school," she snapped, "faster than any of the boys, so shut up." She moved back to stand with Edgwick and the others, shaking out her shoulders before throwing again.

"You could just stand closer," I suggested. Maria breathed in sharply... then took a few more steps towards the Stone Man without another word, lips pressed tightly together. Paul opened his mouth to say something wise, but a glare from me stopped him.

The old dickhead Paul was still in there somewhere, it seemed, and that was another thing to feel hopeful about.

Maria threw the ball, fast and hard enough this time; it *papped* off the Stone Man's chest. I'd now managed to make the arm move when I wanted it, but her latest throw had been much quicker than I'd expected. She looked my way.

"Little fast, there," I told her.

"Make your mind up," she said, but she was smiling. She took a freshly-screwed-up ball from Edgwick and threw it before I was ready.

"*Easy*, Jesus—" I began, almost flinching for some reason even though the ball was harmless and not even aimed at me, but I felt Maria and Paul's threads twitch in time. The Stone Man's right arm snapped up in a clumsy *wax off* motion. The paper ball made loose contact with the arm's outside edge, just catching it, and lightly ricocheted away. Paul breathed out.

"Wow. Good job, Andy."

"It helped when you two helped," I told them, excited. "You helped just now, right?"

"Yeah!" Maria said, grinning.

"I need you to, just like the walking," I told them, already wondering *can we do it under pressure because we already completely broke once—*

"Yes, yes," Maria said quickly, gesturing to Edgwick to roll up another ball of paper. "One more and then we can practice as we walk. We can walk and throw."

"Okay, yeah." We were firing together, wiring together. Maria was already throwing, she and Paul concentrating hard, and I now brought the Stone Man's left arm straight up. It met the paper ball well; the projectile shot high up into the air before coming down in a lazy arc near the Stone Man's right arm. Still within range—

"Again, quick!" Eric said, urging the one-two hit, but I wasn't ready, too busy being delighted with myself for the well-timed swing. I could feel that an impromptu mental command would only half-move the Stone Man's arm in the right direction... and then something came down Maria's thread.

Gimme a sec. I need to think how to describe it.

Okay. I think I have it.

It was as if Maria's thread *took hold of mine.*

No... wait.

Okay. It was as if there was suddenly *another* thread of mine—a copy—and Maria's working with—

Fuck's sake. All I know for certain is this:

Maria moved the Stone Man's arm. Somehow, she used my thread—or my gift—to do it.

"Heyyyyy, slick!" Eric laughed, and Edgwick grinned, neither of them knowing what had just happened. Paul had noticed though.

"Woah," he said. "That felt funny. What happened?"

I was in shock. Maria looked alive.

"Did you do that on purpose?" I asked. Was I... angry? I couldn't tell. My heart was suddenly beating fast. I almost felt violated, I guess, but that was just *stupid.*

"No," Maria said, "I just … we were trying to hit the ball …" She looked sideways for a moment, confused. "*Uh*—"

Maria made a sudden gagging sound and threw up.

Her left knee buckled but she stayed upright, blindly holding up a hand to tell us to wait. Then she sat down suddenly.

"What's going on?" Eric asked, taking his pack off his shoulder and opening it only to find what he wanted was no longer there. He looked at the rest of us. "Someone give her some water." Edgwick fished his out of his bag. To his credit, the big man said nothing, silently passing the bottle to Maria. She took it gratefully.

"Thanks," she said.

"*What happened?*" Eric insisted, looking at me.

"I didn't fully make the arm move in time, the second time," I said. My heartbeat was slowing down. "She did."

"*Maria* made it move?" Eric asked.

"*I* made it move," I said quickly, "but … it was like she *made* me make it move somehow. So you didn't do that on purpose?"

"I told you, no," Maria croaked, "trust me, I don't think I want to do that again."

"Why do you keep asking her if she did it on purpose?" Paul asked, eyeballing me.

"It just felt weird, that's all," I said, holding up my hands. But Paul was still staring at me. "*What?* Alright, I didn't like it, okay? If we start overstepping each other's commands," I added quickly, finding a reason after the fact, "then that's just going to create chaos, the big bastard will be all over the place." I couldn't admit the real reason I was wound up: I was the driver. I was *Dispensatori*... but I didn't truly want to be anymore, so what was my problem? "Look, the most important thing is that Maria's alright. You are, yeah?" Maria nodded, standing up slowly. "And we hit the ball together when I would have missed. That, uh, that's a trick that could be very useful."

"So you did that how, on instinct?" Eric asked. "Maria, did you have any Stone Sight?"

"*No,*" I said, answering for her. Everyone stared at me. "Sorry, I'm just tired. I'm tired."

But that was the thing; I wasn't tired at all.

I'd been worrying about the sleep element ever since we'd left the Chisel, and yet I felt as fresh as when we'd first set off. Paul and Maria looked as flat as an elephant's mattress. I'd just claimed tiredness so I didn't have to get into it, and my blood was up. *Fuck it*, this was a good point to get onto the car situation. "We all are," I lied. "Let's try and get keys for the next parked car we see. Caementum can walk, one of us drives the car behind it, the others can sleep. We'll take turns."

"Andy," Maria said. "You're talking about us sleeping? We need *all three* of us to make it walk. You need me to keep us hidden." The question wasn't confrontational; Maria looked scared.

"Well," Edgwick said, "regarding the hiding side of things: after the helicopter crashed, you said that hiding us was instinctive now, something like *it's automatic like breathing*, words to that effect. Right?"

Of course; with all the chaos I'd forgotten that Maria had been unconscious for *nearly the entire flight* until right before we splash-landed.

"Well... yes," Maria said, seeing Edgwick's point.

"Were you hiding us when you were asleep? Automatically?"

"I don't know."

"Hell of a gamble," Paul said, "if we want to find out for sure if she was or not. She passes out and then we discover that the Stone Giant is charging straight up our arses. We've cut that way too close too many times already."

"It's how many days at walking pace to Coventry, Edgwick?" Maria asked.

"Six, but that's non-stop," Edgwick said. "More with sleep, obviously, but I don't know how you'll ... " He trailed off.

"*Shit,*" Maria said running her hands through her hair. "We can't stay awake for six days, even with chemical intervention. I mean, maybe it's possible, but we'll barely be able to think, and then what happens to the circuit? To our control?"

"Hold on," I said. I was getting an idea. "Maria just used *my* gift. Right? She effectively used my brain like a tool." *Without permission,* Twat-Andy grumbled, but I keep him quiet.

"I see where you're going with that, bud," Eric said, rubbing his chin, his still-bloodshot eyes lost in thought. I clocked his use of *bud.* Over-familiarity... I'm never sure about it. Depends on the person. "But, again: what happens when *you* need to sleep?"

"Then I hand control back to Maria."

"Andy, I just threw up because I moved the Stone Man's *arm,*" Maria said. "I can't make it walk!"

"Not yet, maybe," I said, "but you saw how quickly we got its arm movements down. Maybe we just need to get you used to it." Maria puffed out her cheeks, blowing air out of her mouth.

"God..." she said.

"Paul," Eric asked. "Do you need to concentrate when the Stone Man is doing the lawnmower walk?"

"The what, now?"

"He means the autopilot, the sample loop," I explained. Paul scowled at me, confused.

"How is it a bloody lawnmower—"

"Never*mind,* just... answer the question."

"Concentrate, no," Paul said, "not really. I can feel myself helping Andy and Maria—and even the Stone Man in a way—but it's not something I'm thinking about. The juice is just constantly coming out of me, low-level, until they need more."

"So you only really needed to concentrate when you were helping Andy hit the ball?" Eric asked.

"Oh aye, definitely."

"So that's Paul that can sleep, surely?" Eric asked me. He didn't look at the others.

That was the moment I understood that Eric thought I was in charge.

"Well... that's one we can test fairly safely," I said. "If Paul sleeps and we lose control, Maria and I can wake him up and get Caementum back under pretty easily."

"And when the Stone Man is auto-walking," Eric said, scratching unconsciously at the stump where a hand used to be, "you're mostly hands-off, right?"

"Mostly. I keep adjusting its angle so it doesn't walk into things. The sample loop is coming out of Maria."

"So why," Eric asked, "can't we use the Lawnmower Theory for Paul and Maria's gifts too? The sample loop is a stored idea, but it's a form of energy. So, if you can make functional loops and set them on auto-repeat, why couldn't Maria do the same with whatever she does to hide us, and contains Caementum's energy?" Eric turned to Maria. "How does it feel when you do it?"

"Like a blanket," she said immediately, looking just above our heads as she did so. The funny thing was it felt that way to me too. We were a circuit, after all. "Like I'm keeping you all covered under a big thick blanket. Covering the Stone Man too."

"You could test that too as *you* were dropping off," Edgwick said. "If we noticed any difference in the blanket or whatever, if it felt thinner, or like it was disappearing."

"So I'm the one who has to stay awake?" I asked.

"Maria got sick," Eric said, "when she used your gift to do something really focused. I bet if you set the lawnmower loop going—who cares what the Stone Man hits along the way— she could keep a hand on the reins without too much trouble. Only for a couple of hours while *you* sleep, especially if she's sitting comfortably in a slow-moving car. And we could test that easily."

Maria turned to me.

"Ready to put me in, Coach?" she asked.

Did she look excited?

"Okay." I didn't really know what to do, though. I looked at the Stone Man as it twitched on the spot. "Okay," I repeated. "Are *you* ready?"

"Yeah."

She was. The energy of her thread was pulsing a little more. Paul was already there; he was right, it really was constantly washing out of him.

I thought of the countless hours of meditation back at the Project.

"All yours," I said, and made my mind go blank. I may have many, many doubts about who I am and what my qualities are—or lack thereof—but one thing can be said about Andy Pointer: he learned how to meditate.

Maria's thread sang; Paul's became a little stronger as he joined in. That strange doubling effect I'd felt earlier moved between Maria and I, as if I were still running the show but still distant from it, involved yet absent.

The Stone Man walked.

I knew I could wrest back control at any time, but all I had to do right now was be there. I watched the Stone Man's movements as the road gently turned right; Caementum's angle of approach turned with it. Not smoothly—the monster's shoulders jerked as it made a series of sharp adjustments—but Maria was controlling it.

"Maria, you're doing that?" Edgwick asked. I heard Eric give a little chuckle of delight, pleased with both his idea and the result.

"Yeah," Maria murmured. "Lemme concentrate though."

Maria's head was up, eyes still bright.

I could feel the concentration it took for her to do this, the same way I could feel her being energised by it. Paul and Eric gave each other a little high five. Another brick in the small wall of hope we were building.

At the barest sign of her starting to tremble, I took back over.

"Okay, great," I said quickly. "Excellent, that's really good to know."

I pulled on the thread in my mind as if it were reins; I reset the loop in motion, knowing that the hand gently resting on the tiller belonged to me. I glanced at Maria; she blinked, a little surprised, and darkened some. Her weariness was returning along with her equilibrium. I watched to see if she felt sick again. Maria breathed hard a few times and then gave a shaking thumbs-up, the effort of controlling the auto-walking clearly much less than specific, real-time movements. But was the glance she shot me in the dark one of reproach?

"Let's find a car," Edgwick said. "Go another two hours and then make camp. A rest in a car is one thing, but I think if we're only going to sleep in short bursts then that sleep needs to be lying down, fully out." A murmur of agreement passed around the group. "Obviously we'll stop in a house if one is available, but distance is key over home comforts right now. We'll stop once we get past Loch Long." He paused. "I guess we'll have to come to a group consensus over the kind of sleep protocol once we get there."

I didn't think I'd need it. I kept that thought to myself.

***

Chapter Eight

If Andy Had to do the Same Again, Eric Warns the Group, and Getting Beneath the Surface

***

We got out of the car to make camp.

We'd been crawling along inside a Volkswagen Touran, discovered parked outside a farmhouse. Its keys were found surprisingly quickly inside the building, hanging on a hook in the cosy hallway next to two child-sized coats. I took the keys and left before anyone could comment on the environment.

It was odd crawling along in a vehicle at walking pace, but we were all glad of the rest, monitoring the Stone Man from our seats. Eventually we set up camp in a roadside field, the option to break into another house and sleep there having long since passed. Getting another few hours' walking-pace driving under our belts was more important than comfort, but that choice had placed us in the middle of nowhere. It was Edgwick that had to insist we stop; to my surprise Paul, Maria and Eric tried to refuse. Once the tents were thrown up, however—Edgwick setting up some kind of floodlight-flashlight in the centre of the camp—everyone's carry mats and sleeping bags were rolled out quickly.

I set Caementum walking in a circle about fifty feet to the west of our campsite; if the thing had any kind of leftover muscle memory from its days at the Project, it would certainly have no issue carrying out that particular motion. It seemed more comfortable walking continuously than twitching in place.

"This shite isn't as bad as I thought it might be," Paul said, hungrily fishing out another spoonful of the rations that Straub's people had provided. I disagreed but said nothing. Paul was doing better, I thought. Perhaps the major doses of hope we'd recently had were settling him down. He certainly seemed more comfortable around the Stone Man, making little jokes now and then like his old self.

Maria was so tense though, her thread like a tightrope.

"You okay?" I asked her. The speed at which she looked up told me she wasn't.

"Just thinking," she said, "about Linda. And my friend Ruth, the one the Empty Men took."

"Oh. I'm so sorry."

"Thanks. Linda's husband, Jason, too… He was away with work. I don't know if he's still alive. And if he is, he won't know what happened to her. It's just …" She shook her head. I thought about the List on the tablets. Maria had turned down looking up her ex; she knew the option was there if she wanted it. There was something more here.

"But what is it really?" I asked. The question was so alien to me; reading between the lines of people's responses was never my strong point. Maria's tension seemed different.

"What do you—" she began and stopped. "It's just hard, that's all. Like quitting cigarettes."

"What is?" Paul asked. Maria looked embarrassed.

"At the Project," she said. "When I was fully boosted and went into the Signal, I was so … *wow*. It was indescribable. And I've not been allowed to go back in since. I get it, it's too dangerous, I have to hide us. But I can't stop thinking about it." She looked away to the Stone Man as it paced in the darkness. I understood it then. The desire. I'd felt the energy of driving it. I felt a rush of empathy so uncommon to me that I spoke without thinking, without ego.

"It's not fair that you're not GALE, Maria," I told her. "That you can't fully be Dispensatori. You're stronger, more disciplined. You'd be better at it than me."

Maria looked shocked—I was too, to be fair—and then she came right back with a truth of her own.

"I lied earlier," she said. "When I said I moved the Stone Man's arm by accident. I *did* do it on purpose. I can feel how it feels to drive it the way you do, I feel the echo from your thread. I was …" She hesitated. "I *am* … jealous. It won't happen again. Thanks for saying what you just said, Andy."

"That's okay." I smiled at her, sincere, and she smiled back.

Well look at me, I thought. *Dispensatori as fuck.*

"The Blues that are walking," Paul said. "Not the ones at the Prism," he added quickly for Eric's sake, who was sitting nearby. Paul knew how much closer those Blues were to Aiden than the others. "I wonder when they're going to reach their Targets? Can't be long now. I know Maria's muting everything, but I wonder if we'll still … you know. Feel it."

"Harry's the only one that's been taken so far," Eric said. "Guess the two at the Prism were made from, you know." He coughed. "His Harvest."

"Yeah," Edgwick said, swigging from his water bottle. "It's always two after every Harvest."

I avoided Paul's eye.

"I should have listened to Straub," Eric said. "She told me Harry had the Quarry Response and that I should shoot him right away. I didn't listen. I did it as quick as I could the *moment* his bubble disappeared and the Harvesting began. He only felt it for a second, I'm telling you, but—"

His brow suddenly furrowed. His hand went to the back of his head.

"Eric," Edgwick said, using a soft tone I hadn't heard him use before. "You aren't a soldier. The fact that you could do it all speaks to your strength of character, man. I had to carry out a mercy killing in Afghanistan. He was gut shot with no chance of rescue for two days. Already a dead man. I watched him in excruciating pain until I couldn't take it anymore and put one right between his eyes." Edgwick's gaze was steady, relaxed. "I've regretted that delay every day since. It sounds as if you were far, far quicker, and as someone that had never previously taken a life. You did right by your friend."

No-one spoke. *Good man, Edgwick,* I thought.

"He's right, Eric," Maria added, but now Eric's head came up.

"No," he said. "It's not that."

Eric looked furious.

"Two Stone Men," Eric said. "From each Harvest."

I froze.

"There were three in the Second Arrival," Eric said, his eyes narrowing. "Aaron … *died,* so his Stone Man went home without Harvesting. When the Stone Man came back the next time, there were four more of them, making seven. *Two of them had to have Harvested their Targets.*"

He paused. No-one spoke.

"One of those Harvested Targets had to be Theresa," Eric said.

His hand slowly went to his mouth.

I didn't need an Eric thread to know what he was picturing: the screaming of the short-lived Harvesting he'd witnessed, that of Harry. but longer, drawn out all the way to completion, this time with the Target alive.

And the Target as his sister.

"Straub lied," Eric said, his voice creaking like a coffin lid. "Straub *lied*." He turned to me. "Did you know? Did you know?"

His gaze was a laser drill. The guilt was instant and all-encompassing, and here was a chance to confess. Could I?

You just got done patting yourself on the back for being Dispensatori, I thought. *What would* he *do?*

"I did," I said.

My eyes found Paul, checking. He nodded almost imperceptibly.

"Paul and I," I said, "our job during the Arrivals was to sense and find the Targets. To end the Arrival as quickly as possible, to save lives. Whoever those Targets might be. That's how we became a part of all this. It's why we're the ones trying to *stop* this."

But Eric—my biggest fan, at least before now—looked like I'd just slapped him.

"Is that what Dispensatori means, then?" he said, his eyes black holes in his face. "*Hitman?*"

To my amazement, my response came without hesitation. Even after all those years of therapy on the base, the guilt, never, ever went away … but it turned out I had my answer.

"Eric," I told him. "I am so very deeply sorry for your loss. The Targets whose faces I saw—I never saw your nephew's—have been burned into my brain every night for the last five years. Patrick Marshall, Sergeant Henry Williams, and yes, Theresa Pettifer. And I am sorry—more sorry than words can ever say—that Paul and I *had to do what we did*. But if I had to do it all again? *I would,* Eric. I wouldn't have a choice." Eric didn't respond. I continued. "The only thing I would do differently, knowing what we know now, is—if we were going to let them be Harvested, which we wouldn't now—I would make sure they had the mercy of a bullet, the same way you showed that mercy to your friend."

Eric stood, his posture hunched as if to pounce, but he didn't step towards me. I saw Edgwick tense.

"Fuck … you … " he said.

"I understand, Eric," I said. "But you need to understand what being Dispensatori really is—"

"Yeah?" Eric said. Tears were now beginning to roll silently down his face. "That and being a one-man power trip. I've seen the way your eyes light up when you drive that thing."

"I'm sorry it doesn't hurt me more, Eric."

"Don't talk to me like you've been in the trenches," Eric said, stepping forward. Edgwick stood, ready. "You talk like you got your hands dirty, but there's a difference between dirt and blood. You have plenty of the latter—"

"Eric—" Paul began quietly, but Eric cut him off.

"Shut it," Eric said. "At least he had the balls to actually say it."

Paul's eyes dropped.

"I'm sorry too, Eric," he said. "But Andy's right."

"Neither of you ever had to pull the trigger yourselves, have you?" he said. "You just lead the killers to the victim and then, what, back away telling yourselves how bad you feel about it? Well done. I'm sure the families appreciate that."

"We would if we had to," I said. "Eric ... I can't imagine how this feels to you, but you surely *must* understand in your rational mind why we had no—"

Eric thrust two fingers in my direction, his face tight like a fist, his arm spasming. "You really think you would pull the trigger?" He stepped close by me now, leaning forward until his fingers were about a foot from my face. "You really think you could fucking do it?"

"Hatton," Edgwick warned quietly, but Eric just spun away, clenching his fist, saving me from having to answer. I'd wanted to say *of course* ... but it felt like it might be a lie. I watched Eric as he screamed at the sky, the sound wet and ragged. Then he fell silent.

"Are you going to leave, Eric?" Edgwick asked. "However you feel right now, we need you—"

"Fuck off," Eric spat.

He stomped towards his tent before pausing to answer through gritted teeth. His response sounded as if it took all he had to give it.

"*No,*" he said.

Then he thrust the flaps of his tent's entrance aside and disappeared within. Maria broke the silence.

"*You knew?*" she whispered.

"Enough," Edgwick said after a deep breath, "This isn't the most important thing right now. Figure out how you three are going to make the sleep thing work. Then sleep however you can. Everything else can wait until the morning."

Paul and I exchanged a glance. Edgwick was right.

"Okay," I said.

We figured it out: Maria and Paul would sleep. I would stay awake a little longer to closely watch what happened, me also taking 'watch' of the Stone Man's hands-off control. Once I became tired, I would wake Maria up so she could make sure the Stone Man's loop kept going. She'd also be close enough to wake me in an emergency.

She went off to her tent. I thought she'd be too stressed to sleep but, almost as soon as she entered her tent, I felt her immediately pass out; her thread became calm and still, even if it quietly hummed with a low-level tension. If Eric was asleep too, I didn't know. As furious as he was, I knew he was also exhausted.

The next ten minutes seemed to drag out interminably while we waited for the Stone Giant's presence in the air; that moment never came. Maria's thread quietened further and, once the last of the tension dissipated from it, I was confident she was fully asleep. Paul nodded, confirming that nothing had changed. The blanket of Maria's protection was clearly still all around us.

"We happy?" Edgwick said.

"Jesus," I said. "Did you not hear the exchange ten minutes ago? I think *happy* is a long way off. But if you mean Maria's protection, I think we're safe."

"Okay. You now," Edgwick said to Paul, who nodded and headed to his tent. A few minutes passed and then Paul's snoring could be heard. I checked his thread; Paul's sending of energy continued unabated, keeping the Stone Man walking on its loop. The basics, it seemed, were now automatic, even if they still took a physical toll on Paul and Maria.

"We're good," I told Edgwick.

"Okay. Two hours, tops," he said, moving to the mini floodlight and flicking it blessedly off. Halogens are horrible. The dark that instantly descended felt as cool as the night air. "Then you wake her, check she can run your control basics okay, and get two hours yourself. Right?"

"Right," I said, even though I didn't think I'd sleep at all that night, and not just because of what had happened with Eric. Edgwick disappeared into his tent. I tucked my rolled-up sleeping bag under my arm—I would be sitting in it for warmth—and walked away from the camp into the darkness of the field. Ahead of me I could just make out two shapes, my eyes already adjusting: the thudding, steady gait of the Stone Man, and a nearby tree stump that I'd seen earlier. I was going to rest my back against it and keep an eye on the most important responsibility on Earth.

I was unrolling my sleeping bag by the stump when I heard Paul's tent unzip. His outline emerged in the darkness, as dense and black in the night as that of the Stone Man, only a lot smaller. He saw me, and approached.

"Need to pee," he said. "Hey, have you drank any water today, Andy?"

I had to think about that.

"I don't think so," I said. "I've not been thirsty."

"Take a water break in an hour," Paul said. "So. Eric, eh."

I shook my head. I knew Paul felt even worse than I did.

"Yeah," I said. "Horrible fucking situation. He must hate us. But I meant it. I'd do it again."

"Me too. Theresa Pettifer's *brother*," he said, his tone one of quiet disbelief.

"Christ. Yeah."

There was nothing more to say about it.

"Do you think it'll work?" I asked him. "Straub's plan?"

"I can't think of a better one," Paul said. "And I just want us to finally do some damage to these bastards." He watched the Stone Man's circling shadow for a moment before adding: "You don't *need* to sleep. Do you, Andy?"

"No," I confessed. "Not yet at least, and I should need to. I wanted to wait a little—to be sure—before I told everyone."

"Even with the block on your thread," Paul said. "Your secret was obvious. You have a spring in your step that we don't. But hell, as long as you can keep going then it's only good news right now, and we need lots of that. How's your state of mind?"

"Honestly?" I said. "I can't say I feel *good*– with everything that's happened I shouldn't feel able to even breathe—but I feel … Paul, there's something in the driving of Caementum that brings everything into such focus. It's like it stops me being overwhelmed. I don't know how you're doing this, Paul."

"Mm. Gotta be done," Paul grunted.

I wished Paul could respect himself one ounce of the amount that I respected him. He had severe PTSD regarding the Stone Man and yet here he was, managing to face it, connect to it, be near it.

"You've been a great friend, Paul," I said. I couldn't make eye contact while I said it. "I don't know if I told you that. I'd have laid down and died after Sophie without you."

"Oh. Well … thanks. You've been a great friend too. Sincerely."

"You're doing great. Dealing with *that*, up close."

Now Paul snorted.

"I'm just tired of feeling helpless and afraid, Andy."

"And you're still afraid of the Stone Man now?" I asked.

"Terrified."

We both watched the silhouette of the creature in question began the return leg of its lap.

"But all the same; the Stone Man walks," Paul said quietly. The phrase caught my attention.

"Sorry?"

Paul shrugged in the dark.

"Just something I used to think to myself sometimes," he said. "Back in the cabin. Kind of like... hmm. I dunno. Like *death and taxes*, you know?"

I did.

"Sooner or later," Paul said softly. I waited for him to finish the sentence, but he just shrugged again. "I'm gonna piss and pass out. If you notice anything different with the Right Honourable Gentleman, wake me up right away."

"I will. Thanks for checking in, bud."

"You got it."

He walked away, his gait looking almost as heavy as the Stone Man's. After a moment I heard the flaps of his tent move and then zip up.

Straub's voice spoke up in my head.

Just get everyone to Coventry, it said. *Everything else can wait. The world, the whole world rests on this.*

It was true, but Jesus. He was my friend, albeit a friend I had just lied to, or at least only told half the truth.

Brings everything into such focus had been the understatement of the year.

I'd begun to notice it over the last few hours. I didn't say anything because I'd wanted to be sure—that part was true—but operating the Stone Man was beginning to give me a clarity of thought I had never experienced in my lifetime. The *power* of the thing, being connected to it, in control of it; I felt alive for the first time since my Sophie was taken from me. Operating the Stone Man felt incredible, so much so that I felt like I was cheating by not sharing the same level of suffering as the others.

You don't have to be a cheat, I thought. *You can be their backbone.*

That made me feel a little better. I had never been that to anyone.

You can be Dispensatori in a way you never have before.

Maybe. Or maybe it was one of the blessings of duty, of following orders: the removal of the agony of choice.

Until duty means making choices of your own.

I leaned back against the old tree stump, unzipping my sleeping bag flat and pulling it up over myself. The silence was pleasant, even if the reason for it—no cars, no planes, no industry—wasn't, and then I was suddenly out from under my sleeping bag and walking across the field, my arms and legs swinging effortlessly, seeing the field stretching ahead of me, the camp away to my left, and a rhythm pumping in my brain as I lifted my right arm to my face in confusion and saw a wrist that wasn't my own—

I sat upright. The Stone Man continued its circuit, and I was no longer inside its head. For a moment there I'd fully flashed in; I'd never connected with it like that, able not just to feel its limbs as if they were mine but to move them at my command. I looked to the Stone Man, seeing the arm I had just lifted now dropping back into the swing of its gait. It had been brief, but the *Stone Sight* control had been there. Soon, it seemed, I would be able to sit in the driving seat and actually drive, without needing conscious thought commands sent from the threads on the outside. The idea was thrilling, to say the least.

The Core.

It was an intriguing thought. I'd treated the walk from the Skye Bridge as a period of bedding in, of getting to grips with the Stone Man's fundamentals. Now I had some down time. If my connection to the creature was growing, then—now the Core had been brought up from the depths of the Stone Man's inner space—might it be the next piece of the puzzle? The thing had seemed utterly impenetrable, but maybe after Maria and Paul had some rest …?

But what if the Core really was the thing's mind? What if I woke something up, some emergency subroutine, and lost control? What if getting in there meant pushing the factory reset button?

I didn't know what concerned me more; the potential risk involved or the sense of detached contentment I was feeling as I sat against that tree stump under the stars. It was safest to wait for the others before attempting to open the Core again.

I laid back under my blanket and continued to walk in a slow, steady circuit at the same time. All thoughts of the incalculable losses we'd all suffered were effortlessly tucked away inside an unassailable Core of my own.

***

Eric was the first awake.

I thought it would have been Edgwick, and perhaps it would have been in a few minutes; the sky was only just starting to get some light and colour, and the total of four hours we'd agreed upon was nearly up. I hadn't moved in that time. I knew Edgwick wouldn't be happy, but I hadn't felt even a little sleepy.

I'd been busy, too.

As the night progressed, I'd flashed in and out of the Stone Man's driving seat many times. So much so that, to my amazement, I discovered I could do so at will. Only briefly at first, being *in* it and feeling its limbs, but also slowly gaining more and more control. As the others slept, I found could command Caementum's arms and legs internally for longer and longer periods. There was still about a second's delay between intention to raise an arm and the corresponding movement, but it was there. I thought afterwards that I should have woken Paul and Maria in case something went wrong, but the control I had was so strong that it didn't occur to me. Plus, they *had* to sleep.

Eric hadn't seemed to notice me; my tree stump was a little way from the tents. He stood outside his, rubbing sleep from his eyes while twitching his head all around him as if bothered by a fly.

"You okay?" I called. He looked at me, then away; I wasn't surprised after our last conversation, but it seemed he was listening to something rather than just brushing me off.

That meant something important. His anger would have to wait.

I stood up, shaking off and snatching up my sleeping bag before jogging over to Eric.

"Something's happening," he said, looking up at the sky. His voice was grim. "They're chattering like mad, and whether it's good or bad, they're certainly excited."

Eric was all business, then. Good. I could work with that, and I didn't have to ask who *they* were. I glanced back at the Stone Man, needlessly checking it was still circling on autopilot. It was of course, the immense, heavy stumps of its feet having worn the grass underneath them into mud.

"Is it the Red one?" I asked, rolling up my sleeping bag. Eric cocked his head.

"No," he said. "*Agh,* these low-level threads aren't great to use. I'd go higher but I think that's just too risky. And... *hm.* The nearest Blue is approaching ... I think it's in the Midlands somewhere, like the north of the Midlands. Its already long past Aiden, in that case." He shook his head, annoyed. "I can't tell where it's going, though, and I can't be any more accurate without using a bubble."

"Are we in danger?" I asked him. "The Crawlers?"

"I don't want to say for sure but... maybe. If I had to guess? Yes." He pulled a blister pack of tablets from his pocket and thumbed one free, grabbing it with his teeth. Eric was adapting well to life with one hand, it seemed. "Either way: we need to get up and get moving. If it *is* them, we don't have anywhere near enough of a head start. Based on how fast they were moving before, and how long we've been walking, I think they'd be on us in just a few hours, don't you?"

"... yeah."

He looked over at the Stone Man.

"Can you get that thing moving any faster?"

"Afraid not, and I've gained more control overnight too." I'd tried making the Stone Man run; I could move its limbs quickly individually, but all of them at speed at once, correctly? More than impossible, so much so that I didn't think Paul and Maria could have much conscious effect. I didn't think the Stone Man *could* run.

We were in big trouble.

"*Shit,*" Eric hissed. I could see his pulse beating a rhythm in his neck. "We need to wake the others up and get going. Now."

He turned away and began to dismantle his tent. We were done.

***

Soon after we were on the road again, Paul and Maria in the middle seats, me in the passenger seat with Edgwick at the wheel. Eric sat in the back row of the seven seater, our restuffed packs safely stashed in the vehicle's large storage space. Upon waking, Maria had been surprised I hadn't woken her to take her two-hour watch, but didn't complain, grateful for the rest. Edgwick had simply shaken his head.

Ahead of us the Stone Man led the way, ever marching as the new day's sun continued to rise. Eric was becoming more and more restless, fidgeting quietly in his seat. There was nothing that could be done; we were moving as quickly as we could. I'd informed Paul and Maria of my progress and with them to try and accelerate Caementum's forward locomotion but my earlier, pessimistic predictions had proved correct.

The Touran smelled new because it was; no scented air freshener necessary here, the leather trim luxurious, the car tricked out to the highest spec. For now, we were in physical comfort, even if our mood was anything but, especially with the now-inscrutable Eric inside the car with us. If the

Crawlers were coming, they would be here very soon. All we could do was follow the Stone Man.

It was Edgwick who broke the silence.

"I'm thinking of something," he said, drumming his fingers on the wheel.

"Okay," I replied. I waited for him to elaborate.

"Go on then," he said.

"What?"

"Animal, vegetable or mineral?"

The question was quiet, grim, and coming from the back seat: Eric. I think it was the first time he'd asked Edgwick anything. He was joining in? And furthermore ... really? We were going to play a game, now?

"Animal," Edgwick said, looking in the rearview mirror. "And that's one."

There wasn't a lot else we could do right now other than play Twenty Questions at the end of the world.

"Is it found in this country?"

That was Maria. Her voice was barely audible.

"This country specifically being..."

"United Kingdom," she clarified.

"Okay. Yes. Two."

"Wait," Paul said. "Is this animal fictional?"

"... possibly. Three."

"Well," Paul said, "you just needed to clarify the statement of *where we currently are* to answer Maria's question. So more specifically, is this *possibly fictional* animal also found in England, Wales, or Northern Ireland—"

"Paul," I said, "you can't take two questions back-to-back—"

"You see that?" Eric interrupted. He was leaning between Paul and Maria, pointing through the windscreen at something blue in the distance. It was a motorbike, lying on its side by the opposite roadside hedge. Its mostly blue surface was of course covered in a spray of red that reached all the way down to the chrome of the exhaust. "Stop, stop the car a sec," Eric said, and Edgwick obliged. Paul and Maria shuffled aside, and Eric clambered through before jogging over to the motorbike. He gave the Stone Man a wide berth as he passed it, eventually reaching the fallen vehicle.

"We'd have driven to it in like thirty seconds," Paul muttered. As we drew closer I could see it was a café racer.

"Keys are still in the ignition," Eric said as we pulled up alongside him, Caementum striding ahead. "One of you help me get it up and we'll see if we can use this."

March of the Stone Men

"We're still some way off the roads being clogged," Maria said kindly. "And I've spent enough time on motorbikes this week if you're looking for someone to ride it alongside the car." But Edgwick was getting out and crossing to the bike. Eric didn't initially move as the big soldier approached but then seemed to concede; he moved to the other side of the fallen racer and, using his remaining hand, helped Edgwick raise the bike. Amazingly, despite having clearly skidded to a halt, the bike looked mostly intact apart from a deep-but-uncracked gouge in the left-hand side of the fuel tank.

"We could use this for scouting," Eric said. "We *have* to be faster. Something's coming and I think it's going to be the Crawlers."

Edgwick kicked down the stand before swinging his leg up and over the seat and testing the ignition. The bike growled into life. Eric nodded, satisfied. The thing was still operational. Edgwick pumped the throttle twice and the machine responded. I saw Eric glance at the matching blue helmet in the ditch and instantly dismiss the idea. The inside of that helmet would not be pleasant. Paul took Edgwick's place in the Touran's driving seat. I leaned over him to talk through the driver's side window to our... friend? Maybe Eric wasn't that anymore, but maybe he was starting to come around already. If he'd discovered last night's news a few days ago, then perhaps Eric might have shot Paul and I on the spot. But Eric had dealt with the workings of the Stone Men first hand now, and had to execute a friend himself. Maybe that had given him a different perspective, even if he couldn't accept it yet. "As it stands," Eric continued, "if they're coming, that's a matter of *when* they catch up to us and not *if*. I can go ahead up the road quickly on this," Eric said, slapping the bike. "Surely I'll eventually pass some kind of lorry or truck. I'll just have to suck up sitting in the crusty cab, maybe clean the windscreen, but I can bring it back here and then we can load up The Stone Man—"

"We already tried that, Eric," Paul said. "The Stone Man just flattened the truck."

"*But that was then,*" Eric said, the tension clear in his body. Eric *needed* us to move. "You've already got way more control than previously, right? And you've got between now and the time I get back to figure it out."

"We can talk and walk," I said. Paul started the car rolling after the Stone Man. Eric walked alongside the Touran as Edgwick kicked up the stand and began to walk the bike forward, keeping slow pace.

"Worst case," Eric said, "what would we lose? You'll all still be walking. But if this works it not only massively cuts our walking time—until the roads are blocked again at least—but puts a lot of distance between us and whatever's in pursuit. *It buys us time.*"

The unspoken thought passed around the group, even Edgwick.

"*I'll come back,*" Eric said, looking offended. "Jesus."

"I'll go with you," Edgwick said.

Eric's response was immediate.

"No."

"You're going to ride a bike one-handed?" Edgwick asked. "How are you going to brake safely?"

Eric reddened. In his desperation to be off, he hadn't thought of that.

"Listen," Edgwick said. "It's a great idea and the bike could be useful in future, we'll want to keep it, right? If you find a lorry, could you lift the bike into the trailer by yourself?"

Eric glowered, unable to dismiss Edgwick's points.

"You sure you won't need this guy?" Eric asked Maria, jerking a thumb at Edgwick. Asking *Maria,* I noticed.

"Unless we meet any locals freaking out about us being with the Stone Man," Maria said, "I think we'll be okay."

"Okay. Let's go then, I guess." Eric swung his leg over the seat, sitting snug behind Edgwick, and put his intact hand behind himself to grab the seat's handle. "Stay on the main road," he called as the Touran move away from the still-stationary bike. "I don't know how we'll find you otherwise."

"Okay," Maria called, leaning out of the window and raising a hand. "Good luck." I caught her face in the wingmirror, lit by the growing grey sunlight. The few hours' sleep didn't seem to have helped.

"That thing," Eric said, "needs to be able to ride in the back of a truck by the time we get back. Figure it out."

Edgwick pulled the throttle and the bike rumbled forward, accelerating. Edgwick raised a hand as he passed us, a grim expression on his face. A mischievous idea occurred to me; as the bike moved further away and drew level with the Stone Man, I slowly raised the monster's hand in a goodbye gesture.

Paul and Maria snorted; not a full laugh, but it was something. They didn't have to ask if I was responsible. There was a moment of brief panic—and immediate regret—as I saw the motorbike wobble. What a stupid, unnecessary risk that had been, but I heard Edgwick burst into faraway, full-throated laughter, audible even over the distant engine. Eric was just staring at the back of Edgwick's head. A few moments later the bike was a bright blue dot on the horizon.

"I don't want to die," Maria said quietly, watching them go.

I looked at her in the rear-view mirror, mildly surprised. Paul didn't look up.

"A little while ago," Maria continued, "I thought I did. I *did*. I don't want to now. Even with all this."

"Well..." I fumbled. "I don't either, if that's any consolation."

"Eric's right," Maria said. "We need to get the Stone Man on a transport."

"I didn't want to say while the kid was here," Paul said, "but I don't think it's possible. We might have a little more finesse now but all I feel from that thing is weight. Do *you* think we can control its weight?"

"*It* obviously knows how to," Maria countered. "Right?"

"There's a saying in trauma therapy," she said. "*The body remembers*. If that thing has a system for doing that—a process—we just have to access it."

"Unless that system is inside the Core," I said.

"So you wanna start there then?" Maria asked. "Trying to get inside again?"

"Okay," I said. "Stop the car." The Touran halted, and I told the Stone Man *wait*. If everyone had to be inside Stone Space trying to find a way into the Core, fully focused on the task, then we couldn't let the car drive off the road and into a slow crash in the meantime. That meant Caementum had to be kept paused within our stationary range.

"If you two feel rested enough, let's do it. I wanted you with me for that in case something goes wrong."

I needn't have worried. We spent the next twenty minutes in Stone Space trying to find an entrance to that immense ... *object*, and got absolutely nowhere. We couldn't spend any more time standing still trying this.

"The thing is already heavy," Maria said, sounding frustrated. "Making it *heavier* has got to be easier than making it lighter. Perhaps we start with that, then try to figure out how the process works so we can, you know. Reverse engineer it."

"Makes sense," Paul said. "Fuck it. Try it."

Maria gestured towards to the Stone Man, and I followed her gaze and took conscious, internal control of the monster. I was firmly in its driving seat again, seeing what it saw. Its limbs were mine again, heavy and slow, and— unlike having to be fully present in Stone Space with the others and the core - I was simultaneously seated inside a Volkswagen. It was bizarre. I could feel

- 153 -

the three threads trailing away behind me, each one a part of a puzzle that was keeping me moving.

Andy, are you there?

Yeah Maria, why?

It's weird is all, I can feel your thread but you're distant.

Don't worry, it's a little different when I'm in the Stone Man's driver's seat—

I felt my Stone limbs, their weight. Became aware of how the ends of my legs met the road, even if I couldn't feel it the way flesh would. It was if they were numb but aware of contact. I thought the command:

Heavy.

Nothing seemed to happen.

Heavy.

Nothing. Maria spoke, her voice always so powerful and unnerving in Stone Space.

Wait, she said. *Feel around the Stone Man. I just did. There's something there.*

I did, trying to feel out from the driver's seat. Maria was right.

Woah, Paul said, feeling it remotely.

There was a field all around the Stone Man.

Are you both getting this, I asked them.

Yeah—

These motherfuckers really did love bubbles and barriers and fields, it seemed; I felt this one extend several feet below the ground as I traced it up and around Caementum, a perfect sphere. It didn't crackle or fizz or pulse; it just was *there,* surrounding the Stone Man like a magnetic field. Or a field that could, to an extent, counter the *four forces of particle physics,* or whatever Straub's crew had said.

What is that, Maria asked. *The default setting you think?*

So it can walk you mean? I asked. *I guess so—*

Wait, Paul said. *We're talking about making it heavier, but it's not really about weight, remember? Don't think* heavier. *Think* deeper.

Uh—deeper—

The field expanded, the sphere growing in size.

Yes!

That was Maria. I expanded the sphere again, and I suddenly became aware of a detached feeling of depth, of the press of the soil below and above. I realised that my awareness had moved lower with the sphere, out of the driver's seat and into the expansion of this field surrounding the Stone Man.

"Andy, look!"

Maria's voice from the car's back seat snapped me out of Stone Space. I looked with my own eyes, blinking away the mild disorientation of the shift in perspective and looked where Maria was pointing.

The concrete was cracking under the Stone Man's feet.

"It's working," Paul grunted.

"But that's not right," I said. "It shouldn't crack the floor. It didn't make a trench when it resisted the helicopters in the First Arrival. It's just supposed to be, I don't know, anchored, we're not supposed to be pulling it *down*—"

"Doesn't matter," Maria said, "we're doing something, and that's the idea here. See if you can—"

But already my mind was shooting back out along the thread, carried away by the exciting possibilities. Fine, if pulling the Stone Man lower was okay, then I wanted to see if I could pull the Stone Man all the way down through the fucking *road*.

I shot back into the Stone Man's driving seat and pushed the field again; once more I went with it, but this time the expansion was far greater. I was again aware of that detached-feeling of the press of earth, but now there was a different energy to it; not that of thrumming life, of bugs and roots and soil—of animal and vegetable, even—but of solidity, of almost motionless molecules. Mineral. I was in some kind of bedrock—

I couldn't help it. The energy of it all was overwhelming. I pushed the field as wide I could.

Andy, wai—

I was in darkness.

All the distant sound my body's ears were transmitting to me in Stone Space was completely gone. I have never known a silence like it, before or since; I was so far below that I don't even like to think about it now, frankly. Had I been more connected to my body, I imagine many kinds of instincts would have kicked in and I would be beyond panic. As it was, remote from the various powerful chemicals that could override rational thought, I was frightened ... but not panicking. I believed I had control. All around me was this sense of depth, solidity of a different kind.

And something farther below me still. Something familiar.

The Barrier. It was the bottom side of the Barrier that surrounded the country.

Far above me I could hear Paul and Maria, their voices growing closer along their threads as they tried to plunge after me. I worried that I would lose control of the Stone Man, then remembered that, right now, even though I felt far from it, this *was* the Stone Man's function, my consciousness a part of its field.

I tried to move back up. I couldn't. I reached for Maria and Paul. I could feel them drawing closer along their threads yet still so far away.

Down here—

I reached blindly, up, up, up as far as I could. Something like mental fingertips came along and met my reaching grasp at full stretch.

—*dy where the hell are you, CAN YOU HEAR US, ANDY, AND*—

Our consciousnesses collided. At depth, and at speed.

None of us were prepared, our minds coming together too fast, too unguarded; they cracked open and our recent lives washed over one another, all context of feeling intact.

—*Maria in Barcelona, only a few months ago, and Marcus, her ex, has come all this way to see her, her heart flutters at the sight of him even after all this time and knowing, despite her promises to herself, that she will sleep with him while he's here, she'd needed to feel close to someone for long, she's been so lonely ever since they split, ever since she lost*—

—*Maria at her mother's funeral and wrestling with her guilt over her desperation to be away as soon as possible, her nerves over being back on UK soil are overpowering, it's all she can do to keep her breathing steady*—

—*Paul receiving the phone call from his wife's lawyer. Not even a text, he thinks. The kitchen around him becomes blurry as his legs suddenly feel too insubstantial to support him*—

—*Paul working out at the Project gym, his body feeling stronger ever since the Stone Man shut down, ever since he started putting in the hours, but something is still missing from himself, something that he is beginning to understand will never come back*—

—*Maria, trapped here,* truly *trapped here the last place she ever, ever, wanted to be*—

—*Paul wants to die. He wants this to be over, for his duty to finally be carried out, so he can die*—

The shock of this last was kicked aside by the pulling apart of ourselves, our threads untangling and falling back into order. Silence fell again. Paul and Maria's threads were nearby, aching, their pain laid bare to the elements, white-hot embers from a fire only just put beginning to die. It horrified me. Instinctively I reached out along the threads and—

... I don't have another way to put it, I'm afraid.

I sent them love.

I felt each of them lean into it, melting. Suddenly, ascension was easy. Without another word, I rose us as one, shrinking the Stone Man's field and bringing us all back to the surface. As the awareness of rock gave way to awareness of earth, I released them both and I felt them drift away along their threads. I returned to the Stone Man and went through it and back out into myself, opening my body's eyes; the vehicle rocked slightly as Maria opened the car door and stepped down onto the road, her hands to her face. I got out too and followed, opening my arms wide, and she turned and fell against me. I held her tight even as I discovered that nausea was quickly settling into me; moving the field like that was to me, it seemed, as performing more advanced control movements with the Stone Man was to Maria. I looked to Paul; he was now standing on the opposite side of the car, his arms outstretched and resting on the roof, his head hanging.

"Paul."

He shook his head but straightened and walked around the car towards me anyway, one hand still on his face, the other feeling blindly ahead of himself. I found his wrist before his body met mine and pulled him into the embrace.

They both wept onto my shoulders.

"It's alright," I told them. "It's alright." We were standing to the rear of the car, my view of Caementum mostly obscured by the Touran; we had a little time before the Stone Man walked out of range, and I wanted to stay present rather than making it wait.

Then all of a sudden I was way too present, because I was about to puke.

"Shit, get off me, get *uff, uff*—" I babbled, yanking my arms free as I ran a few steps clear so I wouldn't throw up on my friends. This wasn't some little step-off-the-boat sea sickness clear out, this was a full-on purge. White spots danced before my eyes, my body convulsing and I dropped to the floor. It was all I could do to stop my connection to the Stone Man's threads from disappearing. I knew then, without doubt, that I had pushed things *way* too far with the Stone Man's field. I didn't think I would go so heavy again, or anywhere near it; that was far too risky. Once my vomiting slowed to a hitching stop, Maria and Paul's hands moved under my armpits, gently pulling me to my feet.

"Thanks," I mumbled, dry heaving. I kept my eyes closed, watching the white spots slowly subside. Further acknowledgement of what had just happened between us was not needed. They helped me to the car, putting me in the passenger seat. I heard the rear door and the driver's door open and close.

"Put your seatbelt on," Maria said, sitting next to me. She was driving, then. The engine started and I felt the car swing slowly out to the right. We'd driven around something.

"Whawuzz that," I muttered.

"That," Paul said, his voice sounding as if he was talking close to the window glass, "is proof that our little test was a success." I didn't know what he meant, still thinking about that last piece of knowledge I'd picked up from Paul. We'd have to talk about that. "Look behind you," he said. I did, squinting my eyes open to look through the rear window and immediately seeing what he meant. The angle of our departure meant I could see behind the huge mound of broken concrete and earth that had been smashed out of the road, could see the deep trench beyond that had formed it.

The Stone Man had sunken into the ground and kept going. We'd pulled it into the earth. By the looks of it, as we'd moved the field back up, it's mass (level of anchoring? Control of its matter?) had reduced to the point that it walked up and over the mound at the end of the trench it had created. Then it had continued on its way once the field was back to its default radius.

"*Shit,*" I breathed. I looked through the front windscreen, towards the Stone Man. It was of course walking as if nothing had happened. "Good job, team."

Faint smiles passed around the car.

"Let me get my breath back," I said, "and when we find something to test it with, we'll try going the other way. Lighter."

"As long as the Crawlers or whatever's coming doesn't get us first," Paul said. No one replied, and we drove on in silence. Then:

"The Twenty Questions answer," Paul said, "was the Loch Ness Monster, you know."

"Yeah, I know," I told him.

"*Ohh,*" Maria said, sounding genuinely surprised. "I thought it was a unicorn."

This time the laughter that followed was loud and hearty.

✳ ✳ ✳

March of the Stone Men

Chapter Nine

The Crawlers

***

There were woods either side of the road now. This point would have been at around nine am, I remember seeing the clock on the car's dash and being surprised. Not sleeping really throws off your sense of time.

I knew that Edgwick and Eric would have passed through here some time ago; we were still crawling along—poor choice of words—in the car, keeping pace with the Stone Man. Maria and Paul were asleep again, exhaustion outranking even their fear of the potentially approaching Crawlers. I'd taken over driving, switching seats with Maria. I had the window down, the temperature control keeping things nicely warm in the car so that the colder air outside was refreshing on my skin and face. It helped with my nerves. I tried to stay in that Stone flow state, and for a while I even managed it.

Then I became aware of the distant rumbling.

My flow state vanished, fear exploding through as if someone had smashed the glass of an internal fire alarm; I looked in the rearview mirror. Nothing.

"Paul. Maria."

Sleepy eyes opened.

"Wake up," I said, shoulders tensing. "Wake up. I think it might be go-time. Something's here—"

"What is that?" Maria said, hearing it too. Something heavy was approaching fast; the road in front and behind us was one long bend right now. Our sightlines were limited. Paul opened his door and jumped down to the concrete, running on ahead of us before I had time to say stop, passing the Stone Man. He paused just before the bend ahead of us. I thought he was trying to get to higher ground so he could see behind us better, but then I saw he was staring ahead along the section of road that I still couldn't see. Whatever was approaching was coming on fast *ahead* of us, I could now hear.

Fast and... rattling?

Paul waved both of his hands over his head before dropping his left arm and tugging his right up and down in the air in a gesture I recognised; the response echoed up the silent road, a loud and unmistakable double blast.

Baa-baaaaaaaaaaaaaaaah.

Maria gave a little laugh of delight in the passenger seat. Eric and Edgwick were on their way back. By the sounds of it they were now truckers.

Paul ran back to the car.

"They did it," he said. "They got a lorry. A real eighteen-wheeler."

I walked the Stone Man over to the left of the road, so it was more squarely in line with us; the last thing I wanted was for the boys to drive around the corner and straight into Caementum. We knew who would come off worse from that encounter. The blue and white of a large Wincanton lorry was rounding the bend towards us, Edgwick grinning at the wheel, Eric looking serious in the passenger seat like the world's most miserable driver's mate. Whoever owned the lorry before had a placed a large stuffed SpongeBob up against the cab's windscreen. We pulled up alongside each other, the lorry's idling deafening that of the VW.

"There you are," Edgwick called, smiling. *"We're gonna go a little further back down the road. There's not enough room to turn around here. I saw a lot of places to do it on our way through earlier, so we shouldn't be more than a couple of minutes."*

"Okay!" I called, but then Edgwick was sitting back awkwardly as Eric pushed past him, leaning over to the window.

"Did you do it?" he asked, anxiety written all over his face. *"Did you make it lighter?"*

Once the nausea from my over-exerted efforts from expanding the Stone Man's field had passed—which took a long time—we'd had a try at going the other way. It had proved very difficult compared to anchoring the Stone Man deeper, which wasn't surprising. With the Stone Man being designed to be unstoppable, one could assume its default was, for want of a better term, *heavy*. It only seemed possible to take the field up and in as close as the Stone Man's actual body; how it had ever been as light as it was when dormant, I don't know. I'd hoped that contracting the field would mean the Stone Man would become nimbler; this was not the case. After several failed attempts to contract the field even smaller, we'd given up on doing so and tested the Stone Man on the next car we came across, an old Ford Fiesta. Caementum's impressive height meant it was able to raise a leg and step straight up onto the back of the Fiesta, and as its foot came down the metal immediately buckled and bent... but the car was not flattened into the earth. The Stone Man's other foot stepped up on top of the car. The noise was absolutely deafening as it walked, both windows blowing out as the roof caved in *but not all the way in*, the tyres cracking inwards on their axles but not flattening to the floor. By the time the Stone Man walked off the other end, the Fiesta was a crumpled wreck, but it's undercarriage still had clearance from the ground. Previously, that car would have been crushed totally flat. And this was only our first attempt! There were tired high fives inside the Touran.

Another piece of hope.

"*Yes, but only just,*" I called to Eric. "*I think we should be able to get away with it.*"

I thought Eric might smile or look relieved. Instead, he just nodded quickly.

"*Okay,*" he called, and then moved back into his seat. Edgwick raised his eyebrows at us as if to say *what do you make of that?*

"*See you shortly,*" he called, and then their truck was rumbling away passing us back along the road. "*Keep going, we'll catch up.*"

"Are we going to abandon the car," Maria asked, "if we can get the Stone Man in the back of the lorry?" Maria asked.

"No," Paul said, flat. "Fuck squashing five of us into a truck's cab. We'll use both vehicles."

"You could all lie down in the back of the truck though," I said. "Put down the carry mats. We wouldn't even need tents any more..." I trailed off, realising that sleeping in the truck would mean being inside the trailer with the Stone Man. I looked in the rearview mirror for the Wincanton truck coming back up the road. There was no sign, and I wasn't surprised; it was much too soon to expect them to be returning yet. I rolled the Touran after the Stone Man. The road's incline was becoming much steeper. As we continued, the incline was soon so steep that we had a perfect vantage point to look the landscape below and behind us when we heard the first tree fall.

It was far enough away that, on a regular day along this stretch of quiet road, even the sound of distant cars would have been enough to drown it out. As it was, with almost every single driver dead for hundreds of miles, it was clear enough for me to stop the car and kill the engine.

KrrrrrRRRSSSSSCHHHHH...

"Was—that a tree falling?" Maria asked. None of us replied. All of us stepped out of the car and walked to the back of the vehicle, looking out at the view now before us. Once upon a time this would have been the kind of sight that might have got me to take my phone out for a picture; the forest curving away and down along the hill like a lush carpet, the single lane road slicing through it like a grey river. In the far distance the trees began to peter out like a crowd dispersing, giving way to fields and the occasional farmhouse and small industrial site. More worryingly, there was still no sign of Eric and Edgwick.

"Where are they?" I asked Maria. Before her burden of keeping our Stone-Man-included circuit hidden, she might have been able to call Eric telepathically. Such efforts were off the table now. "I can't see them on the road!"

"They might be turning around in one of the farmhouse's yards or something," I said, but I was worried too. I looked to the clusters of trees below in an impossible attempt to try and see where one had fallen, to figure out how long we had, but suddenly it wasn't necessary. A spray of birds erupted into the air, their cries floating to us across the sky. This plume of airborne creatures had emerged from a section of the forest in the middle distance. As we watched, a segment of the green canopy rattled before our eyes and this time we saw it as well as heard it; the faint crack and crush as another tree fell amid its brethren, giving the effect at this range of a head of broccoli eating itself. Paul gasped as we watched what looked like—at this distance—a gentle rustle moving quickly through the forest, but what was, in reality, more likely to be a devastating, smashing onslaught. Another tree went, then another a short distance in front of that, reminding me of the path of Bugs Bunny's impossibly rapid undersoil digging, busily on his way to wherever he should have turned left at Albuquerque to reach.

Our pursuers, I knew, would not be turning anywhere.

"The Crawlers," Maria said.

"Get in the car," I said, and no-one needed to be told a second time; I looked over my shoulder as we ran back to the vehicle and *yes,* now I could see the distant blue of the Wincanton truck emerging from one of the industrial sites below, but goddamn it the thing was so much further away than the falling trees. The truck was faster than the Crawlers could run, surely? But a hill this steep—

"We can't just *hope* to drive out of this!" Maria said, slamming the passenger door shut. "We're not gonna get any faster than walking pace and those things will be here—"

"I know, I know," I babbled, my hand shaking so badly it took me two attempts to press the Start button. Where was my flow state now? Adrenaline had smashed it to pieces. "We'll... we'll..."

We weren't ready, and now we were fucked.

"We can move the Stone Man's arms now," Maria said. "Can we, can we fight them?"

"We're still too slow," Paul said, rocking in his seat. "And those things are fast—"

"Then can we hide?" Maria said. She pointed to the woods, looking out through the windscreen, the vein in her neck clearly pulsing. "We don't know if they know where we are! They could just be heading to Coventry, trying to stop us?"

We didn't have any better plans, and it might work; Maria *was* hiding us, and there were very good odds that the Crawlers couldn't find us either. If the Caeterus had figured out where we were going, they could have just set the Crawlers after us in the same direction. Maybe they would just race past? But what if Eric and Edgwick drove straight past us while we were hiding? The timing would be everything.

"Could we get up in the trees?" Maria asked. "Hide in the boughs in case they can sense us and come searching around on the ground?"

I didn't like it—I'm not good with heights—but it made sense.

"We send the Stone Man away," I said. "As far away from us as our connection range will allow and we send it into the trees on the opposite side of the road. Hide the Stone Man, hide ourselves separately."

"But what if they find it and take it?!" Paul cried. "Or they fix it or something, and then we have nothing left to try and smash the—" He caught himself, slapping rapidly at his cheeks. "*Fuck it*, let's go, let's go. Grab the packs in case the car gets crushed."

We got out, ran to the back, and grabbed everyone's packs, including Eric and Edgwick's. While Paul and Maria broke for the treeline on the right-hand side of the road, I visually picked a point opposite. I sent a command to the Stone Man, telling it to head into the trees on left hand side then remain in place, twitching or otherwise. I turned back to see Maria racing headlong towards an oak tree with low branches and throwing her and Edgwick's pack at the base of its trunk. I caught up to her quickly, passing Paul—I can run fast when I'm shitting bricks—and threw my and Eric's pack down too before squatting down by the tree's trunk. I laced my fingers together for Maria, and she didn't need telling twice, planting her foot on my palms. She jumped as I rose, pushing upwards with my legs and hands and propelling Maria to the lowest branch. She clambered the rest of the way up using only one good hand and a forearm. Paul next. He was considerably heavier but, being much taller than Maria, he was able to reach up and grab the branch. He pulled, I grunted and pushed, and then he was up. Behind me the distant, crashing sounds of trunk and leaf were getting steadily louder. Could I hear the truck?

"Andy," Maria breathed, settling herself across the sturdy-looking branch and leaning down for me with her good hand, Paul doing the same. I took a deep breath and jumped for their hands, trying to walk up the trunk at the same time, and then I was swinging my leg over a branch for the first time in a good thirty years. I could hardly see the road below us anymore through the thick leaves around my head. It was so dense that all of us sat bent at the waist, our legs straddling the thick branch, in order to have enough room. Vision wasn't a problem though. I could use the Stone Man's sight if needed, even if all it showed me right now was the back of a large approaching tree as the Stone Man moved into the hiding position I'd chosen. I told it to turn, trying to see the road but worrying that the Stone Man wasn't hidden enough. As it circled, I saw that I'd been extremely lucky in choosing that hiding spot. I could see the Stone Man was now placed behind several trees that, fortunately, had enough low-hanging branches and leaves to provide substantial cover. There was also a just-big-enough gap for a clear-ish sightline back down the hill. I moved my vision fully back to my own body. The transition was quick; another area in which the circuit was improving.

"Are you sure this is where we want to be," Paul whispered, breathing hard, "given that those things are coming through the trees—"

"The angle of approach is wrong for that," I told him, struggling to get my breath myself. "They'll be out of the lower forest and onto the road again long before they get to us." The sound of my voice was mingling with that of many approaching, hammering feet. The Crawlers were close now; the vibrations coming through the ground, up the tree's trunk, into my bones, were not in my imagination this time. I froze, listening as the noise grew louder, not daring to look through the Stone Man's sight.

I heard the distant sound of the returning truck. Now I leapt back into the Stone Man's eyes to see how far away the truck was; instead I was struck by the sight of the grotesque things scrabbling up the hill towards us.

The Crawlers were stampeding up the road, trailing leaves and clouds of brown dirt as they stormed up the hill. The sight of them rising toward me imbued them with a surreal sense of relentless pursuit, as if any were needed. Their bulk thundered up the rise as if released from some infernal pit, their unspeakable multi-limbed bodies huge and eager as they ground up the concrete beneath their stump-like feet. I recoiled from the sight of them so powerfully that I found myself back on the tree branch, the noise of the two monstrosities' machine-gun-drumming legs now sickening in its volume. Would they storm past us, racing on to Coventry? Would they sense us and begin to hunt, much as they had at the Project? Or would they, as Paul feared—as *I* feared—somehow find the Stone Man and take it home, vanishing much like Caementum itself once a Harvest was complete?

I didn't need to go back into the Stone Man's sight to know where they were; seconds later the cacophony of their charge drew level with our tree, then stormed straight past it. The three pairs of eyes hidden in the boughs goggled at each other as it became immediately clear where they were going. The angle of their passing made it obvious.

They were heading straight for the Stone Man.

"*Move it away!*" Maria hissed as noise of the Crawlers passed us. "*Further into the woods over there!*"

But it was too late. Even if I began to walk it now, the Crawlers would be on it in seconds, and there was about as much point in trying to make the lumbering Stone Man outpace the charging Crawlers as there would be in trying to get Paul to eat tofu. Somehow Maria's hiding didn't work with these monsters, their hunting instincts working differently, more accurately, than the wider circuit of the Prism.

I dropped into the Stone Man's sight again. I had to. My mind was as tense as a clenched fist, and not just I was about to witness the Crawlers up close. It was because the only choice left now was to fight.

I walked the Stone Man out towards the road to meet them. Our only hope was to try and get the first shot in, and I told the Stone Man to get its hands up. As I felt its limbs respond all too slowly, I knew we were in trouble. The Stone Man quickly reached the edge of the treeline. The Crawlers filled the Stone Man's vision at the side of the road, monstrous, horrifying; my fear shot the sight of it out along our threads and I felt Paul and Maria see it too; both of them cried out.

Then I was looking at the sky, and also I wasn't.

My sight was filled with that strange rhino-like hide that the Crawlers possessed. I realised what had happened: the Crawlers had knocked the Caementum down and were now on top of it, so close that I could no longer see, and I immediately became aware of sensations in both Caementum's left arm and right leg.

I don't think it hurt the Stone Man. I don't think Stone Men even have a remote concept of pain. But I can say that I became acutely aware of a searing pain in *my* limbs, the signal of the Crawler's attachment—for it was attaching itself—perhaps converting into a pain signal in my brain. It was so forceful that I shot back into my body without meaning to. I nearly fell off the branch but Maria and Paul caught me, crying out, their grip shaky. They'd felt it too.

"*Andy!*" Maria hissed.

"*They're not here to fix it, or to take it back!*" I hissed back, my teeth gritted; the pain was becoming a burning sensation and rapidly getting worse. I knew nothing was happening to my own limbs, but fuck me, it hurt. "*The Caeterus have called in the hit squad! Lower me down! Now! Now!*" I scootched my backside forward on the branch as they stared at me in disbelief.

"*Are you fucking nuts?*" Maria snapped.

"*They're not here for us!*" I hissed back. "*They know Caementum is working for the other side and these bastards are here to take it out! They can't let us have their asset!*" I was going to jump. "I have to get down there, the Stone Man's sight is covered, I need to see what's going on with my own eyes or I can't—*they're trying to take the Stone Man!* Lower me *down!*"

Maria looked at Paul, completely stunned, her chest rapidly rising and falling, but she moved to help me. Paul stopped her.

"*You know what happened to the soldiers at the Project!*" he hissed. "*When those things saw them! Any humans that got near were turned into paste!*"

"Just gimme the juice when I need it, okay—" We all heard something beginning to build in the air around us. It wasn't Eric and Edgwick's truck, still sounding far too goddamn far away; no, this was that low, creaking noise that we'd all heard today, heard at Isle of Skye right before the Crawlers appeared. The same one we'd heard at the project the day we finally stopped the Stone Man.

Paul, torn, shook his head and then gripped me under one armpit. Maria did the same, and between the three of us I made it to the ground. I pressed my back to the tree, able to see the road-level struggle from here while still trying to stay unnoticed by our attackers.

The Stone Man was helplessly pinned underneath the two Crawlers, each of whom had fastened the tips of one of their legs onto the Stone Man's left arm and right leg. I didn't know for sure what they were doing, but I thought I knew a feeding frenzy when I saw it. The noise, rapidly increasing in volume, was coming from the Stone Man.

The distress signal.

The call for help that had twice summoned the Crawlers as backup. But now the Stone Man was about to call again, perhaps trying to signal the Blues, the Red. But the connections of the Stone Man—or its core processes, at least—were now silenced, unable to talk directly, internally to its circuit. It was unaware that its comrades had already turned against it, unaware that its recent, external distress signal at the Housing had been heard just fine. Unaware that the Crawlers were the response, sent to kill a rogue agent. If that sound built to its peak, what would that mean in terms of the Caeterus—or the Stone Giant—knowing where we were now? The Crawlers seemed to be able to hunt within short range, at least, unaffected by Maria's hiding. But what would happen if the Stone Man's distress signal could pinpoint us under the Barrier's map?

I ran closer, seeing the unstoppable Stone Man pinned in place. Its helplessness was horrifying. Even without my command it was trying to rise on autopilot, to get up and keep walking, but the two Crawlers forced it back down each time and recommenced... feeding? That seemed to be it; I could now see that the limbs fastened onto the Stone Man's were gently pulsing *upwards*, as if drawing something out.

I swung Caementum's free right arm as I dropped back into Stone Sight. The response was slow but the arm still came up in a heavy arc, colliding with the Crawler perched above Caementum's face and chest. The weight of the limb, even moving at that glacial speed, was still enough to knock the Crawler away, and suddenly I had a clear line of sight through the Stone Man's vision again, knowing what was where—

I kicked out with the Stone Man's leg, thinking the word *Kick* as I did so, hoping a conscious, simultaneous command would create a faster response. It made no difference, but the Stone Man's free leg swung sideways all the same, colliding with the Crawler latched onto the opposite limb. The connection was again hard enough to knock the multi-legged monstrosity away, this time even knocking the attacker over onto its back, but already it was curling its legs back and forth around itself in a horribly limp, octopus-like motion, rocking its main body to and fro as it began to right itself. I pushed down with Caementum's previously pinned arm, using it to balance as I tried to get Caementum back up to a vertical base to defend itself, but the previously knocked-away Crawler was already upon us. It stamped its lead leg onto the Stone Man's already-attacked arm, pinning it to the floor once more. The other Crawler finished flipping itself upright and scrabbled over the Stone Man's torso to latch onto the opposite arm, leaving the Stone Man spread eagled on the road. I managed to plant our feet against the concrete, trying to push.

Stand. Stand!

My intention spoke to Paul and Maria's threads and they obliged, giving me everything they had. It wasn't enough. The Crawlers upon either of the

Stone Man's arms were simply too much for the previously invincible Caementum, our force met with superior counterforce. The distress signal was growing ever-more deafening; if Maria couldn't continue to hide us once it reached its peak then our mission was over before it had started.

Something thumped heavily to the floor next to my human body: Paul. He stared at the chaos in front of us, eyes wide, and yelled up to Maria, having to raise his voice over the Stone Man's rapidly building signal.

"*Gimme a branch! Thickest you can break off!*" He grabbed my shoulder. "*You'll need to move it quick! I think you'll only have a second at most!*"

"*What?!*"

A thick-ish branch dropped down, followed by Maria. Paul snatched the branch up and addressed us both.

"*I've been giving Caementum more since we got to the mainland!*" he yelled. "*Just in case! There might be enough juice in there to get it to Coventry without me!*"

"*What are you talking about?*" Maria yelled, but Paul just stared at the two of us.

Then he started screaming like a berserker. The tendons in his neck stood out like ropes, his face instantly becoming blood red, and Paul turned and charged towards the Crawlers I finally understood what was happening.

A second at most, he'd said. He was going to try and give us an opening.

I went to run after him, but both of Maria's hands flew out and caught my arm, stopping me.

"*Get off me!*" I screamed, but then I glanced down the road and saw why she'd stopped me.

Everything happened at once.

The Wincanton truck was almost upon us, the noise of its approach masked by the now-deafening volume of the distress signal. I would have run straight into its path. Paul, with his two second head start, was already at the nearest Crawler. I had time to see him raise the branch over his head to strike before the truck pulled up, Edgwick leaning on the horn as the vehicle completely blocked Paul from view.

I immediately dropped into a Stone Sight partially filled with the Crawlers pinning my limbs. I could see Eric jumping down from the cab of the truck; Maria darting back to the tree for the packs. I saw Eric rush towards Paul as the latter struck uselessly with his branch at the back of the huge Crawler, the two of them only visible in flashes as the Crawler's twitching legs blocked my Stone Sightline in and out. Then I could see clearly; the Crawler

Paul had struck unlatched itself and spun around to face him, alerted to Paul's presence and temporarily snapped out of its feeding frenzy.

Sweeping the Crawler's legs wasn't intentional.

I'd only meant to try and raise the Stone Man as quickly as possible, to take advantage of the moment Paul had bought us, swinging arm and torso sideways to lumber upright. But the Crawler had turned, placing most of its legs on the ground *around* the Stone Man's arm and fortunately not on *top* of it; this meant my swinging arm managed to go sweep through most of its supporting limbs, dropping the thing to the floor. I saw this and didn't stop; I immediately carried the movement up and over and across the Stone Man's chest, punching away the Crawler on the opposite arm before swinging that arm *back* the other way, knowing the swept-Crawler would already be trying to right itself. The blow connected, sending that Crawler in a skidding gouge across the tarmac and through the roadside barrier, the metal blasting apart with an almighty, yanking screech. It smashed into the trees, momentarily disappearing from sight.

I rolled the Stone Man back over and got it to its knees just in time to catch the other, previously punched-away Crawler charging back in; on instinct I swung both of the Stone Man's arms down in a clumsy chopping motion, the strike slamming down onto the top of the Crawler's bulky, mushroom-like head. It pitched forward and I continued to push down with both Stone hands, using it as an assist to get the Stone Man's feet under itself and finally getting the thing standing.

Now I could properly swing; I again raised and hammered down both Stone arms as hard as I could, knocking the Crawler fully flat and stopping its attempt to rise—

"*Get in the truck!*" Maria's voice screamed right next to my human ears. "*Edgwick, get it moving!*" The distress signal was still building; even in the chaos of the fight I knew I needed to stop it, even as I felt my blows becoming less and less impactful. *Now* I was getting tired? Stone Sight showed Eric dragging Paul towards the back of the trailer. Maria was apparently right next to my human body, wait, *where the fuck was my body*—

Fuck that, I thought, *stop the distress signal!*

But what fucking command would—

Hang up.

The noise died—it had worked!—only to be replaced by sounds of heavily cracking wood and thundering weight rushing towards me as the Stone Man's eyes turned and saw the other Crawler charging out of the trees. I spun the Stone Man to fully face its—our—attacker, panicking, and my Stone arms scooped upwards towards our face, matching my human body's flinching response in an instinctive *get away* gesture. The timing of my cowardly defensive movement turned out to be wonderful, the lipstick tips of the Stone Man's arms catching the underside of the onrushing Crawlers torso. The creature went over sideways, again landing on its back; soon it would be on its feet again, and I had to get the Stone Man to the back of the truck, but already the other, recently flattened Crawler was up and behind the Stone Man. I felt it land on the Stone Man's back and a feeling akin to swimming through tar began to overwhelm me. Fighting two Crawlers at once was like fighting an avalanche.

    I managed to step the Stone Man's left leg forward just in time to brace its body, preventing it from being knocked over forwards. I swung its arms backwards, hitting the the Crawler and swatting it away to the Stone Man's right, but it didn't fall far. The lorry rumbled into life, moving forward. The back of its trailer moved past the Stone Man, stopping just a few steps in front. The rear gate was wide open like a cave mouth, Eric and Paul and Maria and *yes,* my body inside, my friends all screaming, gesturing, the only motionless expression belonging to my strangely vacant face. My body's eyes were open. It stared, unblinking, at what was happening outside of the trailer, face totally slack. On autopilot too? There wasn't time to contemplate it. I began to walk the Stone Man towards them but its steps were sloppy now; slow, swaying, elephantine, the fight having taken something out of either my brain or Caementum itself.

    The flipped-over Crawler away to the Stone Man's left was almost back on its feet. The Crawler I'd just swatted away now rearing up on the right like a biting spider, preparing to pounce. I raised the Stone Man's arms out in a T shape just as the two Crawlers struck, holding them at bay by planting a Stone palm in the centre of each of their torsos and propping them up. I desperately wished the Stone Man had proper hands instead of these useless rounded tips. I needed to grip, to throw, and then the front leg of the Crawler on the left managed to latch on hungrily once more, this time to the Stone Man's left shoulder. The fresh pain exploded inside my mind, threatening to buckle my control, but I shoved with the Stone Man's left hand. The move was slower than ever despite the immense effort it took, but it still just managed to push the latched-on Crawler away. Its leg detached with a horrible ripping sensation, the Crawler toppling onto its back again, but the clumsy, heavy push had meant the Stone Man had leaned over too far with the motion, its hand moving off the centre of the right-hand Crawler's torso. The Crawler took the opening and slid eagerly down the Stone Man's right arm. Panicked, I spun the Stone Man in a lumbering, clotheslining circle, swinging its left arm around in a wild haymaker that landed with solid force, felling its target. Both attackers were down now, and I plunged the Stone Man forward, using it to kick the nearest Crawler for good measure as I did so. The back of the truck was mere feet away and getting closer as Eric reversed extremely slowly, clearly wary of flattening the trailer against the approaching Stone Man. The distance was quickly closed, blessedly so, as it felt as if the Stone Man were walking with ankle weights—

Weight. We had to reduce the field of the Stone Man's connection to the earth, or the Stone Man would flatten the back of the truck.

Paul and Maria wordlessly obliged my intention, but the timing was very bad indeed. I became aware of the Stone Man's field retracting and suddenly I was lost in the haze of crazy perspective shifts; I was rising up around the Stone Man's torso, then seeing it's vision, then switching to my own eyes inside the truck's trailer, watching the greyish-brown bulk of the Stone Man staggering towards me, seeing the two Crawlers rising to their feet behind it and beginning to rush in.

I dived back along the thread and into the Stone Man's sight, mentally blinking away all other visual feeds, and with my last bit of mental juice I dove the Stone Man's torso forwards onto the rear lip of the trailer's exposed bed, seeing Eric, Paul and Maria dragging my unresisting human body hurriedly backwards. As the Stone Man fell forward, I knew this was it; we were either light enough, or the Stone Man was about to smash straight through the metal and into the road below.

BANGGG.

All I could see was blackness ... but it didn't give way to light.

The trailer bed had held. Dented, certainly, but held—

Kick now! Maria's thread bellowed. *Kick behind you now, now, now!*

Fucking KICK! Paul agreed, and I kicked blindly backwards with the Stone Man's legs like a toddler having a face-down temper tantrum on the floor. There was that dull feeling of connection again followed by the sound of a distant crunch, the audible aftershock of which quickly died as we accelerated away.

Hold, I told the Stone Man, and jumped back into myself, feeling the metal against my back and the three pairs of hands that were holding my arms and shoulders. All was noise: the rattling of the trailer, the acceleration of the truck, the frantic breathing of the three people around me. Before me lay the entrance to the trailer, a rectangle of light at the end of a darkened metal hallway. Its floor was badly dented, the Stone Man lying face down in a shallow crater of metal. Beyond it, framed by the trailer's opening, I could see the kicked-over Crawlers rolling back to their feet and beginning to give chase. Were we accelerating fast enough to leave them behind? Yes; already they were shrinking in our sight as the truck got up to speed.

We had escaped by the thinnest of margins. Maria patted me on the chest.

"You... okay?" she wheezed. All I could do was weakly raise my hand. No-one spoke, all stunned and breathing hard.

"Fuck me," Eric gasped. "Fuck *me*." Then: "Good job, everyone. *Christ*. Good job."

Paul's shaking hand ruffled my hair. My raised one came down limply and squeezed his wrist back as acknowledgement. He and I, I knew, needed a serious chat after that little display; after the revelation I'd had from his mind when we figured out how to make the Stone Man lighter. But that could wait. We had very pressing concerns to consider.

This was only a stay of execution. The Crawlers would not stop, and we would have to sleep again. Soon the roads would be full and our lead would be slowly eaten away, our pursuers rapidly gaining ground. We had experienced the up-close horror of the Crawlers twice, barely survived, and now it was very likely we would see them again. Our escapes so far had not been due to defeating them in a fight.

We now knew that the Stone Man was no match for two of them. We were completely outclassed.

Sobering news indeed—in a situation that was already pretty damn sober—but apparently even damning news at the end of the world was no match for my ego.

You still took them on, I thought. *You fought two of them.*

More doublethink: physical exhaustion and a sense of impossible, unbridled power.

Don't get cocky, dickhead. You still got your backside kicked.

I scooted backwards, wincing, the others helping and moving aside to give me room. I propped my back against one of the packs lying against the rear wall of the trailer. To my right, Paul moved himself into the corner and drew his knees up to his chest, not taking his eyes off the Stone Man. Eric and Maria moved against the opposite walls; a noticed a gentle smile of encouragement pass between the two of them. We sat like that for a while.

The trailer continued to rattle noisily as we sped away towards England. The noise of it all was a blessing. It saved any of us from having to talk for a while.

***

Chapter Ten

Licking Wounds, the Group Separates, and the Perils of the Law of Attraction

***

Paul was the first one to break the silence.

"That hurt," he said, having to raise his voice. The back of the truck was fucking *loud*. "When they attacked the Right Honourable Gentleman. Right? You two felt it as well?" Maria and I just nodded, neither of us wanting to address the issue. The implication was too frightening: yes, it had indeed hurt, but we were very likely to experience it again. Or worse.

The damage done to Caementum was visual proof of how fortunate we'd been to escape at all. I'd inspected the body of our prone, twitching, erstwhile ally as we drove, moving around it extremely carefully as I held it mentally in place. Everyone knew what had happened to the people who made physical contact with it during the First Arrival.

There were now small divots in the Stone Man's right leg, left shoulder and arm where the legs of Crawlers had fastened. They were ragged, sharp looking even, as if teeth had nibbled away pieces of Caementum's body. There was no doubting it: the Caeterus' attack dogs were on a kill mission. I asked Maria she was having to work any harder to contain the Stone Man's leaks now it had taken a hit. *A tiny bit,* she'd said, *but it's okay.*

It was unnerving to see literal chinks in the hitherto untouchable Stone Man's armour. Yes, the amount of damage done was minimal, but the sight perfectly represented the chunks taken out of our already limited belief in the mission.

The sight of my mindless-self had rattled me too. I'd looked utterly... well, like I said. Mindless. I knew that, when I was in and out of Stone Space, my body seemed to go into an autopilot of its own, remaining standing, but I'd believed the experience was akin to some kind of inner peace. Seeing it from the outside had revealed the truth: it was only the equivalent of mainlining Xanax.

I looked a drooling blob.

It's okay, I told myself, *that's just what it* looked *like,* but the words rang false. They *felt* false.

"We're not moving fast enough," Paul said. He meant the truck, and he was right. We would slowly pick up speed for a short distance—a truck's acceleration being cumbersome at best—before slowing as Edgwick manoeuvred around some dead car or similar in our path, and accelerating again. "Those things are so *quick.*"

"The Stone military police, you mean?" I said. Paul just looked confused. "Sent to take out rogue agents, to keep their own in line?"

"Oh. Yeah, I was thinking something similar."

"How far ahead of them do you think we are?" Maria asked.

"Not far enough," I said. "And worse—"

"I know," Maria said. "They found us without any trouble. Whatever I'm doing to hide us from the Caeterus and the Red, it doesn't work on them."

"If they're attack dogs," Paul said, "it would make sense that they're a more refined version of the Stone Men. They're certainly faster. Maybe they're designed to hunt, and if so, then perhaps they track using something we can't influence. Smell or something."

"And the distress signal nearly went all the way off again," I said. "Caementum trying to call for backup. Even if it doesn't know that its own side have turned against it, we can't have that happen if we get into another skirmish. Who knows what happens if it manages to communicate with the Red or the Blues? Does that connection become permanent once established?"

"You said *it doesn't know,*" Maria quoted. "You think it ... understands things like that then?" She looked at Caementum and drew her knees a little closer to her chest. "Like it really does have a mind?" She shivered. "If you'd have told me a week ago that I'd be in the back of a lorry with that thing ..."

"That's been debated a long time," Paul said, shrugging. "Especially after Andy felt the Core down inside the thing back at the Project; the Right Honourable Gentleman went dormant immediately after that, so we never got to find out. But a lot of Straub's people are convinced that the Core *is* its mind, whether that be a conscious intelligence or just some kind of Stone CPU—"

"But what," I asked, "if it's not any of those things?"

"Go on."

I'd been pondering this as we drove. Now I wanted to get the others' opinion.

"What if the Core is the storage battery?" I asked. "Something certainly purged when the Detonation went off at the Project. What if the Core feels central to everything because it's a power source?"

"You mean whatever exploded out of it when it was flown off to Greenland?" Maria asked. "Or rather, Skye, as it turned out."

"Yeah."

"If you're right, that could be useful," Paul says. "Especially if we—" He stopped himself, wiped his forehead. "*When* we meet those things again. The Detonation killed the Crawlers at the Project. If the Core is a battery, its depleted, but it might be enough to take these ones out too."

"We still weren't fast enough mentally," Maria said, "as a unit. If Eric and Edgwick hadn't shown up when they did, the Crawlers would have destroyed the Stone Man and then us next."

I thought of the Crawlers at the Project, turning men and women into paste beneath their hammering feet. Fighting them felt like Caementum had weights on its ankles, and those weights were our lack of cognitive speed. If we didn't improve, we might all get stamped into oblivion.

"We'll get faster," I said, needing to believe it. "We've been getting better quickly, haven't we? We just need to keep it up, being present in-circuit, building up those cognitive pathways." I tapped at my forehead. "Look how far we've come already." It was meant to be a Dispensatori speech but I kept seeing my own blank-faced expression as it had stared back at me from the truck. Paul and Maria looked unconvinced. I couldn't blame them. We were light years away from having enough control to stand a chance against the Crawlers.

Let alone the Stone Giant.

I was suddenly unable to look at them, so much so that I even chanced a glance at Eric. Instead of looking sullen and resentful, Eric was looking at all three of us with an expression of amazement.

"What is it?" I asked.

"Do you know you're doing that?" he asked.

"Doing what?"

"You're answering questions out loud that none of you are asking," he said. He pointed at me. "You just said *yeah* a minute ago and then you both looked at Paul for a bit, and then you," he said, pointing at Maria, "said *we still weren't fast enough mentally* and then you all went quiet again. Are you...?"

He tapped his own forehead now.

"We weren't talking out loud for all that?" Maria said.

"No," Eric said. "Did you not realise you weren't?" There was silence then, apart from the rumbling of the truck. It was shocking, knowing that the in-circuit talk had become indistinguishable from the regular talk, but also reassuring. Here was yet more improvement.

"Sorry," Maria said. "We didn't mean to be rude."

Eric shook his head quickly, as if realising that he'd allowed himself to be drawn back into conversation with Paul and me. "It's okay," he said to Maria—and Maria only—before putting his head onto his forearms where they rested on his knees. It didn't look like Eric was going to be a team player anytime soon.

Conversation stopped for the next two hours of noisy, rattling and slow progress. I thought about trying to open the Core again, but my strength still wasn't recharged enough. The energised feeling I'd had since we started walking with the Stone Man had returned some, but another attempt at the Core would have to wait a little longer.

We left the Highlands behind. The dead traffic was a little thicker now, but not yet impassable. Maybe it would never get that way; the roads had been gridlocked around the coastal areas when the Empty Men first turned up on the beaches, but we didn't know if that would be the case nationwide. After all, the nation's motorways only became a nightmare during the first three Arrivals because of people fleeing the actual *path* of the Stone Man. The whole country didn't just jump into its cars in a panic. Perhaps, once the Empty Men chaos had settled somewhat—and before the Barrier hit—the only mass flight would have been from the cities around Coventry? People wanting to escape the Prism? If so, maybe the motorways would not be the clogged arteries we anticipated, packed with empty, burst-driver cars. The A roads might be even less so. Maybe we would be lucky.

But I thought we'd used up the last of our luck with the Crawlers.

The truck began to slow, pulling over to the left. We were stopping, pulling into a large roadside services forecourt, a stab of the industrial world into a backdrop that was still green and hilly. We heard the cab's door open, followed by footsteps, and then Edgwick appeared in the rectangle of light that was the truck's rear gate. The reason for his grim expression was clear: the forecourt was covered in burst and desiccated blood, the dead vehicles and pumps lightly coated in crumbling red. This forecourt had clearly been busy when the Barrier hit. The sight reminded me of images seen in my childhood mind's eye, conjured by music and narration: the Martians' red weed from The War of the Worlds, sprayed all over our cities.

"Fuel stop," Edgwick said. "Stretch your legs. I'm going to try and figure out how to turn on the pump at the counter. We're still good for supplies but it can't hurt to grab some water and snacks while we're here. Have a think about our next move; do we keep the truck or figure something else out? The roads haven't really started to thicken up yet, but they might. Truck might not be the best option." He looked around himself for a moment, stiffening a little as he took in the red carnage. *Even Edgwick*, I thought. My hands were beginning to shake.

Edgwick walked away, and Eric hopped down out of the truck, head down as he silently followed the soldier to the small building on the other side of the of the pumps. The only sound was the light breeze and the distant crunch of Eric and Edgwick's boots in the dried remains. It sounded like footsteps in fresh snow.

"I'm gonna ..." Paul began, gesturing towards the shop. Then he sighed heavily before carefully moving around Caementum's prone, face-down body and getting out. I didn't move. The shaking in my hands was quickly getting worse. I couldn't take my eyes off the red spray that was draped over nearly everything in sight. Maria looked at me as she began to move towards the trailer's opening.

"You coming?" she said, her voice low but steady.

"Yeah," I said. "Yeah. Just gimme a sec." She hesitated. "It's okay," I told her. "Just gathering my thoughts." Maria turned away, stepping down. I waited a few seconds before I fell back against the inside of the truck, my vision spinning.

The whole country. The whole country. The whole country.

I managed to do a Carl Baker, strengthening my block in-circuit so the others wouldn't notice, but the panic attack was getting worse, and fast. I wasn't sure the block would be enough. My whole body felt cold and stiff and limp at the same time. I began to hyperventilate. I kept waiting for it to end, but it didn't. Minutes passed. It only seemed to get worse.

The whole country—

The others will be back soon, they'll see—

THE WHOLE COUNTRY—

Just when I thought it would begin to affect Caementum, the panic attack began to die off. I sat up, my hands still shaking and my stomach still nauseous. I needed food, or maybe just sugar. I needed to get myself level again before the others noticed. I carefully made my way around the prone Stone Man on shaky legs and stepped down from the truck. I immediately felt light-headed. I took a deep breath, straightened, and turned around to see Maria standing there with a carrier bag full of food and water.

"You were ... quick ..." I said, my voice a croak.

"You block wasn't very good," she said. I looked beyond her; I couldn't see the others. They had to still be inside the forecourt shop. "Don't worry," she said. "I stopped it reaching Paul. As soon as your block tried to get denser—it didn't, by the way—I could tell something was different, so I helped shore it up. What set you off? This?" She nodded her head towards the red-covered pumps. I nodded.

"Yeah."

Maria's gaze was steady, her composure solid. She noticed me noticing.

"I've had more practice with trauma," she said. "The circuit helps, too. But I think we're going to see a lot of things like this."

"... yeah," I repeated.

"Do you want me to help? Or try to?" she asked, pointing at her head.

"No," I said, moving away. "Thank you. I'm okay." I stood up straight and realised that I was telling the truth. I was okay now.

"You have to let it—"

"I know," I told her, giving a thumbs up and heading for the shop. "I'm not resisting it. It's just passed, that's all. It's okay, I'm okay ... are you okay?"

She looked as if she wanted to press the issue, but she dropped it.

"I'm just nauseous," Maria said. "I don't know if that's from keeping everything together with the Stone Man, the stress of it all, or what. But I feel pretty sick, to be honest."

"I'll look in the petrol station for some travel sickness pills," I said briskly, and walked away before she could say anything else. I felt like the Stone Man, all the chinks in my armour on full display. I was exposed like the fraud I was beginning to believe myself to be. As I drew closer to the shop, Edgwick appeared and gave me a thumbs up. "Pump's on," he said. "I'll have the truck refuelled quickly." He gestured at the truck. "You think you could drive that if I gave you a few pointers? You'll be messy as hell behind the wheel but you won't have to worry about moving traffic."

"Why?" I asked, and then Eric appeared behind him. He made direct eye contact with me for the first time since he'd picked us up in the truck.

"We're leaving," he said.

The kid. Aiden. But how would they—

Eric pointed towards the motorbike still connected to pump six. A dried gunk-covered Triumph cruiser was parked there, the fuel nozzle sticking up out of its tank. Keys in the ignition. Helmet on the seat. Desiccated red remains of a human body coating the side nearest to the pump. Edgwick nodded at me and headed towards the bike.

"We grabbed the truck so quickly that we left the bike," Eric said. "And a cruiser will be a lot more comfortable for the long ride." I'd wondered why the smaller bike was missing from the trailer, but Eric hadn't exactly been inviting conversation. Why was he now? "You're gonna be taking the lorry along A roads from here to Coventry, right?" he said. "You'd be mad to take the motorways." The A roads were, in terms of actual mileage, a route several hours longer than the more direct motorways. But they would be faster for the truck than the potentially-three-stationary-lanes-thick M roads. Sure, we could use the Stone Man to clear cars out of the way, but if we were doing that for the entire journey then it would be quicker to walk.

"I think so, yes."

That's just gonna be too long for me," Eric said, rubbing the back of his neck, "I'm under no illusions about whether I'll be back in time to save the kid. But I have to try, and me and Edgwick will be twice as fast by bike. We can get past the motorway traffic at speed."

I watched Edgwick remove the pump's nozzle from the bike's tank.

"You two already talked about this just now?" I asked. "That was quick—"

"Edgwick had a nephew," Eric interrupted. "Did you know that?"

"No," I said. Edgwick had family then ... or did. "The nephew wasn't Stone Sensitive. Was he."

"No," Eric said. I marvelled at Edgwick's resilience. He hadn't missed a beat since the Barrier went up.

"Is he—" I began, but Eric cut me off.

"I don't know," Eric said, "but he just told me about his nephew, and that he'll ride me to Aiden. I'm going with him now before he changes his mind."

"I didn't think you two were particularly—"

"We're not."

I was leaping from a low-level panic attack to making a key leadership decision. Eric and Edgwick leaving meant were losing our soldier, our most capable member in terms of *getting shit done*. We were also losing the only person that could safely monitor Stone communications—even if Eric's abilities weren't as advanced as Maria's had been—and the person that could free us if we got bubbled.

But Eric had nearly died—I guess kind of *had* died—getting us through the Barrier and back in again. He owed us nothing, we owed him everything. But the *mission*—

"Eric ..."

"You're not going to try changing my mind, are you Andy?" Eric said, inhaling through his nose, his jaw set.

"I don't think so," I said. "I'm not, in fact, not really. But I have to say one thing."

"Okay."

"We might need you. We might need you both. We're talking about the end of—"

"I know. But I'm not like you."

I bristled a little, but Eric had a right to his resentment.

"... how so?"

"I can't just lay it all at the door of the mission," Eric said. "If I just let that kid get Harvested, I wouldn't be able to go on living. Simple as that. Maybe that's even selfish—what was it, twenty Arrivals or something and then the whole world is gone—but I can't let him die. Not like that."

"Okay," I said. "I can't make you stay, and you heard me out, at least. But promise me that you'll wait for us outside Coventry, whatever happens?"

"Done. We'll camp by the A45. Come in that way. If you change your route of approach, send up a flare. Send up a few. I'd say I'll just keep an ear out," Eric said, pointing a finger skywards to indicate the Threads of the Caeterus, "but I don't know how reliable that is."

"Will you be able to use the kid's bubble again to communicate with us? Let us know you made it? Only if it's safe."

"Yeah. And it should be safe. I mean, what are they gonna do? Try and bubble *me*?"

"Okay." I decided to take a chance and held out a hand. Eric looked at it, his expression a little surprised. Then he took it, shook it, and looked me in the eyes.

"Good luck," he said, taking the words from my mouth. "We might not see each other again, Andy." Was this him forgiving me? I didn't think so.

"Yeah. Yeah."

"I hope we do," Eric said, before adding: "I think we have more to talk about, don't you?"

"For what it's worth," I said, "I hope we have that conversation."

"Mm."

I thought we were thinking the same thing: neither of us truly expected to have that conversation. Not after the encounter with the Crawlers, and we weren't even in England yet. I looked over at the bike. Paul and Maria had joined Edgwick there; the soldier was talking, no doubt explaining that which Eric had just told me. "I'm gonna go back in there," Eric said, jerking a thumb over his shoulder at the shop, "and see if I can find an extra layer. Maybe a staff polo shirt or something. I know it's still reasonably early, but I don't see the day getting much warmer than this, and I was freezing earlier on the bike. Long day ahead." He turned and headed inside without waiting for a response. I followed, branching away from Eric once inside the main building and heading for the restrooms, the surprising air conditioning colder than I liked on my skin. The panic attack had loosened my bladder as well, it seemed, and to my relief the spray of dried red indoors seemed to be limited to an area near the counter. I realised that would have been a line of people waiting to be served when the Barrier passed through here. I pushed the thought away but decided that if the men's room was full of that horrific redness I would simply take a piss round the back of the building. To my great relief it seemed that the gents had been empty when the Barrier struck.

I was standing at the urinal when the door opened; Paul joined me, standing at the opposite end of the trough.

"Eric and Edgwick are buggering off," he sighed.

"So I gather."

"You try to talk him out of it?"

"You think he'd listen to me, of all people? Or you?"

"Nope."

I heard the flow of liquid start to hit the metal as I zipped up and began to wash my hands.

"Hey," I said. "I have to ask you something."

"Shoot."

"What was that about back when ... the Crawlers attacked?" I asked, changing from my original question about what I'd felt from him when we'd collided in-circuit. That felt too nosy. I tried to keep my tone light. "When you jumped down from the tree and tried to get their attention? You saw what happened to the soldiers at the Project."

"... I do."

The words hung in the air.

"Paul—"

"I know you think about them," Paul said. "The original Targets. We talked about them a lot. But I think it's different for you." I turned off the water and turned around. Paul was still peeing, his back to me.

"How so?"

"You turned yourself in to Straub as soon as you understood that you were a Target. You did it right away."

I sighed. I'd heard him say this kind of thing before.

"I did the exact same things as you, Paul. Hunted the same Targets—"

"You turned yourself in *right away*," Paul repeated, shaking himself off and zipping up. "I tried to weasel out of something that I was prepared to put upon other people." He crossed to the sink without making eye contact. I stepped back to let him in. "I learned who I am that day. Nothing's been the same since." He ran his hands under the water, hesitating before saying: "When you lie in bed at night thinking about those faces, Andy, *you* can at least know you *were* going to jump out of that window, or would have done if Straub hadn't stopped you. I can't say that, and I have to live with that. Or rather—" He stopped again. "Doesn't matter."

"I thought you were past this?" I asked as softly as I could. "You said your therapy had been—"

"I was, sort of. I don't know," Paul said, shaking off his hands. "I just ... with everything that's happening ..." He finally made eye contact. His expression made me take a small step backward in surprise. His eyes held so much longing. "I want this to be over," Paul said. "All of it. I'll do whatever I have to do to get this job done, and I will give *everything* I have. You don't have to worry about that. But, other than that ... I'm done, Andy. I'm done."

I just stood there. I just fucking *stood* there, my mouth open like an idiot. I didn't hug him. I didn't even pat him on the shoulder. I didn't. Know. What. To. Fucking. Say.

Then he patted me on *my* shoulder.

"It's okay," he said. "It's okay, Andy. I know."

Then he walked out of the restroom.

I stood there alone for a minute or two before making my way back outside.

By the time I got there, Paul and Maria were shaking hands with Eric. Edgwick approached me.

"Let's go to the truck a sec," he said. "I'll give you those pointers, Pointer."

"Nice."

"You should generally be fine even if you drive it like a dodgem all the way to Cov."

Once the brief lesson was done—I thought I could handle the big rig okay, seeing as the roads had no other drivers—we came back to the bike where the others were waiting. Edgwick and Eric mounted up, Edgwick of course at the handlebars, Eric on the back. Eric had found a black sweater and was now wearing it under his jacket.

"You sure about this?" I asked the soldier.

"He is," Eric said, answering for him.

I looked at Maria, suddenly wanting backup, panicking.

"I already tried," she said. "And besides, we already agreed to this. We can't make him stay."

"... fucking *hell*," I muttered, unable to keep it in, but I offered my hand for Edgwick to shake. His big paw covered mine.

"See you on the A45," he told me.

"Make sure you do," I said, before adding to my own surprise: "You're a good man, Edgwick. I always thought that. You were always decent to me at the base."

Edgwick's red moustache widened as his lips spread in a smile.

"That's because you were generally decent," he said, and started the engine. The two men walked the bike backwards and turned it to face the service station exit. Edgwick raised a hand as they slowly accelerated, then opened up the throttle once they reached the slip road. The bike quickly disappeared from our sight with a roar that drowned out Maria's words, a quiet prayer muttered so softly that I nearly didn't catch it:

Please let us see them both again.

Then we—

... Jesus. Ah, sweet Jesus.

...

The prayer didn't work, you see.

We wouldn't see them both again.

...

So. I offered to take the first stint driving.

Maria asked if I was sure, and I said I was. Paul and Maria needed to sleep in the cab. I saw the way they swayed as if in a breeze, saw their hooded eyes, their sullen expressions. Panic attacks or not, I was still somehow energised from running the Stone Man. *Paul will feel better if he sleeps*, I thought, sweeping our conversation nicely under the carpet. *He'll be fine and we can get on with saving the world.*

"Okay," Maria said, looking at the trailer and shivering. "Riding with that thing anymore ... just no." Paul just nodded and headed towards the truck's cab without another word.

He'll be fine, I told myself. *He'll be fine.*

***

It took me much longer than I thought to get used to driving such a big vehicle, but after the first hour I at least felt vaguely in control.

The A roads remained fairly clear for the first few hours, but all too regularly we would have to slow down to manoeuvre carefully around cars—the same issue that had bled so much speed from our truck journey so far—and this was now even slower thanks to my inferior truck driving skills. Every time I carefully eased the big semi around whatever was in our way, I pictured the Crawlers getting that much closer.

Paul and Maria, seated to my left, spent most of this time blessedly asleep.

In the early afternoon we received a very mild Stone vision. Its impact was so heavily watered down by Maria's blanketing—it was like a brief, mild nausea—all it really did was awaken my friends and break me out in a cold sweat. I could even drive while it passed. The moment only lasted for a few seconds; the image overlaid upon the road ahead. It was almost fully transparent, the face of a white, balding man hanging impossibly in front of us. He looked to be in his sixties. We would save him, or we wouldn't. The main thing, I told myself, was that the Target wasn't a kid. It wasn't Eric's Aiden. The vision faded quickly, and we continued on our way.

Neither Paul nor Maria went back to sleep after that.

Soon after that we came to our first full blockade. It was on the main street of what looked like a small market town. The only buildings either side of the road were a butcher's shop and an estate agent, but a two-vehicle pileup between them had managed to perfectly knock each other sideways to fill the road. The inside windscreens of both vehicles involved were filled with an all-too-familiar dried red spray. I thought about just ramming between them with the truck, but if I somehow crippled our vehicle in doing so then it might take a long time to find another truck here. Paul agreed with me, Maria wanted to try blasting on through, so mine was the casting vote.

We would use the Stone Man to clear the way.

Getting it to crawl backwards out of the trailer without damaging it was difficult, but I didn't tell the other two how much of a relief it was to let it walk again. Guiding the Stone Man on walking autopilot was easy, but keeping it still—lying prone in the trailer—actually required far more effort, like trying to ignore a constant itch. Setting the Stone Man to work felt like stretching my mental legs after a long time cooped up.

Paul and Maria remained in the cab—there was no need for them to get out—while I marched Caementum over to the two ruined vehicles, a Volvo and a Transit van.

I stood about fifteen feet away from the vehicles and sent the Stone Man towards them, picking the van first. I felt unbelievably tempted to make it punch or kick the van aside, just to see how far it could punt objects that weighed several tons. But Maria had made me agree beforehand: *don't hit them in case you strike a spark. Then we'd have exploding and burning cars to get past. Just* push *them.*

As it turned out, the agreement was irrelevant; as Caementum drew closer to the van, stone hands by its hips, palms out and ready to push, the van was caught by the Caementum's lead foot as it stepped forward. The van cleared the ground with an immense metallic *bang*. It flew through the air all the way to the butcher's shop, destroying both the display window and the entire front of the building housing it. The smell of leaking fuel filled the air. I spun around, open mouthed—holding my hands up unintentionally in the same manner as the Stone Man—and looked up at Maria. Paul's eyebrows were raised, a small smile on his face, but Maria was slowly shaking her head.

"*I swear,*" I mouthed, but she just pointed behind me to the flames that were slowly beginning to rise inside the ruins of both butcher's shop and van.

"*Just smash the other one,*" she mouthed. I quickly walked the Stone Man over to the Volvo and swatted the car's front end as gently as I could manage. The Volvo crumpled but, more importantly, it spun sideways like an opening door before stopping, leaving the road clear. I ran back to the cab, expecting an imminent explosion from the butcher's shop, only to see both Paul and Maria pointing out through the windscreen. I looked. The Stone Man was slowly walking away up the road, autopilot having kicked in now that the consciously controlled task was at an end.

"Oh, shit," I said, turning the Stone Man around before beginning the careful, slow and noisy process of manoeuvring it back into the trailer. I thought the trailer's floor was definitely going to give way this time, but it didn't.

"That took too long," I told the other two once the truck was back in motion. The whole process had taken around ten minutes. How much ground had the Crawlers gained in the meantime? Their top speed had to be at least thirty mph. We were only occasionally getting up to sixty, but with the constant slow-downs, I wasn't sure if our average and their average were that far removed from one another.

"Well at least you had fun," Maria said, raising an eyebrow, but she was smiling faintly. She knew I hadn't done it on purpose. Her eyelids were already drooping again and I was glad; I didn't want her to see the exhilaration in my eyes. That *had* been fun. A break from the constant worry, but that was already over; I was thinking about how we would handle it when the A roads got clogged, *if* the A roads would get clogged.

"Go to sleep," I said, faking a smile.

We wouldn't be able to outrun the Crawlers for much longer.

***

Three more hours passed., and I still had my doubts.

We'd passed Edinburgh and made it as far as Dunkeld. Still no sign of the Crawlers. We'd had to use Caementum as a vehicle mover six times by this point, and when we next stopped to use the bathroom at a roadside services—one with a brand-new, un-damaged, and fully fuelled Eddie Stobart truck sitting right there—we all agreed it was time to switch vehicles. Even with our ever-greater control of the Stone Man, the back of our existing trailer was practically ready to give way, battered by Caementum's exits and entrances. Paul reckoned it would normally have taken about four hours on the A roads to get this far; given that it had taken us six made me think that we were still making good time.

The roads were indeed becoming more difficult to traverse but a combination of my improving truck driving and becoming accustomed to sending the Stone Man in and out of the trailer meant that we were now pretty efficient ... but still stopping too much. Still giving up little pieces of our lead to those things.

Paul and Maria somehow looked worse despite having rested, their eyes puffier, their breathing heavier. What could I do? Except to—literally—keep on trucking. My lower back was screaming at me by this point with all the driving, but here finally was some physical suffering for me. I wore it like a badge of honour.

Around hour seven, my friends passed out. Around hour eight, I woke them up. I didn't want to, but hope was important.

"Guys. Guys."

No answer. I used their threads.

Guys.

They opened their eyes, blinking.

"I thought you should see this."

They looked through the windscreen. Took in the empty fields either side of the road.

"We're in England," I told them. "We've crossed the border. We're getting there."

They didn't say anything. I thought it could be a moment. That it could shore them up, let them know we were progressing. The mental side of all this was so important.

"How much further to go?" Maria asked. "How long?"

Based on the map I knew it would normally be about another six hours with a clear run. So potentially at least another seven or eight, most likely more.

"About five hours," I lied, hoping the block on my thread would cover it. Maria nodded and closed her eyes, wincing. Paul's were already shut.

I put my foot down as much as the straightening road would allow.

***

By the time we reached a street-lit Loughborough, on our way inland to the Midlands, I was starting to believe that we might have lost the Crawlers completely. More than that; I was starting to believe that we might actually win.

We were nearly there, after all. I'd expected *something* to stop us even getting this far, yet here we were. Maybe we could go all the way and actually pull this off?

As it was, even my least-optimistic guess about getting to Coventry inside seven hours had been ambitious. It had taken us that long to get to Loughborough, passing the village of Seagrave, to be more specific. We were about to begin our route around Leicester to avoid its clogged-up arteries and head down into Coventry, driving under a dark sky devoid of stars thanks to the streetlights in the surrounding area. The driving had become unbearable, the boredom and the anxiousness all seeming to mingle perfectly with my restricted, constant driving position, fucking with my spine. Not driving for five years followed by a thirteen hour stretch behind the wheel of an articulated lorry was not, apparently, a good idea.

The lack of Crawlers kept my spirits up. Whatever they had used to track us at the Isle of Skye surely had to be limited to short range pursuit. But did that mean the Stone Men could find us if we came within range of any of them?

That would likely be happening soon; drawing near to Seagrave meant we were only about an hour's regular drive from Coventry. We were so fucking close! Maria and Paul had been sitting silently, peering out of the windscreen through eyes that were narrowed to slits.

"Another hour," I said, shifting in my seat in another pointless attempt to ease the pain.

"Take a break," Maria said. "I can feel the tension in you. That's not going to help the mission."

I opened my mouth to protest but immediately realised she was right. I'd been mentally checking in with the Stone Man about every thirty minutes or so; a body scan, to use the meditation terminology so beloved of the late Doctor Holbrooks and his staff. Just checking that I still had the full awareness of its limbs, its presence, when required. On my last check-in, however, I'd noticed that the connection was a fraction fuzzier, requiring more effort, more concentration, and the cause was becoming clear: I was too stiff, tense, and in pain. I did need a break.

"I can last another hour—"

"Hold up your hand," Maria said. "Hold it flat, and steady."

I did. My hand shook noticeably, and not just from Eddie Stobart's lousy suspension.

"And you still haven't slept?" she asked me.

"I can't," I said.

"You're having a break," she said, her voice weak but determined. "Taking fifteen minutes for a reset will be worth it. We need you as good as you can be as we … head in …" She rubbed her eyes, her dozy thoughts unable to complete the sentence. "You know what I'm trying to say. Pull over here."

We were driving along a pleasant residential through road, the kind of place that was nice enough when on your way to somewhere else. Identical, bland houses lined either side of the street, but I could see a petrol station a way off in the distance, seated where the road met a roundabout. The limited streetlighting here was enough to have a clear view as I pulled the now slightly incongruous lorry over to the kerb. It was almost unthinkable to picture that, most likely, all of the houses in this clean, inoffensive semi-neighbourhood were empty save for dried blood coating their internal walls. The country would have shut down the moment the latest Arrivals began, people leaving work and going or staying home to be with their loved ones. It's the only reason, I think, we were able to make the passage to the Midlands as relatively quickly as we had. If the Barrier had spread earlier, we'd probably still be stuck in Scotland clearing cars.

"Maria—" I protested, even as I killed the engine.

"Don't argue."

"What if someone dies because I took a fucking break?"

"What if," she said, her voice cold, "everyone left under the Barrier, and everyone in the world—what was it, twenty or thirty Arrivals and the planet's population is gone?—dies because you went into Coventry that much less effective, that much more mentally slow? All because you wouldn't take a break when you needed to?"

The impact of her words must have been clear in my face, because she shrugged, her expression blank.

"If you want to play hardball," Maria said, "I'll play hardball."

"She's right," Paul added, finally speaking up. His voice was low, and he looked at his feet as he spoke. "I'll even have a go at cracking your back, if you like."

"You think you can help?"

Paul mimed putting on a backpack.

"Back-to-back, you know the trick," he said,

"Okay, okay," I said, opening the door, thinking there was no fucking way in hell Paul was going to be able to do that. He looked like he could barely stand. "Fifteen minutes." I eyeballed the houses. The thought that one of them might have a bed I could lie on for a minute was suddenly very tempting. "You two getting out? Bathroom break?" They hadn't had one for a while. They nodded and stepped down from the cab; I did the same, groaning and slowly twisting myself back and forth to try and loosen up. It had rained a little while ago, and the trees and front-garden grass surrounding us were covered in droplets. I heard Paul call weakly to me.

"Come here." His voice moved around the truck's cab along with the sound of Maria's footsteps. In this manner they were out of my sightline when the Horns sounded.

This was the loudest I'd ever heard them. How were they getting through like this? I think to myself now that, if we were driving, we would have crashed. I cried out, my voice lost in the Horns' blast as my vision suddenly received an overlay again, that extra visual layer on top of the reality my eyes were seeing. I was seeing Targets—laid over the sights of houses and gardens and trees and hanging before me like faint reflections seen in a window. But they were brighter now, and there were so many more faces than I'd ever seen at once. Even in my amazement I tried to count them, aware that I was still upright and in control of my faculties. How was this even happening? Why was this breaking through Maria's blanket in this way? As the faces continued to spin on their visual carousel, I thought they passed into double digits. At least ten faces ... and one shining, golden light. Eric had told Straub that, when he'd received the vision of Jenny Drewett—she who was consumed by the Pale Stone Man—he'd seen a golden light. Her *bubble* had been golden.

And he'd said that Aiden's was golden as well.

I understood what was happening: it wasn't coincidence that there were so many Targets in a vision hitting this hard, and one accompanied by the Horns at that. The sheer number of Targets had to be the *reason* the signal was strong enough for its feedback to affect us like this.

The Horns stopped and the faces began to fade. I staggered my way around to Paul and Maria's side of the truck's trailer. Maria was breathing hard, but Paul looked far worse, his back against the trailer as if he were about to fall down.

"The Horns," I croaked, moving to the back of the trailer to open it. "And the visions. At the same time. They've Targeted and started walking *at the same time.* They *are* getting faster." The Prism. Could it be getting more efficient with time, the same as our circuit?

Neither answered. The street was still soaking wet from earlier, heavy rain. Paul clearly needed to lie down immediately, but if he did so in the road he'd spend the rest of this ordeal in wet clothes. I went to Paul and put my arm around him, shocked anew by how narrow his once-broad shoulders had become. He allowed me to guide him to the back of the truck, his legs threatening to give way.

"Just lie down in here until you get your equilibrium back," I told him, opening the trailer's gate. Paul hesitated at the trailer's entrance. I was almost surprised. Then I realised this reluctance had less to do with the Stone Man, and more to do with having spent years inside a trailer of his own. Then he softened, laying his shaking hands onto the bottom of the trailer's gate. Paul clambered unsteadily inside, moving around the prone Stone Man and scuttling the fifty-plus feet to the back of the trailer on his hands and knees. He collapsed heavily against the trailer's rear wall.

"Gimme ... gimme a minute," he called. "That one hit hard." He was a dark figure now, tucked far away in the pitch-black recesses of the trailer's long insides. "That was so many—"

"I know," I said, interrupting as kindly as I could. I needed to check on Maria. I began to turn away but Paul called after me.

"I counted them."

"I tried to."

"There were twelve Targets. That makes sense."

"... it does?"

Paul sighed as his outline shifted in the darkness, propping his back upright against the head of the trailer.

"Six Blues," he grunted, "at the start, coming out of the Prism once the Red got made. They've had plenty of time to all complete a Harvest each. That means how many *new* Stone Men?" *Twelve more*, I thought. *Two from each Harvest.* I'd previously feared it might have been more, having heard the Horns more than just six times as we drove. I'd reminded myself that the Stone Men sounded the Horns for many things, from Harvesting to starting to walk. "Twelve Targets," Paul said, "and all those new Stone Men setting off for them at once. No wonder we saw it. So eighteen of the buggers at large now. With the original six continuing their journeys."

"Nineteen if you include the big one," I said. "The red."

"Yeah. And Eric said the kid's bubble was gold. I saw gold just now, you?"

"Yeah. Shit."

One of the new Blues would now be on their way to the boy, Aiden ... unless Eric got there first. Surely he was there by now? It had been, what, twelve or thirteen hours since he left on a motorbike, taking the motorways?

"It's *all* getting quicker," Paul said.

"I'm ... gonna check on Maria," I replied, and moved away to see Maria circling on the spot, her hands still in her hair, her head down. "Maria?" I asked.

"Just gimme a minute, just gimme a minute," she snapped. I approached carefully. Should I hug her? She was clearly having some kind of trauma response to what we just witnessed, but everything about her now screamed *leave me alone*. Was she freaking out about the kid? She'd communicated remotely with the boy and knew that a Blue was now on its way to him. He wasn't just a name to her.

Your team just took a hit, I thought. *Talk to them. They're really fucked right now and this is when you have to step up.* Of course, I had zero clue what to say. I straightened up though, biting back a gasp as my suffering back protested the movement—

Fuck your back, I thought. *Say something.*

"Paul," I called to the inside of the trailer. "Can you hear me in there?"

"Yeah."

""We, uh, we're gonna take a break, like we planned. The plan doesn't change." That was good. That was what Brigadier Straub would say if she were here. "I know we're worried about the kid, hell, I know we're worried about Eric and Edgwick." That was a lie. I'd barely thought about them since they left. Not because I didn't care—I did—but because the focus the Stone Man gave me had blocked out almost everything except the pain in my back. "I know I don't need to remind you," I said, searching for the words. "But this is literally about *the whole world*. I can't put it any more succinctly than that. Those targeted people…" I trailed off, watching Maria continue to circle. *We let those people go? They aren't our problem? They'll die as heroes?* Jesus. But what *could* we actually do about it? "The best way to stand a chance of helping those people is *keeping going*. We'll be in Coventry soon. Maybe we can stop all this, but we won't if we lose our shit now." That felt like a good resolution. I'd redeemed the speech. "Right? Paul?"

"Yeah," Paul called weakly.

"Maria—"

"*Shhh!*"

That wasn't the effect I'd hoped for.

"Well, okay," I said, reddening. "But I think—"

"Andy, please, *please*," Maria said. "I'm trying to check the … *remnants* of the vision, it's hard enough to keep it here—"

"What? You're still seeing it?" What was she doing monkeying around with the vision?

"There's something in it, something important," Maria hissed, eyes screwed tightly shut, her hands pulled into clubs either side of her head. "I don't know what it is but it's… snagging—please just gimme—"

She suddenly took a jerking step backwards.

"*Ah*—"

Her eyes flew open, staring through me and seeing something terrible. I moved to her, held her up, but her body began to shake so violently in my hand that I let her fall against me so I could quickly lower her to the ground. It was that or drop her. The knees of my jeans instantly soaked through with standing water as I knelt to lay Maria across my thighs, holding her back upright against me as best I could. I knew what was happening. I'd experienced the same only that morning. Maria was having a panic attack.

"Don't fight it," I told her. "Just let it come and it will pass—"

She clutched my arm. Her fingers were claws.

"*Mar—Mar—Mar—*" she babbled.

"Tell me after, tell me after—"

"*Marcus, it's Marcus—*"

I just had time to register the name, who it was—*Maria's* Marcus—before I felt the shaking move out of Maria and into me, into our circuit.

Into our threads.

Suddenly here was another thing bigger than our personal circumstances.

"Maria, the circuit—"

"*Andy!*" Paul screamed from inside the truck.

"*I know! Maria—*"

I felt Maria's hiding influence begin to tear, her blanket of protection shredding.

Sleeping was one thing, it seemed, but the primal soul-twisting of a panic attack was shaking our control completely apart. What could I do? If I told her to get it together, it would only make things worse; if she did as I told her and let this thing come then the tearing would continue—

I felt it then. Sudden, cold, and terribly aware, scuttling quickly towards the three of us and coming from all directions.

The eye of the Stone Giant.

I heard banging from inside the trailer as Paul tried to get up. My mind instantly became blank, this had happened so quickly—

"Ma-Maria—"

Her eyes rolled up in their sockets, she started to convulse, and I knew this was going beyond a panic attack. The lens of the Stone Giant's encircling presence was closing eagerly, and then it was upon us.

Many things happened at once.

My body immediately began to constrict as it had by the shores of Loch Alshe, falling backwards onto the concrete. I was dimly aware of Maria's weight sliding off my lap. I curled into a ball as the banging of Paul's own constrictions hammered against the trailer. Everything intensified. It was faster this time. Was that due to the hardening, embedded Barrier carrying the many signals of the Caeterus everywhere at lightning speed? Perhaps due to having found us once and being more prepared a second time? What I do know is that only seconds passed before I felt another sensation quickly joining the presence of the Stone Giant. A joining. A connecting, and not just of the Red and whatever it was bringing to that sleepy residential road outside of Leicester.

Of course, I thought, even as my body gibbered on the ground.

The original six Blues had been walking for a long time, ever since they emerged from the Prism. We knew that. They'd all completed their first run, made more Stone Men, and were now well underway with their second journey. We should have expected that many of them would be walking away through the Midlands right now. We should have expected something like this.

The Stone Giant connected the same Blue that had been sent after me five years ago. It *connected* to me. Not to the circuit. Not to Maria. Not to Paul. Me. I recognised the sensation immediately. We had, after all, been connected once before, and that had been a sensation I will never forget for the rest of my life. The presence reached out to seize me, my worst nightmare immediately manifest.

The *click* into place in my head was like a physical punch. Immediately the Quarry Response began, but infinitely worse than before; the double hit of the Response itself combined with the shock of instantly recalled trauma. I tried to scream but all I could do was gag. I rolled onto my back, dimly aware of the swirling light that was beginning to appear around me in a circle; my bubble, already beginning to form, and we no longer had Eric around to do anything about it. I felt as if I were dying.

Any sense of control we had over the Stone Man completely disappeared.

There was a sensation of deep emptiness. Even as I continued to buck and thrash—the distant, conscious, rational part of my mind begging me to remember how I broke to the Quarry Response in the past, to save myself, completely unable to access my tumbling mind's memories—the sounds from the trailer turned from dull metallic thumps to the deafening, eager rending of steel.

Any shred of remaining hope vanished.

Damaged, or just worn out, Caementum had used Paul's unique nature as a battery to keep itself going, leaks and all. The Detonation had then dumped out what little energy the Stone Man had left, and the rest had been bleeding out into the earth while it lay dormant. Then we'd shored up its holes and woken it up with a plan for Paul to power it all the way to Coventry. Fine. Good plan.

What we hadn't counted on was the Maria-repaired Stone Man using Paul to recharge its own battery over time, never considering that the no-longer-leaking monster would be able to store energy again. It's the only theory we have that makes sense. What I know for sure is that when Maria lost it and we fell under the gaze of the Stone Giant, two things happened.

We lost control of the Stone Man, and now it had some of its own power.

The metallic screeching of the truck hit a sharp crescendo as the legs of the rising Stone Man tore through the bottom of the trailer. Paul's screams were drowned out as those legs began to walk forward, carving through the metal. The rending sounded to my helpless ears like the end of the world, which of course it was, Maria and I twitched and thrashed uselessly on the road as the Stone Man walked, closing in on its original Target: Paul.

Paul, sitting less than fifty feet away from it, trapped at the other end of the truck's trailer.

***

Chapter Eleven

Dead Meat, the Will of the Caeterus, and Things Get Much, Much Worse

***

Something fastened itself onto my ankle and squeezed.

Then my other ankle. Then the back of my head was scraping painfully along the concrete as a wide-eyed and shaking Maria tried to drag me out of the bubble. It didn't work. The ugly, few-inches-high halo of the growing bubble followed me, Maria gripping my legs and holding them high to avoid her touching it.

"*Fuck!*" she screamed. I could barely hear her over the noise from the trailer, from the screams of both metal and man. Maria screwed up her eyes, her grip tightened a moment, and then the Quarry Response was gone. *Click.* I let out a gasp as Maria dragged me clear of the ugly circle; now it remained in place, unable to feel me. She released my ankles as I rolled onto my side, the knowledge of the now-approaching Blue suddenly absent as the almost physical sensation of Maria's blanketing wrapped around me. Her hands shot out.

"Get up!" she screamed, as I took her outstretched hands and staggered upright.

"How—how did you break—"

"*Fucking help Paul!*"

We ran around to the back of the screaming, shaking trailer to see the hulking form of the Stone Man closing in on Paul. He was trapped, his own Quarry Response was in full effect, rendering him helpless and panicking. His threads were nothing but white noise.

"*Snap him out of it!*" I yelled. "*We're still connected, why can't we reach him?*"

"*I can't!*" Maria yelled back. "*The Stone Man is creating his Quarry Response, it's too close to him—*"

We couldn't get to him either. The huge Stone Man was walking up the trailer's centre, the metal walls too close to its elongated, moving limbs for us to get past. If we touched the Stone Man we'd be rendered catatonic, unable to help. We had seconds until it finished its walk across the length of the trailer and reached Paul. Maria finally got the threads working between us again and our two-person circuit flickered into life. I tried to flash into Caementum. It was useless; without Paul, I couldn't gain any kind of purchase. I needed a mental handhold, something to grip—

The gap in Caementum's internal works. The place I'd mentally dived into back at the Project, throwing myself into the Stone Man's gears, but I'd been so lucky to find it—

No. We'd plugged it up again when we restarted it.

"Maria! Are you still keeping that thing's energy together?"

Her mouth opened in surprise; she'd been doing it so long, so automatically, that she hadn't even thought of it. We'd lost control but we were still connected—

Maria pulled the plug and the Stone Man's energy released. The streetlights around us pulsed spasmodically in and out—but didn't go completely off—and the screeching of metal ground to a halt.

We called Paul's name as we moved forward, trying to see him in the dark. We could hear his hitching, gasping breaths that mirrored our own, but his Quarry Response was over, ceasing the moment Caementum was shut down.

"You're okay Paul!" I cried. "We stopped it!" I looked at Maria. Her face was ghostly. I wrapped her up in my arms in relief. She held me back. "Thank you, *shit,*" I said. "You saved me, oh my God." Maria nodded against my chest and released me, looking up into my eyes. "How did you do that?"

"A-as soon as I felt the Stone Giant," she said, "You know, affecting me. I just hid myself instinctively. I've done it before. The shock of cutting off the Quarry Response kind of reset me. I saw the bubble growing around you and just—"

"You said you saw Marcus—"

"No," she said, holding up a hand and backing away. "I mean … not now, Andy."

She turned back to the trailer.

"Paul?" she called. "Can you get around it safely now it's not moving?"

There was heavy coughing in the darkness, followed by moans of relief.

"I need ... light," Paul quietly called back. I pulled my signal-free phone from my pocket, my trembling grip a useless, fumbling thing. Our actual torches were in our backpacks at the other end of the trailer with Paul. He wouldn't be able to root through them properly in the dark.

"Here, here," I said, switching my phone's light on. I held back a gasp as I took in the suddenly illuminated sight in front of me.

"*Oh my God,*" Maria whispered.

Paul was cowering right up against the back of the trailer, squinting in the bright light and holding up a hand to shield his face. The immense back and silhouette of the Stone Man almost blocked him entirely from view. Once again, it had been far too close; the Stone Man had been thwarted only two or three steps away from its quarry. All around its thighs the trailer's bed was buckled and bent upwards in small, frozen waves of metal. Paul looked up and saw how close it had been.

He let out a scream and his feet began to pedal uselessly backward on the trailer's floor, trying to propel his body through the solid bulkhead and away from his now-dormant pursuer.

"It's okay, it's okay!" I yelled. I am deeply ashamed to admit that I couldn't bear to hear him whimpering. "It's shut down, you're safe! You're okay, *breathe* mate, breathe." Paul stopped scrabbling, putting both hands down at his sides, but his eyes remained on the Stone Man's head. "Look at me, Paul. Look at me." Paul did, reluctant to take his eyes off his motionless pursuer. "You can get past it. See? You can get by on the right, there. See the gap? Look at the gap, Paul." To my surprise, Paul began to crawl forward quickly, as if moving before he lost the nerve. He scuttled around the Stone Man, flattening himself against the trailer's wall, and out to where we stood with outreached arms at the open gate. He collapsed into us. Despite Paul's greatly reduced weight, it was an effort for Maria and I to hold him upright. The moment was brief; there was still enough of the old, proud Paul in there for him to straighten up after a few seconds and wipe his face, trying to fake a chuckle.

"Cut that, *uhh,* cut that a bit, *uhh,* a bit—" he mumbled.

"It's okay," Maria said, reaching up for Paul's shoulder, and even as I realised our circuit had clicked fully back into place my thoughts whispered to me:

It had you again. You were nearly bubbled, with no Eric to save you. Done for. You would have ended up like Patrick Marshall, screaming in the middle of the street as your spine was burned out of your body. Like Henry.

I thought of Maria's own revelation: Marcus, the man Maria still clearly loved. A Target. A *bubbled* Target. What the fuck did I say to her?

"You saved us both, Maria," I blurted. "You fucking saved us *both*."

Maria scowled, sniffing heavily, red-eyed.

"It's my fault that happened," she said. "I kept hold of the vision, I knew there was something in it that I couldn't let go of, Andy, and I hung on to find out what, but I didn't *know* it was Marcus, I swear!" Maria began to circle again, fists clenched. "I never would have endangered us intentionally, I just felt something important and I thought—"

"Fuck that, Maria!" I said, genuinely shocked. "Are you *okay,* I mean … Marcus, like you say—"

But Maria was already waving me off, shaking her head.

"I told you, *leave it*," she said. "There's nothing we can do. You were right. The mission first, *duty* first. The best way to, to, to *do* something about all this. You were right. You were right."

"Well … do you …" I'd just given a speech about how this all was so much bigger than us. Now here was Maria, actually walking the Dispensatori walk. "Do you … need a moment, or something…"

"Yeah. Yeah I do."

She walked away then, disappearing around the front of the truck's cab. Her muffled sobs came shortly after. A sting of her pain rippled down her thread; I grimaced with the impact of it before I felt her block come down, locking Maria into an echo chamber of her own hurt. Paul was standing at the trailer's gate, his hands resting upon it, bent at the waist. His breathing was beginning to slow as he stared into the mangled darkness before him.

"Gonna need another transport," he said.

"… yeah."

"How'd you stop it? We weren't …" His finger came up and tapped the side of his lowered head.

"Maria pulled the plug we made," I told him. "I think maybe Caementum had been storing some of your energy and—did you… you see what happened to the streetlights?"

"No."

"They kind of flickered when she broke the seal. They didn't go fully out like with the Big Power Cut."

"Not as much energy in the bastard, I guess."

"Yeah. I hate to say this right now, Paul, but ... how long before you think you'll be good to try and get it moving again?"

Paul sighed, long and heavy. Then he straightened and gazed into the trailer, eyes locked on the huge shadow. I realised he was seeing a frozen snapshot of what was very nearly the moment before his death.

"Give me five minutes," he said.

"Okay—"

Then it hit me.

We were hidden again, and the Blue that had connected to me—*my Blue*— could no longer see where we were in real time.

But what if it was still heading for our last known location?

Shit.

We didn't know how far away it was, and our transport was now totalled. We could easily get another car for ourselves, but we wouldn't be able to move the Stone Man at speed until we found another truck.

Don't panic, I told myself. *You're gonna have time to get Caementum restarted and be out of here well before the Blue arrives.*

That made sense. I breathed out. The best thing I could do, then, was give these two a few minutes, as requested.

"Guys?" I called, backing away and looking at the row of houses behind me. "I'm gonna go sit in the back garden of ..." I looked. "Number 17. Come and get me in fifteen minutes. Then we move." Vaguely murmured acknowledgements floated my way, so I turned and walked across the street to number 17, heading for the back garden.

The garden was small but neat, flanked either side by its own garage and the garage of its neighbours. Its rear security light clicked into life as I rounded the corner. I was very relieved to find no dried red spray illuminated there, only a small garden dining set consisting of a table and four padded chairs sitting on the patio. I sank into one of the chairs, taking in the silence and finding myself suddenly shocked by the sheer normalcy of suburbia.

Regular, dull, safe suburbia. A world I hadn't known, or even visited, in the last five years. A world that, in this country at least, would never return. As my now-only-grumbling back settled against the chair I realised that my convulsing, spasming Quarry Response had achieved one good thing: it had cracked my fucking back.

"Well, that's something," I said out loud, before putting my forearm in my mouth to muffle my cries as I sat in that garden and wept. All I wanted in that exhausted, impossibly weary moment was to just go and be with Sophie. Failing that, silence and nothing. It would at least mean peace. The fight was just endless, endless.

After a few minutes I was calming down, and heard approaching footsteps. Paul rounded the corner just as I finished quickly drying my eyes.

"Ready," he said.

"Is Maria?"

He shrugged.

"Let's find out."

We found out very quickly that none of us were.

The next hour was spent standing around in soaked clothes, the cold in our bodies growing along with our concern as a horrible suspicion slowly gave way to a far worse certainty:

We couldn't restart the Stone Man.

None of us wanted to admit it. We just kept quietly trying, me finding its threads, Maria sealing and containing the Stone Man's remaining energy, Paul sending us the extra power we needed … but it slowly became clear that something was wrong, and it was only getting worse the more time passed. Concerned comments gave way to mild bickering as our frustrations grew, all of us understanding the same thing.

Our timing was off.

It was something that we hadn't really been consciously aware of the first time we'd restarted the Stone Man. An ability that once had been instinctive was now noteable by its absence, like an aging athlete abandoned by the flow state he once took for granted. We could barely even make our own circuit work properly now, let alone make Caementum dance to our tune. What was wrong? There was one fleeting moment when we thought we had it, the high cries of gently moving metal reaching our ears as the connection between us and the Stone Man fused briefly together. Then whatever innate rhythm we'd previously have used to catch this moment and move it onto the next functional beat abandoned us. The metal fell silent, our awareness of the Stone Man's processes died, and I screamed my frustration into the night sky.

"You can't set off the automatic walking, even?" Maria asked, her tone pleading rather than accusatory.

"*No*," I hissed. I didn't say the nasty, unforgivable thought that lurched into my mind: *if you weren't so busy pining over your fucking boyfriend then maybe we'd be moving by now.* I was beginning to feel tired again—the source of that delightful thought—so these two had to be practically dead. "Look," I said, "I didn't want to say anything earlier but … when I was Targeted just now? The Red–the Giant—it sent a Blue our way. I don't know if it's still coming or not, or exactly how far away it is—"

"Great," Paul said, "but I'm more worried about the fucking Crawlers than one Blue. They'll be here a *lot* quicker than any Stone Man."

My jaw fell open. I couldn't believe I'd forgotten. The *Crawlers*. I'd been so busy obsessing over being Targeted again. And while we could run away—break into the nearest house with a car in the driveway, find the car's keys, and drive ourselves off into the sunset—the Crawlers would destroy the Stone Man and with it the hopes of the fucking human race.

"Let's just … let's just try again," I said.

"We have to face it," Maria said, swaying lightly on the spot. "Me and Paul. We're the reason this isn't working. We're too exhausted, and we're not mentally responding quickly enough to each other's thoughts, not like before. We might be in big trouble, here."

But there was no time to sleep.

"Let's keep trying," I said.

After another thirty minutes I went back to Number 17 to grab three of the garden chairs. If they were exhausted, we could at least do this sitting down. Another thirty minutes after that, it was one in the morning, and things were only getting worse. After the latest failed attempt all three of us slumped in our chairs, me tired and defeated, Paul and Maria spent.

The three of us—and by default, everyone else, *literally* everyone else—were dead meat.

"We *have* to take a break," Maria whispered, pinching the bridge of her nose. "We're only making it worse. Maybe we sleep for ten minutes—"

"There isn't time—"

"We could have slept all *this* time!" Maria snapped, and she was right, but hindsight was, as always, effortlessly perfect. "We'd all be rested and waking up *now*—"

Maria's eyes widened and she leapt to her feet. It was the quickest I'd seen her move since her revelation about Marcus.

"We need to *wake up*," she said.

"We know," Paul began, "but now there's even less time to slee—"

"*Amphetamines*," Maria said.

She looked between Paul and I as if we had an ample supply of amphetamines in our back pockets.

"I see your logic," I said, "but we don't—"

Then I got it.

We didn't have any, but there would be a pharmacy somewhere not too far from here. They would maybe have Ritalin, surely?

This was the ADHD generation, after all! Those Gen Z arseholes were finally useful!

"They wouldn't make us less physically tired," Maria said, her hands animated in the air, "but they'd make us more alert, maybe get the rhythm back that we had when we woke that thing up! And all this, this *Stone shit* seems to be about getting our brains working in sync. Right?" All we had to do, I realised, was find a pharmacy on the map first, and that would be easy with the digital tablet map Straub had given us. Sure, it's GPS wouldn't work, but we could plan a route instantly. It was that, or try to sleep. But how long did we have left before the Crawlers got here, or the Blue? We couldn't know until we started seeing buildings fall on the horizon. So how long could we risk sleeping, an hour? Would that rest wake our minds up more than amphetamines could? I doubted it.

"We get this street name," Paul said, standing up too. He looked excited. "Use it as the start point—"

"Yeah," I said, already heading for number 17. There was a car in its drive, and we would have to be quick. "Good fucking *thinking*, Constance. Go root around in the packs and find that crowbar. The hard drugs will probably be locked up and we'll need to break into a drawer or a cupboard or some shit."

"Okay," Maria said, moving away, a spring temporarily back in her step.

"Paul, go find out the street name—"

"We're gonna just leave it here though?" Paul asked. "The Stone Man?"

I paused. The idea was … weird.

"Yeah," I said. "I guess we have to."

Paul nodded and began to walk away down the street. I paused for a moment, listening. No distant crashing of buildings. No thrumming of heavy, multi-legged feet either. I nearly got down on the wet floor and put my ear to it, but I decided against it. We'd been here hours trying to restart the Stone Man. So much of that gained ground was now lost.

But we had to get on with the latest plan. That was all we could ever do.

***

Fifteen minutes later we pulled up in our technically-stolen car—a Mercedes—at the first pharmacy, a small building wedged in the middle of a quaint high street.

Inside, the place smelled lightly of disinfectant and none of us mentioned the splashes of dried redness coating much of its internal walls. Its lights were still on, the store caught in the middle of opening hours when the Barrier vaporised both staff and customer alike. The three of us were wearing borrowed coats I'd grabbed from number 17, taken to keep us warm in our wet outer wear. There wasn't time to waste checking for clothes that fit. The coats would do.

I'd been right about the locked storage situation, and in this case, it was a whole locked cupboard. I'd taken over crowbar duties, telling the exhausted Paul and Maria to just lie on the floor to wait. It took me several minutes but eventually I got the door open, revealing shelves of medication. The three of us went to work, but after five minutes we had to admit defeat: there was no Ritalin to be found, and none of us knew any other names for amphetamines. *Unless they have little packets labelled 'Speed',* Paul had muttered. It wasn't helpful, but it was another welcome flash of the old Paul. I missed him a lot.

"Next pharmacy," Maria said. "Come on." We'd already identified our next two locations in case the first was a bust; the nearest was another ten minutes away, which probably meant at least twelve or fifteen with moving around dead traffic. That wasn't far, but that meant we would be a whole twenty-five to thirty minutes away from the Stone Man. I didn't like that at all. We could return to find the Crawlers feasting on its corpse.

Tiredness was now fully settling into me like lead. Without my connection to the Stone Man, I was slowing down at an alarming rate. I needed the amphetamines too.

We hustled for the exit but Maria suddenly stopped in the doorway.

"You two get in the car," she said. "I need to grab something."

"You ok?" I asked. Maria shook her head, waving me away.

"Tampons, Andy. Tampons."

"Oh, right, yes. Sorry." I felt myself redden slightly, which made me redden even more; I was becoming flushed because Maria had said *tampons* to me? But I couldn't help it. Maria saw it before I could turn away in time.

"Bloody hell, Andy," she said. "I knew this American woman once. She had a saying for moments like this. *Bless your heart.*"

"Oh," I said, confused. "You're welcome?"

She shook her head.

"Start the car. I'll be there in 30 seconds."

I did. Soon we were on our way again.

***

The second pharmacy was in a larger, more modern building in the middle of a small just-out-of-town retail park. That strange sensation of stepping into a world gone by washed through our circuit again. If not for the eerie silence—and splashes of red dotted around the car park—one could almost believe everything was still normal. A faint sensation of longing thrummed through my circuit's threads.

Inside, we found the meds, and easily; I kicked myself for not going there first. Of *course* the larger place was more likely to have what we needed. I opened the packet and handed out tablets to Paul and Maria, swallowing them with water we'd grabbed out of the pharmacy fridge.

"Can I see the instruction thing?" Maria asked. We were back in the car, Maria in the front, Paul stretched out on the back seat. The light was gone from her eyes now. I hoped that would change shortly, thanks to the miracle of chemical intervention. I handed the folded piece of paper to her. "Says it's gonna take at least twenty minutes before we feel anything," she said.

"That's okay," Paul said. "Should be bright-eyed and bushy tailed by the time we get back, right?"

No-one replied. I started the engine and we set off. After a few minutes, Maria said:

"Do you have your phone, Andy?"

"Yeah?"

"Do you have songs downloaded? Can I connect it to the car Bluetooth?"

This was a surprise.

"Yeah. Yeah, sure." I handed my phone to her.

"Thanks," she said. "Outside of the circuit is … too quiet."

She scrolled through my Spotify for a moment and found something she wanted. After a moment the sounds of Shania Twain began to filter its syrupy way out of the speakers. I looked at Maria, but she was looking out of the window, her hands to her mouth. I couldn't see her expression in her reflection; her eyes were lost in the shadows.

***

I snapped off the stereo when we were five minutes away from the Stone Man.

"What is it?" Paul asked. Maria continued to stare out of the window.

"Hold on."

I listened. I rolled down the window. I began to think maybe I'd imagined it and then I heard it again. Distant, but unmistakable. Loud.

The dull but explosive crash of a falling building.

Now Maria turned around. I rolled the window back up and gripped the steering wheel as if trying to crush it, taking a deep breath.

"How awake are you both," I asked them. I thought I already knew the answer; I had noticed no difference in my own alertness since taking the amphetamines.

"Same as before."

"Same as before."

I stared at the road ahead, the white line rolling away beneath us.

"*Bollocks*," I said.

* * *

It was nearly 2am by the time we made it back to the ruined truck.

It looked completely out of place parked smack in the middle of a residential road. We got out of the car just in time to hear another crash, this one much louder. Much closer.

"*Look,*" Maria said, pointing away over the houses nearby. I nearly couldn't see where she was looking—it was dark, remember—but then I had it.

A thin line of smoke, only just visible in the upward glow of distant streetlights.

My pulse immediately spiked, and the threads of my circuit suddenly felt harsh and pointed.

"You feel anything? The Ritalin?" I asked, but Maria ignored the question.

"It can't be the Crawlers," she said. "That smoke, the noise, it's all coming from the wrong direction." She didn't have to say what that *did* mean was coming.

"Ok, *can you feel anything?*" I asked again. "Either of you?" That's when I realised that maybe *I could.* Maybe my adrenaline and heart rate weren't going haywire simply because of the situation.

"Maybe," Paul said. He looked a little more alert, but that could just have been fear.

"Let's just get to work on—" Maria began, but her sentence was cut off by another crash. That was *loud*, only a few streets away now. Paul and I had been in this situation before, and it was no easier the second time. If anything, it was worse; this time, I not just the Stone Man—could well be the Target. There was no Patrick Marshall here to take the fall for me. "Get to work on that fucking thing!" Maria said, hurrying to the black mouth of the trailer. We followed, and tried to begin the process.

Already it was different ... but only a little.

"*Oh!*"

We nearly had it, right off the bat! The connection our minds snagged a little, and there was an audible scraping of metal as the Stone Man stirred ... but it wasn't quite there yet.

"Concentrate, concentrate—" Maria began, but again her words were cut off by a deafening bang from behind us. "For fuck's *sake! Just concentrate on Caementum, nothing else!*" Now we could hear the faint sound of splattering water as it sprayed out into the air; somewhere nearby, some house's pipes had been torn free of their settings, its walls smashed. Paul's breathing was frantic, but I could feel the determination in his thread, in Maria's. There was something else there too; a rapidly growing quickness in the back and forth of our circuit at work.

The amphetamines were working.

"*That's it*—" I began, and the Stone Man started to move, my voice drowned out by the sound of the tearing metal. We were waking it up ... but something was wrong. I wanted to head it up the road, just to get it moving away—we could just walk it in any direction, through buildings, if we had to get it *away* quickly—but instead it was turning on the spot where its waist was wedged in the trailer's base, not responding the way I wanted. I sent the command to just *walk,* but all that did was briefly pause it.

"Make it walk Andy," Maria barked. "Just make it walk!"

That was when I understood two things.

One was that the amphetamines either weren't yet absorbed into our systems enough to have full control, or they were and still weren't enough.

The other thing was that the Stone Man was still going for Paul.

We'd woken it, yes, but we didn't yet *have* it, and Caementum's programming still held underneath everything. Until we again broke it to our will, it was focusing on Paul and nothing else.

The Stone Man completed its turning circle and began to walk back out of the trailer.

"Back up!" I said. "Just walk back, don't lose focus, keep trying!"

Our eyes stayed locked on the Stone Man as we backed away, watching it slowly approach along the trailer's black tunnel like a beast of legend emerging from its cave. The roaring of the rending metal sounded like a hunting cry, the Stone Man's heavy feet pounding on the road as it waded free. Its head and shoulders cleared the trailer's gate, and I noticed the terrible thudding sound of its feet seemed to be doubling before I understood that similar footsteps were now coming from behind the houses nearby.

There was an immense smashing sound, followed by that of crumbling brick and popping circuitry that became a rushing noise as internal walls and ceilings collapsed. The air was filled with madness as I turned to see a roof fall in and a front wall of brick explode outwards, destroyed as if it were nothing more than plaster.

The Blue Stone Man—*my* Blue Stone Man—walked through a house behind us to our left, trailing dust, and began to cross the street towards the trailer.

It was perhaps around sixty feet away.

"Back ... back up," I repeated, "back up around the trailer." My heart seemed to pulse in my eyes, the sheer pressure in my blood confirming this really wasn't just fear, that the amphetamines' effect was continuing to increase. I spread my arms as I walked backwards, scooping my friends either side of me and moving my gaze between the advancing Caementum as it turned to follow our path. The oncoming Blue was approaching behind it. "Just draw Caementum away from it, keep this distance between us! We need to buy some time until we can get the Stone Man back under control, we have to keep it away from—"

"It's faster," Paul gasped. My hand was on his chest. His heart was like a hardcore techno beat. *"The Blue is walking faster than Caementum."* He was right. It wasn't walking much quicker, but quick enough to slowly walk us down. This was clearly a full-powered Blue with more in the tank than our damaged and drained Stone Man. The Blue was about forty feet away now and slowly gaining. What the fuck would it do to Caementum if it reached him?

It. Not him. It.

We continued to reverse in an arc, passing around the cab, Caementum steadily following as its arm caught the cab and bounced it aside with a screech of rubber, crumpling metal, and suspension. All the while the Blue continued to close in behind it, the houses either side of us forming a killing chute under a jet black sky, the stars non-existent above the streetlights.

"Focus," I said, "Focus. *We have to get it back.*"

We tried again as we backed up. We had to draw the Stone Man along, either under our steam or its own, keeping away from the closing Blue for as long as we could. I tried to make the Stone Man raise its arm as it walked, just to try and re-establish a modicum of control. Its arm slightly fluttered up and down. That was better than a few moments ago, the connection a little stronger, my presence in that limb more *there*. Yes, I could feel inside its shoulders now, its head, the bond was becoming clearer, the lines between my own body and the Stone Man's becoming blurred again.

"Together," I said. "*Together—*"

I felt their concentration catch, the timing better, and this time Caementum's arm raised about a foot away from its body before dropping back into the swing of its relentless gait. "We're getting it, we're getting it," I said, realising I was fucking repeating everything I was saying.

I also realised that we absolutely were not going to outrun the Blue. It was now at thirty feet, our pace keeping Caementum at a constant ten feet behind Paul.

I tried the arm again. It responded more quickly. I tried the other. Likewise. Could I make Caementum's legs move even a little faster? Its legs responded, but all that did was make it stumble, same as they had when I'd tried to make Caementum run. We were constantly fighting against the will of the Caementum's original internal commands, failing each time. It now felt like we'd tried to restart an old car too many times too quickly and had flooded the engine, trying to do too much at once.

I glanced behind us, seeing the street beginning to curve around to the left. I changed our angle of retreat as the Blue moved within twenty feet of Caementum. I saw Paul and Maria's eyes constantly flicking from Caementum to me, Caementum to me. They were looking to me for answers. Sweet Jesus Christ, they were looking to me for answers. The Blue moved within fifteen feet of its quarry.

Something invisible crackled between them.

Caementum certainly felt it; the creature slowly began to straighten.

Then it stopped. We kept backing up.

"Did you do that?" Maria gasped.

"No," I said. The three of us backed up another ten feet or so and stopped. The Stone Man did not follow. The Blue continued its approach as Caementum began to slowly turn around on the spot.

"What the fuck is it *doing*?" Maria asked as the Stone Man completed its circle and stood motionless in the road. The only sound now was the crunching footsteps of the oncoming Blue, bearing down on the former lynchpin of its previous missions. We stood and watched, helpless to do anything else.

"Try and move it," Paul whispered. "Andy, try and back it up."

'Wait," I said, swaying in the middle of the street, but already I could feel my mind recharging. The fog of the constant effort was lifting already as my thoughts became clearer. The amphetamines, surely? I quickly sent a mental image along our circuit of a flooded engine. "We need a second, don't you feel that?" Both nodded. "Let's ..." There was nothing else we could do. We just had to see what was going to happen.

The Blue strode up to the waiting Caementum. Would it attack? What would happen to us if it did? The Crawlers' attacks had hurt us, but that had been a biting, devouring of the Stone Man's body. Would the Blue's attack be the same? Did it have the same capability?

"Holy shit," Paul muttered. "I can't believe this." I couldn't either. As the Blue drew to a halt in front of Caementum I was struck by just how much larger it was. I always knew that the Blues were taller than Caementum, but it had been a long time since I'd seen them standing next to one another, and even that had been on a TV screen. The Blue was healthier, fresher; even from where we were standing, I could feel the energy radiating from it. The two Stone Men faced one another. Now the only sound was that distant rush of water from destroyed pipes. Neither of the two creatures moved.

"What is it *doing?*" Maria repeated, just as a noise rang out, buffeting off the houses. We winced. This wasn't like the Horns. This was a high pitched, tinnitus-like sound, not dissimilar to the chatter of the Caeterus I'd heard in Stone Space at the Project. This was harsher, more distorted. Blessedly, it only lasted a few seconds, but then we all jumped as we felt something—a thread—shoot out of the Blue and into somewhere deep inside the Stone Man. We might not have had control of it, but we were still connected to the creature. Now the two Stone Men were connecting, creating a circuit of their own. What did *that* mean?

"Do we disconnect?" Paul whispered. "What if it detects us?"

"No," I whispered back. "I don't know if we'll get it back—"

My eyelids began to flicker. My vision began to blur as I felt a flow of information that I couldn't understand passing from the Stone Man to the Blue. Maria must have felt it too because she called it before I did.

"I think," she said, "it's trying to find out what's wrong with Caementum."

"Shit," Paul said, "like it's running a diagnostic?"

I didn't answer, trying to feel where that thread was going inside the Stone Man; would the Blue become aware of my presence in there? I didn't know, but I had a feeling I knew where that thread was heading, and I was quickly proved right. I didn't follow too closely, not wanting to be caught, but as I felt that thread disappear into Caementum's depths, I knew the Blue was connecting with that unbreachable something that I called the Core. It must have connected too, because something lanced up from deep inside me and buried itself in the back of my skull.

I would have fallen were it not for Paul and Maria holding me up. Apparently only Dispensatori was feeling it, channelled through my now-limited control connection to the Stone Man.

"What's happening?" Paul asked; whatever was happening was *really* hurting me, that would have been clear. A lancing pain was boring into a specific spot right at the back of my head, like the world's ugliest, rustiest acupuncture needle was jammed in there and slowly beginning to twist. It was so excruciating that I could barely see.

"Andy," Maria said, "how do we help?"

"The Core," I grunted. "Inside the Stone Man. The Blue is accessing it, I think—"

Something invisible shot up out of Caementum and into the sky.

All of us looked up pointlessly, feeling it but not seeing it; it was almost like a change in the air pressure, something that rippled across our faces as it rose like a missile. All of us flinched as we felt it connect home with the Barrier, out of sight between us and the equally unseen stars.

Paul expressed our thoughts perfectly.

"Fucking hell," he said. "That can't be good."

We waited for the next part of the process. The pain in my head lessened. Whatever stage of whatever sequence was occurring was perhaps complete, but that thread between the Blue and Caementum continued to sing loud and clear. Whatever information was passing between them continued to flow, and now it was also coming back the other way.

"Is it trying to repair Caementum?" I asked.

"We can't let that happen!" Maria said, suddenly panicking. "If it does that it's all over! Andy, we have to try and take control *now*, we have to fight the Blue!" My pulse was thrumming, surging thickly. Paul and Maria's threads felt alive in a way they hadn't for some time; the amphetamines were busy in us, and we'd waited to let that flooded engine settle. But even if the thread between the Stone Man and the Blue didn't somehow stop us re-asserting control … we were going to try and *fight* the Blue? I thought that would only go one way. The power of the Blue was abundantly clear. But what else could we do? Try and walk it away? The Blue was faster, it would walk us down. They walked everyone down, eventually. "Andy? Andy, take control and *hit it!*"

"Wait," Paul said. "You think they're connected brain to brain? CPU to CPU?"

"Yeah—"

Paul sent his idea down his thread; we were connected to the Stone Man. That meant we currently had a direct connection to the Blue's brain—

"You want to try and control the *Blue?*" Maria said. "We already tried that, remember? You remember how successful that was?" I did. We'd tried to remotely stop the Blue that had been coming for Eric's friend Harry. We'd been able to flash inside it at range but, when we'd tried to stop it walking, we hadn't even been able to access any of its functionality, let alone stop it.

"But *the Stone Man wasn't in our circuit then*," I said, beginning to hop from foot to foot.

"Oh—"

"You see? The Stone Man isn't just a part of their circuit, it was the *lynchpin* of that circuit. There has to be some kind of internal connection protocol between them, they communicated with each other even when the Prism wasn't here. If that connection's still there, we can use it to get *inside*, inside!" There it was, another faint sniff of our drug of choice: not amphetamines, but hope. "Plus, we were doing it remotely before, and right now they're face to face—

"If you're gonna do it," Paul said, "do it *now*—"

"But the Red," Maria said. "Even if we didn't have the Stone Man, lynchpin or not, its gonna know we're doing it. It pushed us out of itself when we tried to get into the Red before—"

"I know," I said, talking fast. "and if I can get in there, you're right, it's going to notice. If it pushes me out of the Blue, I need you to try and keep me in there."

"How?" Maria said, throwing up her hands.

"How do you do any of this shit?" I snapped back. "Just fucking do it!"

"*Just fucking take control and punch the Blue!*"

"You wanted Dispensatori, right? Then this is my call! Okay?"

"*Okay!*"

"*Whatever you're going to do*—" Paul repeated, eyes locked onto the two Stone Men, and without another word I flashed into Caementum. I briefly felt it light up as it received a fresh burst of information—the connected Blue had sensed I was in there. The connection didn't feel like a thread, though; I quickly understood that I couldn't use it. Fine. If Caementum was the lynchpin, then it must know how to form communications with its Blues; there had to be an existing protocol, I just didn't know how to use it. But then, I thought, I didn't understand how my iPhone connected to other people's phones; the important thing was that my *phone* understood: *Hey Siri, call Person X.* The phone did the rest. I didn't understand how the Stone Man worked either, but it seemed to understand my commands.

Connect, I told it, and suddenly I was flying between the two Stone Men. *It had worked,* and the noise inside the Blue was terrible. Its internal Stone Space was filled with that horrible, high-pitched, distorted noise that was presumably the Blue in diagnostic mode. But this was only as far as we'd been before; this wasn't deep enough. If two Stone Men could form an integral diagnostic connection, then surely it could access the deeper systems?

Take me deeper, I thought, and suddenly that distorted noise was deafening and the pressure around me increased. *Holy shit,* I thought, *this is easy—*

I immediately began to feel the Blues limbs, its head, its whole body, it was fucking working—

The diagnostic noise stopped. There was then only a rushing sound of rapidly changing information inside the Blue before I felt my Stone Space consciousness being compressed, the sensation of the Blue's limbs disappearing from my awareness, and a coldness all around.

Maria—

I couldn't hear her from here, but her energy was all around me, sent to me along whatever the Stone Man had automatically created for me. The compression eased, and *we were still in there ...* but then that coldness became stronger, covering everything. It was suddenly an all-too-familiar presence, and I understood that we now had the Red's attention. There was a short, concussive slamming sensation and then all three of us were staggering backwards in the street, seeing through our eyes once more. We had been pushed out.

"I-I couldn't keep us in—" Maria was saying, but the Blue was drawing back its left arm.

"*Move it—*" Paul yelled, but my brain was still stunned from the forceful displacement out of the Blue. I had time to say *catch me* to the others, hoping they would move my mindless body as I dropped mentally back into our Stone Man's limbs as quickly as I could. The degree of amphetamine-powered control felt much larger now and I was in its arms, trying to get them up in time, but it was all still too slow. The Blue's arm swung sideways, and I leapt out just in time as the Blue's hand smashed into the Stone Man's head.

The Stone Man was knocked clean off its feet.

It sailed through the air and a low fizzing sound emitted from Caementum as it smashed through the front wall of the nearest house. The crash of brick and glass only emphasised the explosion that went off inside our circuit, sending my vision flickering between my own eyes and Caementum's Stone Sight. I was very glad I hadn't still been inside Caementum as that punch landed. The remote shock was so great I couldn't even speak as I heard Paul and Maria cry out.

"It's coming," Paul gasped, watching the Blue advance on the fallen Caementum, the knowledge of what was happening pinballing around our circuit: the Blue was officially attacking us. It had sensed our presence when we tried to commandeer it and now it, or the Red, had decided that Caementum was beyond repair. Worse: it had decided that the Stone Man was a liability. I ran to the side of the road, hoping it was distant enough to avoid being caught in the fight, and leapt back into Caementum's limbs. I put one of its arms down to try and help it rise as it shifted under the burial of the collapsed house's frontage, but something was different. Its arms and legs were shaking, and it fell back onto its behind with an immense *whoomph*.

That blow had affected the integrity of the Stone Man's energy, whatever power was holding its body together. The force of the punch had gone *through* it.

I managed to sit the Stone Man up as quickly as I could, looking through its sight. The lights were off in the still-intact ceiling so the whole space was a shadowy cave. The only illumination was coming from the streetlights, seen through the gaping opening in the front wall of the house. The advancing Blue followed the Stone Man inside the building, its head scraping along the ceiling causing plaster to cascade behind it. I got the Stone Man to its knees in cripplingly perfect time for its head to be directly in the path of the now-swinging leg of the Blue. Again I leapt out just as the blow landed, knocking the Stone Man upright and sideways. I saw Caementum crash sideways through the house's outer wall, across the separating alley, and in through the outer wall of the house next door. The force hit me and I clutched my stomach in pain, seeing Paul dropping to his knees, as Maria vomited onto the road, that second energy-damaging blow rippling out along our circuit. We were in big trouble. I jumped back into Stone Sight but it was fully dark. Caementum was buried once more under a tsunami of bricks and breeze blocks. Outside, I knew, my circuit was on the deck, literally and figuratively. The Blue was advancing once again.

Get up!

I meant all of them. The Stone Man, Paul, Maria.

GET UP—GET THE FUCK UP—HELP ME—

I leapt back to my human eyes, lurching to Paul and Maria and grabbing them under an armpit. I watched the sea of debris ripple and shift as I remotely commanded Caementum to turn over, trying to get it to its feet, to fucking *stand*. Rubble poured from the Stone Man's shoulders as it finally stood.

Fine, I thought. *If this is what it has to be—*

Something else was rising, screaming up from within my own depths, something intense and angry. It was unfamiliar but primal as it kicked in, found in the moment when my back, the backs of my friends, were against the wall. Was this what Sophie meant about me? I watched the Blue close in, already swinging, and I knew this was it. I sent the command—

Fucking block *it—*

The Stone Man's arms shot up, bent at the elbow. The lipstick hands were up by its head, the most basic defensive gesture, the Blue's blow met the back of Caementum's forearms with a dull, dense *thud*.

We'd blocked the strike.

It hurt even outside of its body, the energy Stone Man's of the Stone Man's physical integrity still rocked. But it was only a little compared to getting struck in our Stone head. How the hell had we moved so—

The amphetamines must have finally peaked—

"*Andy!*"

The Blue's other arm was already swinging and this time—because I was so fucking busy kissing my own backside over stopping one attack—my response command wasn't anywhere near quick enough. The Blue's punch came in low and caught Caementum in its side. As it landed there was a burst of feedback-like noise, as if a microphone had been quickly swung past a speaker. The blow opened a thin crack in Caementum's torso, covering a small section where its ribs would've been. Caementum wasn't knocked backwards this time—the arc of the Blue's strike had swung upwards and into Caementum's body—but the resulting pain left me unable to think. I simply reacted, swinging wildly with the Stone Man's left arm. It barely connected with the Blue's shoulder, only knocking the Blue a half-step backwards.

"*Get it,*" Maria gasped. The realisation that we had landed even a weak strike of our own fired around our circuit like the world's hottest gossip; I knew an advantage when I saw it, however small. I stepped Caementum forward, swinging with its right; the blow only grazed the Blues head, the impact merely rocking it a little. The Blue hadn't come off its feet. I don't think those things can feel pain—perhaps only sensing injury, our human brains converting that knowledge into pain signals—but we hadn't 'hurt' it as much as it had 'hurt' us, and now the Blue was straightening and attacking once more. The air around us was choked with dust; particles fired out of ruined plasterboards, rubble and loft insulation, making it hard to see. It got into my eyes and I was temporarily blinded. "*Back it up!*" Maria yelled, and I did, trying to buy us some time and reset, to clear my fucking eyes, but retreating would only take us so far. We couldn't back the Stone Man up indefinitely; that Blue bastard would always catch up to us, and God help me if I wasn't feeling the absolute *last* thing I expected: exhilaration. Even through the pain, the feeling shot around our circuit like electric fire.

"*We can take it!*" I screamed, finally getting the crap out of my vision. "*Caementum's responding now, we can move—*"

"But *it* is fucked!" Paul yelled, and then pointed a shaking finger at the Blue. "And *that* thing is a powerhouse!" The three of us were backing up too, staggering in a loose line at a ten foot distance from the retreating Stone Man. Paul's arm was wrapped around my waist, and my hand was gripping Maria's shoulder. The Blue emerged through the dust cloud and yes, already it was gaining—

"*Incoming!*" I yelled. "*We don't have a choice!*" Then the Blue was upon the Stone Man, swinging again with its right—

Duck—

The Stone Man did, *beautifully*, moving so well that for one shining moment I knew—I fucking *knew*—that we were going to win, only for that knowledge to be blotted out utterly as the Blue's left arm swung up and caught the Stone Man's lowered head right in the centre of its face. Even remotely I felt the force move through the Stone Man's battered body, spreading and devastating its insides. We scattered sideways, or rather, Paul and Maria did, Paul dragging me out of the way by my shirt collar as the Stone Man staggered backwards. It fell with such speed that it would have flattened all three of us, passing through the point where we'd been standing only a moment ago. It smashed through another house, a bungalow this time, its Stone body perfectly destroying the building's supporting walls. The entire house caved in completely, blasting another cloud of dust and grit up and out into the air. It got into my eyes again and I had to drop back into Stone vision to see our attacker, but the Stone Man's sight was also compromised by the fresh mountain of rubble on top of it. I had the strangest sensation of using my hands to push and rise up awkwardly like a baby deer, only not under my control. Then the Stone Man's eyes showed me it was standing and moving forward, and that was when I realised Paul's thread was thrumming in a very different way.

He was using my gift to take control of the Stone Man.

I leapt back to my body, managing to clear my human sight just in time to see the Stone Man lunging up and forward out of the rubble in an explosion of dust. The massive form of the Blue surged forward and Paul lunged the Stone Man directly at its enemy in the worlds heaviest, messiest rugby tackle. Both Stone Men stumbled backwards, tangled up in one another; I didn't know if the smaller Caementum would be heavy or large enough to take down the Blue, but Paul's clumsy, barely-controlled attack seemed to land just right. The Stone Man's shoulder met the Blue's legs nice and low, getting at the Blue's centre of gravity. The pair of them smashed into the tarmac, the impact forming a shallow crater, but already the Blue was pushing its lipstick-tipped hands up onto Caementum's shoulders, trying to push it away.

"*Andy*," Paul gasped, dropping to one knee as his legs finally buckled with the effort, blood streaming from his nose. He didn't have to ask me twice; I took control, pushing Caementum's hands into the cracked street and awkwardly working its body up the prone Blue's torso as our opponent began to try to club at the Stone Man's sides. The impacts were heavy but again, not as heavy as the blows to Caementum's head had been ... at least until one smashed directly into the fresh, foot-long crack in the Stone Man's waist. That one buckled all of us, including the already-dropped Paul. He fell fully to the ground but there was no time to check on him; I had to complete my objective before the Blue got itself back to a vertical base. I had to keep it down, and that meant getting the Stone Man's knees onto the Blues' shoulders like a schoolyard bully. I needed greater control and flashed back in. The Stone Man's vision was now filled with the thrashing, writhing of the Blue, making the struggle feel like doing battle with a Stone octopus. For a horrible moment the Blue pitched sharply sideways, and the Stone Man was nearly thrown off, but I wildly slapped down with a Stone left arm and managed to solidly connect with the Blue's head. The force was so great that it drove the Blue's skull several inches into the tarmac.

Now, NOW, Maria's thread screamed, just as I finally managed to scrabble Caementum's knees up onto each of the Blues shoulders.

Hit it the way it's hitting us—

What the hell did that mean? I straightened Caementum at the waist just as the Blue's hands came up and around each of the Caementum's hips. The monster on its back was ready to push the monster on top away, ending our one chance at survival; I raised both of Caementum's hands into the air together just as Maria clarified what she meant, the image flying down her thread as clearly as an instructional video. The Blue wasn't just punching, its energy was punching *through* us—

Got it—

Just before I slammed Caementum's hands down as one onto the Blue's head, I tried to tell it what Maria wanted it to do.

Punch through—

We had to hit it the same way it was hitting us.

The Stone Man's hands hammered down, driving the Blue's head even deeper into the street. A spiderweb of cracks exploded around it in the tarmac. I felt our energy push beyond the Blues body—the connection between the two Stone Men was still there, to a degree—and I knew this blow had actually 'hurt' our enemy. We'd at least rattled whatever systems were working inside the Blue's unspeakably powerful body. Its limbs shook beneath the Stone Man, the integrity of the Blue's own energy damaged. *Yes!* The Blue's arm was swinging wildly; I flashed back into my body to run this remotely. I was in position now.

"Do it again!" Maria screamed, her thread filled with a heady mix of fear and bloodlust. The latter was appropriate; I tasted a coppery wetness run over my lips and realised my nose was now leaking blood too. I obeyed all the same, repeating the attack, picturing the Stone Man's strike blasting *through* the Blue's head as it wrenched itself free from the artificial surface and began to sit up. Caementum's pressed-together hands came down hard, the energy slamming out beyond the strike alone. *Boom.* Again. *Boom.* Again. *We were winning*, so much so that I nearly didn't even register the sound of another collapsing building coming from behind us. Another followed almost instantly after it, louder, then another, louder again, coming on much, much faster than any of the Blues ever had. The noise reached our street, a house exploding outwards so forcefully that its flying rubble smashed through windows on the other side of the road.

"Andy!"

One moment we were winning. The next, all hope was lost. The Blue's backup was here, the Stone military police arriving in the nick of time.

The Crawlers burst out of the remains of the ruined house and began to thunder up the street towards us.

***

Chapter Twelve

For Crying Out Loud

***

It was the most terrifying moment of my life.

My human body froze in sheer panic, even as I dropped one more desperate strike onto the Blue. I had to try and buy the Stone Man time to stand up unimpeded so it could defend itself against this fresh attack.

I tried to call *get back* to Paul and Maria but the sight of the Crawlers hammering down that street—streaming dust and cracking the tarmac with every step of their heavy, terrible feet—took my voice. All that came out was a dry squawk, but Maria was already backing her body up anyway, dragging Paul with her by his armpits, his feet limply pushing backwards to help. The Stone Man stood. I backed it up remotely moving it away and giving the Blue a hard stomp to the head as I did so. I imagined the strike driving all the way through the Blue's body like a piledriver from hell, *boom,* and our opponent's body twitched with the impact. I could do it remotely, it seemed, if not as impactfully as from the driving seat. Had we done permanent damage to the Blue? I thought we'd at least slowed it down, but at what cost to the Stone Man?

The Crawlers roared across the space between us and themselves and I staggered backwards behind the retreating Stone Man. The Blue was beginning to rise now, but more slowly than before, its movements juddery; *yes,* we'd damaged it, but we knew that even a damaged Stone Man was still an unfathomable force to be reckoned with. Then one of the Crawlers reached the Blue and lunged onto it.

The Crawler knocked the Blue flat once more, latched on, and began to feed.

Time seemed to stand still for a moment. Then the other Crawler was darting across the remaining space between it and the Stone Man as my head spun:

The distress signal, my spinning, adrenaline-and-amphetamine-amped thoughts babbled, *it wasn't what summoned the Crawlers to the Project. The Stone Man* was *calling for help. But it wasn't calling the Crawlers.*

It was calling for help because *the Crawlers were coming.*

I broke and ran to the side of the road, realising that my fight or flight instincts—which seemed to have been choosing fight until now—had decided, in my moment of terror, to very helpfully select the third option of *freeze.* The Crawler stampeded across five or six more feet before actually leaping towards the Stone Man like a enormous jumping spider. Time again slowed to, ironically, a crawl as the Stone Man's attacker seemed to hang impossibly in the air, it's disgusting multi-legged bulk flying towards the Stone Man with its limbs hungrily outstretched.

Amphetamines and adrenaline fired in what felt like every cell of my body as I moved on instinct. Paul and Maria's assistance came to me automatically down their threads, giving me what I needed without perhaps even knowing they were doing so. I'm almost certain Paul didn't. What I *do* know for certain is that complete focus fell for a moment. I waited until the last bizarrely stretched-out second before torquing the Stone Man's waist with everything I had, swinging a Stone right arm in a hellaciously forceful arc. It connected with the Crawler's side in an impact that sounded like a freight train hitting a boulder. The Crawler was knocked sideways, flying through the air. It smashed through a lamp post, sending up a shower of sparks, before turning a FOR SALE sign into kindling and staving in a house's front wall like a fist punching through a paper bag.

"*Come on!*" I yelled to Paul and Maria, just as the Blue kicked away the Crawler attacking it and struggled to its feet. That Crawler landed the wrong way up, but already it was beginning to twist and buck its humped turtle shell of a back to get itself upright. The Blue followed the Stone Man immediately, and gaining, whatever programming it was following overriding any instinct to press its advantage against the Crawler. The monstrosity that I'd knocked through the house burst free of the rubble and charged after us. My focus was torn between the two attackers, distracted at the fatal moment; I watched, helpless, as the onrushing Crawler leapt onto the Stone Man and knocked it to the floor, pinning it. The Blue would be there too in only a few seconds. I had to flash in, risk of greater damage to myself or not; the busy legs of the Crawler were too much to handle remotely. I flailed the Stone Man's arms in circles, a desperate and crude *wax on wax off* motion as I attempted to stop those horrible feet from latching onto the Stone Man's body. I tried not to mentally pull away from the Stone Man's sight, looking up at the horrible writhing underbelly of the Crawler and thinking of the underside of a giant, clawing woodlouse. The Blue loomed into my Stone view alongside it, just as the Blue's attacking Crawler finally got itself right side up and leapt back in, latching onto the Blue's back. The Blue reared backwards, writhing.

"*Thuppul,*" I heard Paul call, his words slurred. My human eyes looked to my left to see Maria holding Paul up—

The plug, Paul said in my head. *Pull the plug—*

I understood; if we pulled the plug on Caementum, same as we had a few hours ago, then maybe the resulting dump of energy would render the Crawlers dormant like their comrades at Project Orobouros. But we'd pulled it once already, and the blast had been *pitiful* compared to the one detonated at the Project. The Stone Man had barely even begun to recharge; would another blast even do anything? And Caementum would be shut down afterwards, helpless. Maybe we could restart it again, but it was *currently in a fight*—

The Crawler attacking the Blue wrapped all but two of its legs around the Blue's lower body and latched its foremost two legs onto the back of the Blue's neck. It twisted and the Blue fell forward, landing face down alongside the Stone Man. The Blue began to buck, trying to dislodge its assailant, and I realised that I could feel that same sickening disruption of energy that came with the Crawler's 'bite.' The thread between the two Stone Men was still intact, and I was receiving a second-hand experience of the Blue's internal energies being shredded. The feeling was much more distant, muffled.

Blanketed—

Maria, I said in circuit, wax-on-wax-offing with Caementum's arms and legs as fast as I could. My Stone vision watched the elephant-foot-tipped legs of the Crawler thrusting towards me as they tried to gain purchase. *I'm going to try to get into the Blue again—*

But the Red will push you out!

I want you to blanket the Blue, the Blue, hear me! Can you do it?"

Ye-yes, maybe! Give me a second—

I felt her blanketing begin to stretch, reach; it was becoming thinner around us, the sensation of being so very nearly exposed becoming more and more palpable. I wouldn't want to risk it being this way for more than a few seconds, but we *needed* those seconds.

Paul! Take over and keep the Stone Man's arms and legs moving! Don't let the Crawler get any purchase! Maria, I need you to tell me when the Blue is fully blanket—

Three! Maria's thread barked. She was counting me down; I felt her comprehend the plan. We'd already tried to get *into* the Blue.

But we never thought about getting *around* it.

T-two—

If we could cut it off from the Red that way—and that then meant I could control two Stone Men—then we stood a fighting chance.

One—

I dived out along between Caementum and the Blue as Maria's blanketing of the Blue completed, already telling it to take me deeper this time. As I shot through the outer layers of the Blue's self and dived deep within, the difference to the Blue's insides was immediately clear: our attacks—and the Crawler's current attack—had definitely done something to the Blue's internal energy. Before it had felt like being part of some devastatingly powerful computer. Now it was a computer in the middle of an earthquake. I braced myself for the push back, but it didn't come; the plan was working, but again Paul and Maria's thread communication felt so distant now as to be almost completely absent. I called to them, and a faint response came, growing closer, but I couldn't hear it. There was no time to calibrate and improve the connection; I was in here alone. Okay then; it seemed I didn't need them because I was again becoming aware of the sensation of limbs. The *Blue's* limbs, *yes,* I was fully feeling the Blue's limbs, now uninterrupted and unimpeded by the remote presence of the Stone Giant. I was slowly beginning to see through the Blue's sight now too, but it was hazy, remote, unlike being in Caementum's driving seat. I tried to move the Blue's arms; I could feel them but not move them. Why? Then I had it.

The Crawler had the Blue pinned.

I could feel how the Blue's arms had been seized and pressed behind its back, perfectly preventing it from rising or defending itself. The Blues legs, then, but to my surprise I couldn't even move the unpinned legs either. I may have been able to feel the Blue's limbs, then, but I had no control. The best I could muster was a feeble twitch of its legs.

The pinning Crawler latched its bite onto the Blue and the pain began to pour into me; pinned and uncontrollable, this Blue would not be our weapon; it was time to go. I rushed back out along the connecting thread into the Stone Man. I nearly collided with Paul's consciousness in Stone Space where he was manipulating Caementum's arms and legs. Not very well, it seemed; the pain was continuing here as now the Stone Man's leg was once again pinned and being eaten.

What are you doing, Paul barked. *Get back in there—*

The Blue can't help, it's pinned, and the best I can do is make the bastard twitch—

Andy, I told you, pull the fucking plug—

Can't you feel how weak the Stone Man is!? The blast won't do anything and then it'll be helpless—

Then—then—can we pull the plug on the Blue?

That wasn't an option. The only reason we even had a plug to pull on the Stone Man was because we'd put that energy-blocking plug there ourselves in the first place. The Blue was intact, and had never been—

No. That was wrong.

Paul, keep moving the arms—

I cried out, interrupted as Caementum's other leg was pinned; it was time to move. I went to leap straight back into the Blue before I pulled up short. I had a moment to register that my new plan had nearly just killed the Stone Man for good.

Paul, do you think you can use Maria's gift to pull the plug on Caementum *when I say?*

What, Paul's thread asked in disbelief. *You just said—*

Dispensatori fucking says so! Start counting to ten with me, both of you, and when you get to ten, pull it!

Hurry, Maria said. *Please—*

Count with me, one, two—

Three, Paul said, complying, *four—*

I flew back out into the Blue, telling the Stone Man to send me as deep as it could. If our plan worked, and we could get ourselves and the Stone Man out of this, we wanted it to have taken as little damage as possible. That meant Paul keeping the Stone Man's arms working, fighting until the last possible second. But if we didn't want it to get totally fried, the timing had to be right.

Five, I counted.

The sheer noise and pressure of the Blue's deepest internal processes made my consciousness feel as if it were being squashed flat. We didn't need control anymore; we just needed to be firmly inside its processes. Instead of resisting and trying to remain in place, I let that high pressure waterslide of information carry me around the Blue's networks. I shot around the Blue's system at the speed of thought.

Six—

Before, I'd felt for the snag on the weak point in Caementum's core functions as I washed by them.

Seven—

This time, already connected to the Blue, I also had pain to guide me.

Eight—there

The pain reached a crescendo and I now braced myself; it combined with the intense pressure that came trying to hold myself in place, but I knew I had arrived at the point the Crawler was latching on. I screamed to no-one, feeling the Crawler's bite shredding the integrity of the energy that held the Blue together.

The point at which the unfathomable power of the Blue was being leeched out. The chink in the *Blue's* armour.

Nine—

This Blue *wasn't* intact anymore, I'd realised; not only had Caementum banged it up a little, but the Crawler was eating holes in it too. It didn't have a Maria to seal things back up again either. Maybe the Red could help in that regard, but Maria had the Blue blanketed. It was on Airplane Mode right now.

Ten—

I felt the thread connecting the Blue to Caementum suddenly disappear. Paul's rhythm was good it seemed, doing his job right on cue and pulling the plug we'd placed in the Stone Man. I felt a faint wave of nausea and realised that was the Stone Man's weakened Detonation washing over the Blue. Panic suddenly gripped me; could I get back? Where was my circuit? Was I still connected to Paul and Maria, at least? I hadn't thought about any of that, and I couldn't feel them in here, especially not this deep. The solemn answer came to me right away:

It doesn't matter. Paul can use your gift. Maria too. Not as well as you, but they've absorbed some of it. They can make it to Coventry without you.

The weak point was right in front of me, still just about holding everything inside the Blue. I might not have been able to control the Blue— unless you only needed me to make it twitch like it was quitting coffee—but I knew from experience that fucking up a damaged Stone system was easy. You just had to reach out and twist.

Do your duty, Dispensatori.

Sophie.

The Stone Man was now ready, I knew, rendered dormant as instructed at the last possible second. It had to be. Surely its systems would be overloaded, fried irretrievably if active when the Blue Detonated right next to it?

I gripped the other side of the weak point and wrenched with all my might.

The Blue ... blew.

It's hard to describe what happened next.

I want to describe it as being *washed away*, or maybe *swept away*, but neither of those descriptors would be fast enough; they imply being carried off like a twig in a particularly rapid game of Pooh Sticks. That would only work as a metaphor if rivers moved at the speed of sound. I often wonder what would have happened were it not for Maria's blanketing all around the Blue. Would my consciousness have been propelled out into nothingness, perhaps even carried away as far as the Caeterus? What would I have seen? Would the energy of my Stone form have survived away from my body? Would my *body* have survived, perhaps spending the rest of its days in the vegetative state I'd seen in the back of the truck? I'm glad to say I'll never know. There was a burst of noise and then all I felt was Maria as my Stone Space form was caught by a blanket of nothing but her. The blanket quickly turned into a single thread and I was back in-circuit, snared like a fish on a line, although again, that metaphor only works if the fisherman in question was The Flash. Maria's voice dropped into my awareness.

—*cking worked, oh my God*—

I dropped back into my body as quickly as I could, feeling my wet clothes being pressed against my skin by the pavement and realising I had been lowered to the ground. For a horrible moment I thought I had gone blind, my human eyes ruined by the effort or by the dumping out of the Blue's energy. Then I quickly understood it was because every streetlight, every light that had been on inside some of the houses, was out. The stars were more visible.

I sat up. The Stone Man lay on its back, shut down by Paul. There was, of course, a perhaps equal chance it may have been massively recharged by the Blue's Detonation, but that would have meant Maria having to contain the energy in the Stone Man as its insides potentially erupted with power. My suspicions were that the effort would have killed her, especially as physically drained as she already was.

Paul squatted down by me, breathing as if he had just run a marathon.

"Are you ... are you okay..." he asked.

I patted his hand to let them know that I was, speechless as I took in the motionless Blue, lying on the ground. On top of it lay an equally motionless Crawler, it's colleague also spark out where it lay on top of Caementum. Overloaded and wiped out, just like its brethren back at the Project.

We'd done it.

We'd stopped all three of them.

Maria was sitting with her eyes closed tight; what had the effort done to her? Memories of Sophie flashed across my mind, but now the immediate threat was over I quickly became aware of that *exposed* feeling again. The influence of the Stone Giant, or the Prism itself, was close by in the world around us, and soon it would break through Maria's now-thinned and stretching blanketing—

The exposed feeling was lessening rapidly. Maria was doing something.

"I'm okay," she said, eyes still shut. "I just need to—*uhh*. Got it ..." She opened her eyes and offered me a weak smile. "Keeping us and the Blue blanketed at the same time was hard enough. Shifting it fully back onto just us ... it's just really fucking hard. And slow." She saw my concerned expression and patted my hand. "I'm okay, seriously. It just took a minute." Paul gripped my shoulders.

"Good job, man," he said, shaking me a little. "Good *job*, good job—"

The rushing, crumbling noise of falling rubble came from behind us.

All three of us jumped. We turned to see the barely intact ceiling of a ruined nearby house finally collapsing in a noisy cloud of dust. We covered our eyes and waited for it to pass. When the sounds of trickling debris finally settled Paul—with lousy timing as it took him far too long to think of something vaguely clever—said:

"There goes the neighbourhood."

The two of them pulled me to my feet and, as the movement brought a wave of light-headedness, an idea struck me. It was so big it took a few seconds to comprehend. I was experiencing elation. I took in the sight of the defeated Blue before me. We'd managed to blow out the Blue from its insides.

I had killed 'my' Stone Man.

I stepped forward, spat onto the back of its head, and threw my head back in a scream that carried five years of nightmares away with it.

I turned to Paul and Maria. They were smiling.

"We fucking got them," Maria said softly.

"You were blocking that shit!" I yelled at Paul, giddy, making the *wax on wax off* motions with my hands. "You were right in there and you just started—"

"Yeah!" Paul gasped, swaying where he stood, mirroring the same motion. We looked like a couple of simpletons but we didn't care. "And you *blasted* that son of a bitch's guts out like, like in *Alien!*

"And you caught me!" I yelled to Maria, punching and swinging at the air, *we'd fucking done it*, we'd won. "Like a fish in a net! *Slick!*"

"Yeah," Maria echoed, her tone still soft, quiet, but all I could think about was the enormity of what we'd just done. It was only one battle won in a larger war, but goddammit, it was a win we badly needed. And Paul could use my abilities with greater control now, too! The late Doctor Holbrooks was right. We were evolving, merging, exchanging energy even; *it really wasn't just about genetics.* Maybe someone's genes—or in Paul's case, genes coupled with a bang on the head that made you a unique battery—did set a person up in their initial bracket of abilities. Same as, say, Michael Phelps having the perfect body to be a swimmer. But you still have to get in the pool and do some fucking lengths to see what's what.

I felt alive, *alive,* and I embraced it. Wasn't that what I was supposed to be doing? Embracing being Dispensatori, for good or ill? I jabbed a finger towards Maria again, wanting to bring her into the moment Paul and I were experiencing. Then I saw her face and remembered that the reason for her quietness wasn't exhaustion.

She was, of course, still thinking about Marcus, trapped in a bubble. Of fucking *course* she was—

I noticed then how all of us were holding ourselves, arms pressed to our stomachs, standing slightly bent at the waist. I felt the ache there now, hiding behind the adrenaline. The fight had damaged us. We couldn't keep letting the Stone Man take punishment like that; it seemed to be passed on to us. Even in the darkness I could see the blood around Paul's mouth. I remembered that I had a matching, nosebleed-produced crimson mask of my own.

Then we'll save Marcus, I instantly thought, still lost in my moment of bravado ... but I looked at Maria and the sensation quickly drained. Time was against us, we'd had our celebration, and it was time to re-awaken the Stone Man once more. I wasn't too worried about that now we were no longer in a fist fight. The amphetamines were doing their job—

Shit. Sleep.

It had to be around 3am by this point, and even though Paul and Maria had dozed some on the way here, they hadn't actually had any real, restorative sleep. Ritalin was coursing through their veins and neither of them had any kind of tolerance for it; I didn't know if they'd now be able to sleep at all that night. How long did Ritalin last for? Hadn't the packet said something about extended release, too?

"I can't imagine what you're feeling," I said to her. "But—"

"Don't," she said. "Let's just get to the packs." She headed in the direction of our new Mercedes, miraculously intact and parked by the ruined lorry. "We'll have some water and then get that thing restarted. Physically my whole body feels like lead, but I'm absolutely wired mentally, there's no way I'll be able to—"

"Maria, listen—"

"I don't want a pep talk."

"Okay, I understand—"

"Everyone's dead," she said.

"Yeah," I said, confused. "It's fucking awful. It's—"

Maria spun to face me. Tears streaming down her cheeks.

"*No, Andy, it's worse than that!*" she screamed. "*Everyone in this country is dead and it turns out I could have done something about it!*" Her voice rang off the intact and partially ruined houses either side of us; she looked up sharply, hearing it, and spread her arms, as if to say *do you see?* "Where was I? Hiding in Europe! Five *years* we had to prepare; what difference could I have made?"

Now I understood. This had been a long time coming. I let her talk. "Imagine what Sophie and I could have done," Maria spat, "if we'd been working together? What kind of control we might have had? How many of these homes—" She began to turn on the spot, thrusting her fingers at houses, manic. "Would have people in them still? They're *dead*, all of them *dead*. We could have been ready for all this. We could have had the Stone Man under control and ready to go; we could have had enough control to risk flying it all the way to Ground Zero the minute the Prism showed up. *Linda* might be alive."

Don't say it, I thought. Then she did.

"*Sophie* might be alive."

That took any words I might have had coming, but Paul stepped up.

"You told me at the Chisel," he said, "right before Eric showed up. You said you thought the government had enough people, enough volunteers. And you didn't know what you could do."

"That's not an excuse!" Maria said, her eyes red. I believed that she meant everything she was saying, but the Marcus thing had finally broken the dam. "What about duty? What about *finding out* if I could help?

"You were a trauma victim, Maria," Paul said. "You went through something no-one should ever have to—"

"I don't care! And don't, don't—" She clutched her fists in the air by her head, screwing up her eyes. "Don't fucking try to *talk me down*. This? All this, that I'm saying?" She slapped her hand against her chest. "That's what's keeping me going! Whenever I start to feel like I can't take any of this, like *how the hell am I supposed to save the world, I can barely stand up*, I think of how I could have fucking done something about it all if I hadn't been such a coward and that means *I keep going.* So don't …" She breathed out, lowering her hands, opening her palms. "Just don't try to take it away from me, okay? Please. Don't baby me."

"We won't," Paul said. "Will we, Andy?"

"No, no," I mumbled. "No."

"… but can I say one thing?" Paul added.

Maria's mouth fell open, her head lightly shaking … but then she raised an eyebrow.

"… yes," she said.

"They gave me a lot of therapy for survivor's guilt," Paul said, brushing the damp backs of his trousers with his hands. "Didn't do a lot for me. But one thing they said stuck with me: apparently every study shows that self-compassion works better for motivating yourself, than berating yourself. *I'm not saying you're wrong*," he added quickly as Maria scowled. "If it's working for you, then its working for us. But consider this: maybe if you gave yourself a bit of a break, maybe our circuit could work even better. Smoother."

"Sure. Whatever." Maria began to walk towards the car. "Water," she said, and that was that.

"Fucking hell," I muttered, watching her go. I pictured myself trying to carry out this mission knowing that Sophie was in a bubble, even if we were estranged like Maria and Marcus. It was clear that, at least on Maria's part, they weren't separated because of a lack of love.

"I don't like being a hypocrite," Paul grunted, waving off my move to help him as he stumbled a little on the spot. "Holding court on whatever reasons someone might have to keep …" He shook his head. *"Ah, not my place. That's what I mean. I just care, that's all. Maybe she needed to hear that."* As the endorphins released by our victory began to settle, I realised I had a headache, a bad one.

"Christ," I said, beginning to shuffle up the road after Maria. My stomach hurt on the inside as if it were cramping, but it was nothing compared to the ice pick that was beginning to slide into my brain. Paul fell into limping step alongside me, grimacing.

"Painkillers in the packs," Paul said. "We'll all take them."

"The Crawlers," I said. "They don't work for the Stone Men, then. They *eat* them."

"Yeah. I wonder if they're the main point of the Barrier, in fact."

"… you think?"

"They only got through, by the looks of it, because Eric punched a hole in the thing. Yes, it was sealing over again, but was that a weak spot? As soon as the Stone Man was shut down at the Project—weakened, but maybe bleeding out enough to give them a signal to follow—up they pop. Easy kill. But they got shut down when Caementum went *ploof.* Okay. Then we three arseholes turn up, fill the Stone Man's juice back up some—but still not to full strength—and surprise, here they come, following a weak signal."

We walked in silence. I thought about the Prism, the Red. Carrying out their farming process to create more Stone Men. Cattle in a fenced-off enclosure now, slow and strong.

Then wolves got the scent of a weakened prey. Of a *vulnerable* Stone Man. Even the Blue, when the Crawlers had fed upon it too, had been hurt.

The idea was startling. I'd entertained the theory that the Stone Men were the next step above us in the food chain. It never occurred to me there might be something above *them.*

"But if the Barrier protects the Stone Men," I said, "while they work on their Harvest, then does that mean that those things coming here ..." I pointed back up the road at the immense shadow that was the cluster of dormant, impossible bodies. I didn't like the sight of the Stone Man lying under one of those monstrosities. "Does it mean they're just the start of ..." I trailed off, thinking: *what happens, then, when there are hundreds of Stone Men under the Barrier? Do the Crawlers start to come and never stop? Stronger ones? Or maybe so many that they don't need the Stone Men to be vulnerable?*

"Ugh," Paul said. "I don't like that idea."

I noticed that the streetlights were shining in the distance; the ones around us still hadn't come back on, but I thought they would shortly. They had after a few minutes when the Stone Man's Detonation caused the Big Power Cut.

"Look at that," I said to Paul. "The Blue's Detonation would have been more powerful, but it looks like it didn't carry that far. Why do you think that is? It couldn't have been Maria containing it, surely?"

"No. No way she does that and survives. Not now. She can barely stand."

I looked back to the motionless Crawlers and Stone Men in the road. If the Blue's Detonation had gone nationwide, wouldn't it have fried the other Blues too?

"Do you think maybe the Blue stopped it, then?" I said. "Some kind of dying-breath containment protocol to protect the others?"

"Maybe," Paul said. "Probably had to be, really. It's the only thing I can think of. Damn shame, if so. A full-scale, fully-powered-up Blue Detonation might have made our job a lot easier."

Blue Detonation, I thought. Sounded *like a porn film.* It was a stupid joke that the old Paul would appreciate; I opened my mouth to say it and stopped. I saw Maria's silhouette stumble ahead of us in surprise before I realised another vision was coming. The street around me became hazy as the second sight of an overlaying image began to arrive. But the twelve new Blues had only just started walking, and this couldn't be a vision from one of the now-reduced-to-five original Blues; like the mass vision that had arrived earlier, this was stronger, breaking heavily through Maria's protection. This was also something new entirely; we weren't convulsing or feeling even a little nauseous. Ahead, Maria spun around to face us.

"*Eric,*" she gasped, and she was right. This wasn't the Stone Men's doing, and the fingerprint of Eric's energy was all over it. I hardly knew the man and yet it was as familiar, as evocative, as the smell of fresh-cut grass. Somehow, this was coming from our friend.

Eric was sending us an image.

"What is—" Paul stopped dead as the image began to clarify. The elation we felt—that Eric was still alive and sending us something—vanished as the image clarified.

He was not sending us good news.

Paul slowly sat on the kerb, all the air draining from him. I wanted to do the same, my legs feeling as though they could no longer support me.

"Oh ..." Maria said. "... oh *no.*"

I would not, of course, find out until later what happened to Eric and Edgwick. What they went through after they rode away from us that morning. Their bravery, I believe, is the reason I am alive to tell you *my* story.

They will always, always have my respect.

Excuse me. I need to take a break.

Actually, I'm gonna stop for tonight. I've been at this for hours. I'm going to make something to eat and pick this up again tomorrow.

***

Interlude

France, Now

✱✱✱

The view through Straub's living room window showed dark skies that were only just beginning to spit rain. The long-threatened storm of the day was finally starting now that evening was here.

Nathan hadn't moved from his seat since he'd pressed play, other than for one trip to Straub's bathroom to relieve himself. Around lunchtime, Straub had brought him a tray of cucumber sandwiches. Eating them had been an effort. Not just because he hated cucumber, but because he had no appetite.

Nathan paused the MP3 player, realising how dry his throat was. Where was Straub now? He stood and moved to the doorway.

"Hello?" he called into the depths of the house. Now he had mentally come up for air, he realised he could smell cooking. Straub emerged from the kitchen.

"How are you getting on?" she asked.

"Good," Nathan said "Well, I mean; good as can be."

"It gets worse," Straub said.

Nathan had guessed that.

"I just need some water, please?"

"No problem," she said. "And dinner will be ready soon. Do you like nut roast? Your timing's good if you're taking a break, it'll be ready in five. I've been trying out veganism for a while, but I don't feel any healthier. I'm starting to think it's a load of *B*, if you pardon my French."

"Nut roast is fine. Thank you. By the way: the audio quality of the tape. It's really bad. Hard to hear."

"There's a reason for that. I'll tell you after. I've made up the spare room," she said, turning for the hallway. "But we'll have to leave early in the morning."

Nathan felt a little thrill of excitement; he'd been so lost in the tape he'd forgotten the upcoming occasion. He'd never been to the actual ceremony itself.

"You … really go to the ceremony, then?" he asked.

"Yes."

"Every year?"

"Oh yes."

"Aren't you … seen?"

"You really think I'll be spotted amongst all those people? When I'm disguised? Nathan, they aren't even really *looking* for me. I was always a team player."

"So how did you get … dispensation, as it were, if you have to go incognito? It's hard to get access at the best of times, is my understanding. Money has to change hands."

"I have a hook up. One that costs me nothing."

Nathan held up the MP3 player

"Listen," he said. "I need to thank you. For all of this. I just can't believe I'm …" He shrugged. "Thank you."

"You're welcome. Is it what you wanted?"

"There are … answers, at least."

"But closure?"

Nathan didn't answer.

"I warned you. Let me get you that water."

She turned to the kitchen, back straight, but Nathan called:

"Do you have a tape of Eric?" he asked.

Straub paused in the kitchen doorway.

"I'm afraid not," she said eventually. She didn't turn around. "Like Andy, I was told later what happened."

Straub walked away along the darkened hall.

***

Part Three

Eric and Edgwick

Chapter Thirteen

Riding Bitch then Just Bitching, Making New Friends on the Road, and Eric's Bad News

***

Eric and Edgwick. Earlier the same day.

The Horns had sounded twice since Eric and Edgwick had set off.

The sound had of course been deafening, unpleasant, and startling. Thanks to Edgwick's nerve and riding skills the sudden, impactful noise hadn't caused any major problems for the two men. It was the first *vision* that caused all the chaos.

They'd been making good, relatively steady progress for about four hours, Edgwick handling the bike like an experienced rider. On a straight run, Eric surmised—based on his many years as a road musician—they would have been somewhere near Preston by now. He calculated that the constant winding around dead motorway traffic had added about an hour onto their ride, and now they had to be around or nearing the northernmost end of the Lake District. Even so, the delay was small and, as much as Eric hated to admit it, that was down to Edgwick's riding.

A lot of the motorways had been as bad as Eric had feared.

He'd been unable to observe them from Colin's helicopter during their flight from Aiden's house. The miles of smashed and twisted traffic below them had been too much to look at. Too perfect an indicator of the sheer scale of death left by the Barrier's speed-of-sound passing.

Now, riding through it at ground level, the experience was infinitely worse. Nearly every still-intact windscreen was filled with dried redness, the air reeking of leaked petrol and the lingering smell of burnt-out engines. The stench even reached Eric's nostrils through his helmet, a helmet that, mercifully, wasn't full of crusted, burst and desiccated flesh. By the grace of God, they'd found a second clean helmet for Edgwick; some poor soul had clearly pulled his broken-down bike onto the hard shoulder and placed his helmet on his seat, waiting for help to arrive. The Barrier had arrived first instead. They'd even seen the occasional dead body, though Eric expected this. There would have been Stone Sensitives on the road that had survived the Barrier's passing. They'd been killed instead by hitting the instantly driverless cars around them.

The pair of riders hadn't been talking much, Edgwick only communicating to let Eric know he was about to make a sharp turn or similar.

Then the vision—the first since they'd left—came.

Since his boosting, Eric found he had a head start on knowing when a vision was imminent, even when he'd been under Maria's de-sensitising, heavy protection. He'd had maybe a second to know something was up, like smelling smoke a moment just before realising your hair is on fire. Now he noticed his skin breaking out in gooseflesh a good ten seconds before the vision really hit, a longer warning before the whole world tipped sideways.

The problem—when disaster finally struck—was one of complacency.

Eric got the mental head start on this incoming vision, and hadn't even worried; instead he just gently tapped Edgwick on the shoulder..

"*Uh?*" Edgwick called.

"*Vision incoming,*" Eric told him.

"*Wha'?*" Edgwick said, finger aggressively tapping the side of his helmet.

"*Vision,*" Eric called. "*Incoming.*"

"*Shi—hold on!*"

Eric heard the urgency in Edgwick's voice and had a flash of a second to understand, to his horror, that which Edgwick already did: Eric had already become used to Maria's influence removing the worst of a vision's impact. He had forgotten that they were no longer under the circle of Maria's protection.

Edgwick had that second to squeeze the brakes a little, reducing their speed rapidly without jamming them on and losing control of the bike. The vehicle was still moving as the vision hit them full force. Their bodies, of course, locked up as it did so, and Edgwick's hand clamped violently on the brake.

The bike skidded to an immediate, screeching halt. Momentum, of course, didn't.

Eric would later be grateful, in a small way, for the vision's disconnecting effect; it separated his mind from most of the crash's impact along with the pack he had strapped to his back. They'd made the decision to decant most of the contents of Edgwick's pack into the bike's large twin panniers along with the folded pack itself. The rest had been squeezed into Eric's pack and placed onto his back. As both twitching, fitting men were thrown over the bike's handlebars—Eric faintly aware of the sound of the Triumph slamming sideways onto the tarmac and scraping into a skid—he had time to crazily think *the paintjob, the chrome* before he collided, back first, into the still-intact windscreen of a burnt-out people carrier. The majority of the glass held, cratering but not collapsing, and Eric bounced onto his stomach on the car's bonnet, continuing to fit. The road disappeared and the vision fully came to him: an elderly-looking man. Eric was aware that he couldn't breathe—his wind taken either by the impact or the vision itself—but he found himself wishing, for the first time, that the vision would keep going.

He knew the pain would come when it stopped.

The worst of it, to his amazement, seemed to be in his neck. As the vision faded the pain at least didn't get any worse. His stitched-up shoulder was barking too, jarred by the collision, and his breath came in tight wheezes that simply weren't bringing in enough air. He crawled off the bonnet, amazed by his good luck—his injuries seemed minimal—and needing to find Edgwick. There was no way his associate would have had as fortunate a landing. Edgwick had slowed the bike but they'd still been moving fast enough for them to go over the handlebars. Eric slid off the car's bonnet and his legs buckled, dropping him to his backside. He rolled to his side and stood, trying to see where—

Edgwick lay a few feet away in the road, face down.

He wasn't moving. The back of his right shoulder was sitting up in a manner that it shouldn't. His rifle, previously slung across his back as he rode, was lying several feet away from him.

"*Edgwick!*"

Eric hobble-ran to the fallen soldier, but already Edgwick was stirring. He lifted his left arm and began to push himself up. Then he screamed and fell back down. Eric crouched, breathless and wincing, moving to help Edgwick up. The soldier stopped him immediately, his wide eyes latching onto Eric through the visor of his helmet.

"Don't! Don't touch me!"

Eric withdrew his hand as if Edgwick was on fire.

"I won't, I won't. Tell me what you want me—"

"I think my shoulder's ... out," Edgwick grunted. Eric looked at the ugly bulge under the jacket that they'd taken from the service station.

"I think it is."

"And—*aah*—I think that arm's—*fuck!*" He yelled out in pain and frustration but laid his helmeted head back down on the tarmac. "Okay. *Shit*, put your hand on my shoulder." Eric didn't argue, gently resting his hand and stump where Edgwick had instructed. There was a large bulge there, hard and bulbous, and the feel of it made Eric's stomach turn over. "You gotta push it, hard and fast, like a thrust. Don't tell me when you're gonna—"

Eric pushed. Edgwick screamed, the big man's feet drumming on the road as his voice hit a high register Eric wouldn't have thought possible.

The bulge didn't move. Eric stopped pushing.

"*Jesus Christ!*"

"You told me to push!"

"*Like you fucking mean it! You have to—*"

Eric violently pushed Edgwick's shoulder and the soldier barked like a frightened dog. Edgwick's shoulder dropped back into place with a sickening, muffled *clump*. Edgwick's cries stopped but his breathing turned into a hitching, wet sound as his whole body started to twitch. Eric waited for it—and the rapid and creative stream of curse words—to pass.

"*Good ... man,*" Edgwick said eventually. "*Ohhhh, Christ,* Jesus Christ. Okay. Okay. Turn me over. Roll me over my good shoulder."

"But you said that arm—"

"I can move it but can't push with it. Think it's a break. Just roll me over quickly."

Eric did, using his stump at Edgwick's back and his remaining hand under Edgwick's good shoulder. The big man turned over like a roll of dense carpet, making *ah ah ah ah* sounds all the way until he was lying on his back in the road. He carefully lifted his left arm onto his chest and caressed it with his right hand. Eric could see now how the material of his jacket was shredded where it had been dragged along the road; the heavy material had perhaps protected the rest of his torso and arms from as bad an impact as his legs. The bottoms of his black Chisel-issued combat trousers from the knees down were chewed up, but the shins underneath were mercifully intact. They were, however, scraped and oozing blood.

"We'll have to disinfect your legs," Eric said, relieved that Edgwick was alive. Then the thought of antiseptic and necessary medical intervention made him think of Harry again. He'd done well with that so far today, keeping thoughts of his all-too-brief friendship at bay. Edgwick's helmet twitched briefly up and down in agreement, the helmet that Eric realised had probably saved the soldier's life. "Is there any in the first aid k—"

"Get it," Edgwick said, closing his eyes and groaning.

"Now? Don't you need a second?"

"Do you want to get to the kid or not?" Edgwick grunted and dropped his right hand back to the floor, leaving his left arm on his chest. "Left arm's broken. *Fuck!*"

How would they treat that; a splint? A sling? They had bandages and heavy painkillers and Edgwick was field-trained—

It hit him then. Even if the Triumph had survived the relatively slow-speed crash, Edgwick had a recently dislocated shoulder and a broken arm. Eric only had one hand. They could no longer ride a motorbike. They would have to walk through the clogged motorway—and if Edgwick could—find a car, and drive to Aiden's.

Their journey had just become significantly longer.

Aiden.

Eric slapped at the road with his remaining hand in frustration. He carefully removed his pack from his back, wincing, and began to root through it for the first aid kit. If he had been trying hard not to think of Harry, his efforts to avoid thoughts of Aiden had been constant and torturous. The ride had been interminable, boring enough in itself. But tormented with fear and frustration as he was, and knowing that, at any minute, one of the newborn Blues at the Prism could start walking the boy down. Eric had to remind himself how many hours of walking it would take to cover that distance, how much ground he and Edgwick had been gaining. Each time the Horns had gone off he'd used his boosted ability to carefully listen to the Caeterus.

These long-range checks had been very quick, darting-in-and-out affairs, using the low-frequency threads that he'd discovered since his boosting. Even though those threads were relatively quiet—low-traffic in terms of communication compared to the others—he didn't want to stay in there any longer than necessary. Yes, he could free himself from a bubble—at least, he *assumed* he could, and from the inside at that, having only opened the not-yet-hardened Barrier so far—but it wasn't worth taking any risks if he didn't have to. He'd been trying to glean any hint of whether the Blues standing at the Prism had started walking in Aiden's direction yet. He hadn't found out for *absolutely* sure, but he thought they hadn't. Much clearer was the creation and assembly of more and more new Blues in Coventry. Not good.

He'd tried a few times, unsuccessfully, to see if he could communicate with Maria, but he'd quickly abandoned that idea. She was too well hidden, and he soon realised that getting through might possibly draw Stone attention to his friends. He'd noticed how all these long-range Stone shenanigans seemed to get a little easier the further they rode. He'd initially thought it was due to his repeated efforts acting as a kind of practice, but his gut was beginning to tell him it was because of moving closer to the Prism. He'd been wondering what he'd be able to do once they reached Aiden's, right outside of Coventry.

It would now take them considerably longer to find out.

His hand clenched around the first aid kit's bottle of antiseptic, restraining himself from flinging it into the sky in a fit of rage.

***

"You ever get jealous?" Edgwick said.

They'd been walking for around an hour, and this was the first thing either of them had said. Edgwick, limping silently along, his broken arm bandaged up as tightly as possible and hanging inside a makeshift sling. Eric, lost in his worries about the boy and generally reluctant to talk to one of Straub's lot. Edgwick might only be an underling, someone who'd joined the army to serve his country and simply wound up on the Stone side of things. But he'd still been part of it. Still been part of the cover-up that had taken Eric's sister's life. Eric wasn't so sure how he felt about it all now, he still didn't like Straub, and Edgwick had been part of her inner circle. Eric knew Edgwick wasn't a Private; the man held rank. He may have followed orders, but he'd given them too.

But, he thought, *you're now in a foxhole together, like it or not. So—*

He cut that thought off.

They'd made slow progress along the motorway, walking between the miles of twisted, burnt-out vehicles. Only now were they approaching an off-ramp. Using a car would be pointless here. They'd be changing vehicles every twenty feet. The landscape either side of the road barriers—when they could see it clearly through the ragged late Autumn trees—was a bland, washed-out display of brownish-green and empty fields, interspersed with the odd industrial building. Edgwick had figured out a new route that would take them the rest of the way to Aiden's via the less-congested A roads—essential now they planned to recommence their journey via car—but they would have to get to those roads first, and away from the motorways in order to reap the benefits. Eric knew losing the bike would mean a slowdown, but now he understood the crash had truly devastated their speedy progression.

"Jealous of what?" Eric asked, his hand going to his aching neck. Painkillers had helped only a little.

"The others," Edgwick said, squinting as he looked at the Barrier turning above them, separating earth and sky. "Andy and co. You and I are just bog-standard Targets, pretty much, even if you can hear things or whatever." He paused. "Well, I suppose you're a bit tasty now you've been boosted. But it's the other three that are having all the alien contact. The cool kids are the ones driving the Stone Man."

"I don't know if *bog standard* is right," Eric said. "No offence, but … speak for yourself, you know? I got us through the Barrier and back. You're, what? TIN?"

"Damn," Edgwick said. "Once a grunt, always a grunt."

Eric let out a snort before he could catch himself. He didn't want to start bonding with Edgwick even a little, but that had tickled him.

"Better that," Eric said as they passed a bus. Its windows were blocked with dried red gunk. "Than the alternative. Or at least better if we can do something about *that*." He gestured to the Barrier. A question struck him: if they couldn't affect any change, and the Stone process continued unabated, would he still consider himself lucky? Spending the rest of his life effectively on the run under the Barrier?

"And if we can't?" Edgwick said, as if reading Eric's mind.

"Then … I suppose … we try to slow down the Harvest at least."

But what kind of a life, Eric thought, *would that be?*

"Oof," Edgwick said. "*Harvest.* I hate when people call it that. Can you pass me my water, please?"

Eric stopped and shucked off his pack before fetching Edgwick's bottle and handing it over. They'd had to leave Edgwick's pack. The soldier couldn't carry it anymore, so they'd decanted as much of its contents as they could into Eric's. Eric waited with his hand out to take the bottle back, unsure if Edgwick's reset shoulder would struggle with the bottle's one litre mass.

"I'll drink and walk," Edgwick said, grimacing a little but otherwise okay. They fell back into step.

"I can't think of a better word," Eric said, "than Harvest. I grew up around farmland, you know. Well, until we moved. And we didn't have one of our own. But I was familiar with that life, what was involved. Knew a lot of farm kids. I found myself thinking about that stuff all the while I was holding that bloody Barrier open; about what the Barrier is, what it's supposed to do."

"Yeah?"

"Yeah. And I think it's kinda like crop rotation. With us as the crop."

"Go on."

"Well, maybe not crop rotation, but something like it. Protecting the yield. Managing how it grows, I guess, or at least after you send the Empty Men in first to kill any threats. All the GALE people, like Andy. The ones that had shown they could flash into the Stone Men. Then they move to the next stage of the plan. Once they've cleared the decks of anyone that might be able to throw a spanner in the works." He gestured at the sky again. "Then you send the Prism, and *that* sends out the Barrier. *Whoosh.*" He performed the motion with his hand and instantly regretted it. The coldness of the gesture made him feel sick. "So what's left after that, underneath the Barrier? Nothing but Targets. Varying levels, yes, but only pure Targets to breed with one another. Anything that might water that down—all the non-Targets—gone. There's enough of us here to keep the crop going, but plenty for them to comfortably come and keep their own process moving. And no way for any genetic impurities, as they see it, to ever get in."

Edgwick raised his thick red eyebrows.

"Unless we've just made them nervous," he said.

"What do you mean?"

"Their whole system got screwed up," Edgwick said. "The Stone Man got stuck here, then we shut it down, then the bastard pretty much exploded. They're probably not used to that kind of thing happening. So maybe they decided to pull the plug. Put the Barrier in place to stop anyone from leaving and then just Harvest what they have until we're done. No more trouble. Stops the bad batch getting out of control." He shook his head. "Just my theory, and like I said: I'm a grunt."

Eric shivered. It was time to change the subject. *You're still in a foxhole together,* his mind reminded him. *You might have to save each other's—*

Fine. *Fine.*

"Where were you before you were at Project Orobouros?" Eric asked, almost through gritted teeth. The question wasn't to get any more of his once-desired answers; Andy had willingly explained anything Eric had asked. *Apart from the truth about the Targets,* Eric's brain whispered.

"Ground Zero," Edgwick said. "For the amount of military presence they had there, it was certainly a whole lot of sitting around. It was okay in the warehouse, but not being on the main site. I was glad to get moved over to the Project."

"Warehouse?" Once upon a time Eric's first question would have been *what the fuck were those two dead monsters you had on ice,* but now he'd seen them up close. Now he'd been in the presence of the moving Crawlers and knew all he'd ever want to know. Even so, Eric was still amazed to hear himself talking so casually about subjects he once would have sacrificed years of his life to obtain.

You did, that sad voice inside him said. Eric wished it would shut up.

"Yeah. There was a hangar over in Upper Stoke way, a backup location in case an Arrival occurred and fucked up the main site. Which it did, in fact, so some remarkable foresight from the British brass on that one."

"So that's what was in there? Vehicles?"

"Earth moving equipment," Edgwick said. "In case of another power outage, buildings being demolished. After the Big Power Cut, temporary as it was, the government decided to prepare for more possibilities. A worry after the Big Power Cut was that the Stone Men might somehow use a similar blast to take out anything with electronics, like our vehicles. So at one point there were even horses there as emergency organic travel to get them to the Project, the Chisel, Parliament, wherever." Edgwick smiled. "I liked the horses. That's why I liked working there."

"Huh," Eric said. "I can't see horses being much use if there's a load of Stone chaos going off. They're so skittish."

"These were *army* horses."

Eric snorted again.

"For a soldier," he said, "you certainly seemed to have a lot of soft postings in the last few years of your career."

Edgwick shrugged.

"Yep," he said, "and still not enough, and not soft enough. Gimme some lambs too. Gimme a guard post on a bloody petting zoo."

Now Eric actually laughed. He heard it, realised what he was doing ... and then the question came to him. He stopped walking, the growing ease he felt around Edgwick cutting off as if sliced by a scalpel. Edgwick walking a few feet further forward before noticing. The soldier stopped and turned.

"Hatton?" he said.

"Were you there?" Eric asked. "When they took her? Were you involved?"

Edgwick lowered his eyes.

"No," he said. "I was there for Henry Williams, though. When they took him to the Stone Man."

Silence.

"You've seen it too," Edgwick asked. "Right? Your friend. Harry."

"Yeah," Eric said, blinking rapidly. His shoulders dropped. "It was awful."

He began to walk again, striding past Edgwick. After a few moments, he heard Edgwick's limping steps begin to follow.

Eric slowed a little to let Edgwick catch up, and the two men continued along the off-ramp.

***

"*Shit,*" Eric spat, slapping at the steering wheel. "Fuel light's on."

Edgwick, sitting in the passenger seat, began to fiddle with the map on the tablet.

"We're good," he said. "I think ... yeah. I reckon there's a petrol station about five miles from here. Piece of piss. Don't worry."

"*Ah,* I just wanted to—" Eric slapped the wheel again. He'd wanted to push straight through. *It's okay,* he told himself. *This is gonna take ten minutes, tops. Edgwick goes in, switches the pump on, you fill up, then fuck off. Maybe you can do it in five.*

It was nearly 9pm. The sky—and the mostly unlit roads along which they were driving—were dark. If Eric had been tense before, now he was ready to explode like John Bates.

It had taken about three hours walking to reach a point where the blockages were few enough for a car to make a difference. Even after that, with a car procured, blockages and necessary car changes had meant taking another two hours or so to get to the A roads proper. Things finally started to open up after that, but another two hours later they were still not at Aiden's. They were, according to Edgwick, perhaps an hour away if they were able to put their foot down relatively uninterrupted.

They hadn't stopped since they left Maria, Paul and Andy that morning, and now the Citroen he was currently driving wasn't the only thing that needed refuelling.

This was the end of the third day since the Empty Men arrived. How much sleep had he had since then? A few hours maybe? Even that had been fitful and restless. Despite the incredible tension inside him, Eric's eyelids kept drooping, but he was behind the wheel. They couldn't stop for a nap, either. Not when they were finally getting close. Every time he felt himself starting to drop-off, he would summon an image of the kid's face. He'd even started repurposing an old Beastie Boys song, forming a mantra in his head to mentally yell himself awake: *No! Sleep! Till Ai-den!*

It had worked, for a while. Soon, he knew, it wouldn't.

The Horns had gone off again around 4pm. Eric had pulled their current car over to the side of the road so he could fully concentrate and use the low-frequency threads of the Caeterus. He simply had to do another rapid in-and-out check again or go insane. He hadn't had a vision of Aiden's face yet—or even a vision of a golden light, same as with Jenny's matching gold bubble—so he thought the kid was safe for now. But he still had to *know*. Using the threads had been easier still at that shorter distance to Coventry, and the limited information he scraped made him think Aiden was okay. He could tell a Blue was heading to a Target. The low-frequency threads weren't clear enough to tell which Target it was—out of the visions he'd seen that day—but he thought he got enough of their vibe to know it wasn't the boy.

"Left here," Edgwick said, snapping Eric out of his thoughts. The car's headlights illuminated a left hand turn in the hedge-lined and winding country lane, a pub called the Rose and Crown sitting opposite. The latter was a large white building with a sign advertising a BEER GARDEN and LIVE SPORT. It made Eric think about meeting Luis in the pub the day the Empty Men arrived. He thought of all the people that had been in the building then: the old men pub regulars, the bar staff, the glass collector. Fucking *Luis*. All almost certainly dead.

Eric turned left. The top of the petrol station's still-lit forecourt could be seen rising in the distance over the hedges, its pump prices sign standing out front. Eric accelerated, passing a Renault Clio that had crashed into the ditch along the roadside.

Soon after, Eric was tapping his foot impatiently while he filled the tank. Edgwick was inside the shop, having turned on the pump and fulfilling Eric's request for two large cans of Red Bull. The station was small, with only four pumps on the forecourt. The harsh lights in the roof were buffeted by small clouds of moths trying to worship their God. The pump clicked in Eric's hand. It was time to go.

"Edgwick!" he called. "Come on!"

He got back in the car and began to drum his fingers on the wheel, thinking about Luis again. Had Luis said he'd received visions during the original Arrivals? Eric couldn't remember, but if Luis had, then maybe ...

Edgwick still hadn't emerged from the shop.

What was he *doing*? Another minute passed. Two. Eric stared at the car's ceiling, rocking in his seat with impatience. Was there a toilet inside? The man wasn't taking a shit, was he? *Now?* They were so close. Couldn't Edgwick wait? Three minutes. Four. Eric peered through the windscreen and tried to see into the petrol station shop. He could see the back of Edgwick's head and shoulders. The soldier was moving around on the other side of a divider full of chocolate and other snacks, bent over and rooting around. They already had supplies, what the hell was Edgwick doing?

"Fuck's *sake*," Eric hissed, getting out of the car and slamming the door before striding across the forecourt. He stomped through the shop's sliding doors. Edgwick straightened up at the swishing sound.

Except it wasn't Edgwick.

It was a big man around Edgwick's size, easy to mistake at a distance for the soldier. Up close, this man looked a little older, but no less powerfully built and certainly a lot less relaxed. This man's eyes were wide and wild. The right-hand side of his forehead bulged gruesomely and one of his eyes was swollen shut. His forehead sported a long, deep wound that looked only recently dried. From here, Eric could see a little way around the divider; enough to see Edgwick's boots sticking out. The soldier was flat on the floor, his feet gently twitching.

For a moment Eric wondered how this stranger had got the drop on Edgwick, but then remembered the soldier's severe injuries. It wouldn't have even been a fight. Was Edgwick unconscious? Eric moved to help Edgwick but the stranger stepped forward, blinking rapidly, his head lightly twitching. In one hand he held Edgwick's pistol.

The soldier's rifle, Eric knew, was still in the car, but Edgwick hadn't removed his sidearm holster. Eric had removed his, much to his current regret. He found the shoulder holster a pain, even if he wore it on his non-stitched up shoulder, and now it was in the car, useless. The man was wearing a pair of blue jeans, and a t-shirt that would have once been plain white. Now it was covered almost entirely in dried blood. The man seemed to notice where Eric's gaze fell.

"Blood's not mine," he said. His voice was low, dull. Bovine. "Not mine. S'my mother's. I was taking her—" He blinked again, did the head twitch. "We were driving. She was talking, talking. *Never* shuts up. Then she just. She just. She was there one minute. Then." He froze, looking as if he had shut down for a second. Then he came back. "Gone."

"It's okay," Eric said carefully. It was clear the man had taken a severe blow to the head. Eric moved sideways, trying to see Edgwick's face behind the man's legs. "Is that your car up the road there? The one in the ditch?" Eric understood it all now: the Barrier had come through. Killed this lunatic's mother. The crash, trauma and head injury had all proved too much for someone who, Eric could believe, might need a few less head injuries than the average bear to go full lunatic. And he *was* a bear of a man: perhaps in his mid-fifties, overweight but stocky, his hair a crop of tight curls cut short. The stranger took a few more steps forward and Eric decided that, should the man take any more, Eric would risk a run for the car, and his weapons. Eric only had one hand and a still-injured shoulder. He doubted he'd fare much better than Edgwick in a fist fight against this unit, and Eric hadn't heard the stolen gun being fired. He doubted, therefore, that the man had thought to take the safety off; this was Britain, after all and the average Brit had never held a real firearm. If it took the stranger a few seconds to realise why they couldn't fire, if they realised at all, it would buy Eric time to get to his own gun.

But why had the stranger even attacked Edgwick?

"My car, yeah," the man said. "I've been ... struggling to think straight. Been thinking of ... moving from here but I just keep ... sleeping. Headaches and shit. Do you work for them?"

"What are you doing here?" Eric said, trying to avoid a very loaded-sounding question.

"Told you. Sleeping. Eating." The man's hand went to his head again. "Keeps going dark. Don't know where to go. Easier to hang around here since it all happened. Food's here. Toilet. Do you work for *them?*"

Hanging around here since it all happened, Eric thought. *The Barrier came through yesterday.*

"What's your name, my friend?" Eric tried.

"I'm Dennis, now *answer the question!*" Dennis said, suddenly screaming, wincing.

"No, I'm not with them, Dennis," Eric said, hoping that this was the right answer.

"Are you with this guy?" The man pointed the gun at Edgwick's body. He scowled. "You come together?"

"... no."

"Where's your car?" He looked through the glass. "That it outside?"

"Yeah. I was hoping to get some fuel."

"I think this guy's army."

Now Eric was very glad he hadn't changed into the military fatigues that had been in his pack.

"Army? You think?"

"Look at his clothes. And he had this." Dennis brandished the gun. "This was *his*." Dennis spat on Edgwick's feet. "*He* works for *them*."

"You mean ... the Stone Men?"

"The government. *They* work for the Stone Men. It's all a secret programme. They made a deal. Stone Men get us, the government gets to reduce the population and start over."

"Wow, that's amazing," Eric said. He'd always worried about sounding like this kind of conspiracy theorist. He was trying to sound casual and curious even as his hand shook. He had to get himself and Edgwick—if Edgwick was alive—out of there without either of them getting shot. "So you crashed, eh? That's rough, man."

"Yeah. Yeah," Dennis said. He made a strange choking sound with his throat, *ack-ack-ack,* before continuing. "Taking Mum out of the Midlands. Didn't want her anywhere near Coventry with everything going on. These bastards, these *bastards.* They would have fed anyone they could to those things. *Bastards!*" He spat on Edgwick again. "I was in the toilet when he came in. Heard someone. Snuck out. He wasn't even paying attention. Saw the gun, knew I was right to be sneaky. Knew he was here for me. They need us to feed *them*."

"Yeah," Eric said. "They do. The government want to get ..." Wait. What would the government want in return if they made a deal with the Stone Men?

"Technology. Get their technology."

"Yeah, the technology, that's what I was going to say." Eric said, trying to keep the tremor out of his voice. Dennis blinked a few more times, looking dazed by the effort of conversing. *How fast were you going with your elderly mother in the car, Dennis,* Eric wondered. An idea came: if he couldn't take Dennis down, maybe Eric could get rid of him by giving him the car. Dennis had obviously just been staying where the resources were while his mania ticked quietly away. Eric didn't think Dennis particularly *wanted* to be here. They could find another car if they had to, maybe in the nearby pub car park. "Where were you taking your mother, Dennis?"

"Kidderminster. Have to get back," Dennis said dreamily, looking around himself as if suddenly surprised to find himself in a petrol station.

"Did you not go looking for another car?"

"Car's *gone*," Dennis said, shaking his head quickly and wincing again, hand going to his wound once more. "Told you. Stuck here. We're in the countryside, no cars for miles. Pub car park's empty. I looked. Are you going to

Kidderminster?" It hadn't even occurred to Dennis, then, to look further afield for another car. The damage to Dennis's brain was perhaps even worse than he'd originally surmised. This wasn't just a crash and the trauma of losing a mother; perhaps it had also been affected by a vision, or the Arrival itself, or *something*.

"I'm not," Eric said, "but you see that car outside? That's mine. You can have it. You can drive it all the way to Kidderminster."

Dennis blinked.

"I can?"

"Sure."

"You don't need it?"

Not if it gets you out of here long enough for us to fuck off, Eric thought. "No," he said. "Tell you what: if you give me a minute to get my stuff out of it, you can be on your way. I even just filled the tank."

Dennis squinted and looked Eric up and down.

His eyes fell onto Eric's missing hand.

Shit, Eric thought.

"Where did you say you came from?" Dennis asked, eyes narrowing further and seeming to finally take in Eric's scraped-up appearance. "Were you in a crash too?" Dennis scowled at himself. "No, your car's outside... sorry, can't seem to—"

"That's okay—"

"Hey. Hey. Don't talk a sec."

Dennis's head slowly pitched sideways, giving him the air of an enormous wild-eyed owl. But those eyes never left Eric.

"Let me ... go get ... my stuff," Eric said, slowly backing up towards the door. This was about to go south, fast, and Dennis had a gun. Eric wondered if he was about to die in a Midlands petrol station. "I'll be right b—"

The gun came up quickly.

"You're acting very suspiciously," Dennis said.

"I'm just—"

"Shut up."

The gun in Dennis' hand started to shake.

"You're lying," Dennis said.

Fuck it—

Eric turned and bolted for the door, fear lending him wings as he charged through the sliding doors and bolted towards the car. He didn't look back, not even as he heard the doors glide open again behind him, heard Dennis grunting in frustration—

"Fucking *thing*—"

Then the sound of feet running far too quickly in pursuit. There was copper in Eric's breath already as he drew closer to the car, his adrenaline-fired brain reading the cues his ears delivered and guessing what just happened behind him: Dennis had tried to shoot, got frustrated when he couldn't understand why the gun wasn't firing—the safety, Eric's guess maybe correct—and was now giving chase. If Eric could make it to the car, the rifle was on the back seat, his pistol in the passenger footwell. Front or back? *Front or back?* The car was fifteen feet away, now ten, now five. He could pull the pistol out more quickly, one-handed, the rifle too long to pull out in a hurry and difficult to aim at speed with only one—

Something unspeakably solid collided with the top of Eric's skull. He stumbled against the car as he reached it, knocked physically and mentally off-kilter by the sheer force of the blow. Had Dennis somehow run astonishingly fast for a man of his size and punched Eric in the back of the head. The world went white and, when it came back a split second later, Eric's vision had doubled, the world displayed at a crazy angle. He heard the weighty clatter of a metal object hitting the side of the car, then the concrete and understood what had hit him: Dennis, with a perfectly aimed or just plain lucky throw, had flung the pistol at the back of Eric's skull. It had then bounced off and collided with the car, then the floor. Eric slid off the car's bonnet and dropped to the floor, momentarily stunned, his vision temporarily full of blurry whiteness. He fumbled blindly for the fallen gun. Which way had it landed? To Eric's left? If it fell onto the car, it must have flipped up and over Eric's head after impact, the momentum of the speedy throw carrying it forward—

Find it, find it—

Dennis' heavy footsteps were charging up behind as Eric tried to crawl forward, to expand the range of his blindly searching hand and stump as his sight of the forecourt struggled to return, flicking on and off, switching to white and back again. Why couldn't he—

Dennis' heavy, meaty arms fell over Eric's shoulders, furiously and mindlessly grabbing him around his chest, but Eric pushed upwards with his feet. The top of his head connected perfectly with Dennis' nose. The big man bellowed, releasing his grip, but this second impact on his skull made Eric feel as if a pickaxe were being jabbed into his brain. His vision turned full white and stayed that way. Eric fumbled again for the gun, his remaining hand against the car for support and bearings as his stump frantically and impotently slapped against the floor. He could hear Dennis emitting muffled screams that sounded as if his hands were over his face. Eric's hand crossed over the door handle. *The door handle,* the passenger door—

A heavy foot slammed into Eric's stomach hard enough to spin him around but he still managed to keep his blind grip on the car's doorhandle, Eric's arm remaining raised as his back fell against the car. He tried to hoof in air, his feet splaying out in front of him on the concrete as he weakly popped the door open, but then felt Dennis' heavy, sweaty, breathy weight settle down.

Dennis had dropped into Eric's lap. Now his thick fingers were wrapping around Eric's throat, pressing the back of his head into the car door.

"*Nuh,*" Eric gasped as Dennis' thumbs found his windpipe and began to squeeze. Dennis became an invisible monster in Eric's whitened vision, the big man's breath damp and hot. Droplets of the blood gushing from Dennis' nose sprayed into Eric's face with every frantic madman's grunt.

Eric swung weakly inwards with his stump. It connected with the side of Dennis's head, enough to rock the attacker's weight on his lap but not enough to knock Dennis off entirely or break his grip. Eric's exhaustion meant there was little power in the blow, and now his body was demanding air that wouldn't come. Still blind, Eric swung weakly again, and this time the strike acted as an unintentional range finder to Eric's sightless bearings. He felt his stump connect with Dennis' ear.

The ear. He immediately thought of Duckie, the bouncer at Barrington's, one of Eric's regular gig venues. Duckie had always liked to give what he called *fight tips,* and Eric had always listened. This one in particular had stuck because it sounded so vicious and easy. The image of Duckie's gleeful face swam behind Eric's sightless eyes: the short, heavyset man raising his chunky, calloused hands. Their fingertips were drawn into the upper pads of each palm, his hands curved into scoops—

Eric clubbed at Dennis again with his stump, catching the ear once more, but his body began to buck as it ran out of oxygen and Eric understood that Dennis was killing him. Eric let go of the car door as his vision began to flicker back in and out, knowing he would not be able to get to the gun, that Duckie, *of all fucking people,* was probably his best hope. Duckie, swinging both his palms inwards simultaneously, stopping them either side of an imaginary head before him—

Eric swung with stump and right hand at the same time, cupping his hand slightly; his clubbing stump made up for the lack of fully reliable sight, letting him know by default where Dennis' other ear was. He couldn't bring much power to that either, but if he could get it right, at the same time—

The strike was weak, cuffing ineffectually at Dennis' ears, and now Eric was going to be killed on a petrol station forecourt by someone he could barely see. The thought was so depressing that it just made him want to sleep.

No—

Eric gritted his teeth and swung one last time as hard as he could. His hand and stump finally slammed onto both of Dennis' ears at the same time.

Like this, Duckie had said, *hard as you fuckin' can. You bust the cunt's eardrums, every fuckin' time.*

The result was instantaneous. Suddenly Eric could breathe, his already-bruised throat opening up mercifully as Dennis' fingers flew away, but already Eric was turning his body around to slap his hand on the car, trying to find the door handle again. His flickering, returning vision allowed him to see the car as he leaned back and opened the door, Dennis screaming in agony behind him. Eric's desperate breath filled the footwell as he fumbled for the gun, seeing three pistols, blinking them back into one. He'd never had a concussion before, but from what he knew of them, he thought he had one now. He grabbed the gun on the second try and yanked it from its holster. He turned out of the footwell to face Dennis, who was on his feet and charging back in, screaming and red-faced, blinding pain insufficient to stop his madman's fury.

Eric pulled the trigger. The gun didn't fire.

The fucking safety—

Dennis fell upon Eric again as the younger, smaller man's shaking hand thumbed the safety off, Dennis flattening against Eric without finesse or grip and squashing him against the car. Dennis, now a lunatic seeking only to squish, to *press* Eric out of existence. The gun was trapped against Eric's stomach by Dennis's body as the bigger man shoved a hand against Eric's shoulder, then face, Dennis trying to push himself back to gain enough distance to start punching effectively. The move gave Eric just enough space to twist the gun's barrel into the fleshy mass of Dennis' stomach. Its handle pressed painfully into Eric's hip under Dennis' weight.

For a split-second, Eric thought of telling Dennis *freeze, there's a gun in your stomach, I don't want to kill you, please.* One close-up look into Dennis' eyes told him this was pointless.

Eric pulled the trigger three times, the world flashing white again with the concussive volume of the pistol's deafening discharge. Dennis bucked, his thick body remaining in place even as the bullets ripped through him and exited through his lower back. His weight, like himself, became instantly dead, and his body dropped back down onto Eric's. Eric began to shake, trying to push Dennis' body off him, but not quite managing it; Dennis' upper torso slumped sideways, headfirst, leaving his shoulder resting on Eric's stomach. Eric sat with his back against the car door, breathing hard and staring at Dennis' heavy corpse.

Eric had just killed a man in self-defence.

If it wasn't for Duckie, he thought, *he would have killed* you.

Yes, and God bless Duckie, but still: Eric had now taken a life, and not one already over at the hands of a Harvesting Stone Man. The thought was so big that, as Eric's returning sight of the world began to darken, he almost welcomed the way his body was quickly going limp. He was *exhausted*. He needed this unconsciousness.

But Aiden.

He tried to open his eyes, fighting against the dying of the light, but the darkness was so heavy and rushing in from all sides.

We were so close—

***

"—ton. *Hatton.* Hatton. *Shit.* Can you hear me? Can you—Eric? Hey, *hey,* good, good, easy. Easy."

Eric opened his eyes. Everything was still blurry. Someone was talking to him. Where was he? His head hurt like a *bastard,* and his neck and stomach felt like they'd been hit with a baseball bat.

"Can you hear me okay? Just make a noise."

"*Umm.*"

"Good. Wait a second, let me—"

The speaker moved away. Eric heard and felt the opposite car door open *car door,* he was sitting up against a car, they were at a petrol station, he'd been attacked—

"'g'wick?"

"Yes," Edgwick said, his footsteps moving back around the car, and as Eric blinked he found he could focus. He was seeing single vision again, at least. If he was concussed, he had to hope it was mild ... but he knew even that could still have major repercussions. He glanced to his left. Dennis' body was lying on its back. Edgwick must have pulled it away—with only one intact arm as well, Edgwick had to be strong as shit—and turned it over. Eric tried to lift his hand, but it came away from the ground strangely, as if lifting out of glue.

He looked down, confused for a moment by the sea of red that had pooled under his buttocks, his legs, his finger. Dennis' blood, leaked from his bullet wounds.

"Here," Edgwick said, squatting down and pressing the neck of a water bottle to Eric's lips. Edgwick's face looked relatively untouched. "Drink. Little sips, though," Eric leaned forward slightly to drink, his head coming away from the car. Edgwick whistled. "Shit. Hell of a lump back there."

"Fucker threw the gun," Eric said once he'd swallowed the liquid. "Got me right there."

"Mm. Choked me out from behind. Didn't even see him," Edgwick said. He gave Dennis' leg a light kick. "Sloppy mess like this getting the better of me. I'd never live this down at work." Eric watched the thick, dead limb wobble. *You had to*, he told himself, and then wasn't sure if it was the concussion or the knowledge of what he'd done that made him turn and puke the water all over the floor. The liquid landed on Dennis' congealed blood but didn't wash it away. "He was gonna kill me," Eric said, wiping his mouth. "He'd gone crazy. Barrier *sent* him crazy." He wondered how much of Dennis' mania came from just that; connection with the Barrier. Did he feel the Caeterus in it as it went through him? He'd put Dennis's lunacy down to trauma and a head injury, but none of them, not even Maria, had considered that some of the survivors of the Barrier might be mentally altered by its passing. How many of the survivors did they potentially have to worry about?

"You did well," Edgwick said. "He would have done you, then come back to finish me off." Eric just continued to stare at the water pooling on top of the dried blood, now beginning to mingle. "Hey," Edgwick said. "*Hey*." Eric looked up. Edgwick's eyes were wide and focused. "You did well, and you did right. You saved yourself, you saved me, and now we can get on with our duty. You understand?" Eric just blinked. Edgwick's eyes lowered. "Yeah. That's pretty much how useful the truth always is in these situations. I'm sorry, Eric. But when you remember this in the future—and you will—just try and remember I said that." He rooted in the pack he had brought back from the car. "Keep looking at me a sec?"

Eric did. Edgwick produced a tiny pen torch and shone it in Eric's eyes. Eric winced but continued to look.

"Mm," Edgwick said again. "Mild concussion, perhaps." It wasn't news, but Eric was too busy noticing something about Dennis' blood.

If it was congealed enough to resist water washing it away—

"How long was I out?" Eric said, lifting up his red palm and turning it sleepily back and forth.

"*Yeah,*" Edgwick sighed. "That's the bad news. We've been out quite a while, buddy." *Don't call me buddy,* Eric's brain petulantly spat on instinct. He looked at the sky outside the forecourt; it was still dark. "Eric, it looks like, uh, we went under and stayed under. Must be the exhaustion. We went into full sleep. I think you'd still be out if I hadn't woken you up."

"How lo-*what time is it?*" Eric said, instantly alert as the fear hit him. He remembered it then, flash-recalled the way a casual remark or a song can recall a moment from an otherwise forgotten dream: seeing the forecourt ceiling lights for a moment as the Horns had awoken him. His exhausted and concussed mind had simply been too far under to clamber up from the depths, before dropping under again and failing to make the connection.

The Horns. At least one Stone Man had started walking while he was out.

"Aiden—"

"It's gone 1am," Edgwick said. "I think we got here around 9pm, maybe 10, I don't know. We've been out for about three, maybe four hours."

The truth settled into Eric like mercury, racing around his veins, poisoning, toxifying. Four hours was enough time for a Blue to have walked from Coventry and Harvested the boy. But how long ago had the Horns sounded? Immediately Eric tried to reach for the low-level threads, but all the attempt did was make his headache worse. He tried again.

He couldn't do it.

Mild or not, his concussion was interfering with his ability to read even the low-frequency threads. He winced and Edgwick saw it; he put a hand on the younger man's shoulder.

"If you're trying to listen to them, I'm not sure there's much point right now or even if it's necessarily safe. You've just had some head trauma. At least wake up a bit first, man. Can you stand?"

Eric held up his good hand in reply, his heart now beating in his chest like a combustion engine, the need to *move, move* almost a full-blown panic. They'd fucked up, badly. Eric got to his feet, Edgwick helping as much as he could. The colours of the forecourt became a little washed out for a few seconds, but Eric's vision held. His sight seemed to have corrected itself some while he was out.

"Can you—" Edgwick began, but already Eric was turning on shaky legs and popping open the passenger side doorhandle. The weariness of it all settled onto his shoulders like a yoke: *okay, you had a rest, now put this thing back on. You're going to fail, but you knew that already. Explain to the kid's mother why it wasn't your fault when you get there, I'm sure she'll understand. Let's go—*

"Let's go," Eric said. "Get some painkillers from the pack." He slid down into the passenger seat. Edgwick snatched up the pack from the forecourt's concrete floor and ran around to the driver's side. Eric's pulse raced, each beat making his head throb as if it were being squeezed. Even as the sense of impotent fear returned and wrapped itself around his spine like an icy serpent, Eric still felt a sting of gratitude for Edgwick. He had to admit it: Edgwick didn't fuck about. When it was time to go, Edgwick went—

He caught himself and scowled, his hand going to the lump on the back of his head and imagining passing on that particular insight to Esther. *Isn't it funny, grieving mother, how soldiers are good people to have around when you're trying to get somewhere?*

And the response would come back:

Yeah? Well, you had one with you. So why didn't you get here in time to save my son?

Edgwick started the car.

"Will your head be okay," Edgwick said, "If I really put my foot down?"

"Do it."

"Good job this is an automatic," Edgwick said, swinging the car in a wheel-spinning, head-pounding half-circle out of the forecourt, "or you'd be changing gears for me."

Eric began to pray to a God in which he had long since lost any faith, the darkened hedges around them blurring into a night-time trench run towards Aiden.

***

They were making good time—they had to be less than ten minutes away from Aiden's place now—but Eric's fingernails were leaving marks in the solid plastic of his arm rest. All his desperate attempts at using the low-frequency threads to glean *any* information were thwarted by nausea and pain. The noise of the Caeterus was so loud in his head now they were close to Coventry—proximity did indeed matter, it seemed—but he couldn't focus the sound into an understandable message. The thwarted mental effort reminded Eric of trying to revise for his A-Levels while Theresa blasted goth rock in her bedroom next door.

Eric cursed Dennis, furious at what the maniac had taken from him. The rage had washed away any guilt Eric felt over the man's murder. The only good news was that the painkillers had taken the edge off the constant pain in the head. Eric had taken double the amount directed

"Hatton. Look."

Edgwick was pointing through the drivers' side window.

At first, Eric couldn't spot it. They were close enough to the M6 for the road lights to blot out the stars, so it took a few seconds to make out any details in the landscape below. And it *was* below, their road briefly devoid of any hedge barriers and elevated enough to leave somewhat of a view. "About five fields over," Edgwick said, his voice shaking in a way Eric hadn't heard before. He sounded excited. His finger poked against the glass. "Up *there*," he said.

Eric saw it, and his breath caught.

The expanse of darkened fields covered most of the view to the horizon, divided by the black, heavy lines of hedges. The break in the latter stood out, making it easy for Eric's eye to track from the busted-open gap to that which had broken through. Even so, it was only the thing's size that meant it could be picked out under the night sky. If it wasn't so damn big, Eric didn't think he'd have been able to spot it

A Blue was making its way across the fields.

It wasn't moving quickly—of course it wasn't— and eventually Eric could make out the edges of where its body began and ended in the dark. Part of the seemingly undulating, distant blob visually resolved into an arm, which meant that part was the head, and so on.

The Blue silently continued towards its quarry.

"You see? We're going to beat it," Edgwick said, turning to Eric with a grim smile on his lips. "We're going to beat that fucker there for definite. I don't think we'll have all that long to get the kid out, but we're going to be there ahead of it. Okay?"

Eric almost didn't dare believe it, but relief and hope were still blooming like a rose in the iron ground of a winter field. *The kid hadn't already been Harvested.* All his worst fears had been proved false, debunked when believing otherwise seemed utterly foolish.

"Oh my God ..."

"You need to start getting yourself ready," Edgwick said. "You have to be *ready*, you hear me? So do whatever you gotta do to prep, if anything. Get ready. *Be ready.*"

"I will."

But his head continued to throb, and now weeds also began to break through the snow in Eric's mind's eye. If his concussion affected his ability to use and interpret the Caeterus' threads, would it also—

Eric saw the dark farmhouse then, looming in the far distance as Edgwick turned the car onto the final lane.

"That's it, that's it!" Eric hissed, pointing. "That's his house!"

Light was glowing through the living room window, a faraway point of square brightness in the night. A less experienced person might mistake it for the light from a fireplace. Eric watched how, visible even at this range, that sickening golden light turned and breathed. His body broke out in gooseflesh.

Soon after that their headlights were lighting up the side of the building and Esther's face was appearing at the window, eyes wide, hair sticking up. The woman had clearly been through hell and wouldn't know for sure who was approaching her house. She would of course be hoping it was Eric, but it could of course be any number of survivors.

Edgwick swung the car into the courtyard, pulling the vehicle to a halt behind the Land Rover still parked there. Eric opened the door and leapt out the second the engine died, calling Esther's name and feeling light-headed in a way he knew wasn't anything to do with Dennis. *They'd made it*, and the bubble was still intact. That meant the kid was alive, and they still had time to try and do something to keep him that way. Eric could not fucking believe it—

"*Esther! Esther!*"

Before he'd reached the house's entrance, he heard a bolt being fumbled out of its catch, heard a key turning in the lock and a muffled call of his name emanating through the door, *Eric, Eric*. The courtyard was flooded with light as Esther threw the door open, wide eyes now streaming with tears. Her bathrobe-covered arms stretched out to Eric as she charged towards him in a state of utter disbelief.

"*Oh my God, you came back, you came back—*"

She reached him, fell against him and wrapped her arms around him, and as his head and equilibrium protested Eric didn't care. He was shocked by his own response: he clung to her in return, wrapping his arms right back around her and squeezing hard. Esther's grip was so tight he almost found it hard to breathe, her *relief* so palpable it was as if he could feel it through his skin. He thought *he'd* been going through it? He'd been moving, taking action, having agency. Physical pain, and a lot of it, sure. But all Esther had been allowed to do was sit here, helpless. Trying to believe that the stranger that had been and gone would not only come back but *survive* and come back. Eric knew she wasn't just clinging onto him; she was holding onto her son's survival.

The bathrobe she was wearing felt warm and soft against Eric all the same. For the briefest second, all the smells of the moment—those of disinfectant, leftover cooking, and the fabric conditioner in her robe— washed over him as he was held in a drowning person's grip. He imagined that this was what it felt like to come home.

But—as always—this home wasn't his, and he had work to do.

He savoured it for a whole two seconds. He could be allowed that much. Then he took Esther's shoulders to gently move her off him but already she was turning and pulling him into the house by his wrist. She turned to say something to him and saw his face clearly under the kitchen lights. Eric had managed to clean most of Dennis's blood off his face on the way, using the bottled water and some napkins he'd found in the car. His face was still scratched up however, and a bruise the size and colour of a plum stood out in the centre of his neck, right over his trachea. Further dark discolouration spread around it in a lightening halo. Esther saw all this and slowed—but didn't pause—their progress through the kitchen.

"Shit," she breathed, wiping her eyes. "What happened—" She looked behind Eric at the sound of footsteps in the entranceway. "Hi," she said, still pulling Eric towards the living room, still not stopping.

"Hello Ma'am," Eric heard Edgwick call. "I'm Toby. I'm here to help out."

"Can your friend," Esther asked Eric, ignoring Edgwick now in her desperation, "you know, do anything? He looks hurt too." They moved into the light of the living room, the glow there cast by both the artificial and sickeningly natural. Eric saw Esther more clearly now, her frazzled face sunken and red. In the twenty-four hours or so since Eric had last seen her, this woman had been helplessly simmering away. She'd gone from being frightened but strong and capable to barely able to stand upright. Hope, it seemed, was a ruthless captor.

"Not really," Eric said, before adding: "but I wouldn't have made it here without him."

"Eric?"

That was Aiden.

The boy lay on his back on the floor, his head resting at a painful angle against the golden bubble's side. He looked sleepy and Eric prayed that was just because of the time—it was around 2am, their final leg there more stop and start than Eric would have liked—and not because of a lack of food and water. How long did they have? The Blue might be as close as ten, maybe fifteen minutes away now. Would that be enough? Eric hustled over to the bubble, Esther following right on his heels.

"He's going to get you out, baby, okay?" Esther babbled. Aiden quickly got to his feet, trembling, belief bringing him all the way round, and Eric wished Esther hadn't said that. He didn't know if he could still do as they all hoped. "What did you bring?" Esther asked, terrified but eager. "To get him out, did they give you something, your friends?" She looked Eric over, clearly hoping to see a Stone bubble-bursting gun or similar. She looked to Edgwick, seeing the sling around Edgwick's shoulder. "Does he have it…?"

Eric tapped his forehead for Esther's benefit, not taking his eyes off Aiden. The boy was now on his knees on Eric's side of the bubble, hands pressed flat against its inner surface.

"You remember what I did before?" he said to both mother and son. "How I could do some, but not enough? My friends made me a lot better."

"Do it, do it," Esther said, physically pushing Eric by the small of his back towards the bubble. "Please." Eric didn't need to be told twice. He crouched down, hearing Edgwick emit an amazed *Jesus* at seeing a bubble up-close.

"Okay Aiden," Eric said, raising his own shaking hand towards the bubble. He'd had a close call himself the last time he was here, saved only by a team intervention from Maria and Esther. Such a rescue would not be possible this time. "Maybe back up against the other side for a second, okay?" The threads of the Caeterus were no louder as he drew in close to the bubble, even if he could no longer use them now. The Prism, it seemed, was the source; this bubble was unrelated to the noise.

Then try touching it—

Eric did.

This time—immediately—he *knew* he could open it.

Touching the bubble felt like a new experience. Before, it had been like having a key for the wrong lock. It would go into the keyhole, maybe even most of the way, but it wouldn't click home and certainly wouldn't turn. This time he felt as if the key had just glided all the way in without even touching the sides. All he had to do was turn it.

Eric began to imagine a hole opening under his palm and felt the entire bubble begin to vibrate. His awareness of the bubble's structural integrity washed through him—his awareness of his *command* over it—and he now knew that he could do more than open it.

He could destroy it.

"This ... this is going to work," he breathed, smiling. Up close, he could see Aiden's expression: frightened, hopeful, vibrating with anxiety.

"Do it," Esther whispered. Eric again pictured that hole opening, and again the whole bubble started to tremble.

Then Eric stopped.

"Hatton?" Edgwick said.

"... hold on a sec."

"*Do it,*" Esther insisted.

And yet, Eric didn't.

Here—in the moment he had pictured constantly ever since he left this house—he was presented with a quandary he had not expected. Yes, things were no longer the way they were before. But that meant in ways that were both bad and good. Jenny's bubble had taken everything he had to open up even a hole the size of a side plate. Now it felt like his boosting had gone too far the other way; to open this bubble, he realised, meant to do *nothing else* but destroy it.

"Hold on?" Esther said. "What—is there a problem, what's happen—"

"Just hold on," Eric said, concentrating. "Please."

Not the whole thing. Just a little bit. Just open a little—

The whole bubble shook, violently this time.

"*Dammit!*" Eric snapped.

"That was good!" Esther said, an extra edge was creeping into her already amped-up voice. "Why did you stop, that was working?!"

"Mum?" Aiden asked.

"*Please!*" Eric snapped. "*It's okay, we have time! Please let me work!*"

The room fell silent. Aiden's pleading eyes met Eric's.

Eric swallowed. He'd planned all this on the way here, but he hadn't expected this.

He'd made promises to come back and free the boy, made in this very room, and by God he intended to keep them ... *but if they had time, he had to see what was happening around the country.* Even in his near mania on the interminable drive to Aiden's house, Eric had been planning to *use* the bubble. *Free the boy, use the bubble.*

Now it appeared he didn't have the option to do both.

As soon as the bubble vanished, it would take with it Eric's last chance to know what the others needed. Sure, he could meet them on the A45 outside of Coventry, but what if they had to divert? What if one of them were killed? With Maria's gift occupied, Andy and the others were riding blind. Eric's head had taken a hit, and now he didn't think he could use the Caeterus' threads to find them in an emergency. *Yes,* his first responsibility was to Aiden. But if he had time to free the boy—and he still did—then surely he had to use the bubble first?

"Aiden?" Eric said. "I'm going to get you out of this thing. I just checked, and I know I can do it. What I need right now is for you to hang on for *one minute* while I do something—I need to use the bubble, okay, kind of like the way we did before—and then I'm gonna get you out—"

"Get him out *first*," Esther said, a nervous, death-stressed chuckle leaving her lips. Eric could hear the edge of a madness in it, one that might fully take hold if this situation wasn't resolved quickly. "Then use the bubble. Him first, him first."

"I can't," Eric said, not turning around. "I think we'll lose the bubble."

"I don't care!"

"You will," Eric said, "if my friends don't succeed. Then we're all fu—screwed no matter what. And I need to know if they need my help."

"*What?*"

"You promised," Aiden said. His voice was a whimper. Eric heard it and felt something inside himself change irrevocably. In that moment, he understood that his course would not be diverted by the boy's words. This had to be done. There was more than one kind of duty.

Then he would keep his promise.

"I promised and I'm going to—"

"*Get him out!*" Esther screamed, and now Eric turned around. She must have seen it in Eric's eyes—the man she thought would be her son's unequivocal saviour—because her mouth froze open.

"I *will*," Eric said, his voice shaking, his resolve unshakeable. "And I'm sorry that I have to do this first. But I *do* have to, and I need you to be quiet while I do it. Edgwick?"

"Yeah."

"Get the binoculars and keep an eye on the fields. Keep me posted."

"Roger," Edgwick said, immediately leaving the room. Esther's red face turned white.

"Watch the fields?" she whispered. "Why would he have to watch the fields?"

"It won't matter," Eric said, looking away as shame finally penetrated, colouring his face but not averting his intentions. *This,* then, was what duty meant. "Because he'll be out."

"*Is one of those things—*" Esther began, her hands clutching at her bathrobe's collar before seeing Aiden stiffen.

"Mum? What thing? What's that man looking for?"

Eric saw the knowledge hit her: she didn't have a choice and talking was only slowing things down further.

"Oh ... " she said, blinking back tears. *"Please. Just hurry."*

But Aiden didn't understand, Eric knew. All the boy saw was a man refusing to help him, his mother terrified out of her mind, and a stranger that had gone to keep watch for something frightening. The boy had to know, to some degree, that monsters were afoot that night.

"Mum!" he screamed, flattening himself against the bubble. *"Mummy! Please! Tell him! Make him get me out! Mummy! Mummy!"*

Esther gasped, covering her mouth with her bathrobe's collar.

"You're getting out," she muttered, moving close to Eric and squatting down alongside him. "Just-just listen to Eric—"

"I'm going," Eric said, "to put my hand over yours on this side, like we did before—"

"Get me out! You promised!"

"Aiden! Listen!"

"*Aiden Nowak!*" Esther yelled, her voice choking with tears. "*You do as you are told right now!*" Sobbing, glaring at his mother reproachfully, Aiden moved his hand onto his side of the bubble's surface. He placed it limply off-centre under Eric's just as Edgwick rushed back into the room. The soldier's eyes were alive. Frightened.

"You've got maybe five minutes, Hatton," he said, his voice tense and booming in the small space. It was clear how serious things were. "Maximum. Esther; do you have anything you need to take with you? Anything you need me to pack? You're going to want to move the second we get your son out of there. You're going to get in your car and you're going to head north."

"I-I packed a bag," Esther said. "It's already in the—while we were waiting—"

"Do you know where your keys are? Quickly, now."

"On the hook by the kitchen door—"

Edgwick was already turning to leave.

"I'm going to move our car out of the way, and I'm going to have your engine running," he said, adding just before disappearing out of the room: "Hatton, get a move on."

I'm fucking trying, Eric thought. But he was risking the kid's life, even after *Aaron—*

No. This was about making it so the kid might have a life after this; all the kids under the Barrier, all the Aarons, making it so they had a chance to *not* be under the fucking Barrier—

"Your hand, line up your bloody hand properly, Aiden!" Eric hissed, hearing the way he was speaking to the boy, but he was *trying to save the kid's life*— "Quickly, now." He was repeating Edgwick's words, he realised, as Aiden's palm lined up with and pressed against Eric's—

The living room vanished. Eric would have let out a sigh of half-relief if he had breath to let out inside Stone Space.

He hadn't known if he could do this since his injury. He hadn't been too worried about his control over the bubble; that was a physical, hands-on (or *hand*-on) kind of control. But he'd worried that, even with the inherent mini-router abilities of the bubble, his head injury might have stopped him going into the vision of the country as before. Now, he saw, the opposite was in fact true. The dark shape of the country below him was laid out in even greater clarity, the lights of Stone Sensitives speckling the landscape now like stars. He saw the larger lights—the bubbles—and there was one right by Coventry. Aiden's, the light he was touching right now. The Prism, there in the heart of the Midlands, and behind it all—a lot louder in Stone Space this time but scratching in and out like a badly-tuned radio—was the screech of the Caeterus.

Where are they, he thought, searching frantically for his friends and cursing Maria's hiding of them even as he thanked God for it. The emotions of the bubble captives sang to him, audible even through the screech of the Caeterus. Fear, despair, hope. He had to pull back before it all became too overwhelming, but not before he heard the children mixed in there. Many other Aidens, Aarons. Pointer was right about that—

Eric's greater clarity had, he now saw, added new elements onto the map. They were blurry blue shapes, seen in much lower resolution than everything else, but now they were visible.

Eric could see all eighteen of the Blues.

The outlines of arms, legs and heads were hard to make out, but the colour was unmistakable. Some of them were brighter than the others; the new Blues, Eric surmised. A quick count proved it: twelve of those, six of the duller ones. All were spread over the landscape at different points. Eric noticed something odd moving right next to the next nearest Blue; the *closest* Blue, of course, being the one approaching Aiden's house right this moment.

The next closest looked to be near where Eric thought Loughborough would be, but something strange was moving very close by to it. It was a writhing, blackish-grey mass, *no,* there were *two* of them, having left a faint double trail on the landscape behind them. Eric zoomed out and followed it all the way back to the edge of Scotland. He realised he could now see the faint outline of the Barrier here, unlike before, and saw where the two somethings had crossed through it. Eric couldn't tell for sure, but it looked like the hole had healed over. Even so, the path of the Crawlers—and their representation in Stone Space—was clear.

But they weren't the only things close to the Blue at Loughborough.

That Blue was standing practically on top of something else, so much so that Eric nearly missed it. A little blob of ... nothing, connected to an even smaller blob of nothing. These two little patches on the landscape could easily have been missed. Whatever they were they had been excellently camouflaged, but a thin, near-translucent line was rising out of one camouflaged blob and up into the Barrier above. It was pulsing, and Eric could see that it carried from the point it met the Barrier all the way to Coventry, and the Prism. A thread of some kind? It was hard to tell, but whatever was rising out of those connected, camouflaged blobs illuminated their presence on the map the way a bat uses sonar. Without it, Eric realised, he would never have seen through the camouflage—

He understood.

The large, camouflaged object. The smaller camouflaged object connected to it. That *had* to be the Stone Man and Maria's circuit, masked by Maria ... or rather, no longer fully masked. The Blue was right on top of them; whatever had wrought this change of circumstances must have been carried out in Stone person, up close and personal. The Blue had done something.

Whatever the cause, Maria's Stone Man now had a thread connecting it—and her friends—directly to the Prism. Never mind the fact that a Blue was right on top of them; even if they survived the encounter, the Caeterus now knew exactly where Andy and the others were at all times.

Eric's shock was so great that he nearly fell out of Stone Space. *The camouflage, the blanket,* he told himself, *it's still there, so even if it knows where they are the Red can't hurt them remotely, surely—*

He became dimly aware of the sound of Esther's screaming, coming to him as if from several rooms away. That brought him back a little, and now Edgwick's voice joined in too. He came back to his body, heard all three people screaming at him, but over Esther's pleas and her son's sobs it was Edgwick's words that cut through the noise most clearly:

"*It's nearly here, Hatton! It's nearly here!*"

The boy. The vision. But the others. The other children. Maria and her friends were the only ones who could—

"*Eric!*"

He saw it just as he felt his body begin to shake: a ring of grey, swirling light appearing around him on the floor. He'd been spotted, and his Quarry Response was starting accordingly. Fear flooded his body, but before it could take hold Eric jammed his stump down against the rising silver light. *No*, he told it. The light dissipated with a hissing, crackling sound, and Eric's nerve held.

He closed his eyes and went back into Stone Space.

The screams around him cut off instantly and he reached for that thread at range—that *tracker* on his friends—with his mind, throwing caution to the wind. He was all too aware of time running out for everyone as he tried to latch on, to somehow disrupt the thread's signal. *Yes*, he had it, feeling himself interfere with the information; perhaps he could overload it, short it out—

A familiar whiteness flashed across his perception of both country and thread, snapping his perception. He knew this task was, for now at least, beyond him, his concussion muting his abilities and dooming his friends; he could not stop their position being given away. Now something else was coming: the searching eye of the Stone Giant, or the Prism itself—*perhaps*, Eric thought wildly, *the Red, all the Stone Men, are merely extensions of that thing, perhaps the Prism is the true mind behind this madness*—and Eric dropped back into the shredded and torn chaos of Esther's living room. He felt pain in his stitched-up shoulder and realised that Esther was slapping at him, sobbing hysterically.

"*Get him out! Get him out! You promised!*"

"*Hatton!*" That was Edgwick, and there was no more time to find out what was going on with Maria and the others. The fear in Edgwick's voice told Eric how little time he had left.

"You're getting out now," he told the boy, but Aiden was beyond listening, calling hysterically for his mother. Okay then. Eric pressed his hand onto the bubble and commanded it to open. It began that violent shake once more, increasing in ferocity so quickly that Eric thought the Blue was already in the courtyard and rocking the house with the force of its footsteps. But it was the bubble making the furniture around him vibrate, causing objects to fall off shelves and crash to the floor, but Eric knew that any second it would pass and the bubble would open.

Except it didn't.

"Hatton!"

It was uncanny, this sensation of *almost but not quite* tipping over; it felt like all it needed was the tiniest push, and then Eric would give that much only to find it was still ever so slightly out of reach. *Okay,* he would think, and give it that much more, only for it to somehow still need a tiny bit more to complete. *Fine, you bastard,* Eric thought, leaning mentally and physically into the bubble at maximum effort. His head screamed and his vision flickering again as the hateful thing's rumbling dislodged plaster dust from the ceiling above.

Still the bubble held. Eric couldn't get the boy out.

His exertions sent waves of nausea that seemed to roll outwards directly from the injury on the back of his skull. The national Barrier had been easier than this—

The national Barrier wasn't baked in then, Eric thought, outright panic gripping his entire body. *You said it yourself. You opened a hole in Jenny's but that was new, too. Boosted or not, you've never—*

All it needed was a little more, *but he was giving everything he had—*

Edgwick at his ear—

"Hatton," he said, his voice low and intense, "you have about one minute to get this thing open before the—"

Edgwick's hand rested on Eric's back. Something happened; some sidestep. It wasn't a true circuit—they didn't have a Watchmaker to put it all together—but Eric knew enough from his years of Stone conspiracy research. Stone Sensitives could affect one another if an active Stone Man was abroad in the world. TIN or not, something in Edgwick's touch added to—or removed something important— from Eric's now-boosted but struggling frequency.

The bubble effortlessly burst with a rush of air no more powerful than a leafblower.

One second it was there, the next it wasn't, or rather the full version of it wasn't. The lower ring of a bubble's initial emergence was still intact, remaining in a golden circle seven or eight inches high. The world's largest back burner, but already diminishing. Soon it would be gone entirely, Eric thought. The crying boy leapt to his feet and sprung clean over the low wall of light, landing in Esther's outstretched arms. The mother clutched her son, the pair moaning and sobbing in relief. The sound was relieving and damning to Eric's ears in the now silent room, but already Edgwick was turning Esther by the shoulder and running her to the kitchen, Aiden in her arms. The three of them fled; Eric staggered to his feet but stood too quickly. His head pulsed at him with the movement, and he swayed in whiteness for a few seconds until his equilibrium returned. Then he gave chase, crossing the kitchen and running outside only to find—to his amazement—Edgwick and Esther standing in the driveway, Esther still holding her son.

The adults were staring, motionless, at the fields behind the house.

Aiden looked Eric's way, the lower half of his face covered by Esther's shoulder. His still streaming eyes, red and swollen, stared at Eric reproachfully.

"What are you doing?!" Eric yelled at Esther. "Get in the car! Go—"

"Look," Edgwick said, pointing. Eric stepped down from the doorway and around Edgwick's large frame. The view into the next field was clear from this angle, but the darkness was thick.

"What am I—"

Eric saw it then. The produce being grown in the field at the back of the house was some kind of tall plant; as Eric's eyes adapted to the night's low light, he could see the darker swathe carved through the crop, showing how close the Blue had come.

The trampled down crops led all the way up to the back of the house. This hadn't just been close; it had been over.

The now distant Blue was disappearing through one of the hedges marking the field's opposite boundary. It had almost doubled back on itself, having completely changed direction. It was walking *away*—

Esther, of course, broke the spell, running with her son to the car's passenger side and opening the door.

"Go north, like I said," Edgwick began, following her back to the driver's side. "Get as far as you can from Coventry, all the way to John O' Groats if possible. Don't stop for or talk to any strangers—"

But Eric was turning and running back inside. Even as the knowledge settled into him—however he'd done it, however fucking traumatised the kid might be, however *close* it had been, *he had freed the boy*. The thread going from Caementum to the Prism, the Blue suddenly changing direction, the Blue right on top of Maria and the others—he didn't like this development at all. None of it could be good. As he flew into the living room, hearing Esther's car engine start outside, he saw the slowly fading ring of light was now only two inches high. Would this remaining amount of bubble be able to do anything?

March of the Stone Men

Eric skidded to his knees, head screeching in protest, and pushed the fingers of his remaining hand against the last of the light.

Immediately he was in Stone Space again, the sight of the country far fainter than before and fading all the time, but all the points of interest still stood out in harsh relief: the lights, the bubbles, the Prism ... and the Blues.

The dimmer ones were still quietly going about their business. They were even harder to make out now against the dulled backdrop. Eric looked to where he thought Loughborough was and, yes, he saw them: the two blurry, camouflaged-but-visible shapes. Not only was the Blue previously there no longer visible on the map—*holy shit, did they beat it?!*—but the undulating, greyish-black objects that were the Crawlers were gone, too. The realisation that his team had somehow won—beating not only a Blue, but both Crawlers—would normally have been a cue for ecstatic celebration. But when Eric looked to the newer, brighter Blues, he understood exactly what was happening.

All hope died in him.

Every single one of the new, brighter Blues was facing towards Loughborough. Those further away were still moving, heading inward. None of the brighter Blues were a particularly vast distance away from Loughborough; having not long left Coventry, Loughborough wouldn't be too much of a pivot. The closest of them were standing still, letting their further-away brethren catch up to them. Waiting until they could move in together.

All twelve new Blues were walking towards—or waiting to walk towards—the Stone Man.

No—

Eric tried once more to influence the thread that ran to the Prism from the camouflaged blob that was the Stone Man. Again, that whiteness flashed and interrupted, as it did the next time and the next time. Frantic, knowing he was about to lose this connection entirely, Eric became aware that the twitching energy that made up the larger of the two blobs was now much more stationary than before. The smaller blur—Maria, Paul and Andy—was still flickering too, and with conviction. Eric thought that they were still alive.

But whatever his friends had done to win, the Stone Man itself was now in trouble. Was it damaged? If so, how badly? And the Blues were walking *quickly*. Eric watched helplessly as the newer Blues continued to close in, noticing that the remaining, dull looking original five continued on their individual journeys. The plan was clear: the surviving five originals were to continue with the programme. The rest were being sent together as a unit.

Overkill, but a certain kill. Snuff out the problem for sure while the original six kept the process moving. The Stone Men, always efficient. And Maria and the others had no idea—

He flashed back into his body, seeing the gold light was now only about an inch away from disappearing entirely.

"*Edgwick! Edgwick!*"

It was a Hail Mary, but Edgwick's presence had helped with Eric's concussed energy before. The big man rushed into the room at a run, dropping to Eric's side, his hand again landing on Eric's back—

"*What is i—*" Edgwick's voice began and ended as the sight of the living room gave way to Stone Space once more.; too much this time it seemed, the vision of the country and its varying lights and colours now *futzing* and becoming low-res, but all Eric needed was to see *that* particular thread; *there, yes!* Eric went to it; the thing giving his friends away had to be destroyed. He yanked at it, pulled, twisted, but all he got was whiteness and distant pain.

Use it then—

He grasped the thread with his mind, suddenly overwhelmed by the flow of screeching communication, and tried to create a mental snapshot of the horrible, encroaching sight below him. But he was losing his grip—

"*Edgwick! Focus!*"

Something shifted a little; the thread became a fraction clearer, and Eric's grip strengthened for precious extra seconds. Eric pictured flinging the snapshot along the thread towards those two blurry shapes. Just as the effort brought the concussed whiteness back, he thought he felt something shoot away from him. Had the picture gone through, clear and self-evident? Stone Space was disappearing from Eric's sight, and he screamed uselessly into that place with everything he had:

THEY KNOW WHERE YOU ARE! THEY'RE COMING! THEY'RE ALL COMI—

The image of the landscape below vanished.

Eric dropped to the floor, clutching his head and moaning. He waited for the ice pick in his skull to diminish, wondering all the while *did it go through, did it go through—*

"You... something went out of me."

Eric opened his eyes to see Edgwick eyeing him strangely.

"It did," Eric said.

"Did you do that?"

"You helped," Eric said. "Thank you."

" ... what did you see?"

Eric lay back on the floor, groaning, the words *they're in big trouble* coming to his mouth ... but stopping at the sound of Esther's struggling engine from outside.

She and Aiden were still on the driveway.

***

Eric stepped outside just as the engine finally caught.

Esther's hands snapped back to the steering wheel, her eyes locked on the rear-view mirror, watching the fields; then she saw Eric. She didn't drive away. Eric approached the car, awkward and cautious. Esther put on her seatbelt.

Then her window began to lower.

"Hey," Eric said.

"That thing's not coming here anymore. Is it?"

"No."

Esther nodded, her lips pressed tightly together.

"Where's it going?"

"After my friends. Your son has been, by the looks of it, shunted down the priority list."

Esther breathed out heavily, her mouth quivering with terrified relief ... but then her eyes blazed open.

"Is that what you were doing, then? Using my son to try and contact them?"

"... yeah. Sort of." Esther just nodded again. Silence. "It was to do with trying to save the world." He didn't add *where your son is*. "Why haven't you left?" He'd expected Esther to be nothing but a pair of black, possibly *flaming* tyre tracks leading out to the road and the nearest horizon.

"I rushed, and stalled it," she said. "And I was planning on burning out of here, but ..." She breathed out heavily. "It struck me that maybe driving away from the one person that can help my son if something like this happened again ... I'm not sure if going away from you is a good idea. I wanted to talk to you before I left."

"Edgwick is right," Eric said. "You need to go north. I don't know what's going to happen now. You want to be as far from Coventry as possible because ..." Because what? If Andy and the others couldn't stop this, Aiden being far away would delay the inevitable?

Esther said something quiet that Eric couldn't hear.

"Sorry?" Eric asked.

"Thank you for saving my son," Esther repeated, staring at her feet, before turning to Aiden in the passenger seat. "Aiden," she said. "What do you say to—*oh, Aiden*—"

The boy was hugging his knees, rocking gently, his eyes staring out of the windscreen. It was a sight Eric would remember until the day he died. Esther leaned over, grabbing her child again and embracing him. The pair of them cried together and Eric turned to see Edgwick standing in the doorway. The soldier shrugged and headed back inside without a word. Eric waited.

"Where are you two going now?" Esther said eventually, wiping her face with the hem of her top. When she turned her gaze back to Eric he felt it again: that feeling of home, forever denied him. Then she made it even worse. "Do you have to go where your friends are going?"

"I said I'd meet them—"

"*Come with us,*" Esther suddenly said, turning fully to the window. "You have a pack, right? I gave you one—"

"I ... I have a different one now—"

But Esther was getting out of the car and grabbing Eric by the arms.

"Come with *us*," she said, pleading. "The car's big, we can take turns in driving. Your friend, too."

Eric's chest constricted. The sight of a pretty woman asking for his help was firing off primal neurons in his brain. But the acceleration of his heartbeat made the back of his head throb and whiteness dance before his eyes, and thus the spell was broken. Eric knew why Esther wanted him to join them so badly. She'd even told him; he was the only person she knew of that could get Aiden out of a bubble. He gently pushed Esther's arms down and she lowered her head, looking ashamed.

"Sorry," she said. "It's my *son*—"

"If I had a son and he'd been trapped that way," Eric said, "and *you'd* come along to get him out? I'd be asking you the same thing. Don't worry. Look; there's a reason it was so important that I try to help my friends. If they can pull off the plan, we think we can free *everyone*. Aiden won't need my help."

She looked at the remaining blood stains on his face. Her hand came up and her fingers brushed his cheek.

"What happened to you?" she asked. "What's been happening, what *is* happening?"

He couldn't tell her. What Stone Sensitives knew, the Caeterus might know.

"All I can tell you," Eric said, "is that my friends are somewhere around Loughborough." *The Caeterus knew that much already,* Eric thought. "We were supposed to meet them outside Cov, but they're in trouble, and I don't think they know. I have to warn them, but I don't know how to find—"

He stopped. The Stone Men knew a way to find them: the tracking thread. But he didn't know if he could use it, especially now he was hurt. Eric cursed Dennis for the hundredth time. He'd been improving all the while with the low-frequency threads.

If he'd remained uninjured, perhaps he could have figured out how to use that tracking thread to find his friends, or at least have broken it so the Stone Men couldn't. Now, without some kind of CTE specialist to help his concussion, he had no way of getting any closer to that thread—

No. That wasn't true.

"So are you and Toby heading to wait outside Coventry now?" Esther asked, but Eric didn't think they were. The Stone Man had seemed injured. Eric thought Maria and the others might be a while, if they were to survive and arrive at all. Sitting on the A45 outside Coventry would be a waste of time.

But the threads had been getting louder and louder as he and Edgwick had drawn closer to the Prism. Stronger. Clearer. With Eric's now-muted abilities, the threads still weren't strong enough at this distance for Eric to use.

So he would have to make that distance shorter.

Hope fluttered in Eric's chest. *Also,* he thought, *the Caeterus might be tracking the Stone Man, but you didn't see any bubbles around those camouflaged, blurry blobs.* The Caeterus might know where Caementum was, but Maria's protection clearly still meant she and her friends couldn't be bubbled—or Caementum controlled—long range. The tracking thread was the problem, leading the Blues right to where they could handle things up close.

But threads were still, to a degree, Eric's speciality. If he were to do anything about it, he and Edgwick had to get up close, too. Close enough to the Prism to snap that thread entirely.

Eric said, sighing heavily, impossibly tired ... yet alive. *He'd saved the kid.*

"Me and *Toby*," he said, "are going to Coventry."

✱✱✱

Chapter Fourteen

The Drive Home, Birthday Bumps/Lumps, and Edgwick's Unintended Close Encounter

✳✳✳

"But they must know what we want to do then," Edgwick said, shaking his head. "To send all the new ones after Pointer and the others. They know something's up."

"I guess," Eric said. They were cruising at speed along the A45 now, Eric at the wheel. Edgwick had seen the swaying state of the younger man and expressed uncertainty about letting Eric drive. Eric had insisted.

So far it had only been a relatively short drive from Esther's to this point, but time enough for Edgwick to agree with Eric's plan. *I'm still the grunt here,* he'd said. *You know more about this than I do. Wherever you wanna go, we go. We're probably dead either way, anyway.*

The A45 part of Coventry's outskirts was, of course, still as open and unencumbered as Eric had seen it the day before. The Renault flew along, its headlights illuminating the flow of concrete under the night sky.

"They never seemed to show that kind of concern before, though," Edgwick said, stroking his thick red moustache. "The process always just continued. Must mean we're doing something right."

"Yeah."

"*That* said," Edgwick mused, "isn't all of this—the Empty Men, the bubbles—a counter measure?"

"True."

"You're so chatty and insightful."

"Sorry," Eric said. "Just this headache. Shoulder. Neck. I'm pretty banged up. Hurting." All of that was true, but it wasn't the reason for Eric's silence. The point he'd been dreading was coming up. "Just keep talking. I'm listening."

"I'm just mulling it over," Edgwick said. "Looking at everything from both sides."

"It's okay. It's distracting. I appreciate it."

Edgwick stared out of the window.

"What was I—ah, yeah. They never demonstrated this kind of intelligence before. Rudimentary problem solving, yes, but everything they've done in the last few days seems like their version of … tactics?" He paused. "I guess that doesn't mean they weren't always this smart, or that the Prism doesn't make them better in some way." Edgwick shifted awkwardly in his seat. "I can't lie, Hatton. I'm nervous about this plan of yours."

"Me too. Please: just keep talking."

It was helping, and now they were passing the point Eric had been dreading. The headlights briefly revealed a small patch of red spray by the roadside, one that had clearly emanated from the body lying nearby. Its back was facing the road, the corpse's face was out of sight. Eric was only partially grateful for this as it meant the hole where its spine had been removed was fully on display. Edgwick wouldn't notice it, Eric knew; this, to him, was just another piece of bloody carnage left by the events of the last few days.

Eric had kept his promise to Harry—that he would leave immediately without burying his friend—but this moment was part of the cost. Eric's knuckles tightened on the wheel, he kept his eyes on the centre line of the road as his heart rate sped up. He thought of the storage key Harry had given him, its fob reading I HEART EARLSDON on one side and the lockup's address on the other. Inside the lockup were Harry's paintings, the ones Harry had made Eric promise to get to Harry's daughter in Europe if the mission was successful.

"Easy," Edgwick said. "You're doing ninety and there's a bend coming up."

"Sorry."

Eric eased his foot off the accelerator. He managed to avoid looking in the rear-view mirror at Harry's now rapidly shrinking body. He breathed out as slowly as he could and tried to keep his next inhale steady. He'd gone straight to the Isle of Skye, as promised. Saved the kid, as promised. Now there were no more promises to keep, or at least ones currently within his power to keep. If Eric were to be able to get to Europe, Andy and the others would have had to do their part first and destroy the Barrier. For the time being, then, Eric's promise backlog was clear. Instead of relief—to Eric's great surprise—the sense of choice only seemed to make things much harder. For example: was this current mission the right thing for he and Edgwick to do? Eric had to hope so.

Millennium Place was only five miles away.

***

The screeching of the Caeterus became deafening in Eric's head once the Renault was inside the Ring Road.

Before his head injury, Eric had been able to reduce his awareness of the sound. Now, his still-unhealed brain meant the constant and growing noise had been driving him more and more crazy the closer they drew to Coventry. His headache was a pneumatic drill, one that thrusted with every heartbeat. He didn't dare take any more painkillers in case they messed with his mind at the crucial, upcoming moment. He'd slowly stopped responding to Edgwick altogether. The soldier had noticed and politely ceased talking.

Driving along the Ring Road was surreal. The tall buildings of Coventry's city centre passed by either side of the car like silent watchers, wondering what the hell he was doing back here. Had he really only left a day ago? Already it felt like an alien landscape. Eric understood that he was a very different person than the one who had rushed to Ground Zero, kicking himself for forgetting his listening equipment when the Arrival had started.

Eric saw it then, he slowed, stopped the car. It was time to switch places anyway, but the sight jutting up in the near distance caught Eric's breath in his throat. Not from fear, but from knowledge of the enormity of the unknown ... and of his determination to go through with the plan anyway.

The Prism rose up ahead of them on the Ring Road, dark and dense and impossible.

Both men got out of the car and stood on the concrete. Even in the dark, the feeling was uncanny; standing once more on that surface that Eric rarely ever walked around. His bike had always been his Coventry transportation, and Eric found himself transported to the last time he'd stood upon it: he and Harry, running from the Barrier as it flew over them.

Eric and Edgwick moved around the car, switching sides.

"You ready?" Edgwick said over the roof of the car. "You want to start now, or do you wanna get *close*, close?"

Eric nearly said *yes, now*, but hesitated. How close did he want to be? He deliberately hadn't tried to access that tracking thread yet—any of the threads, in fact—until they were as close as possible to the Prism. They'd debated the best way to go about it. Edgwick had pushed hard for the potential plan of Eric steadily trying to check, check, check it all the way into Coventry. The argument for that plan had been—assuming a maximum range at which Eric could avoid detection—that it would be best to quickly check repeatedly until they knew where that range began. Then they could stay at 'close enough' range and, potentially, be safe. The risk with Edgwick's plan was that they might get caught during the very first little check, and potentially before Eric was close enough to affect the thread at that. If it turned out they only had one chance to interfere, Eric wanted that interference to have the best chance of working. It was maddening. The amount they *didn't* know about both the Caeterus and Eric's damaged abilities made the whole thing a gamble.

Eric had settled on what he called the 'Shit or Bust' plan; drive to Coventry, as close to the Prism as possible—right into Millennium Place if they could—while trying to remain aware of any changes that might arise. They'd out the results when they pulled the trigger. No early, potentially plan-ruining risk. Only one big risk.

The Stone Giant had tried to bubble Eric twice now, but only because Eric was interfering with an existing bubble, and a golden one at that. Eric thought that, if he wasn't in contact with Maria or fucking around with bubbles, he wasn't really on their radar particularly. But what would it—or the Caeterus—do once Eric started monkeying around with things at the Prism?

As if sounding a warning, the Horns filled the air.

Edgwick winced, covering his ears, but Eric screamed. His head felt like it would burst like a pimple at the ugly, distorted brass sound. He rode it out for a few seconds until the Horns mercifully ended.

"Think they know we're here?" Edgwick said, straightening.

"Could ... just be the process," Eric grunted, swaying and holding his fingers to his temples. "Bad timing. Doesn't necessarily mean ..." The discussion was pointless. It didn't change the plan. "Just get us to Millennium Place," he said. "Park as close as you can. Then I'll start."

"You got it."

They opened the car doors and got back in, Edgwick settling into the driver's seat. The car rolled forward, and through the windscreen the shadowy shape of the Prism began to grow.

March of the Stone Men

***

Millennium Place—or Ground Zero, as it had become known—was dimly lit by the lights of the elevated Ring Road nearby. Any closer streetlighting had been flattened by Stone comings and goings. Still, there was enough illumination to show Eric and Edgwick what was going on.

As they'd drawn closer and closer, experiencing no resistance, the decision had been made to get off the Ring Road and head all the way down to street level at Ground Zero. *As close as possible* meant as close as possible, after all. The Stone Giant would be there, along with any returning or recently-born Blues. If it, or any of its colleagues, made a move in their direction, Edgwick was to floor it.

Now Edgwick slowly crawled the car along the former bus lane that led past Millennium Place, passing the row of long-abandoned shops and bars that ran along the front of the plaza. Edgwick had his instructions—no, his *orders* from Eric, an irony not lost on the younger man. Ahead, the Prism stood atop the crumbled ruins of the Ground Zero building, a perfect testament to the manner in which the Stone Men had completely imposed themselves upon Eric's world.

Maybe, Eric thought, *we're about to do something about that.*

"Stop here," Eric whispered. "Leave the engine running."

The Renault drew to a halt. About one hundred and fifty feet to the car's right, lay the Prism. In front of it stood the Stone Giant.

It was upright and unmoving, so still that one could have been forgiven for thinking it a harmless, surreal statue. It wasn't alone, and Eric understood what the recent Horns had been signalling.

A returned Blue was standing in front of the Stone Giant.

Edgwick gently blew air from his cheeks, the sound low and impressed. "The Red Stone Man. That's one *big* bastard."

"It is." It was. Eric leaned over to see through Edgwick's driver side window at the two behemoths standing before the Prism. The Blue was massive but even it was utterly dwarfed by the size of the Stone Giant. The smaller Stone Man's head only came up to the Giant's chest.

The Horns sounded once more, seeming to fill both the outside world and the space inside the car. Eric bit back a scream but managed to keep his eyes open enough to squint through the windscreen. The car was parked at enough of a two-thirds angle to see everything as the process began to play out before them.

Both the Red and the Blue's chests began to extend towards one another, forming wide, rectangular columns. As soon as they met in the middle, the Horns stopped. Eric moaned in relief but then began to feel a faint rumbling coming through the floor of the car. He looked to the Prism; the entire monstrosity was clearly vibrating slightly, operating in tandem with the two Stone Man before them. Eric and Edgwick waited for a few minutes, tense. They watched for any further developments. None came.

"It's come back from a Harvest," Eric whispered. "The Blue. I think it's giving the spines to the Red—"

"Are they using the Prism somehow?" Edgwick whispered. "I think—wait, look, *look.*"

Something was happening to the Red. It was becoming wider, it's shoulders starting to expand outwards a few feet below the point where its collarbone would be.

"I see it."

"Eric," Edgwick said, not taking his eyes off the spreading Red. "I think we might have been very lucky here. It's *busy* right now. If you were going to get away with this unnoticed—if you were ever hoping that thing might be distracted—surely this is the moment. If you're gonna do anything, *now is*—"

"Yeah. Yeah."

Eric felt it then; the first sting of real fear. The Stone Giant truly was just that, a giant ... but did it also look a little different now? Eric wasn't sure if it was just the streetlight affecting the creature's appearance, but was its colour a little off from the last time he'd seen it? It was still crimson, but was it the same crimson?

He realised he was stalling.

"Are you doing it—"

"*Ssh,*" Eric hissed. "And no. Not yet. I'll tell you."

"Sorry."

"... it's okay. Listen, I'm, I'm ... I'm gonna do it now."

"Good luck."

Edgwick offered his hand. Eric hesitated for a moment, then took it.

"Thank you," he said. Edgwick nodded and their hands separated.

Eric closed his eyes and opened his mind.

"*Ah!*"

His eyes flew open. Both men froze after Eric's cry. Could the Stone Men hear? If they could, or had, they made no show of it.

"*What was that?*" Edgwick hissed.

"I'm okay. That was just a shock." The already deafening noise of the Caeterus' threads had become a sharp, shocking cacophony once Eric had tried to use them here. The jump in volume had been like a gunshot, one aimed at Eric's headache at that. "I'm going again—"

The screeching filled Eric's mind once more, and while the source was undoubtedly as powerful as it could be, the feedback from the Prism was as concussive as a thrown pistol bouncing off the back of one's head. Connecting to the tracker thread had been difficult with a bubble, but at this range it was difficult for a different reason: this was like trying to hear a whisper in the middle of a trading floor. Without the visuals provided by actually seeing Stone Space, Eric was doing this blind, operating on feel and instinct alone.

Edgwick had helped though, at Esther's house. Something had shifted once his energy had connected with Eric's. Edgwick wasn't a battery, like Paul, and they hadn't had any of the psychic communication he'd had with Maria. But Edgwick's energy had helped harness Eric's focus a little. That had been with a bubble involved, but perhaps here it would—

"Edgwick. Put your hand on my shoulder."

"Roger."

Edgwick's heavy paw came down.

"*Aah, Christ, the other one—*"

"Sorry, sorry—"

Edgwick's hand switched to Eric's un-stitched up shoulder but already Eric knew that wasn't quite enough. It was like having an eye test: *which is better, number one or number two?* Number Two here was *slightly* better, but the tracker thread was still unclear. He tried using mental muscle memory to unlock what it felt like to connect to it, but he had nothing. How was he supposed to even begin to find it?

The obvious answer hit him like a dry slap. The Prism. One end of the thread he was seeking was connected to the Stone Man, the other to the towering edifice before him. If he wanted to find it, he knew exactly where one end of it was, at least. All he had to do was cut it or interrupt it, not actually use it—

It's too risky, he thought. *They'll see you.* The Prism seemed to be directly connected to the Stone Giant. Even if the latter truly were distracted, surely it would know that Eric was trying to mess around at the Prism itself?

If that happens, Eric thought, *you make sure you cut that thread no matter what. You make it so they can't track the Stone Man anymore.*

Edgwick's grip tightened on Eric's shoulder.

"*Jesus,*" he whispered.

The growths either side of the Stone Giant were now beginning to separate away from its body. Gaps were appearing in what was now becoming thin red webbing, the growths themselves a different colour entirely. The webbing then tore off and slowly retracted back into the Stone Giant, looking like ripped sheets. Two large, mostly formless shapes were left standing either side of the Giant, about the same rough size of the Blue.

The same rough colour.

Two huge, lumpy, formless columns of what looked like rough blue clay now stood either side of the Stone Giant. The birthing process was complete.

"The Prism doesn't make them," Edgwick whispered. "The fucking Stone Giant does."

There was no time for amazement. The two adult Stone Men—the Blue that had brought its Harvest and the Red—were still connected; any second the Horns would sound again, and their chest protrusions would disentangle.

"That's why the Red one hasn't gone anywhere," Edgwick was muttering. "The fucking Prism is part of its birthing process—"

"*Ssh,* please—"

If this truly were a window of sneak opportunity, it would shortly close.

The Prism. Go for the Prism—

Eric closed his eyes and reached for the edifice before him. He couldn't find the thread; the sensations in the air around were too myriad, to endless. How could he find one thread amongst all these—

Eric felt for his friends. Brief as their relationship had been, theirs was a much easier sensation to recall; the feeling of their combined energies as clear as an index card in his mind. It made things much easier, but still felt like rooting blindly in the bottom of a drawer, like trying to find something very familiar to the touch but by touch alone.

Then he had it, *right there!* He fumbled it; his concussion interfered, making a solid grip impossible.

"Edgwick, you need to, I don't know, concentrate or something, you focused last time—"

That helped. *There,* he almost had it. No, *he had it!* Eric had the tracking thread, unmistakably. Immediately he quickly checked if he could communicate with Maria; he couldn't. He screamed down the thread but anything he could produce was simply vaporised by the sheer volume of information emanating from the Prism. He was *too* close for that ... but maybe that closeness meant he could now break the thread, his hold of it stronger here—

Something was coming the other way along the thread. Eric froze, panic seizing him—

It was an image, appearing in Eric's mind.

It appeared to be of some kind of tower. The picture itself was crude, its shape like that of a rook on a chess board, either due to the limited communication on the thread or the lack of imagination of the sender, but the shape was there.

His friends had felt him, even if they couldn't hear him.

Maria—or Andy, or Paul—had noticed his presence and managed to send something back ... that made absolutely zero fucking sense. What the hell did a castle tower have to do with anything? They were in a castle? They were holed up somewhere like they were in a dungeon? *He* should hole up somewhere like a dungeon? What did it mean?

And he didn't have time to figure it out; soon the hopefully distracting-birthing process would complete. There was no time to dither, the job of snapping that fucking tracking thread was paramount—

But it's your last chance to speak to them—

Eric tried with all his might to send them the message *tell me where you are,* but it felt like pissing into a waterfall. Any communication here was only one way and what he'd been sent was useless. He'd have to figure it out later. Eric turned his attention deep into the thread itself and tried to influence it. *Twist, snap, break,* he thought His head felt as if it would pop as he worried at the thread, his mind acting like—his *head* feeling like—a serrated saw blade.

It didn't work. He couldn't do it.

"Eric." The soldier sounded awed. "I can feel something. We're connected to them, aren't we?"

"Yes," Eric breathed, ignoring him. *Break. Break,* he thought. But the connection held. "Edgwick, I don't—I don't—"

He couldn't do it.

Feel along the thread with your mind, Eric thought. *Maybe there's a weak spot.* He did just that; the tracker thread continued, he realised, beyond the Prism. Growing larger, or perhaps it merged with another, longer thread at the point where it began to travel beyond.

To elsewhere—

Suddenly, just the awareness of it was enough. Eric was caught, unable to prevent what was happening. His consciousness became aware of something unfathomably vast; it came upon him so quickly that he had no time to react.

All thought left him then save one, his insufficient human mind beginning to conceive of what lay on the other end of that thread:

They're endless—

The unfiltered, unguarded and fully connected gaze of the Caeterus fell upon Eric's mind.

Awareness faded—the sensation of his body as it began to buck and twist and drool quickly leaving him—as Eric Hatton began the cessation of his being. He tried to let go but it was too late; the thread seemed to seize him like a cord. Part of him heard Edgwick yelling *what is that, Eric, listen to me,* even as Eric felt Edgwick's energy behind him in this sudden circuit, the Caeterus themselves as Watchmaker. Their observation turned Eric and Edgwick's rough connection into a thread of curiosity, the Caeterus turning Eric's disintegrating mind over and examining it like a bug on a slide. He had time to think *Edgwick they'll move onto you next, look into you, you shouldn't see and you shouldn't let them seeeeeeeeeeeeeeee—*

Then his mind was being shunted; his thoughts jolted, jarred, and then came back into lucidity as he became aware that Edgwick's energy had pulled Eric's energy behind his, barging Eric's consciousness away from the thread and taking his place in the process. It was clumsy, desperate; Edgwick didn't have the ability or the finesse for anything else.

Eric dropped fully back into his gasping body to see Edgwick in the Renault's driving seat.

The soldier was holding his face and screaming.

Eric tried helplessly to use his disassembled and reassembled mind, his thoughts stunned and unresponsive. He could only listen as Edgwick's voice slowly turned into a ragged thing; it began to emit the shrieking screams of the truly mad, for that was what Edgwick had become. Somehow the soldier had thrown his consciousness in front of Eric's, knocking Eric free of the thread that had seized him. But now Edgwick had taken Eric's place; the terrible dissolution that was the full, direct gaze of the Caeterus was now Edgwick's to experience.

Eric found his voice, his thoughts, but it was too late.

"Edgwick! Edgwick!"

The soldier began hammering the driver's window with his feet, screeching as he frantically tried to free himself from his metal prison. The window gave way, Edgwick's powerful legs working with a madman's strength. He immediately began to clamber through the small opening, ignoring Eric's effort to stop him as much as his broken, splinted arm and injured shoulder.

"*Edgwick! Stop!*"

Edgwick's hands sliced open on the jagged glass, leaving bloody stains as he squeezed his bulk through the window frame. He made it through with shocking speed, falling out of the door and onto the street. Still shrieking, he lumbered to his feet and ran headlong towards the two Stone Men, clawing at his face all the way. Eric threw open the passenger door to give chase, Edgwick's full-throated hollering ringing off the silent, surrounding buildings as he ran. Eric's fear of being 'seen' by the Stone Men was forgotten, thinking only of saving his friend, but even as he made gasping, head-aching pursuit after the big man, he understood where the now-mindless Edgwick was headed. Eric knew he couldn't stop the soldier in time.

Ahead, the two Stone Men remained entangled. Either side of the Red the two lumps of Blue substance were only just starting to take on some kind of shape. Edgwick was ignoring all three Blue objects before him. He was running directly at the Stone Giant.

"*Edgwick, please—*"

It was pointless. Edgwick ran headlong into the Stone Giant, his face colliding with its hip. There was a stomach-turning crack before Edgwick dropped straight to the floor like a lead marionette.

He didn't bounce off; it was as if the Stone Giant simply absorbed the kinetic energy of the impact, leaving no recoil. Eric let out a moan as he skidded to a halt, holding his head and neck and seeing Edgwick twitching. Eric knew it was, without question, too late. Even if he couldn't hear what Edgwick was saying, Eric knew the sounds that would be leaving Edgwick's mouth.

"*GCATTAGATAATTAGACCGATGACC—*"

Eric dropped to his knees. He didn't even cry out. They had failed utterly. The Horns sounded a moment later, signalling the retraction of the Man and Giant's chest protrusions. Eric slowly stood and began to back away, watching Edgwick's body all the while. There was something he needed in the car.

Once it was retrieved, Eric made his way back across the former Millennium Place. He didn't have a plan outside of the next few moments—the immediate task at hand—but his stunned mind knew he needed to survive. Maria and the others were still being tracked, and the mission might need his help.

Oh God, he thought. *That's true, isn't it.*

There was still a long way to go.

Eric hadn't been this close to a Stone Man since the Red was Pale; he and Harry pummelling it with a sledgehammer. The shrieking of the Caeterus in his ears—a sound now far less impactful after being directly connected to the Caeterus themselves—continued, mingling with the Horns as the Blue and Red's chests continued to retract back into themselves. Eric drew within ten feet of the monster and looked up, up, up to its blank, rough-surfaced face. He felt like a child before it, the scale of the task before him represented in disgusting red sculpture. Then his eyes fell back to Edgwick.

Eric—desperately trying not to lay his tears at this Stone altar—began to cry.

His anger had been enough to carry him through saving the boy, but now he was tired *beyond* anger. Duty remained, though, and this Eric now understood. He raised the pistol he had fetched from the car and levelled it at Edgwick's babbling head.

"—CCATGGATAGATCCAGATAC—"

No one had ever recovered from touching a Stone Man, Eric knew. Instead they moved—over their years in various facilities—from babbling catatonia to full brain death, their central nervous systems eventually shutting down. No-one knew why. They only knew the end result. Edgwick deserved infinitely better than this and Eric couldn't leave him this way. The soldier had not hesitated to protect Eric. Eric would not hesitate now.

Eric pulled the trigger. Edgwick's head rocked violently sideways, a crimson hole appearing in his forehead as a matching spray covered the concrete behind his skull. For the second time within twenty-four hours, Eric had killed a friend.

Eric watched the previously connected Stone Men slowly complete their reformations. He wanted to say something, some angry line, but all such things were beyond him. There was only a howling within him as endless as the Caeterus themselves. Left with no other choice, Eric broke and fell into a hobbling, painful run towards the car. He didn't know where he would go; he only knew that he needed to be away. He didn't think that the Stone Men would come after him. Their attentions were on the *real* threats, those that could actually take down Stone Men and Crawlers alike. Even so, being close when the two monsters fully awoke would be inadvisable.

Eric dropped into the driver's seat, slammed the door, and *now* he screamed.

He leant into the wheel and bellowed for a full minute, the resulting pain and light-headedness in his brain welcome now. Once finished, the stillness of the car and the knuckle-pulsing in his skull was good. He could think, dispassionate and detached.

Move, he thought. *Move the car.*

That he could do. He started the engine and began to head for the Ring Road.

Now where?

Maria and the others. He had to find them somehow, contact them. It looked like they'd received his warning; they'd responded when they felt Eric use the Prism, so maybe they'd been waiting for him. But their message made no sense. If only the picture had been clearer, he would know if it was supposed to be an actual place or just a metaphor.

Edgwick—

Honour him by thinking clearly, Eric thought. *Make a plan. Now.*

He thought the others probably now knew they were being tracked. So maybe Maria wouldn't be hiding them so much, knowing there was no point? Conserving much-needed energy? He couldn't rely on that anyway; even without a bubble, his head injury probably meant long-range comms with Maria were a no-go. Even if he could somehow find them, how would he get to them quickly? Based on what he'd seen on the way here, a car would be slow as hell as soon as he got outside of Coventry, even if his friends were only still in Loughborough.

Then what now, he thought. *You're fucked. What now. What now—*

What *did* he have, then?

They sent you a picture of a castle. They have no reason to think a castle means anything to you; the image had to be literal. So you look for actual castles. They were in Loughborough. Use the tablet map to find the nearest castle to Loughborough—

He already knew it: Mountsorrel Castle. It had to be. He knew it from childhood.

His hand went to the keys, but his head turned automatically. His eyes went to where Edgwick lay at the feet of the Stone Giant. Like Harry, Edgwick would not receive a proper burial. Unlike Harry, Edgwick hadn't told him not to—

Mountsorrel Castle, Eric thought. *That's all that matters. It has to be right. It has to be.*

He started the car, the awakening engine signalling the beginning of his latest mission.

Again, it felt utterly doomed from the start.

✱✱✱

Interlude

France, Now

***

Nathan toyed with the small black MP3 player in his hand.

He'd been sitting in silent thought since Straub left the room to finish dinner. Outside, the storm began to whip across the landscape. Even when the thunder struck, loud and full, it wasn't enough to startle Nathan from his ruminations. The door opened and Straub reappeared. She carried a small tray adorned with a napkin, cutlery, and a steaming helping of delicious-smelling nut roast.

"Did you listen to any more?" she asked.

"Not yet," Nathan said. "I didn't want to start and then stop to eat."

"Why would you stop to eat?"

"Oh," Nathan said, reddening. "I assumed you'd join me."

"Don't let me interrupt," she said. "You keep listening. But I don't like to hear it. Once was enough."

"If you want to put your headphones back on, I can—"

"Don't worry. I'll sit in the other room, watch my Chase reruns. That's as long as this storm doesn't knock the power out. It happens out here from time to time, so don't panic if it does. It comes back quickly."

"Okay. You know, I think when I hit play again, I'm gonna go all the way through to the end."

"You won't have time tonight," she said. "There's a lot more to go, and like I say we'll be up very early. It's a long drive in the morning and I like to get there early. Things don't usually happen down there until a bit later, but I like to be sure. You can listen on the way, and maybe the last of it after we get there. You'll finish before showtime, I'm sure."

Nathan held up the MP3 player.

"How *do* you have this?"

"Amazon."

"The *recording*."

"Couldn't resist," Straub said. "I was never one for jokes in the past. People like jokes, though, so I try." She shrugged. "One can never truly change one's nature, you know. But you can work on it." She raised her eyebrows.

Nathan didn't take the bait. He didn't want another exchange about looking for closure. He couldn't think about that right now. He just wanted to finish the recording.

"Maybe jokes," Nathan said, smiling, "are one thing you're okay to *not* work on."

"Honest feedback," Straub said. "I like it. Anyway: when you've listened to the whole thing, I'll answer your question." She dusted off her hands. "I'll leave you to it."

She left the room, closing the door behind her. Nathan adjusted the tray on his lap and placed the small MP3 player in the corner of it.

This time he didn't hesitate to press play.

***

PART FOUR
DISPENSATORI

Chapter Fifteen

Sky Blue Army, Parting Words, and the Showdown at Old John Hill

✱✱✱

Okay. Morning.

Yeah. *So.*

…

I didn't sleep well, even if the bed here was surprisingly good. I couldn't stop thinking about how much more there is to tell. Just saw the timestamp from yesterday's recording, didn't realise how many hours I'd been at it. That was pretty much the whole bloody day. Gonna try to do the rest in one go, but it's gonna take a while. That's okay. I have food, and water, and I have had some corn flakes and toast. Ready to go.

Where was … right. We'd taken the meds, got the Stone Man running again, fought the Blue and the Crawlers and escaped by the skin of our teeth. Then Eric's message had arrived, and we all—

Hm. All. All three of us.

…

Got to finish. Okay. Okay.

Once we'd calmed down after receiving the news from Eric—his vision of the twelve encroaching Blues arriving as a strange combination of visual data and inherent information—Maria tried unsuccessfully to contact Eric again. She couldn't try too hard. The Caeterus knew exactly where Caementum was anyway, but that didn't mean they couldn't bubble us the second Maria stuck her head too far over the parapet. She also thought something was severely *off* with Eric's energy, noticed in the fading remnants of his transmission. She thought he was hurt.

Based on the rough location from which Eric had transmitted his message, Maria thought he must have used the kid's bubble. At least he'd likely been successful in his mission.

Since then, we'd been debating the next course of action while trying to get our rattled heads back in the game. If the diagnosing Blue had somehow put a kind of tracker in Caementum, could we do something about it? We spent a short while trying, and decided we couldn't. Maria could sense it better than anyone else, but she couldn't affect it. *It's not a thread,* she said. *I can sense it but it's like trying to grab smoke.*

Twelve Blues were closing in. *Twelve.* Could they even catch us? Apparently, they were closing in fast. Perhaps we could race to Coventry and smash the Prism before the Blues caught up to us. Then we could deal with the Blues arrival, our mission complete, if the Blues even kept coming once the Prism was destroyed.

But they walked faster than us, and after a few quick tests, something immediately became clear.

We wouldn't be able to transport the Stone Man by truck anymore.

We'd restarted Caementum without too much trouble and inspected its damage. Along with the few new divots taken out of its body by the Crawlers, Caementum now had a large crack in its side from the blow dealt by the now-dead Blue. Whether due to all this fresh physical damage or not, we could no longer consistently manage Caementum's weight. We tested it by walking it up and onto cars left on driveways, managing to keep it aloft for a few seconds on the only-slightly caved-in roofs. Then Caementum suddenly squashed the vehicles flat. It didn't feel like a control or connection issue; it felt like an internal system problem.

"Did you feel what happened when the Blue was hitting us?" I asked the others. "It wasn't like the Crawlers. They were biting out chunks, but the strikes from Blue seemed to just, I don't know, affect the Stone Man's whole integrity. Like they were damaging the actual energy holding the bastard together."

The other two nodded.

"But you did something like that, didn't you? Like I told you?" Maria asked. "When you made the Stone Man hit the Blue. Like you were kind of ..." She slowly mimed with her hands, punching one through the other.

"Yeah. Like you said: copy what it was doing to us. Punching *through* the Blue, trying to knock its energy ... out of it, maybe? Shake it up? Think about it: they can shrug off missile strikes, but their own punches can leave cracks? It has to be more than just Stone on Stone impact. Whatever energy makes them so unstoppable must also hold their bodies together. When they collide, that integrity is damaged."

"You think that's why we're struggling with its weight now?" Paul asked. "Like Caementum's energy has been banged up, so the system's not working the same?"

"Maybe," I said, "but doesn't it feel a little bit better on the inside already? So maybe it can heal with time. If we had *more* time, maybe it could heal all the way."

But time was the one thing we didn't have, and transport for Caementum—for now—was out. We weren't going to outrun the encroaching Blues all the way to Coventry.

One way or another this was coming down to a twelve-on-one fight.

The thought was just ... stupid. We'd barely survived a fight with one Blue—albeit with two additional Crawlers that *really hadn't helped*—but twelve Blues was still another thing entirely. Panic set in. I set the Stone Man to autopilot, walking up and down the street while we threw ideas around. I was trying to keep everyone calm whilst absolutely shitting my pants.

First on the agenda: transport for *us*. Mentally, my circuit was alert, the amphetamines racing around our brains. Physically, the other two were spent, the wetness of their clothes now mingling with their sweat. We had to return to driving slowly behind the walking Stone Man, conserving our strength. The second item was a little harder to resolve; terror is not conducive to reasonable discussion.

"We can't fight them," Maria said. She had her hands in her hair, pacing almost as relentlessly as the Stone Man itself. "We just ... we just ..." One of her hands found her stomach, clearly thinking about the body blows from the Blue's attacks.

"We can," I said, even though I didn't believe it. My recently arrived headache wasn't abating.

"Not wanting to be negative," Paul grunted, sitting on the kerb and gratefully taking another swig of water. "But can you tell me how you think we're going to beat them?"

I replied, without thinking:

"Well ... maybe we can do the same thing we just did?"

The sudden hope in their eyes was surprising, and I realised what I'd just blurted out, might actually have legs. "Maria: you blanketed the Blue from the Stone Giant. Right? Do you think you could do that again?"

"I think so. It's not easy to spread the cover from us, then to the Blue, and back, but I think I can."

"Then we do the same thing," I said, beginning to pace myself now. Why *couldn't* this work? "We'd only need to do it on one of them, surely? Blanket it, go inside, trigger a dump of its energy—"

"We'd have to hurt it first," Paul said. "You busted out through a weak spot, right? And one the Crawler made in its hide, at that."

"Yeah. But I think we *can* hurt it," I said, miming Maria's punching-through motion again. "If we're smart—and lucky—we only need to hurt one enough to pull off the same trick. One Detonation could take all of them out at once."

"But they'd all have to be in the same place—" Maria began, stopping as the realisation hit us all. They *would* all have to be in the same place.

"Yeah," I told her. "They would. We'd have to let them all come to us. Take out one ... and take out the rest with the blast when they're all together."

"Fuck me," Paul breathed. "How *close* together?"

"The Blue," I said, "seemed to trigger some sort of final containment failsafe at the end. Right? It seemed to catch its own Detonation from going off at full force, a real last-breath action by the looks of it. But its Detonation still hit this street full force. All the lights went out and *stayed* out, unlike with the Big Power Cut. So, it hits hard in the immediate vicinity."

But Paul was shaking his head.

"You think we're gonna be able to pull that off with twelve of the bastards closing in at the same time—"

"Maybe not on this street," I said, my amphetamine-fuelled brain solving problems at lightning speed. *I should have done these things years ago*, I thought, before the rope-thick vein pulsing in my neck told me otherwise. "When these houses got flattened around us, the dust and debris were just horrific. My sight in the Stone Man and my actual sight kept getting fucked. But what if we had open ground? No houses or office buildings to confuse things when they get smashed. *High* ground. We choose the arena in which to meet them. One that suits us."

"No," Paul said, shaking his head. "There has to be a better—"

"Oh, God," Maria said, "No. He's right." She sat down next to Paul and put her hand on his arm. "It's our best bet. And high ground would mean they have to come *up* at us. It'd make their job harder. We only have to get *one*—" She caught herself and smiled sadly. "Listen to me. To us. We aren't action heroes.

We're an ex-yoga instructor, a reporter, and a ..." She closed her eyes for a moment, searching her circuit's knowledge. "Safety officer."

"Thank you," Paul said, smiling and patting Maria's hand.

"In my old life I—" Maria stopped herself. Her 'old life' meant Marcus, clearly. Marcus, trapped in a bubble, waiting to starve to death or for death to walk down his driveway. "My worry," Maria said changing the subject, "is that our only *real* warrior is off somewhere with Eric. Do you think they're—"

"We can't speculate," I said. "We have to assume they're okay until we know otherwise—"

"Old John Castle," Paul said, snapping his fingers. "It has to be. Perfect."

"Where's that? Wait, castle? We don't want to be near *buildings*—"

"Don't worry about that," Paul said. "Old John is literally just one little leftover tower. A *folly*, I believe is the correct expression. You know a castle on a chessboard?"

"Of course."

"The thing looks just like one of those. We always called it Old John Castle when I was a kid but that's not really what it is."

"But why there?"

"Several reasons: it's not far from here, it's in the middle of Bradgate Park—which means open land all around it—and most importantly, it's on top of a good, steep hill. High ground, like Maria said. *Excellent* high ground. Those things' heads would be at foot height if they have to come up towards us. Perfect for an early kick."

That did sound good. I pictured a Blue's head rising up before the Stone Man's leg, Caementum kicking *through* it hard enough to punt it clean off the monster's shoulders. Having struck the Blue in the head—and being struck in the Stone Man's head—it felt like the worst of the damage was done there. That's where the killing blows should land. Even if the Core was somewhere in the depths, the Stone Men's sight definitely saw from where their eyes should be. Some sort of heavy processing in that part of their bodies, perhaps? Impacts there maybe rattling the rest of their complex Stone circuitry?

"How far away from here?" I asked.

"Twenty, thirty minute drive on open roads," Paul said. "So maybe about three hours at Stone Man walking speed? Barring any difficult roadblock clearances."

More than enough time. We'd seen what looked like the closest Blues waiting for the furthest. We'd all individually got the same gist from Eric's message, and had to assume that gist was correct; that they were all planning on meeting us as a unit. Based on the spread of the Blues around the Midlands in Eric's vision—even with their greater walking speed—they had to be a good nine or ten hours away.

"The amphetamines should start to wear off after we get there," I said. "That's a good thing; you'll have time to sleep and get some rest, then take a fresh dose before they all …" I trailed off. The next word was *arrive*.

The glibness of my idea was wearing off and the reality was settling in.

Twelve of them. All at once.

"… before the sun comes up," I finished, but everyone knew what I'd meant to say.

Maria shivered, holding herself.

"It sent *all* the new ones," she said, and I didn't need to ask who *it* was. "It wants to rub us out. Not taking any chances. I know that's nothing new, but just knowing it made that decision. To stand a better chance of killing *us*, personally."

Paul's face twitched. He glanced up quickly, to see if I'd seen it.

"It's okay," I said.

"I'm sorry," he said. "Powering that thing, even with you two helping. Now there's going to be this … fight. I can't—" He coughed. Sniffed. "I should have been dead. I should have been dead a long time ago."

Maria put her arms around Paul's still-broad shoulders, and for once I didn't look away. I wanted to encourage him, to say something that would give him hope. But even though I believed in the new plan, even though I had more stamina than Paul did … I felt the same way. Every time I thought I had a grasp on this shit, or some hope, my brave new direction was revealed to be bullshit. A lie I'd convinced myself was true. And every time that was discovered, it was another notch harder to get back to my feet. I had no flowery words to make it better for Paul.

Then Maria said it perfectly.

"We just have to, Paul," she said. "I'm sorry."

He looked at Maria, his brow furrowed.

"I know," he said. "I know. But … how much longer …"

She rubbed the back of his head. Sniffed up her own tears.

"As long as it takes," she said sadly.

Both of them turned to me, and I realised I was supposed to follow up.

"Let's quickly find some dry clothes," I said, copping out. Our clothes were even wetter now post-fight. They needed to sleep at Old John Hill; we would simply have to raid the nearby wardrobes of the dead. "Then we'll get in the Merc and on the road. Meet back there in five."

I turned away before either of them could reply, heading for the nearest intact house.

***

Seven minutes later we were on the road.

Maybe an hour after that, around 3am, Maria thought she could hear Eric. I checked. I couldn't hear a thing.

"Are you sure?" I asked her. I was wearing my new-but-ill-fitting sweater, jeans and jacket. Paul was wearing jeans, a grey hoodie, and a blue baseball cap, a combination that made him look like a young thug. Maria was sporting an absolutely shocking lime green tracksuit. *It's warm* had been her justification, and I couldn't blame her.

The Stone Man walked ahead of our slowly trundling car as we traversed the darkened A roads, looming large in the semicircle of our headlights. Damaged or not, slowed down or not, make no mistake about it: the Stone Man was a monstrosity. But it was once again *our* monstrosity.

"I—*yes*," Maria said. I stopped the car. "You can't hear that?"

"No," I said. "Paul?"

"No," Paul said from the back seat. "Are you sure you're not—"

"It's like he's … underwater." Maria paused, frowning.

"Can you hear Edgwick?" I asked. "Are they both—"

"No Edgwick," Maria said, her face tensing and relaxing, tensing and relaxing. "Eric's flickering in and out. He's hurt or something. *Shit,* I don't know how long—"

"Tell him where we're going, quickly."

She winced.

"I can't," she said. "Words aren't going—*pictures* then, Paul, you said it Old John looked like—"

"Castle on a chessboard—"

Maria's eyes flew open.

"*Oh!*"

"What?!"

"Something happened at the end! Something happened to Eric!"

Ahead of us, the Stone Man continued to walk. I kept an eye on its range.

"Like what?"

"I don't know! There was something huge coming in, then he was gone."

"Like the Stone Giant?"

"Bigger. Much, much bigger."

Silence apart from a ticking sound. I realised it was the indicator, flicked on before I pulled over. Old habits dying hard.

"Did you send the picture of Old John?"

"I-I tried to send an image of a tower shaped like a chessboard castle," Maria replied, "like you said, and on a hill. That was so quick, I don't-I don't know if it went! Do you think Eric's okay?"

I restarted the engine. What was it Maria had said? *We have to.*

"Let's keep going," I said. Nobody responded, so I just rolled the Mercedes after the Stone Man. Ten minutes later I had to use the Stone Man to smash a Range Rover out of our path. I let out an involuntary little chuckle of delight as I did so. The icy silence that followed—them still thinking about Eric, me lost in the power of Caementum again like an arsehole—made me wish my phone was already hooked up to the Bluetooth. That way I could easily just press play on some music. I *was* worried about Eric; I was just very, very worried about us too. No-one was talking about the other thing: the slowly tightening circle of Blues on their way to kill us.

I watched the Stone Man walk for the next hour. On the plus side, the thing was at least beginning to feel a little more responsive. Maybe healing as hoped, or at least its internal energies. The divots and cracks in its body were no different than earlier. I didn't think that would change.

"Did you think," Maria suddenly said, "did you think the Blue's energy dump was more powerful than Caementum's original one back at the Project? At least before the Blue auto-stopped it?"

"Yes," Paul said. "A much bigger and more powerful dump. Definitely."

I glanced at Maria's reflection in the glass. *There* was a tiny smile, brief and vanishing, but it had appeared nonetheless.

"You think Caementum *came* here on its last legs then?" I asked. "If the Blue's Detonation was larger, Caementum obviously didn't have as much juice inside it. No wonder it latched onto Paul and started drawing from him."

"The bigger question," Paul said, "is why they didn't just set off something like that the second they first came here? Really shut us down. Make sure we had no chance at all."

"Because they're like Gods," Maria said quietly. "They don't think they need to." She turned away from the window now, looking through the windscreen at the walking Stone Man.

"And maybe they're right," she added.

***

We reached Bradgate Park around 5am.

After using Caementum to kick a few bollards and trees out of the way, we drove the car right into the park itself. Our headlights revealed a surprisingly vast expanse of green that stretched away for what looked—incorrectly—like miles in either direction. Old John Hill itself was right by the car park, its hill much closer to the entrance than I'd expected, and it was indeed a good, steep incline. The landscape was more of an issue than I'd expected, though. I parked the car by the hill's base and got out, looking up the rise. The moon was high and clear that night, and the shadow of Old John—or the ancient, man-made folly part at least—stood proud at the summit.

"Hmm," Paul muttered, seeing the same problem. "Didn't really remember that."

The hillside itself was dotted with large, jagged boulders. They were large enough to necessitate physically climbing over them if someone were to take any route up the hill rather than the path. I wasn't worried about Caementum getting round them—it would go through them—but who knew what chaos might occur when the Blues descended? Or rather, as it would now be with the hill, ascended? The boulders might be in our human way if we had to move fast. *Flying* boulders might be added into the mix, chunks of lethal rocky shrapnel blasted into the air by striding Blue legs.

I jogged up the path, shocked by how out of breath I was at the top, and turned around, surprised to see Paul and Maria clambering slowly up the hill behind me.

"You can rest in the car," I told them, but Paul shushed me. A minute later, they were standing alongside me, turning on the spot to take in the horizon. We could see for miles beyond the park. Paul really had, in one sense, picked a perfect spot … if not for a few apparently forgotten issues.

"This might not be right at all," Maria said. "The hill is like an obstacle course. That'll only hamper us and won't affect them but look, there's a fucking *forest* blocking all that part of our sightline over there." She was right; it was only a small forest, but still a forest nonetheless. I was more than happy to solve all of these problems.

"Don't worry about any of that," I told them. I turned to look at the folly. It was exactly as Paul had described it: just like the castle on a chess board. It stood fully intact and alone atop this windy lookout point here at the end of the world. The folly had a little stone archway to nowhere stuck against its side, presumably once part of a much larger building. I'd asked Paul if this was the case, but he didn't know. *We just used to play Robin Hood here,* he'd said, *and kick the shit out of each other with sticks.*

The building had a large wooden door—one added in modern times but designed to look as period as possible—set into the space where the original had been. Presumably this was so the small, ancient tower could perhaps be closed to the public outside of visiting times. It was cold tonight and I thought we'd need to make a fire. A fire inside the tower would be even warmer. A quick *knock-knock* from Caementum would render the visiting hours permanently open, letting us inside, but sadly we had to do more damage than that. We would have to flatten Old John.

We'd have to flatten *everything* except the hill.

Hey, I didn't like it either. Ancient landmarks are ancient landmarks, but we were there to save the world. We couldn't have a collapsible stone structure in the middle of our high ground, and we couldn't have any physical obstacles here. Same for any blockages in our sightlines. Fortunately, we had the single greatest piece of heavy machinery ever driven by man. It was 5am, and we thought the Blues would be here by nine or ten. More than enough time for me to go to work while the others rested.

"First thing to go," I sighed, "is the tower. Then I'll pulverise all these boulders around the hill. We don't know the direction we'll be retreating up the slope, so they've all got to go. You two get a fire going at the top, then get in your sleeping bags and rest."

"What are you going to be doing?" Maria asked. I pointed at the forest.

"Honestly?" I told her. "I feel bad admitting it, but … I'm going to be having fun." I headed back down the hill to where the Stone Man was patrolling back and forth by the car. I opened the boot and grabbed my pack to get my torch. I was going to need it.

"You're serious?" Maria called down, finally getting it. "You're going to flatten the *forest*?"

"Yep," I called back up. "We have to. Think it'll take me long?" I found the torch and grabbed both of their packs. I didn't want them to have to carry them to the top of the hill; I did that for them. "Have a bite to eat," I said. "You have to be hungry by now."

"Do you need us to do anything?" Paul asked, sounding reluctant. I don't think he liked being babied, but he appreciated it all the same.

"Just over here one sec," I said, summoning the Stone Man. It turned and began to thud its way up the steep incline. I pictured its brothers doing the same. "I'll take care of the tower now. We can use that door for firewood."

March of the Stone Men

"We have the camping stove," Maria said, but I shook my head.

"Come on now," I said. "Don't you want a real fire? It'll be a lot warmer than a crappy stove."

They exchanged a glance; I understood. A fire in general was maybe unnecessary, after all. The sun would be up in just a few hours and, while chilly, their sleeping bags would do the job. They just wanted to lie down, their amphetamines clearly wearing off. That was good. Perhaps ordinarily they would have lasted a little longer, but I thought Paul and Maria had burned through the meds quicker than most. That's just what it took to drive the Stone Man.

Once I'd used Caementum to quickly reduce the ancient landmark to rubble, I got the fire going. I left Paul and Maria laying with their heads on their rolled-up camping mats. I don't know if they watched me work in the nearby forest. They had a perfect view of the foliage below, but by the time I was done and returned they looked asleep. The whole flattening process took less than an hour. I sent Caementum back and forth in straight lines, felling every tree in the process before sending it back over it all again, stamping down the undergrowth. The hardest part was seeing what was going on in the dark, but the Maglite torch was ultra-powerful. I could stand at a distance, controlling the carnage.

Yeah. I enjoyed it. I'm the only one who knows what it was like, and if you think you wouldn't, believe me: you would enjoy it. I have no guilt about it.

I set Caementum to pacing in a circle around the summit and went to sit by the fire. It was still high—one thing I can do is build a good fire, especially when I have a camping stove full of propane to cheat with—and I enjoyed its warmth, sitting with my back against my still-packed pack and letting my heartrate come back down. I was a Super Lumberjack, and I was indeed okay, at least for that moment. Of course, I wasn't even a little bit sleepy. I looked up to see Paul and Maria watching me through puffy eyes.

"Felt good?" Paul murmured.

"Yeah," I said, not bothering to deny it. "Don't think what's coming is going to feel good, though. I think that's going to hurt quite a lot." But right now, everything was strangely fine. Still. "When's the last time you went camping, Maria?"

"Last night, genius," she said, a smirk breaking through.

"I meant *before* then," I said, rolling my eyes.

"About five years ago," Maria said. The smile remained, but her eyes looked faraway. "Just after I found out I was pregnant. Marcus and I went."

"Oh," I said, immediately feeling bad about the question, but Maria sleepily waved a hand.

"It's okay, Andy," she said, smiling sadly. "This is a nice memory." She looked at the flames and her smile gently widened. "Marcus was so worried about me going, but I insisted. The trip had been planned for months. It wasn't even really camping; we slept in his van. Lying on his crappy old mattress with the back doors open, watching the fire. his hands on my stomach." She pulled the top of her sleeping bag closer to her chin. Her expression was in shadow now. "You know ... it was probably the most peaceful I've ever felt."

She fell silent.

"You okay?" I asked, thinking about Marcus inside his bubble. The memory might have been nice, but the man in it was currently in trouble.

"I'm good," Maria said quietly, but her gaze stayed on the fire.

I couldn't read her face. I decided to switch her out.

"What about you Paul?"

"Ten years. Easy."

"Hmm. Last time I went camping," I said, "has to be even longer than that. It was with this girlfriend of mine. I'd have been in my early twenties" I looked at the stars, remembering the story. "She was nice but she was *convinced* that we were gonna get attacked by wild animals, right? And I kept telling her *hey, there aren't really any animals in the British Isles that would attack us. It's fine.* And she'd kind of nod and go *yeah, but you can't be too careful, can't be too careful*. And I'd think: *what do you mean? What wild animals are actually gonna get us?* But I didn't say it. Eventually I snapped and said *okay, exactly what animals do you think are gonna eat us?* And she couldn't name one." The fire looked ready for a larger piece of wood now. I grabbed one.

"So what happened?" Maria asked, making me jump a little. I hadn't heard her stir. Her eyes were heavy with sleep. I thought about the question, trying to remember. What *did* happen?

Oh, yeah.

"Well," I muttered, placing a large fragment of National Trust door on the fire. God knew what the thing was coated with. That wood was giving out a lot of smoke. "Well, as I recall, we kind of got into an argument."

"Why?"

I rubbed the back of my head, embarrassed. Why the hell did I bring this up?

"I just kept asking," I said. "*Tell me one. Tell me just* one. I was ... fixated. Frustrated by her not accepting that there weren't any wild animals for us to worry about."

"How did it end?"

"She, uh, she went home. Left me alone in my tent. Good job we took separate cars." The fire continued to crackle. No-one said anything. My headache throbbed patiently. "I guess it was pretty stupid of me to make such a big deal of it," I said. "I just ... I couldn't help it." I could see it then: looking up at the blackness that was the roof of my tent, laying awake all night trying to figure out what just happened. Knowing we were over. The fire popped. "I liked her a lot, actually. Rebecca. Blew *that*." I shrugged. "She was no Sophie, of course, but ..."

"Can you show me?" Maria said,

"Show you?"

"Send me the memory," she said. "Pass it along. You know how."

I did know. I saw the memory in my mind's eye. With a mental push, I could send it to her. But I hesitated.

Then I sent it to them both.

They closed their eyes, watching it, feeling my experience of it. Maybe not as real as the real thing, maybe real enough. After a moment something came back down along their threads: empathy, from both. It gently washed over me like a cooling breeze on a sweltering day.

Maria opened her eyes.

"That was awful," she said.

I didn't know what to say. I knew I'd been in the wrong that night, that I hadn't needed to browbeat Rebecca like that ... but Maria and Paul knew that too. I wasn't the victim of the story, but my friends were only speaking to the fallout of my own actions, the anguish I'd experienced afterwards. There was no judgement or blame. Just an acknowledgement that the situation I'd created for myself was difficult.

Not since Sophie had I felt so understood.

"Still fucked up, though," I mumbled.

"Oh, totally," Paul said. "Brought it on yourself. Damn shame, though. Did you apologise?"

"Yeah," I said, clearing my throat. "But. You know. She'd seen me for who I was, by then."

"Not that person now," Paul said, eyes closing, sleep beginning to take him once more. I was glad; I wasn't sure what he said was true, at least not completely. I sent something back along our threads: my gratitude, heartfelt and complete. To my shame—and my eternal regret—I didn't send them what I really felt in that moment.

That I realised I loved them both very much. Even Maria, who I had known for only the briefest time, but who I now knew intimately through the nature of our intensely shared experience. How scared I felt at the possibility I might lose them.

The sense of Stone calm gained from my busywork flew away. *Now* I was frightened.

The platoon of Stone Men coming for us was finally starting to feel like a reality. Paul and Maria suddenly seemed very frail and fragile. Paul might have already been broken for a while but Maria had changed since the news about Marcus. They were at their wits' end, meaning our circuit was far from optimal efficiency. We needed to be at our best if my friends were to survive.

I was even starting to worry about my own capabilities. This headache had crept in ever since our encounter with the Blue, having started when that thing was 'scanning' Caementum. Had it done something to me in the process? Or worse, was this my brain starting to blow a gasket from constantly driving the Stone Man? I pulled my sleeping bag up to my shoulders, closed my eyes to the fire, and stepped into Stone Space.

Out along the thread between myself and Caementum, down into its depths.

Before me hung the Core.

I'd pretty much given up on the idea of ever getting into it, but I had nothing better to do for the next few hours. It didn't hurt to look some more, and I had to try *something* to help my friends. I slowly circled the Core. There wasn't an inch of it I hadn't already repeatedly traced. Doing so eventually seemed pointless, but I still kept thinking this might have been that which the Blue accessed. If so, it was another vote for the Core potentially being the Stone Man's mind, or at least its equivalent of a central processor. I noticed how my headache felt more distant and dulled in Stone Space, a welcome reprieve. I could stay in here for a while—

The headache. The bloody headache. It really *had* been a bastard, hadn't it, at the moment it kicked in? Right when the Blue was scanning ... but the pain had been so acute and localised, that pickaxe-in-the-head feeling coming from a very specific point at the back of my skull. *Precise.* Did that mean something?

The idea snagged.

If the Core is related to whatever the Blue did during its scan, I thought, *and my pain is related to* that ... *could that pain lead me somewhere? Reverse engineering a thread, almost?*

I pictured the moment in my mind, recalling that specific blooming of pain as much as I could. I looked at the Core and felt compelled to move around to the other side of the immense object. The specific memory of the now-dulled pain was taking me somewhere, like a metal detector beeping more frequently. *Don't get excited,* I thought. I'd been at this vantage point on the Core's surface before, many times, along with every other point. and I'd discovered zero cracks or fissures. Perhaps, though, I now had a better idea of where to knock?

According to the vision Eric sent, I thought, *the Blue put something in the Stone Man. I can't see it or feel it, so maybe it isn't even a thread at all, or maybe it's a different kind than any we've seen before. Whatever it is, it goes all the way back to the Prism. Is that of any use here?*

Not yet, certainly, but something told me I was getting warmer. I let my brain tick over, continuing to reason it out: *If this thread/not thread/whatever goes into the* Core, *then it's around here somewhere, even if you can't see it. If you could maybe cut it and use it, or just somehow* connect *with it, then you could—*

Cut threads. I already had some, didn't I?

I'd found them right at the start of all this, when we woke the Stone Man; the ones lying broken, snapped the moment the weakened and dormant Caementum had been wrenched away from Paul. I'd found them, held them, used them to take control of the monster. Were they still—

I felt around. Yes, the remaining unused and broken threads were still there, hanging loose. These were dull, dead, hard to see and completely forgettable compared to the threads we'd used to drive. Those had become bright and alive once I'd grasped them with my mind. Could these broken threads be put to use? I hesitated. What would happen if I connected them to the Core and the whole system shorted out, the circuit blowing back in on itself?

I considered the zombie-like state of Paul and Maria, and figured that it was a risk that had to be taken.

Face it, Dispensatori, I thought. *It's twelve-on-one, and a damaged one at that. You're already dead. You might as well try.*

I lightly connected the ends of the Stone Man's broken threads to the Core. I barely had time to think the command *open* before the thing unfurled like a flower.

It was like a cavern yawning open before my eyes. Inside was ... nothing. Even when I moved into it—only realising later what a potentially dangerous move this was—there was still nothing, other than a sense of cold. Was it just empty, then? Perhaps a feature of the creature's design that never got utilised by its creator; a covered gap in the dashboard for an optional stereo that was never fitted? As I floated around the space, trying to figure my next move, I became aware that there were differences in that coldness, subtle but there. So there was *something* here, even if I couldn't comprehend what it was. There was a sensation then that felt vaguely familiar on my skin—

No. No, I'm not explaining it right. There was a sensation of *déjà vu,* only one I hadn't actually felt bef—

Dammit. There was the faintest sense of *familiarity.* That's the best way I can put it.

I reached out for it instinctively.

Then I was inside an immense tent.

Not a tent like in my Rebecca story, but a field tent; literally a field tent, beneath my feet was grass, the construction all around me something like an immense canvas marquee. For a second, I thought it was Paul's hangar, but this covering wasn't made of metal and, while still big, wasn't anywhere near as large as Paul's was. I was walking forwards, standing tall, and as I saw the cluster of people in the near distance—military fatigues, machinery, lanyard-wearing civilians—the person standing out in the centre of the marquee by themselves was immediately and horribly familiar.

Alone and wearing a hospital gown, upright but with his eyes rolling back up into his head, was former Sergeant Henry Williams. I was the Stone Man, and I was bearing down upon my quarry.

I understood immediately, the sight making the conclusion inescapable: what I was seeing was some kind of stored memory from the Stone Man's visual feed. *Familiar,* oh yes, my experience with Henry Williams familiar indeed, seared into my mental DNA. I never saw Henry's Harvesting myself, but I'd read the file. Henry, taken to the nearest open space by the walking Stone Man, in this case a field. The immediate area and air space were cleared, but the military still hastily erected a field tent over the space to ensure the actual Harvest would be unseen—

I panicked, pushing backwards with my mind from this connection that had drawn me to it, desperate to be away from the image of Henry growing closer and closer, searching for its opposite, anything, to be away *as far as I could,* and when I felt a temperature and pressure completely different to my current situation, I seized it with all my might and dived towards it.

I saw a blackness that slowly became a red sky.

Not red like a sunset; red like nothing I have ever seen in my life.

Before me was an immense sea of hairless faces.

Even though they clearly weren't human, it seems that fear is truly universal; I could see it in every one of the creatures gathered at the front. Their heads were elongated and narrow, but their tiny black eyes still communicated terror. They wore no clothes, their humanoid bodies—their arms as proportionally elongated as their faces—smooth and featureless. The faces of the larger creatures standing further back simply looked stern, standing tall, their shoulders erect. They formed a wall with their bodies, seeming to hem in the creatures before them.

A single creature stood at the very front of the crowd, placed directly in front of me. Its hands were curled at its chest, its body bent at the waist, its black eyes turned to the sky as its head lolled backwards against its thin, wiry neck.

I looked out of the corner of this memory's eye, seeing 'my' chest. It was pale, like bleached chicken, with a network of wiry veins visible beneath the surface. I knew that, were I able to look behind me, I would see the Prism from which I had just emerged.

The image started to fade quickly; I couldn't hold it, couldn't bring it back. Then the image was gone entirely and I was back inside the cold, empty cavern of the Core. More than that, though; I was coming out of Stone Space altogether as if on autopilot. As I drew out of the Core, it began to close, the threads I'd attached dropping limply free. I was going back to my body? Why? The second I came fully back to myself, to physical awareness, I felt my body jerk and I had the answer. I'd caught myself falling asleep.

I was suddenly so tired I could barely function.

I jerked again, passing out once more already, sitting upright. Opening the Core, it seemed, had finally done something to whatever had been keeping me awake. Darkness was falling again, fast. I had a second to double check that Caementum was still circling on autopilot before I dropped, ironically, like a stone.

***

When I awoke, the Stone Man was no longer walking in a circle.

I shot upright. The sky was full of washed-out light and Paul and Maria's sleeping bags were empty. I checked my watch; it was gone 8am! How long until the Blues arrived? An hour? Two at most? I clambered out of my bag, clearing my throat to call my friends' names, but once I was standing, I could see down the steep rise of the hill to where Paul was sitting. He'd parked himself in the now-pounded gravel that remained of the many boulders that had been jutting from the earth. His arms were wrapped around his knees and he was staring ahead of himself, his face hidden by the shadow of his baseball cap's brim. About twenty feet below him, closer to the bottom of the slope, the Stone Man was slowly swinging its arms back and forth in front of its body, feet planted. As the sleep bled out of my brain, I did what I should have done in the first place and checked Paul in our circuit; yes, he was controlling the Stone Man. As I watched, Caementum's arm movements switched from back and forth to up and down.

Paul was practicing.

I breathed out, looking around for Maria. I couldn't see her.

"Hey," I called. Paul looked up and raised a hand.

"Are you seeing this?" he said. He was smiling.

"I am," I said. "Very nice."

"It's not the Bolshoi ballet," he said, "but it's something." I made my way down the rise and patted Paul's shoulder, sitting down beside him.

"How come you're awake?" I said. "You set an alarm?"

"Yeah."

I realised to my horror that I hadn't set one; I'd passed out too quickly. I shivered, thinking of the near miss, but then realised we'd have felt them coming long before they arrived. I looked to the horizon. There were no traces of Blue there other than the pale colour of the sky. We'd see them soon.

"Where's Maria?"

Paul gestured with his head.

"Down the other side of the hill," he said. "Said she needed some alone time. We can call her on the circuit hotline if we need her quickly."

"Okay."

"I'm worried about her, man."

"Me too," I said, not adding *but what about you, dude?* "Knowing what's happening to Marcus, along with everything else she has to do. Damn."

"You think she's DIGGS level now?" Paul asked.

"How do you mean?"

"I mean do you think it's possible, after everything that's happened? The boosting, spending time in-circuit."

"Anything's possible—"

"Actually, that's not really what I mean," Paul said. "Do you think *she* thinks she's DIGGS level now?"

"Why would she?"

"She heard Holbrooks say it's possible," Paul said, shrugging and playing with a piece of grass. Before us, the Stone Man started to slowly turn in a circle, its arms held out either side of itself. "People can go up a level on the Stone Spectrum. Epigenetics or whatever. She has to wonder if it's possible."

I'd heard all the Stone Spectrum theories at the Project, up to and including a Fung Shui rearrangement of the hangar. That one lasted about a week.

"But it's not," I told him. "You know the score: it's possible to go up *one* bracket. But Maria is LION. At best, she'd be GALE, like me. Just because she's powerful doesn't mean she's in that DIGGS bracket. Remember: you're talking about it all wrong, they're not *levels*, they're brackets. I hate it when people say levels."

"Doesn't mean she doesn't believe she's somehow managed to go up two whole levels," Paul said, and I wasn't sure if he'd used the word *up* deliberately.

"Okay. Let's say she does believe that," I said, carefully checking my own circuit block in case Maria might be listening. I mentally nudged Paul to do the same. "What's your concern?"

"My concern is what her concerns might be," Paul said. "Like, maybe she's worrying about what might happen to her now she's been boosted. Now she's more on the Caeterus' radar. Maybe that's what she's sitting over there being frightened of right now. And if she's *not* worried, I am."

"I won't let anything happen to her." The words were out before I could stop them. Paul's lips turned up in a friendly smirk.

"Well, you know," he said "Good lad, I guess."

His smirk broke into a grin. I started to chuckle. We both did.

"We're gonna fuckin' *die*," I said, and the chuckles turned into laughter as the fear and madness of the situation collapsed all the way into the inverse of itself. It was suddenly so bizarre it was hilarious. Paul slapped me on the back, shaking his head and wiping his eyes, and for a moment we were just two friends hanging out and shooting the shit.

Then I heard the sound of approaching footsteps. Maria was heading over, a sad smile on her face as she watched us, her eyes dry but red. She nodded towards the Stone Man.

"Can it do the Hustle?" she asked. Paul stood, smiling, and arched his back.

"One dance step at a time," he said. The three of us silently watched the Stone Man continue to turn. Maria cocked her head, watching Paul.

"You're not afraid of it anymore," she said quietly. "Are you?"

Paul considered it for a second.

"I don't think I am now, no," Paul said. "Not this one, anyway. You?"

"Not this one," Maria repeated. "No."

Paul stood and took his baseball cap from his head. He hefted it for a moment, and then began to walk towards the Stone Man. It stopped turning; I didn't know if Paul could trigger the autopilot so I quietly took over and made it shift its weight from foot to foot on the spot. A moment was occurring, I could see, and I just wanted to make sure it went smoothly. Paul stopped about five feet away from the Stone Man, then took a deep breath before walking four of the remaining feet towards it.

"Paul—" Maria began.

"Wait," I whispered.

Paul tossed his hat up towards the Stone Man's head.

It bounced off and landed at Paul's feet; he picked it up and tried once more. This time it landed perfectly, the blue cap looking ludicrous on top of the monster. Paul stepped back and spun around to grin at us as he sent the Stone Man off walking in a circle. I let him. The sight of the Stone Man walking and wearing that ridiculous cap set me and Paul off again—Maria even joined in—but this time, as Paul turned the Stone Man to walk towards us, the laughter drained away almost as quickly as it had come.

Paul watched the Stone Man approach, blue cap and all. He stayed calm, letting it draw close to him; he even straightened up, sticking his chest out a little. Once the Stone Man was again within five feet of him, Paul stopped it walking. He snatched up a stick from the ground and stepped forward, the smile gone from his face. He drew close to the Stone Man, raised the stick above his head, and jumped straight up, using the stick to knock the very tip of the cap's brim up and off the Stone Man's head. He bent to grab the hat, hesitated, and then picked it up. He straightened and looked the Stone Man in the face. Nodded.

Then he walked back over to join us, head down.

"Fucking thing," he said.

I thought about telling them what I'd seen in the Core and decided not to. If we survived, I would. What I'd seen didn't matter now and would only be a distraction we could ill afford. We couldn't do anything with the Core anyway; the way I'd been wiped out by going inside meant it wasn't a risk we could take again, not with the Blues' imminent arrival.

"We should take our amphetamines," I said. "Make sure they're in our system before the Blues get here."

"Why isn't the Stone Giant coming with them?" Maria asked. "That's what I don't get. If the idea is to send a wave at us, why not throw *everything* at us?"

"Same reason that the original six are still at work," I said. "The process never stops. Always efficient. And you said it yourself: they're Gods. Jupiter doesn't get his hands dirty if he can just send Mars to do it. Can you blame them? If they know how things went down with the Blue we fought, then they think twelve is plenty." *They're right,* I thought, glad again for the blocks in our circuit.

"I want them here now," Maria said quietly, amazing me. "I want this done. I want it over, and I want to hurt them."

"You'll at least get a chance," Paul said.

"Well, I don't think we actually *hurt* them—" I began, but Maria cut me off.

"However it works," she said, watching the Stone Man with eyes that were, I understood, full of hate. "I want to kill them. I want to kill all of them."

There wasn't a lot I could say to that. If Maria was in kill mode, that was probably for the best.

"I'll get the tablets," I said.

Then I—

...

Sorry. I, uh ...

Hold on.

***

Sorry. I needed a moment. We're coming to a difficult part of the story, and—

...

Sorry. Thought I was ready. Let me just get a glass of water and I'll start again. Hang on.

***

Okay.

Around an hour later, we saw the first Blue on the horizon.

We'd been watching the northeast so carefully—having seen a very faint plume of smoke in that direction—that I nearly ignored the movement I glimpsed away to the northwest. I caught it, though, sitting up in surprise. I'd expected our first glimpse of them to be much smaller, but this Blue was close enough for me to easily make out its shape. It stood out clearly against the muddy green and brown landscape, heading steadily towards us.

"There," I said. The amphetamines were now well into our bloodstreams and brains, our circuit turbocharged, and while I couldn't say for sure, it felt like the Stone Man's back and forth pacing was a little higher now. A little more pep in the step. The three of us had been sitting on the hill, but now we stood, as one. With the folly flattened we had full line of sight in all directions, easily seeing over the pile of thick gravel where the tower Paul called Old John Castle once stood. I looked behind us; four more Blues could now be seen at about the same distance away, spread, of course, all around us. They hadn't been there the last time we looked. We'd somehow become complacent in our watching, but who could blame us; seeing them, there was still no reason to panic (other than, obviously, our impending deaths). The circle of Blues would not close upon Old John Hill for a good twenty minutes, at least. I turned further left. Now I could see the faint shapes of four more Blues. The rest heaved into view soon after, the circle perhaps not closing as perfectly as I thought it would. Maybe they would co-ordinate more as they came into closer range.

"Maria?" I said. "Pick one."

Our fear had been flattened out much like Old John; still present but tamped down to something that, while still hard and permanent, was not in our way. Our blood was all the way up. Even my damn headache was background noise. Maria turned in a circle and pointed at a Blue on the horizon at random.

"That one," she said.

"Okay," I said. "Everyone knows the plan."

"Yes—"

"Let them get close to us, nice and close together," I said. We did know the plan, but I wanted zero confusion. "Then we move on *that* one. We blanket it, then hit it, damage it. Stone Giant can't push us out. Then you two keep it busy while I get inside and burst the fucker out."

"Okay," the other two replied. Their eyes were darting between each of the Blues as they continued to make their silent way towards us. They were still too far away for us to feel or hear the steady, heavy thudding of their feet. We weren't going to blanket it until we were ready to make our move. We didn't want to give the Stone Giant any more time than necessary to respond in any way. So we watched, we waited, and it was interminable. There was no avoiding this, and so perversely, I wanted this to at least begin now so it could be over one way or another. I *wanted* it.

More waiting. Watching. I observed their pace as they closed in. Thought about the timing involved, and the thought popped into my head:

We should go towards them now—

That would mean giving up the high ground, the high ground we came here to use, but the *timing*, the grouping—

"Listen," I said. "I-I might have a potential change of plan. I think our plan is wrong."

"You're kidding," Maria said. "*No.* Not now."

"They're quicker than us," I said, "but there's getting close and there's getting close. Look at the timing of their pace. I think if we wait until they get to the hill there's too much chance of a pile-on from the ones we're not fighting. If we go now, while they're spread out, we'd still have time to get back here if—"

"While they're still spread out?" Paul asked. "The whole idea was to have them all *close together*, so even if it caps the Detonation like earlier—"

"Yes," I said, shaking my fingers, "but look at the *timing,* look! By the time we get down to them they'll be pretty damn close to one another ... but not so close for the others to physically pile on while we take care of our target. I don't think that's a luxury we'll have on the hill, high ground or not!"

"Shit ... " Paul murmured. Maria didn't respond, looking from Blue to Blue.

"And if we run into any problems," I said, talking quickly, "then I think—*as long as we land the first punch*—we can at least put the fucker down, and then get a stamp in on its head while there. We'd buy ourselves enough time to get back to the high ground, where we can go with the original plan. We give ourselves two bites of the cherry! And if the change of plan *does* work, then it'll all be over with the first encounter."

"*Why* did you wait to say this now?" Maria asked.

"I-I just thought of it; maybe it's the amphetamines talking, but I feel a lot more confident about getting close than I did earlier. Don't you?" *Confident* wasn't the word—there was no confidence here—but I was Dispensatori, and the word *hopeful* felt too damn weak. "I think Caementum's healed a lot, and we're starting with full control, unlike last time. Look, fuck it, this is as good as its going to get. What do you think? Answer quickly."

"Shit," Paul repeated, moving from foot to foot as he watched the Blues grow larger. "Yeah. Okay, yeah. Let's do it. Maria?"

"… yes."

There was only the gentle breeze then, buffeting our hair and our faces while death closed in.

"Are you re—"

"We're waiting for *you*, Andy," Maria said, and I realised I was stalling. Even now, after everything, staring down the barrel of my own demise was a real bastard.

"Just in case," I said, trying to think of the right words as I set the Stone Man off walking towards its supposed comrade. "It's been a pleas—"

No. That wasn't what I meant. I sent what I *did* mean around our circuit. It still wasn't as honest or open as it should have been, but I felt them both receive it, confirm it, and then the Stone Man was walking and so were we.

We headed down the steep hill, following a few feet behind the Stone Man and aiming at the Blue that Maria had selected. I looked to the other encroaching Blues to see if they were following our change of location. Even at a distance it was obvious that they were; shoulders of that size do not turn in a subtle manner. I tried to make myself as aware of the Stone Man's limbs as I could while operating them remotely, outside the driver's seat, my vision entirely my own. I would only use the Stone Man's full sight at the last possible moment, needing to easily see the whole battlefield, and wanting to avoid the combat complication of having my body becoming a zombie. Most importantly, if the last fight was anything to go by, I couldn't afford to take many hits while inside the Stone Man. Even one could take me out, and then we would be utterly screwed.

I looked behind me, assessing our possible line of retreat: if this failed, we would have to move efficiently to get back to the top of the hill before the net closed. Kicking attackers in the head, ones over ten feet tall—kicking *through* them—would be a lot easier when standing above them. Maria and Paul's eyes were alive, their jaws set. No talking now. Maria looked as if she were about to burst, her expression utterly fearless but full of pain.

We drew within twenty feet of the target Blue.

I went to say *now* but I didn't need to; I felt Maria's blanket around us already beginning to shift, to stretch and become thin as it spread to cover the Blue as well. If the Blue noticed in any way, it didn't show, or slow. It just kept coming. I felt Maria's blanketing connect and complete, removing the Blue from its wider circuit and the aid of the Stone Giant. Paul, Maria, and I halted as the two Stone Men moved into striking distance of one another. We didn't need to get any closer than this; it was all on Caementum now.

"*This is it!*" I yelled, my heart in my throat, my body feeling plugged into some Stone power socket, Paul and Maria gasping as we saw the Blue drawing its arm back to strike. This time, we were ready, and the amphetamines already at full power.

I saw the Blue's heavily telegraphed punch; I reacted just in time.

I bent the Stone Man quickly at the waist, sending the Blue's arm swinging harmlessly overhead, before swinging the Stone Man lipstick-tipped arms upward. They moved together in a crossbody, clubbing motion that started at its right hip and ended over its shoulder; exhilaration whipped through me as I saw the blow was going to land, and well. I pictured the strike moving *through* the Blue's head as the Stone Man's hands connected beautifully. They struck so hard that the force of it staggered the larger monster backward at the waist. I could have sworn I heard a faint fizzing noise at the point of impact.

"*Yes!*" Maria yelled, but already I was pressing the advantage, unable to believe our luck. I stepped the Stone Man forward and drove a straight left smack into the centre of the Blue's face. I then followed it up with a clumsy, looping pub-haymaker right into the Blue's torso, me picturing Caementum's hand blasting out through the Blue's back. The fizzing was unmistakable now, the noise clear in the air without the sound of crumbling buildings to drown it out. The Blue was doubled forward by this last punch and, seizing the opportunity, I swung Caementum's arm down onto the back of its head.

The Blue was driven flat into the deck like a paving slab.

"*Now!*" Paul yelled. "*Oh my God, now! It's down, It's fucking down!*"

"*Take over!*" I yelled to Paul, feeling him take the Stone Man's reins as I quickly looked around us for the other Blues. I froze as I saw how much larger they looked already. If this didn't work and we needed to beat a retreat, we would have less time than I thought. "*Move the Stone Man in and stamp the bastard twice, then stop!*" Paul obliged, moving the Stone Man's feet into stamping distance. "*I'm going in!*"

The second after Paul drove Caementum's foot down onto the fallen Blue's head, I gave the Stone Man the command—

Connect—

And connect it did, my consciousness shooting across the gap between myself and the blanketed Blue like a psychic bullet.

Take me deeper—

But something was different.

I knew it as soon as I went inside this Blue, hearing the noise of its inner Stone Space and feeling it trying to rise up off the floor under its own volition … but the sensation was only faint. Everything jolted as Paul dropped another boot onto the Blue; that *hurt*. I was glad I'd told him to only do it twice, suspecting that unloading on the Blue while I was connected to it would go very badly for me. But I wasn't as deep inside its systems as I should be; I'd told the Stone Man to send me *inside,* into its *inner* systems. I could feel its limbs a little, but instead of feeling them as my own—even if I had no real control—they felt separate, like I was wearing a living suit.

Connect, connect fully—

But nothing was happening. There was no way into its networks here. Paul was done hitting it, as instructed; now I felt the Blue around me beginning to stand. I tried to halt its upward motion but, as before, the best I could make it do was that fucking feeble twitch. That much, at least, was the same as before; but what the hell was different now? The Stone Man was the Blue's lynchpin, always had been! What was the problem—

I realised our terrible mistake.

The Blues and the Caementum had always been connected; Caementum had always been the lynchpin, after all. We'd proved all that in Loughborough when we'd used Caementum to get inside the Blue's systems. But in our planning for this battle, we'd missed a key part of that encounter.

That Blue had been one of the six originals. Caementum was *their* lynchpin, starting their Harvest cycle and leading them back and forth across their departures and Arrivals. But *these* Blues were never a part of that; the only leader they'd ever had was the Stone Giant. Caementum, it seemed, only held rank over the Blues it had a lipstick-tipped hand in creating.

Caementum had no connection to these twelve. There was no way in.

In desperation I tried to tell the Blue to stop, to lie down, but it was pointless; I'd learned in Loughborough that I couldn't command the Blue's limbs. At best, all I could do was make them twitch. There was nothing I could do here. I snapped back into my body, blinking and sitting up. "Hit the bastard," I gasped at Paul, "and don't stop." Paul used Caementum's remote reins to drive its foot down against the rising Blue's head with an almighty *clonk.* Our opponent was driven flat once more.

"You're bleeding again!" Maria said, and she was right; taking Caementum's attack while I was inside the Blue had messed me up, my nose gushing anew.

"*What's happening?*" Paul yelled, but instead of responding I took over remotely; my greater control would allow the Stone Man to stamp faster, harder. It took a second to get full control back, Paul's release of the Stone reins clumsy and sticky. Once I had full control, I set the Stone Man's feet to frantically stamping. Maybe we could kill the Blue like this?

"*Andy, why are we out?*" Maria asked. I looked around us; shortly all the approaching Blues behind us would pincer shut, and the point of no return would be crossed. If we didn't retreat soon, the Blues, walking faster than us, would have closed the exit between ourselves and the base of the hill.

"*We can't get inside these Blue's systems!*" I told her. "*Maria, blanket just us again, move it fully back to just us, quickly now!*" The Blue tried to rise again and, *yes,* its limbs were shaking and loose. The fizzing noise was accompanying its every attempt to move. I dropped the Stone Man to its knees, using it to punch the back of the fallen Blue's head—*through* the Blue's head—over and over, watching the slow horror of the other eleven Blues getting larger in my sight. Now we could feel their footsteps. It felt like being at the epicentre of a low-level earthquake. I willed the Blue to break, to die. I felt Maria's full blanketing of us dropped back into place; she was right, moving it back from the Blue did take far too much fucking time—

A crack appeared in the back of the Blue's neck. It was jerking limply on the floor now, but no longer trying to rise. Had I ... was it dead? I carried on hammering, sweat running down my back as I focused. I wanted to take the thing's head off, maybe that would release the—

No. Despite my best striking efforts, the head held. The net was about to close around us; even if it were possible, there was no time to Detonate the bastard this way. If we needed to do it quickly—and we did—that had to be done from the inside, a place we had no way to get to.

The Blue stopped moving. I stopped punching.

I didn't know what to do.

I didn't know what to do.

"What ... what do we do?" Paul breathed. If we were going to move to the hill it was now or never. We needed to regroup—

"*Let's go!*" I shouted, standing the Stone Man and setting it off marching. We strode back across the park. The Blues were so near now that it felt like we were in the middle of a football match, making a run on goal. No one spoke as the three of us ran around the Stone Man, passing its thudding, ponderous steps as we left it temporarily behind. The first encounter had gone well, but I thought we'd been deceptively lucky. We raced all the way to the base of Old

John Hill, its steep slope zooming rapidly towards us. Paul and Maria turned to look back once we'd reached its base but I charged past them, sprinting breathlessly to the top, wanting to look beyond. The other half of the circle of Blues were the same distance from us as those this side, six of them heading steadily inward, still spread out like their comrades. They would reach Old John Hill at roughly the same time as their brothers. I turned and saw Paul and Maria moving backwards up the slope towards me, and Caementum reaching the bottom of the hill. It began to stride upwards, the relentlessly pursuing Blues behind it. *Now it's the hunted,* I thought. Even in the chaos of the moment, the idea was insane. Behind them lay the fallen Blue we'd taken down. It still wasn't moving, lying face down in the grass. So maybe they *could* be purely beaten out of commission, but there were far too many of them to take out that way. Our only hope had been a Detonation, and that hadn't been possible. That only left ...

Nothing.

There was nothing left.

My throat began to close.

"If we can't get into their systems," Maria began, but there was no need for her to finish. We now had no plan at all, and eleven unstoppable monsters were now making their way up the hill to kill us.

"Then we—" I began. "Then we—"

I grabbed Maria's arm, Paul's arm, dug my nails into them.

"Then we take as many as we can with us," I said, and that felt right. A lunatic's confidence suddenly surged inside me. I started shouting, spit flying from my lips. *"We take them! We take them!"* I sounded insane, and maybe in that moment I was. What other choice was there? *"Okay! Okay!"*

Maria looked at me, and then her face twisted horribly as she began to scream. There were no words in it, no sorrow, only pure rage as her lips curled back from her teeth. Her whole body began to shake and Paul joined in with a deep, soul-bellow of his own that had only power behind it. *Here* was Paul, and as we prepared to go out in a blaze of screaming glory, my brain spoke up:

Oops. WAIT. Hold on a sec.

My pinwheeling mind had caught one of the thoughts screaming around its echo chamber, my awareness trying to remind me of something I'd failed to fully register.

Something happened, my mind whispered, *with the Blue's limbs. THINK.*

"Wait!" I said, yanking Paul and Maria back as they surged forward. I stood still, letting the thoughts play out.

"What!?" Maria screamed, still in full raging flow. *"Let's go!"*

Nothing happened with its limbs! I thought. *I couldn't even do anything in Loughborough! There* and *here, all I could do is make them twitch—*

The penny finally dropped.

We'd have to be careful. Quick. Make not one single goddamn mistake.

And we'd have to be very, very lucky.

"We can—" I began, then explained it the quick way instead: forming a hastily sketched mental montage of my plan, seeing it *working*, and then flinging it around the circuit. They got it; both their eyes opened wide, their rage disappearing into hyper-focus.

The Blues were at the base of the hill now. The Stone Man was just over halfway up.

I told it to turn.

"That one!" I yelled, and as Paul walked the Stone Man down towards our selected enemy, Maria stretched and shifted her blanketing of us, smothering the selected Blue. I waited a few seconds for the process to complete and sat my body down. I had to hope that the Blues had been programmed to take out only the Stone Man, ignoring my human form. Failing that, I had to hope Paul and Maria had the time and the awareness to move me in an emergency.

"I'm going in!"

I flashed into the Blue's upper systems, immediately feeling its limbs again like a useless, living skin. I didn't waste time trying to get into the Blue's deeper systems; Detonation was no longer the plan. A dim measure of the Blue's sight came to me and I saw hazily through its eyes, seeing the Stone Man striding down towards my new body. This was a poor, distant facsimile of a driving seat, one with almost no control, but there was the key word: *almost*. No, I couldn't control the Blue, but I didn't need to. My job now was to do something for which I have always had a natural gift.

I only had to get in the way and make a mess.

Strike first has always been my approach to the limited number of fights I've been in. That's a lot easier to do when your enemy isn't striking you.

The Blue tried to raise its arms, to draw them back to attack; I felt the impulse and tried to control it, knowing I would fail, but the actual desired result happened beautifully. The Blue's arms twitched for a moment. Its impulse to move continued, and again I tried to send a competing impulse. *Twitch.*

The constant interruptions were making the Blue's arms move in slow motion.

They were still barely raised from the Blues sides as Paul drew our Stone Man up close; I was the assistant to the schoolyard bully, effectively keeping the victim's arms held behind its back. The Stone Man had no need to duck for the next second or two, no need to waste energy or effort—or accuracy—on evading an enemy.

Paul only had to absolutely *twat it.*

My distant dim sight through the Blue's eyes was lousy and hazy but I waited, waited as Caementum's arms raised over its head, ready to slam down an elevated, double-handed piledriver of a blow. I waited until the very last millisecond before Caementum's arms plunged downwards toward the Blue's head. I flashed out and into my body in time to hear a *fizz* rip through the air, sounding like a professional-grade firework as Paul and Maria helped me to my feet.

The Blue crashed to the floor. Paul knew to *punch through the energy*, and he certainly had.

"*Yes!*" I yelled, watching Paul drive Caementum forward to give the fallen Blue a trademark follow-up stamp on the head, trying to kill it off. He got it wrong this time, though; in his haste he was no longer striking Caementum's energy through the Blue's. The resulting fizz still sounded like someone had thrown water over an entire server farm, but it wasn't enough. "*Again!*" I yelled. "*But* through, *through*—" Too late. We now had to move before we would be caught by the Blue's comrades. "*Back it up!*" I shouted, and Paul complied, driving the Stone Man backwards up the hill, the three of us backing up above it. It didn't feel like a retreat. We watched the Blue we'd just dropped trying to get unsteadily to its feet ... before, *yes,* falling limply to the deck and beginning twitching on the floor. Maybe not completely dead, but for the time being, no longer a threat, and that was exactly the plan. Maria was already beginning the too-damn-slow process of moving her full blanketing from the Blue to us. If the Stone Giant's presence was lurking nearby, trying to get to us while our concealment was thin, I was too damn fired up to notice. Maybe we *had* been lucky in our first battlefield skirmish, but the second had been won easily, and by design, in a way that could be repeated. Now maybe—if we could just manage the crowd—we had a chance. Detonation had been abandoned. We were going to try and *beat* them.

The plan was now to blanket the nearest Blue and move into it. Twitch its arms, slow it down, and create an opening. The Stone Man hitting it as much as we can and then backing up the hill in a spiral, keeping moving, leading them upwards to the beat of our tune. There was still plenty of high ground behind us; plenty of space to use in a fighting retreat. The Blues advancing behind us would soon be in front of us, albeit below us, as we looped up and around Old John Hill. We'd put two of our attackers down already, reducing their numbers to the ten Blues below, following us up and around the hill like the world's deadliest sheep.

"Which one now?" Paul shouted, the Stone Man's shoulders turning left and right as Paul prepared for the next attack, the Blues striding up the rise.

"Nearest!" I yelled, "always nearest! Maria, are—"

"Ready—"

Maria's blanketing surrounded the nearest Blue and I dove in, twitching the Blue's arms to an almost-standstill, but Paul's limited control caused us problems. He took too long to get the Stone Man up close to the Blue, but with an immense effort I managed to keep the twitching going until he arrived. I flashed out into my body just in time to avoid a pulverising blow from Paul that I was really, really glad I hadn't taken. That was too close. I felt Paul's hand on my collar as I was dragged sharply backwards, my recovering feet dawdling as the three of us continued our circling, leading, reversing path up and around the hill. It was messy and it was scrappy, but holy shit, this was working—

"Move your fucking feet!" Maria yelled, moving her blanketing off the second, now twitching Blue as it took several stomps to the head. That one, too, wasn't rising off the floor. It was neutralised, at least for now.

"That one, that one there!" I shouted.

From there our timing swung from the sublime to the ridiculous; we'd managed to drop the third Blue almost immediately, but as the fourth reached us, our timing was off. Maybe holding that third Blue for so long had taken more out of me than I realised, or Maria was tiring, moving her blanketing slower than needed. Either way, I flashed into the fourth Blue and the Stone Giant's influence was still inside.

It was severely weakened, and lessening all the time as Maria's blanketing closed; not strong enough to push me out but its presence still enough to prevent me from becoming present in the Blue's body. By the time the blanketing had fully taken hold and I was in place, looking hazily through the Blue's distant sight, its limbs were nearly all the way up to defend itself. Paul couldn't get the Stone man all the way inside its guard. I flashed out as Paul landed a punch, but the blow was sloppy, not clean enough, merely grazing our enemy and knocking it off-balance. The Blue didn't fall.

And I'd already flashed out. Everything went disastrously wrong at once.

Maria was already moving her blanketing back onto us, following the plan and preparing for the next Blue. She realised her mistake, but it was too late; the Blue's counter-attack was already launched and I couldn't get back inside to stop it, its right arm swinging hard and full of devastating momentum. There was no way to twitch it in time. Paul got the Stone Man's arm up by its head to block the strike, backing Caementum up all the while, but it was an instinctive, thoughtless movement; we did indeed have the high ground, but the Blue was taller, and its punch was coming in low. Paul was blocking in completely the wrong place.

The Blue's hand connected perfectly with the crack in the Stone Man's torso.

I was still in my body when I saw it all happen: blood spraying out of Paul's mouth, Maria stumbling as the shock of the impact slammed into our circuit. My world was rocked too, but not just from the feedback of the Blue's attack; as Paul and Maria stumbled into one another and fell to the ground, I heard—I *felt*—the click as Paul's weight fell onto Maria's hand, catching it underneath her body. Maria's broken and splinted fingers bent violently backwards.

She screamed, clutching her hand, as the pain shattered her focus. The moving of her blanketing back onto her circuit was blasted from her mind; interrupted, incomplete, and then lost entirely. Her pain sang to me down her thread, but I could still feel her struggling to get us all back under, she was *doing* it, moving the psychic blanket from herself as quickly as she could, out to Paul—

I was briefly aware of the onrushing psychic presence of the Stone Giant and then my world became terror.

It filled my body, paralysing me. I saw the circle of ugly, silvery light already forming around my fallen body and knew what it meant, but unbridled, enforced fear held my limbs in place. I could hear Paul and Maria struggling to their feet. I tried to call to them for help but had no voice. The Blues nearest to me turned my way. *Now* they were aware of me, and as I felt something in their gaze intensify, the circle of light immediately and rapidly responded under their direct command.

The bubble closed around me.

The second it snapped shut, the injected terror was gone, the Quarry Response complete. I shot upright, able to make out Paul and Maria through that horrible, dirty-silver light, the pair of them backing away behind the Stone Man. The Blues nearest the bubble turned and began to follow.

"*Andy!*" Paul and Maria screamed. Maria was holding her hand under her armpit, her whole body shaking as she called my name.

"*What do we do!*" Paul yelled. I tried to use our threads to respond—

Keep going—

But the thought went nowhere. The threads of my circuit felt distant, deadened. I yelled to my circuit instead:

"*Keep-keep going!*"

I tried to leap my consciousness out along our threads, but I couldn't. The bubble had me. I looked helplessly at the closing gap between the Blues and my friends. Paul and Maria had been bought a little space by the Blues' pausing to rapid-close the bubble, but that said space was now meaningless.

If I couldn't leap out of the bubble, then I couldn't leap into the Blues to halt them. It was now nine on one, with no advantage. Once they had finished with Caementum, they would come back for me. Then, like Patrick, like Henry, they would finally—

Now the terror was real, organic.

I became aware of the noise of a nearby car engine. It sounded like the driver was trying to press the accelerator pedal through the floor. I had a second to register the noise before it became deafening, the car flying up over the top of the hill so fast that its front end crashed down once it crested the rise, nearly flattening its suspension. It screeched to a halt a few feet away from the bubble and its door flew open, the driver rushing over to me and sliding to his knees.

Eric had just rocked up.

"*Andy, hold on!*" he yelled, flattening his good hand onto the bubble.

"*Eric!*" Maria screamed. She, Paul and Caementum were near the top of the hill now, partially hidden by the advancing Blues.

"*Keep moving!*" Eric yelled back. The bubble started to shake violently as Eric pressed against it. "*Come on ... come on ...*"

The bubble wasn't bursting.

"*Where's Edgwick?!*" I asked, my eyes locked onto the gap between the lead Blue and the retreating Stone Man.

"Not now," Eric hissed. "*Fucking hell, come on!!*" The bubble was shaking so violently that I could barely see through it, trying to see Paul and Maria—

I saw Paul say something to Maria that I couldn't hear. Maria straightened up sharply, looking from the Blues to Paul, the Blues to Paul —

Paul sat down on the floor, and then his body fell over backwards.

I saw the nearest Blue to the Stone Man immediately freeze, twitching on the spot, and watched as Maria's hands flew to either side of her head in despair.

Then the Stone Man strode forward and raised both its arms.

As Maria howled in horrified determination, I understood what Paul's idea had been.

The Stone Man's arms came down, and as they connected with the lead Blue's head, Paul's limp body bucked on the floor, fresh blood spraying from his mouth.

"*No!*" I screamed, my bubble continuing to rattle but not burst, Eric gritting his teeth and growling way back in his throat. Paul sat up for a moment, upper torso swaying, looking through lidded eyes, before pointing limply at the next Blue that was advancing. Then he fell back down. Maria wept openly now, shaking her head over and over, holding her injured fingers as she sent the Stone Man—for Maria was now driving—towards the now near-frozen Blue.

Maria driving. Paul jumping into the Blues to pause them. But Paul didn't have enough skill to jump out in time.

Down the heavy, clubbing arms of the Stone Man came. Paul rocked violently before sitting up again, but this time he couldn't even point. Maria had to continue backing up Old John Hill, leaving Paul on the ground, the pursuing Blues striding past his body in their pursuit of Caementum.

"*Eric! You have to get me out of here! Paul's still in there when Maria hits—*"

"*I'm trying, I'm trying—*"

Maria was calling Paul's name as we watched him roll limply onto his belly, trying to again see which Blue was closest; he must have found it because the next lead Blue froze, twitching in position just before Caementum took it down. That left six; now five, Maria and Paul smashing another Blue onto the deck as Paul's body continued to twitch and cough blood. Maria and Caementum then disappeared out of sight as they continued their spiral around the hill.

"*Feel where I am, Paul!*" Maria's disappearing voice screamed. "*It's in front of me NOW, do you feel it—*"

Then she was out of sight and earshot. If she was guiding Paul in-circuit, I couldn't hear it from my bubble.

"*Eric!*" I screamed. "*Please! He's dying!*"

Eric's growls became a bellow, the bubble shaking became a crescendo, and suddenly it wasn't there anymore. Eric fell backwards, gasping in air and looking amazed.

"*Fucking DID it, go, go!*"

I didn't need him to tell me. I was already leaping out of the dying silver circle of the bubble and charging up the hill towards Paul. He was trying to get to his hands and knees. I could hear Maria yelling instructions in-circuit now before I heard an enormous explosion of fizzing, causing Paul to cough up a fresh gush of blood. Between them, Paul and Maria had just reduced the Blues' numbers to four. Paul collapsed back to the ground. I wanted to hold him, to fix him, but the best way to help was to take over.

"*I'm here, I have it, you did it,*" I told him, before sprinting away—*I left him there*—up on the hill. "*Help him!*" I barked uselessly to Eric and then I was running, running, and I rounded the rise to see Maria and the Stone Man as they were starting to complete their latest upward lap. The four remaining Blues were close, encircling the Stone Man on all sides at a distance of perhaps fifteen feet. Could the plan of moving in and moving back work for these last few, this close, now I was back? Maria saw me running; she was standing outside of the tightening Blue circle now, pointing back to the opposite side of the hill, meaning *Paul*. Her wide-eyed face was streaked with tears. She knew what was happening there. We were a circuit, after all. I just pointed at the nearest Blue to Caementum and Maria nodded, her face glistening. She went to work, and seconds later I was seated and throwing my mind towards the selected Blue. I felt Maria expertly catch my consciousness in mid-air, firing it through Caementum and powering it like an arrow into the Blue. I watched through dim and distant eyes as Caementum closed in before flashing out with timing and control that Paul didn't have. Maria brought the Stone Man's arms down. Smack, fizz, down to three.

I flashed out, standing and running to Maria. She was already moving her blanketing to the next Blue. I fell into step backing-up alongside her as we circled the rest of the way around the hill's summit. Now I could see Paul again. Eric had my friend on his back, checking him, but Paul wasn't moving. The feeling was clear in our circuit: Paul was still there, but only just.

"*It's ready,*" Maria said, and I dropped quickly to the floor before we went to work.

We put the next Blue down quickly, but now the final two Blues had closed in around the Stone Man and there was nowhere left to go. The Stone Man was trapped between them.

"*That one—*"

Maria worked, I worked, and then I was watching Caementum advance through the Blue's eyes. Over Caementum's shoulder I could see the Blue's comrade looming large, sandwiching Caementum between its two enemies. As I twitched my Blue's arms, slowing them to a standstill. I watched its ally draw back an arm to strike. I bore down, feeling my consciousness threaten to shred as I *twitched* my Blue, held it, held it—

Behind you, I told Maria in circuit. *I'll hold this one, I can hold it, I CAN HOLD IT—*

I watched the Stone Man pivot clumsily on the spot as my Blue fought against my control. I began to falter, having to twitch this Blue's limbs in place far longer than I had its predecessors. I could only hold it a second or two more, watching the Stone Man sway as it threatened to overbalance under Maria's less experienced control.

Maria—

The Stone Man managed to keep its feet and completed the quick turn, bringing its arm around in a messy but thunderous clubbing strike. It slammed into the head of the Blue behind it with an explosion of fizzing noise, Maria remembering to strike through her target. The Blue staggered backwards and fell—not out of commission, but off its feet—and now the Stone Man turned back to my Blue just as my control gave way.

Quick—

I flashed out.

My human eyes saw the Stone Man's arms come down. The Blue's arms were only just starting to rise, far too late. Its body was driven onto the deck, and Maria moved the Stone Man in to quickly stomp its head into oblivion. I turned away for a moment, looking around myself. We had made our circling, reversing way to the very top of the hill. Old John was now littered with our fallen enemies; a quick glance at the ones I could see told me that almost all of them were twitching and unable to rise. One or two had made it back to their feet, but their movements were stuttering and broken-looking. They seemed so damaged that I thought we wouldn't even need to twitch them to drop them. This was now a simple clean-up job. If you'd told me beforehand that this was the sight I would see, I would have been delirious with joy. But the price paid to achieve it was far, far too high. and the victory was meaningless. I couldn't even go to Paul yet. We weren't finished. In the short term that always made it easier. Job first. It kept you distracted from anything else.

The last, down-but-not-out Blue had risen and was coming towards us.

"Plant your feet," I told Maria. I meant the Caementum, but Maria, silent now, her cheeks shining, did so with her own body. Caementum mirrored her. The last Blue met us; we ran our process, but right before I flashed out of the Blue again, I saw through its eyes. Maria's mouth was opened in a scream, her Stone aura visible around her in the Blue's sight, flaring out as if she were bursting into coloured flames. Then the Stone Man's arms were coming down and I flashed free into a world that rang with Maria's fury and grief. Once Maria had stamped the Blue goodbye, I quickly set Caementum to circling. We ran to where Paul lay dying on the grass.

Paul's open mouth and teeth were streaked with red. As Maria and I dropped to our knees beside him and Eric, Paul opened his heavily bloodshot eyes and turned them my way.

To my amazement, he broke into a smile.

"We. Get. All," he said. I looked around at the Blues, those now half-standing and struggling to move freely, and those still on the floor. It made me think of an infestation of flying ants I'd once had to kill, smothering them with ant powder and watching their pathetic efforts to stay alive. We had been the ants in the eyes of the Caeterus; for this skirmish at least, we had managed to turn the tables.

"Pretty much," I said, barely able to respond.

Paul was leaving us.

"Half—half job," he coughed. "Finish off."

"Paul—"

"I'll wait," he said. Maria and I didn't move. "S'okay," he said.

We still didn't move. Now Paul's smile vanished.

"You'd. Deny me. Fucking. Satisfaction—" He grunted. A small, bubbling trickle of red ran from the corner of his mouth. "Of knowing. We finished—"

"Yes, yes, we're going," Maria croaked, "Andy. Come. It'll be quicker with both of us." I babbled my agreement and stood, feeling as if my insides had been scooped out. I glared at Eric, and he nodded.

"I'll tell you," he said quietly. "If anything ... I'll tell you. But be quick."

Maria and I took the Stone Man on as quick a killing tour as we could manage, circling the hill and watching Paul and Eric whenever they were in our sightlines.

We had to put the Blues down permanently.

I wish we could have just left them. Had more time with Paul. But we knew—*Paul* knew—that Caementum had healed after the encounter with the Crawlers. If the Blues recovered and came after us once more, Paul's heroism would be for nothing, and I doubted we would be this lucky again. Clear, high, expansive ground like this was not easy to find. We didn't even know for sure if we could Detonate them by force alone; in the heat of battle, with Blues closing in on all sides, we hadn't had time.

The big problem now, however, was that the Stone Man would have to be shut down to avoid being overloaded by a Detonation, if we could even make one happen; how could a shut-down Stone Man deliver a killing blow? Our only option here was to tenderise the prone Blues as much as possible, crippling them if not killing them. We'd just have to hope they couldn't heal in time—if they could at all—to interfere with our mission to destroy the Prism. If we survived that and were successful, we'd figure the rest out later.

We spent the next twenty minutes doing our worst to the ruined Blues. We may have had time to work now, but Paul didn't. We worked as quickly as we could, punching through each Blue until even their twitching stopped. If we were ending them without Detonating them, we didn't know; a check of their insides showed activity, but even the dormant Stone Man had showed that. We took no satisfaction in it. We were too nervous, too frantic. The sense of time with Paul was trickling away, and the job was taking far too long.

"Good … good job," I mumbled to Maria as the last Blue lay still, but she was already turning and running back to Paul. I followed. We arrived to find that, to my immense relief, he was still with us. The light in his eyes was lower, but as we crouched down that funny smile came to his lips again.

"Ss." He coughed a little and tried again. "Sorted?"

"Sorted, mate. Sorted."

His right hand came up, shaking. I took it. Squeezed it. He raised his left.

"Maria."

She scuttled around to the other side of him, took his hand with her good one, her splinted fingers held against her chest. They would have to be reset, I thought. Paul closed his eyes, smiling wider.

"Good," he said. "Eric. Nothing left to hold. 'less you wanna. Grab me old fella."

Paul's teeth bared in a bloody grin, pleased with himself. Here he was, himself once more, right at the end.

"That's okay," Eric whispered, chuckling through his rapid, wet breathing. He put his hand on Paul's shoulder. "That's okay."

"Does it hurt?" I asked.

Paul shook his head.

"Nuh." He opened his eyes again. "Getting out, Andy. I'm getting *out*." He suddenly looked worried. "*For something.* That was something. Makes up for every ... *thing*. Doesn't it? It does. Doesn't it."

"Yes Paul, there was never—*yes*, yes man, you balanced the books."

Paul closed his eyes again, the contented smile returning to his face.

"*Ahhhhh*," he said, breathing out slowly and looking as if all was right with his world even as he lay bloody and dying in a park in Leicestershire. "Can feel our circuit. Feels good." I looked at Maria; she nodded quickly, and both of us sent as much peace, or soothing, or whatever you want to fucking call—

...

Sorry. Gimme a second.

***

Okay.

We sent it down our threads. Paul's eyes flew open again in wonder.

"*Ah*," he gasped. "If *this!* This." He settled back down. "*This* is what Linda—" His wide bloodshot eyes looking at Maria, then me. "Then I feel. Lot better. About her, too."

His hands tightened around mine and Maria's. He was finally leaving, and he knew it. I started to cry.

"S'ok," he said, smiling at me sadly. "Really. It is." He suddenly became stern. "Andy. Maria. *Eric*. I'm. Lucky one. You're the ones that have to—dd—deal with this shit." Now he looked sad, shaking his head. "So sorry I can't help. You. I'm sorry—"

The moist chorus of responses, all along the lines of *no, nothing to be sorry for* drowned out the rest of his sentence, but Paul scowled so we stopped. He wanted to finish. "Gonna try and put. Everything. Left in *me.* Into the Right Hon—" He coughed again. "*Him.* Think I can move it over. I see it. I see it. It really is just ..." He scowled, trying to find the words, then twitched his head. "Movement of energy. Should be plenty. To get to Cov—"

His face became deadly serious.

Paul's hand gripped mine even tighter, and with great effort he lifted his head to look me dead in the eye. "The Stone Man better ... fucking *walk*. Hear me?"

"I promise, Paul. I promise, I promise."

He lay back.

"The Stone Man. Always walks," he said. The smile crept back onto his face. "Thank God."

"I love you."

The words spat out of me, unbidden. Paul heard it; I believe he did. His eyes stayed on mine, his smile widening so much that his eyes narrowed.

Then it began to relax, his face becoming slack, and I realised that Paul Winter was gone.

No one moved. Maria and I stayed by Paul's side, still holding his hands. Eric, kneeling by Paul's head, reached out and carefully closed Paul's eyes with his fingertips. Maria lowered her head, her hair hiding her face.

Then the force of everything that was Paul slammed into our circuit.

It arrived like a tsunami. We'd experienced this with Linda's death, but this was so much more intense. The combination of our greater connection to Paul and a heavy dose of amphetamines amplified the impact to staggering levels. I could hear Eric barking *what, what's happening*, but neither Maria nor I could answer as every muscle in our bodies locked up like we were being tasered. The energy moved in us ... then *through* us, firing out along our threads and into the Stone Man. Paul's final gift, literally given with his last breath.

It went on for a few moments; I was aware of Eric standing and pacing, clearly wondering what the hell to do. Then suddenly, it was over. Maria and I fell back onto the grass, limp.

"What was that, are you—" Eric began, but fell silent when I lifted a weak OK sign. "I'm sorry, I'm sorry, I got here as quick as I could, if I'd been a minute sooner—"

"Not your fault," Maria said, sitting up and gently stroking Paul's face. "You saved Andy. You saved the mission." She looked up at Eric. "You did your duty." She stood, moving away as I crawled over to Paul. I got one of my arms under his broad back as Maria moved to Eric and held him. The young man was beginning to shake.

"*If I'd been quicker,*" he said. "*If I'd been quicker—*"

"Ssh," Maria said. "Don't ever say that again. How did you find us?"

"Checked ... I checked all the castles around here. Had to keep changing cars to get round blockages, even with the quieter roads. Took hours. Then I came here and saw a Blue, I followed it—"

"Where's Edgwick?" Maria asked, stepping back suddenly.

When Eric broke and began to bawl into her shoulder, I knew we had lost another comrade.

I pulled Paul into my lap and rested his upper body on my knees. I held him tight as I wept, my face buried in his hair.

✱✱✱

Chapter Sixteen

The Last Leg

✳✳✳

We were able to bury Paul quickly. The Stone Man was a hundred times better than any earth mover.

Eric and I lifted Paul's body into the grave. That took twice as long as the initial digging, but I wouldn't have the Stone Man handle Paul. That felt too close to it finally getting him. Soon there was a mound of earth covering Paul's body; it struck me how Paul hadn't known when we arrived that he would never leave this park. That set me off again, but I remembered how relieved he'd seemed to go. Then, as always, there was the job to focus on, and everything else could be pushed aside.

Maria asked if we should say a few words—we'd reset her fingers as best we could—but I wasn't sure. Paul had been very clear; the mission was priority number one, and even a burial this rapid was a time-luxury he wouldn't have wanted. But I couldn't leave him there on the hill, surrounded by the bodies of the Blues we'd defeated. If we'd buried him, we could take a minute to say something. And so, when the burying was done, we did just that. Even Eric did.

What was said that morning was our business alone. I don't want to repeat it here. This is hard enough as it is. All you need to know is that we stood by his grave and spoke his name.

We knew Edgwick deserved the same treatment, but he wasn't here to receive it; we said words for him too, even though it felt wrong to throw his eulogy in as some kind of a two-fer for Paul. Eric said he didn't think Edgwick would mind. Eric had of course told us by then—through tears of his own—what had happened to Edgwick. What they'd tried, and failed, to do in Coventry.

"He saved me," Eric had told us. "Threw himself in harm's way when there was only a second to act. He was a fucking hero."

The guilt was deep and clear in Eric's face as the two of us clumsily lowered Paul into the earth. If Edgwick's body was still by the Prism, and we survived, I swore we'd give him a proper burial.

"He was," I said, "both he and Paul. So now we have to be worthy of them. You know that, right?"

"I know that," Eric said. "You know that?"

"Of course," I said, a little irritated by the question. *I* didn't need to understand what I was saying. I was the one that said it, and Paul had been my friend. Then I realised this was twatty old Andy coming out, and let it go.

By now the sun was fully up. Maria was getting herself some food out from her pack before we set off, and Eric and I were standing awkwardly by the car Eric had driven here. Eric stared out across the expanse of the park, arms folded, backside resting on the car's bonnet. The numbers of the Stone Men were never going to be lower than they were right now, but experience had shown us that those things could adapt. Would we be able to pull off the same trick against the remaining Stone Men if it came down to a fight, and on low ground at that? We didn't know, but we had to strike while we had something of an advantage; grief would have to wait. At least six Blue Stone Men were afield—eight if you included the two box-fresh ones Eric told us he'd seen being born at the Prism. Would we have to deal with any of them?

And then there was the Stone Giant itself.

"I take a lot of comfort," I said, "in Paul seeming at peace at the end."

"Yeah. Sounded like he wanted it."

I sighed.

"I think he wanted it for a long time, Eric. And now his duty's done."

But ours wasn't. My mind suddenly felt very, very weary. After the fight my body didn't feel the same Stone-energised way as it did before. I was awake, but just normal awake, even with the amphetamines. The really odd thing was that, despite this, the actual moving and controlling of the Stone Man now felt easier than ever.

Yes, it had taken a little more damage, and perhaps seemed slower still now than when we first set off. But—and I'd yet to confirm this with Maria— when we were digging Paul's grave I felt that my connection to it had improved. Paul had, I thought, been right about putting what was left in him into our circuit. Even if the Stone Man had taken damage, it felt like there was real *power* inside the Stone Man again. Enough to deal with the Stone Giant?

"I have to tell you something," Eric said, his voice slow and careful.

"Go on."

"I've been thinking," he said. "A lot's happened within the last few days."

"That's a big fucking understatement."

"Yeah. Look. It's hard to admit, especially to you. I-I didn't kill Harry when I first had the chance, Andy. I didn't do what needed to be done." He snorted bitterly. "There's always a role no-one wants, isn't there? But doing nothing and letting other people clean up the mess is easy."

I thought I knew where he was going with this.

"I don't know if it's that simple, Eric. I've felt so much guilt since the First Arrival. But then I think to myself ... I've been *enjoying* running that thing ever since we woke it up." I looked to the Stone Man, watching it slowly turn back the way it came. "It's the second time it's made me feel like the most important man in the world. But Paul is dead. Edgwick is dead." I threw my hands up. "I don't know what I'm saying."

"Well, either way," Eric said, reddening. He looked away. "I was *thinking* ... I have these taped interviews from Project Orobouros."

Now he had my full attention.

"Yes?"

"They're in one of my stashes in Cov," Eric said. "And one of them has an interview with Sophie Warrender. If we survive, I think you should have it."

I'd already cried enough that day. As it was, I felt the pulse thrumming in my neck and quietly said:

"I'd like that very much. Thank you."

"Yeah, sure, no problem, yeah man," Eric said quickly, wanting to move on. "So ... now we go to Cov?" Eric asked.

"Uh-huh."

My eyes fell onto the mound of earth where Paul was buried. Eric saw me looking.

"You think we can take down the Giant?" he asked, as if reading my mind.

Maria approached, carrying a pouch of army-rationed protein gel and unintentionally saving me from having to answer Eric. Behind her, the Stone Man continued to walk up and down.

"I'm assuming we're going to try and find a truck along the way?" she asked, her voice so quiet I could barely hear it. She didn't look up as she peeled the pouch open and put it to her mouth.

"Why d'you say that?" I asked. I thought I knew why, but I wanted her to say it without me influencing her. She jerked her head towards the Stone Man, still not meeting my gaze, eyes on that protein pouch.

"You feel it, don't you? We have better control again? I assumed you do."

"I do."

"At least enough to lay it in the back of a truck again without destroying the trailer," she said. "We're back to where we were and then some. Maybe we can even get it inside a van."

"There's a van in the car park," Eric said.

"I saw it," I said. "Windscreen's all red on the inside so it's a good bet that the keys …" I trailed off. It didn't feel like the right time to be so glib about death. "Let's grab the packs and check it out," I said. "Then maybe we can try getting Caementum inside."

"I'll get my pack," Eric said, heading over to the now-ruined Ford he'd showed up in.

"Let's get ours," I told Maria, gently patting her shoulder as we walked down the hill to the Renault. It was still parked at the hill's base and miraculously untouched. I opened its boot and my heart caught in my mouth. Paul's backpack was lying alongside mine and Maria's.

"Are we … are we taking that one too …" Maria said, pulling out her pack.

"Yes. We might need its supplies, and he'd have wanted … yeah."

I pulled out the two remaining packs without another word. The three of us walked towards the car park, leaving behind us the ruined bodies of twelve Blue Stone Men. I cast a glance back, wanting to feel at least a sense of victory; they'd fucked around with us—tried to kill us—and found out. *We* were marching now, momentum on our side. But they'd killed Paul. They'd taken our hearts. We were broken. And now we were heading into battle, relying on a resolve that felt as if it could withstand almost nothing.

"I was thinking," Maria said quietly as we began to approach the blue Toyota van, "about your camping story."

"Oh. Yeah."

She smiled sadly.

"Reminded me of one of mine—hold on." She closed her eyes for a moment and her memory flowed to me across our circuit, now clearer and sharper than anything that had passed between us before. The story was told in double-quick time, everything landing almost at once yet still somehow making sense. Then it was over. I saw the sad half-smirk on her face.

It took a second for my brain to play catch up, the hook of the story fully landing.

Then it did, and I let out a loud laugh.

"Yeah," Maria said, "in front of all my friends."

"What?" Eric asked, smirking at my reaction even though he was outside the joke.

"And I had to take those clothes *home*," Maria said, and I laughed again, a blessed release after the maelstrom of emotions that had been the last twenty four hours.

"What?" Eric insisted, a confused grin on his face. Maria just smiled, her hand coming up to rest on my shoulder, patting it.

Soon we would be on our way. But right then, we had that moment, and I never wanted it to end.

***

"If we get bubbled," Maria said, "no matter what, we mustn't let ourselves be taken. No matter *what*. Do we all agree?"

We knew what she meant. Each of the packs still carried a pistol and a holster, after all. I would not be Harvested.

"Yeah," Eric said. "I've seen it happen, so don't worry. I wouldn't stick around for it."

"We'll put the holsters on before we head into Coventry," I told them.

The van was approaching the Coventry Ring Road now. It was the first time I had been back to the city since the Third Arrival.

My headache had worsened considerably as we'd passed through Coventry's streets. Soon after that the nausea had begun. That was unexpected and deeply unwelcome. I hadn't felt anything like this since Paul and I had been hunting down Targets during the first three Arrivals. Fortunately, Maria's blanketing of us seemed to stop the sensation from reaching the same peaks as those dark days.

Hm. *Those* dark days? If what I'm talking about now aren't dark days too, what the fuck are? I mean, think about—

Sorry. I'm stalling again.

... maybe Paul was right, you know. Maybe he *was* the lucky one

Anyway. Cov ring road.

As we drove along it, I thought that maybe we would all soon be lucky too. I looked at the dead and ruined streets of my former home and didn't know how to feel about this potentially approaching 'luck'. *Rest.* It called to me.

We stopped to fuel up just outside of Cov and put on our pistol holsters. Maria went to use the bathroom and I started to record a little bit of what I've been telling you here. Partially for a test, using my phone's audio memo function, and partially because I didn't know if I'd get another chance. I'd wanted to try and record a little bit, but I couldn't get into it. I was too nervous.

Maria came back and asked what I'd been doing. I was sitting on the floor and Eric had gone inside the petrol station shop to get some chocolate. I noticed he went in with his pistol held at his side, thumbing the safety off. He'd told us what had happened on their way to Coventry. I didn't blame him for being cautious.

"Recording," I told her.

"Like a ... last will and testament, sort of thing?"

"I hope not."

" ... can I say something into it?"

"Oh. Yeah. Sure, of course."

I handed the phone to her and she lifted it to her mouth, her thumb hovering over the on-screen record button. She hesitated.

"What do you want to say?" I asked, wanting to help.

"I want to just ... leave a message," she said. "Just in case."

She still didn't press record.

"Do you want me to leave you alone?" I asked.

She handed the phone back to me.

"It doesn't matter," she said. "I can't. Let's go."

I took the phone and stood.

"You'll tell Marcus yourself," I told her, and the look in her eyes told me that, for once, I'd read the situation perfectly. "Okay? As Paul would say," I added, forcing a smile, "don't be a silly *tit*."

For the first time in my life, my voice broke on the word *tit*. Maria smiled sadly and reached her hand out for mine.

"Maybe I should just tell *you* something, Andy. You helped me."

"That isn't something I hear a lot, but go on."

"Just before we met," she said, "I'd already started to fight back. I didn't have much choice, but still: I did. But I don't think I was truly a *fighter* until we started all this together."

I had to look away, but I was smiling.

"Only because you had to pick up our slack," I told her, staring at the nearest petrol pump. "I guess my weaponised incompetence was finally good for something."

"We both needed the circuit," she said. "The three of us did. It was the one—the only—wonderful thing about all of this."

I didn't know what to say. I couldn't even look at her.

"He loved you a lot," Maria said. "You know that, don't you?"

The tears behind my eyes were deeply bittersweet.

"Yeah," I said. "Yeah, I do. Even before our circuit, I knew how he felt." Now I looked at her, taking her offered hand. "And *we* are still a circuit. You know that? You and me." I hesitated, and then just gently patted my chest. Even now, I still couldn't say the words aloud to my friend. Maria smiled, squeezing my hand.

"I do, Andy," she said, her voice clear. "I know."

We turned and walked towards the car, hand in hand, as Eric appeared in the shop's doorway.

In each fist he carried two king size Mars Bars.

***

As we drew further down the Ring Road the pressure inside the van's cab felt like it was increasing.

"Are you doing that?" I asked.

"Yes," Maria said, breathing slow. "The Stone Giant … its everywhere here. It knows where the Stone Man is and it's trying very hard to interfere. I'm okay. But if I'm quiet, that's why." I shifted in the driver's seat, resisting the urge to brush off the surface of my clothes, my skin. It felt like something was crawling over me.

As we headed around the empty Ring Road I found myself feeling amazed and horrified by what the city had become. When I'd come back here before the Second Arrival—and with a film crew to boot, those were the fuckin' days—the actual City Centre had been partially smashed up but a substantial population still remained. Now the place was truly abandoned. Eric had said that a few stragglers still called it home, but all we saw as we passed through was a total ghost town. There were now far more flattened buildings than during the first few Arrivals, so much so that the place looked like it had been bombed worse than in World War II. But, of course, eighteen Stone Men had set off in different directions recently. We were extremely lucky that the elevated parts of the Ring Road we needed to use were still intact.

"Nice to be home, eh guys?" Eric asked, his voice grim. I realised that, of course, Maria had once lived here too.

"Different," I said. "Very different."

"I hate it," Maria said.

Silence fell. We were taking the exit that would bring us to the former Ground Zero, and the Prism. We could see the top of that horrible structure in the greyish sunlight, standing tall and sighted through a space where an apartment block stood half-collapsed. I was sweating. The van's cab now smelling musty and salty, feeling as if it were a low-temperature sauna. A couple of thick veins stood out in Maria's forehead. The Stone Giant truly was trying to get in here, and Maria was doing her best to keep it out.

I saw the entirety of the Prism in person for the first time.

We were moving past the empty shops that lined the road alongside the former Millennium Place plaza, the immense, uneven shape of the Prism rising up like something from a nightmare. It stood totally incongruent to its surroundings. It looked as if some god-powered nerd had taken a *fortress of ultimate darkness* or some shit from a D&D game and photoshopped it into the middle of a suburban landscape for shits and giggles. I could see the strange patterning of its rough-looking surface, those tracks and whorls covering the structure's every inch.

"It's *hideous*," Maria whispered, and it was, this immense carbuncle, this alien barnacle that had fastened itself onto my city, my country, my planet, and doled out so much death. Here, in sight of it, was my anger again. Something had to break through the spell that had held us all captive since the recent deaths of our friends, I knew, and I was very glad it wasn't fear. In the back of the van, carefully laid down so well that the chassis remained intact, was our weapon, our somehow-ally, and in a few moments we would be going to war. Our eyes fell on what stood—and what lay—before the Prism. My stomach turned over at both sights, but I felt my nerve hold. I was Dispensatori, perhaps, here at the end. There couldn't have been a better time.

"It's darker still," Eric mused aloud. "The Stone Giant. Look at it. I wasn't sure before, but it's definitely gotten darker *again* since I last saw it."

Whether what Eric saw was true or not, The Stone Giant stood tall before the Prism. The sickening crimson stood out in bold relief against the greyness of its surroundings, its colouring intense even in the grey light of the weak autumn sun. Behind it stood two smaller Blue shapes; they were almost fully formed, but not completely. The outlines of their arms, for example, were visible within the overall Blue mass, but not yet separated away from their sides. Their metamorphosis was clearly within some latter, but not final, stage.

Edgwick's body lay where it had fallen at the feet of the Stone Giant.

A small spray of red coated the ground near his head. Even a big man like Edgwick looked tiny compared to the towering red hulk, but the sight only intensified my anger; Edgwick looked like an offering laid at the literal feet of the Gods. Yes, he had been sacrificed. But Edgwick's had been a sacrifice of the self, an act of sheer bravery, not an appeasement given to these parasites to curry their favour.

Edgwick's last act had been one of defiance. I would do my absolute best to honour that.

Where were these thoughts coming from? I didn't recognise myself in them, and that was perhaps a very, very good thing. Andy Pointer, reporter and general misanthrope, was not needed here.

"Andy?" I'd stopped the van. I turned at the sound of Maria's voice to see she and Eric staring at me. "Are you ready? You've been quiet for like a whole minute."

They looked terrified. But their faces were set, jaws clenched.

"Yes." Something else needed to be said. "We... we can do this. Think of Linda, and Edgwick, and Paul." That felt right. I nearly added *Patrick, Henry, Theresa*, but I hadn't known them the way I'd known—

"Theresa," Eric added, saying it for me, but there was no malice in it. "Aaron. *Harry.*"

"And Ruth," Maria said. Her mouth stayed open as if she was going to add something else, but then decided against it. She grabbed both of our hands instead. "Let's go," she said.

We stepped down from the van.

The wind had picked up some, buffeting my ears a little. That was good. I liked it. We moved to the back of the van and opened its rear doors. The Stone Man lay within, on its back. I was relieved to get it out of there; keeping the Stone Man still on the road was trying indeed. I lowered its arms to the van's inner bed and the Stone Man pushed itself across the metal surface with a loud screech before stepping down onto the road. I turned the Stone Man to face the Prism, moving it from foot to foot once it was facing the right way. I wanted it to stay loose and mobile. We watched the Stone Giant for a second. I'd wondered if it would come alive the second Caementum was within visual range, but it hadn't. It just continued to stand there. Waiting?

Millennium Place had been levelled ever since the Ground Zero building had been established; gone now were the railings, concrete benches, and various other accoutrements of the previous gathering place. The base of the Prism lay over the now-flattened fencing that had surrounded Ground Zero. We had a straight run at the Stone Giant. It stood maybe eighty feet away from us.

It was time.

An idea occurred to me, one that felt utterly stupid and utterly appropriate at the same time.

"Group hug," I said. I wasn't joking. Eric and Maria stepped forward and wrapped their arms around me, and I held them back.

"Let's give 'em hell," Maria said. Then we broke, and it was on; the Stone Man was striding forward, the three of us walking at a short distance behind it.

Still the Stone Giant didn't move.

"Any sight of silver, gold, or any of that bubble shit starting," I whispered to Eric as we walked. "The slightest hint. You get on that, do what you can."

"Got it."

Sixty feet.

"You know the plan, Maria," I said.

"I do."

Fifty feet.

Our idea was simple, in that it wasn't much of a plan at all. It was a theory at best, and if that failed, two lipstick-tipped pseudo-fists would be all we had. We thought it highly unlikely that we could get inside and affect the Stone Giant—to freeze its limbs temporarily the way we had the Blues'—based on the way it could push us out of its progenies. We'd had to come up with something else.

Forty feet. The Stone Giant remained still.

It occurred to me, the thought bizarre and surprising, that we were the ones closing in on a Target, walking inexorably towards it, unshakable and relentless. The idea was satisfying. I clenched my fists, my palms slick with sweat.

Thirty feet.

"Plenty close enough for us," I said. We stopped walking, watching the Stone Man begin to grow smaller in our sight as it continued to stride forward. "I'm going in." I sat down on the ground. "If we have to move quickly—"

"Drag you, we know—"

Then I was inside the Stone Man's eyes as it walked.

The sight of the Giant grew larger before me with every step Caementum took. It was so tall that I wasn't even sure we could strike at its head while it was upright. The size of the thing finally shook the core of my newfound spirit, but not enough to kill it; thoughts of Paul and Edgwick—Sophie—straightened my mental spine and drove us—myself and Caementum—onward. The Stone Man moved within twenty feet of the enormous red monstrosity.

Then the Stone Giant finally stepped forward and started to walk towards the Stone Man.

There were no Horns for the first movement of the Giant. Again, I faltered, but again, it was only brief, even as the most unstoppable force this world had ever seen strode forward to meet me, the concrete cracking beneath its feet. Even at a distance I could feel the power within it, even when experienced second-hand through the body of the Stone Man. This was happening. This was *happening*.

Ten feet apart. Maria had been told to wait until the last minute.

Five. Okay, *now* she should be—

Maria—

I felt her move through me, her thread silent but utterly determined, as Maria poured herself over the Stone Giant.

We'd come up with the plan on the way there.

What, Eric had reasoned, *if it and the Prism are a unit? They seem to act as one. Maybe, if we tried to blanket the Stone Giant from the Prism, it would be lessened somehow? Disoriented, perhaps? That would have to even the odds?*

We didn't have any other insights. That was our best option. If it didn't work, this was going to be a straight-up dust-up.

Stone Man and Giant moved to within striking distance of one another now. The size difference between them was completely overwhelming, especially viewed from the much lower height of Caementum. As Maria's blanketing of the Stone Giant continued, I saw that our opponent wasn't slowing.

Andy, Maria's distant thread called to me. *It's—it's harder to blanket than the Blues—*

Just keep trying—don't stop—

There wasn't time for further conversation; the Red was already twisting its shoulders and swinging a sideways blow at Caementum's head. It was so much taller that it had to bend at the waist to swing properly. This was encouraging and terrifying at the same time. I'd wondered if Maria's protection of us would count for much at close range, but the fact that we weren't dealing with psychic attacks told me the good and bad news.

The good news was this looked to be a purely physical confrontation.

The bad news, however, was this looked to be a physical confrontation.

Duck—

But I already was, having had practice against the Blues, experience enabling me to read where the Red was going to go. The punch flew over

Caementum's head but already a second was coming the other way, the Stone Giant's left arm following up. A one-two of this speed was new, but I managed to lean the Stone Man backward in time to avoid the second. I hadn't been in a physical fight since I was sixteen years old, but my heightened awareness of the Caementum's body—and whatever Paul had given us at the end—seemed to give me far greater presence of mind, moving far better in Caementum than my body would. A third blow was swung by the Stone Giant, this time in an overhand, downward motion as the creature stepped forward; I wouldn't be able to get out of the way of this one in time. I swung the Stone Man's arms straight up above my head, crossed at the wrists, to try and halt the attack. I could only hope it didn't crush us flat.

The Stone Giant's arm met both of mine. The pain made me cry out in Stone Space, Maria's thread shrieking too as the blow seemed to pass all the way through the Stone Man's body down to its feet. Like the Blues, it seemed, the Stone Giant knew all about striking through. This attack hadn't even fully landed, but it felt as if it had sapped our strength.

Maria, I said, the Stone Giant continuing to force its arm downwards against Caementum's, pushing its arms and body down. In a moment Caementum would be driven onto its knees. *Are you okay—*

Ye—yes—

Please—just get the fucker blanketed—

I lifted the Stone Man's right leg and thrust it forwards into the Stone Giant's leading thigh. *Bang.* The monster staggered back a few steps, but didn't fall like I'd hoped. I drove the Stone Man forward, intending to follow up, but its arms were taking a moment to recover. Their integrity, or our control, had been rattled by that punching-through energy the Stone Giant seemed to have in abundance. I was now within striking distance and the Stone Man's arms were still low. Not knowing what else to do, I snapped the Stone Man forward at the waist and drove its head straight into the Stone Giant's torso, hoping that our driving energy could drop our opponent to the floor.

My Stone vision went white as the concussive impact bounced out to my human brain and back to my consciousness. That had been a bad idea. The Stone Giant had been rocked backwards again, swaying, but remained upright. Caementum took two stumbling steps forward, remaining upright too, but I'd lost the sensation of its limbs. Already it was returning, but not quickly enough. The Stone Giant was now straightening, barreling towards Caementum—

Maria!

I'm trying! MOVE—

But I couldn't. The Stone Giant's arm drove forward and hit the Stone Man square in the chest.

The next thing I knew I was looking out of my own eyes, lying on my back, my human hands flying up in a warding-off, flinching gesture to try and protect myself from the incoming attack. I heard an almighty crash and saw the Stone Man landing several feet away from where it had been standing, its unguarded weight carving a short, shallow trench in the concrete. I couldn't understand what was happening, disorientated utterly by this unexpected shift in location, even as delayed pain began to bloom in my chest. Eric noticed the movement of my hands.

"Andy?!" he said. "You're here? Why aren't you in there?"

I realised what had happened, even as I found that I couldn't speak, couldn't breathe as my hands went to my chest. The Stone Giant's blow had been so hard that my presence inside the Stone Man had been blasted back into my body; some kind of auto-protect feature of our own circuit, then? Some aspect of the greater control we had since absorbing Paul's energy?

If that was true, I realised with horror, then the impact from the Stone Giant's single punch could have perhaps killed me.

Even the small amount of force I'd taken before my exit was still preventing my body from drawing in air. I glanced at Maria; she was concentrating so hard on the scene before her, watching the Stone Giant advance on the fallen Stone Man, that she hadn't even noticed my return. Suddenly I could take a deep, whooping breath, tasting blood in it, but already I was leaping back into the Stone Man, seeing the grey sky above through its sight. I could still feel its limbs and tried to roll it onto its side to stand, but something was badly wrong. The Stone Man's body not responding to my commands. In a second or two the Stone Giant would be stomping it into fragments, along with the last of our hope. I focused my efforts; something that had been knocked out of place suddenly dropped back into alignment. I could move the Stone Man again, but as I sat the thing upright and began to rise, I saw that it was too late. The Giant was already upon the Man before I could get it to its feet. I braced, hoping that whatever speed-of-thought process had saved me before would do so again—

ANDY, Maria's thread sang. *I'VE DONE IT, NOW, NOW—*

She'd done it. I saw the Stone Giant hesitate.

I didn't know how long we had it for, didn't care, all I knew was it was briefly cut off from the Prism. How that affected its systems—or if it was just simply confused—the bastard's guard was down for a second. I had to hit it as hard as I could. I made the Stone Man take a wobbling step forward and delivered a two-handed chop to the side of the Giant's waist. It staggered, stunned, and I followed, delivering another double-handed punch to its other side, this one hard enough to double the Giant over. The back of its head was momentarily exposed and within range. I didn't know how long Maria could keep it disconnected, disoriented, but I planned to keep hitting the monster until it fell; I raised the Stone Man's arms together and as they hammered down into the Stone Giant's neck *it dropped to one knee.* Yes! I raised the Stone Man's arms together one last time, planning to drive them down with absolutely everything I had left, but then Maria's thread screamed out in pain and fell silent.

The Stone Giant came alive. It threw a rising uppercut from its low position, it's head a little lower than the Stone Man's now it was kneeling. I had a moment to understand two things: that the Stone Giant—or the Prism—had just thrown off Maria's influence, and that our offence was over. The Stone Giant's punch connected with the Stone Man's head, and the next thing I knew I was staring up at Eric through eyes that wouldn't focus.

"*Andy!*"

That was Eric's voice. My face was covered with something hot and wet. My nose had given way again. Eric dragged me to a sitting position so I could see; to my left, a dazed Maria was staggering upright, trying to get her bearings. In front of the Prism lay the Stone Man, having been knocked farther backwards this time. The force of the Stone Giant's last blow had nearly carried Caementum out of the plaza entirely.

"Helpper," I slurred, pushing Eric towards the stumbling Maria, and then lay down and dived back into the Stone Man. I had to get it back to its feet, to fight, but all I could do was flop its legs uselessly around like a dying bug as the Stone Giant moved in for the kill. I blinked, realised I *was* blinking, and understood I was back in my body again, disoriented and losing my Stone grip. I dived back along the thread once more. Back in the Stone Man's sight the Stone Giant grew larger, larger as it reached the Stone Man and stood over it. The Giant bent at the waist, reaching one lipstick-tipped palm down towards the Stone Man's shoulder as it drew its other arm back. Its intention was clear: to pin the Stone Man in place with one palm and to strike down with the other. My stunned mind saw this and managed to tell me:

Wait—

I did, hesitating until the Stone Giant's bending-down head came close enough., waiting until just before the Giant's pinning arm touched Caementum.

Then I screamed and jerked the Stone Man's torso sideways where it lay on the deck—

Punch through, I thought, *punch through*—

—and struck the Stone Giant's head hard enough to knock it clear out of my frame of Stone vision. There was an almighty rushing fizz that sounded like the world's biggest fire hydrant. I tried to stand the Stone Man to follow. It couldn't; its equilibrium was shot. That last strike might have been exactly that.

Come on, I pleaded, the Stone Man's sight still staring at the sky, my monster rocking weakly back and forth on its back it tried to move. I needed to see where the Stone Giant was; I jumped back to my body to see the Stone Giant was down! It had been knocked some way backwards and crashed to the deck—

Where was Eric? He wasn't with me, and neither was Maria. I spun around and saw Eric bundling Maria into the van. *What the fuck was he doing*—

The Stone Giant tried to get up, then shook for a moment, as if something had gummed up its works. We'd hurt it! Then it was back on its feet but not yet advancing. Its shoulders twisted, then jerked, as if it were trying to turn but not managing it. That last hit had really seemed to have done something? There was a screech of tires and then Eric was driving the van full pelt across the short distance to the Stone Man. He skidded the vehicle to a halt by the Stone Man's right side and leapt out, the van far enough over that I could still see the Stone Giant as it seemed to get itself back in order. Whatever it was doing seemed to work: the Stone Giant was advancing once more. I flashed back into the Stone Man's driving seat, but it was no use. The Stone Man was damaged, and badly. I could get its upper body to sit up a little, its arms stiffly held out at its sides but unable to swing or push itself to its feet. I tried its legs; I could flail those but was unable to get it to stand without the use of its arms. The Stone Giant was coming on fast as I saw, to the right of my Stone Sight, that Eric had taken the rope from one of the packs and was quickly tying one end to the van's tow hook. His back was to the Stone Giant, his hands frantically busy. The Stone Giant was mere feet from the Stone Man, and then it was close enough to raise a foot to stamp down onto Caementum's head. It had learned its lesson; it was keeping its head up this time, out of the Stone Man's range, even though such an attack was now beyond us.

"Eric, hurry!" That was Maria from inside the van. In desperation I tried to flail the Stone Man's foot at the front of the Stone Giant's standing leg. As a kick it was wild and aimless but managed to connect beautifully with the Giant's instep. Our attacker's legs flew out behind it, its head crashing straight down into the concrete by the Stone Man's feet. I tried to kick at the Giant's head again, but this time I wasn't so lucky. I only got half contact, the Red getting its hand mostly in the way of its craggy skull just in time. It began to crawl forward, pinning Caementum's left leg with its arm, raising its free arm to club at Caementum's right, kicking leg. I saw the Giant's arm come down and flashed out at the last second.

I was glad I did. The *crack* of the Stone Man's right leg was audible even from where I stood, the sound like a gunshot as it pinged off the dead buildings all around us. A very familiar fizzing sound followed.

Maria! I called frantically down the circuit. *Get ready to contain us! I think the Giant's trying to—*

The Stone Giant struck again, breaking the Stone Man's right leg clean off its body.

I heard Maria let out a torn scream through the circuit as I braced myself for a Detonation that didn't come; she'd caught it, or she and Caementum's own auto-containment protocol had worked together to do so. Her screams mingled with the distorted fizzing that rang off the buildings around us. I saw Eric waving his arms at me, face red, his eyes white circles.

"*Sit it up!*" he screamed. "*Sit it up and go* light!"

Commands: I could follow commands, even as I recoiled in horror at the sight of our only weapon now completely neutralised. I flashed back into the Stone Man, performing that weak sit-up motion and managing to hold its torso upright long enough for Eric to loop something over my Stone eyes; Eric had thrown the rope over the Stone Man's head and stuck-out arm and pulled it tight. The Stone Giant shifted, raising its leg-pinning arm to take out Caementum's other leg, and that was our last chance; I flailed the Stone Man's remaining leg straight up and caught the Stone Giant in its left shoulder. It was already rising up before swinging down; I don't think the kick damaged it—I could barely kick, let alone properly kick *through*—but the Red was knocked sideways. Too far: its flailing limb slammed into the van's back left tyre, knocking it into an angle.

Go light, Eric had said, could the last of my control do that? I tried, and it must have worked enough, for suddenly my Stone Sight was travelling backwards at great speed as Eric sped the van noisily across the former Millennium Place. That last half-assed kick had knocked the Stone Giant off Caementum enough to give us the window needed to escape. My Stone Sight quickly stopped moving and I flashed back into my body, understanding that Eric had stopped the van. I blinked, my human eyes were full of navy blue aluminium; Eric had stopped the van broadsides—

"*Get in!*"

I staggered to my feet and lumbered around to the van's passenger side, my mouth and sinuses full of the taste and smell of my own blood, my head screaming. I glanced back to the Prism to see a terrible sight: the Stone Giant, getting to its feet, its gait and motion steady. Already it was beginning the pursuit of its Quarry. I glanced at the van's back wheel, knocked askance; I didn't think this vehicle would get us very far.

The Stone Giant walked towards us. Slow. Unstoppable. Every one of its footsteps a dull, heavy, and undeniable chime of doom.

We'd failed. Worse; we'd just had the living shit kicked out of us.

"*Come on!*"

There was no other choice. I jumped into the van. Maria's bloodshot eyes looked at me with an enquiring, pleading expression that *needed* me to tell her that I had a plan. I didn't. Dispensatori was truly all out of ideas, his big beliefs proved empty once more.

"Go," I gasped, the word coming out as a slurred mess. Eric stomped on the accelerator and we flew away up the road in a clatter of broken noise, a ruined Stone Man dragging behind us and our tails firmly between our legs. The van's suspension was beyond fucked now, and we were bounced around the cab as if we were driving over cobblestones. This van would not be taking us far, and a cold truth stung me as I remembered where we were:

Coventry.

There would be little to no abandoned cars left lying around the city centre. No-one but the homeless and the mad had lived here. No people driving around at the time of the Barrier's expansion to be burst by it, leaving us transport, and certainly none with keys in the ignition.

I looked into the van's wing mirror just before we rounded the bend.

Behind us, the Stone Giant walked out onto the road and continued to follow.

***

PART FIVE

A LIFELONG PROCESS

Chapter Seventeen

All is Loss

***

The van only lasted another minute or two before finally giving out.

The back end dropped with a loud wrenching crash, followed by the sound of metal grinding and sparking on the concrete as the damaged back left wheel finally broke all the way off. Eric stopped driving. The only sound in the cab was our pained and exhausted breathing.

"Check ... check the Stone Man," Eric said. I didn't argue. A strange sense of peace was beginning to wash over me. Was this what Paul felt? The knowledge that you had given everything, and that the struggle was over? I thought I'd be more afraid. I touched Maria's leg as I opened the passenger door.

"Are you hurt?" I asked her, still trying to be Dispensatori, even now. Maria's eyes were fixed on the windscreen and she didn't look at me. She just gave a brief shake of her head. "Hold on," I told her. "I'll be back in a second." I turned to get out, but then paused. "Everything's going to be okay soon," I said. My voice was settling down. I meant what I said. Everything *would* be okay as far as we were concerned.

We'd already agreed before we got to Coventry: no matter what, we would not let ourselves be taken. Now we had lost our greatest weapon, it was over. Maria and I were too powerful now to risk even a chance that we might eventually be taken. Who knew what a Harvest of ourselves would mean for the Stone Men?

I wouldn't make any choices for anyone, though. They had their own pistols now, strapped snugly to their bodies. They could make their own choices. For me, I felt like I could feel Sophie all around me. I wanted to go to her, to Paul. I was beyond tired. Five years of these monsters devouring every aspect of my life. The fight was over. I stepped down from the van and moved around to see the Stone Man.

The van was parked outside what had once been a takeaway; the sign was missing now, but I knew it well from my student days. It was the site of the former Express Diner. The weekend fights that happened outside—and inside—this place on a weekly basis had been ugly and depressing; a good friend of mine had been glassed here once. That this would be the place our struggle ended should have been infinitely more depressing, but somehow my sense of quiet completion held. We'd given everything. I understood it then. I truly had become Dispensatori. There was nothing left to give, no duty left to execute. The feeling was unlike any I had ever known.

The Stone Man lay before me, on its back. The crack in its side and its missing leg making me think of my friends and I, the way we had been beaten and dragged and abused—and killed—throughout this entire ordeal. The break in the Stone Man's leg was relatively clean, a neat cross section of the same greyish brown substance as its exterior. I'd expected there to maybe be hitherto unseen seams of *something* running through it, the way Eric had described those beneath the skin of the Pale Stone Man, but they were absent.

I looked around us, just to be sure. There were no other cars here. Maybe we could find one, but the Stone Giant would arrive in a few minutes; we hadn't gone very far at all. There was no way we could get one in time, and even if we could, by the time we got back the Red would be stamping Caementum's head clean off its shoulders. Where would we even go? Where could we take the Stone Man, now that it couldn't even walk, let alone fight?

The van's passenger door was still open. Maria's voice could be clearly heard on the silent street, talking to Eric. The sound of a distant crash suddenly echoed from the direction of the former Millennium Place. The Stone Giant was on its way. I moved to the van's cab, catching the back end of the conversation. Maria was looking at her hands in her lap, her face ashen. Eric was staring through the windscreen at nothing as he replied to Maria, dead-eyed,.

"What ... thing again?" Eric was asking.

"The thing you said earlier," Maria said. Her voice was flatter than I had ever heard it. "About the Red. About it being darker. Say it again."

"Ah," Eric began. "Um." He sounded as if he could barely think. "When I was by the Prism before. With Edgwick. I thought then that it looked darker than when I'd first seen it. And just now—after it had birthed those two Blues—it looked darker again. Maybe losing colour, I don't know."

My brow furrowed as I thought of the Core, reminded of what I'd seen in there. The vision from the Stone Man's own memories, emerging out of something, its body incomplete like that of the Pale Stone Man. Its own birth, Pale as it emerged from a Prism? From *the* Prism, before it came here?

And then it had consumed Jenny Drewitt and turned Red.

"So it's been getting darker as it's made more Blues," Maria said. Her voice was almost a whisper.

First pale, I thought, *then Red. Then darker, less colourful with each birth. All the way to ...*

I thought about how the Stone Man had begun to slow at the Project. About the way it needed to connect to Paul, to take energy from him. That need would make sense if it had come here on its last legs, after it had been used up, or nearly used up.

But still enough left in its tank to birth at least six more Blues.

"And if it kept going," I said. "Maybe it would end up the same colour as the Stone Man ..."

Something was stirring in me, some revelation. *Not now,* the exhausted part of me whispered. *Let it go. We're so close. So close to being finished.*

We were clutching at straws, though. There was nothing here at all.

"Yeah," Eric said, running his hands through his hair and looking at the cab's ceiling. He sighed heavily. "That's what I've been wondering. When I saw the Stone Giant just now, that confirmed it for me. That maybe *our* Stone Man was sent here without the Prism—hell, maybe a last fact-finding mission—to hopefully find a Super Target like Jenny to absorb. Maybe restart the whole process, you know? Nothing to lose; if it couldn't find a Super, it'd make a few last Blues for the folks back home." His hands lightly slapped upon the steering wheel. "Fuckers. *Fuckers.*"

"And that could be why the Stone Man became weak at the Project," I said. "Because it wasn't supposed to be here this long, chasing its Target."

"Uh-huh," Eric sighed, "And they didn't like that. So they got serious and sent the Prism."

I looked at Maria

She was trembling.

"That," she said, her voice barely audible, "is what I'm ... I'm *very afraid of.*" Before either of us could respond, she added: "Eric. Tell me again about Jenny Drewett. She was absorbed. Created the Red."

"... yeah."

"Do you think we could do that with our Stone Man?"

She looked up. Her shaking was increasing; she looked as if she was freezing.

"Absorb someone," she said, "and be recharged to full power?"

I understood, then. This was her last gasp of hope, fear making her think ridiculous things. I felt that strange sense of relief again; what she was suggesting wasn't even possible. We *were* done.

"Maria," I said, touching her arm gently, kindly. "Maria, even if that could work—and if we were somehow prepared to do that to someone—Jenny Drewett was DIGGS. There's no-one—" I thought of Holbrooks and felt cold. The doctor had said someone could potentially move up a whole bracket. Was Maria thinking she could—

No. Maria was LION, I knew. Even going up one would only make her the same level as me—

I realised that Maria *meant* me. If I moved into the next bracket, I would be DIGGS.

If she was right, I could be absorbed.

"Not you," she said, seeing my face, trembling so hard it looked like she were shaking her head *no*. "If you were DIGGS, I think we'd know about it by now. And your bubble was silver, grey—"

"Hey, hey," I said, taking her by the shoulders. "Maria. Listen. It's over. It's over now. Just breathe—" But she knocked my hands away as tears began to leak down each cheek.

"Holbrooks—he-he said—when two Stone Sensitives—*two* Stone Sensitives—"

Her face fell into her hands just as everything dropped into place.

No, I thought. *No. No. No.*

But the truth couldn't be denied so easily. *Yes,* she'd gone back into the pharmacy. She'd said she was getting tampons. She was not, I realised, getting tampons.

Marcus was alive under the Barrier. Bubbled, but alive. If he'd survived the Barrier, he was a Stone Sensitive, like us. Like Maria.

Maria threw her head back, trying to breathe, to talk. Did Eric understand? I didn't dare speak, as if doing so might confirm the terrible, impossible-to-accept truth that was playing out in front of me.

"It's why I didn't call Marcus," she croaked. "I couldn't tell him. After we'd met up, when he'd flown out to Barcelona to see me about a month ago—" She coughed, screwed her eyes shut tight. "I missed my period right after my mother died. Didn't worry about it with all the stress. Then with all the chaos since the Arrivals—" She suddenly gasped, shaking her head. "Didn't realise until the other day. I missed my next period too."

Eric's face whitened. *Now* he understood.

Maria tried to pull something from her pocket. It caught, and she flapped around in her seat, frustrated, before it came free. She held up the pregnancy test, the one she had secretly fetched from the pharmacy when we got the amphetamines.

The small window showed two lines.

I didn't know for sure what they meant, but Maria's head dropped and she began to sob hysterically. I thought two didn't mean she *wasn't* pregnant with Marcus' child.

And Holbrooks had told us that the child of two Stone Sensitives was always DIGGS.

A Super Target. A starter battery.

"No."

My voice was firm, or at least I intended it to be. It cracked as I said the word.

"*You ... said it yourself,*" Maria sobbed. "*This is about stopping the. Stopping the. En-end of the fucking world.*"

"No. No." This was beyond duty, beyond reason. "We can, we can—it's about moving energy! Paul even said it—" If we could somehow move the energy from the child—*two months*, I thought, *it's barely even formed*, the idea now horrifying beyond measure—then surely I could take that energy into me, I could take their place—

"You can't Andy," Eric said quietly. "Because you can't communicate with it."

Surely I could, somehow! I tried to feel along our circuit, to search inside Maria's energy ... but Eric was right. There was nothing else there to grasp.

And the Stone Giant would be here in minutes.

Maria's red eyes met mine. I didn't need to listen to her thread to know what she was thinking: this was our only chance. Our duty wasn't over yet, and it was now infinitely worse than I could imagine.

"The world, Andy," Maria said. "The world." Her tears were now a silent flood. "That day. The First Arrival. When the Stone Man walked through that bus with me and the kids. And it turned to look at me. I was pregnant then, too. Marcus' baby—" She screwed up her face. This was her second time. It was beyond cruel. "It didn't have the Prism to target me accurately, did it? And I thought *leave me alone,* and that hid me—" She lunged forward and grabbed my shoulders now. "Do you think you'll even be able make the Stone Man do it? Maybe it's not possible?" She wanted me to say *no*, and I wanted to so badly ... but already that sentence—that death sentence—was turning in my brain. *The world, Andy. The world.*

"I don't know," I said. This was insane. There was no way we could even consider this.

But the Stone Giant would soon be here. *The world, Andy.*

Maria barged forward, pushing me aside, and stepped out of the cab and down into the road. She fell against the side of the van as she staggered blindly along it, wiping her eyes with her right forearm. Eric got down from the driver's seat and rushed around to Maria's side, but I jumped down too and put a hand against his chest to stop him reaching her. Eric's heart hammered through his thin chest, the feeling clear under my fingers, but this had to be Maria's choice. How could it be anyone else's?

You made that choice for enough people before, Andy, a voice whispered. The world around me seemed to turn grey, the horror of what was happening sinking deeper. *Not like this, though,* I wheedled at myself. *Not like this.* Maria reached the back edge of the van and let out a small moan as she looked down at the Stone Man. When her hands went softly to her stomach, I couldn't take it anymore. Now I grabbed Eric and marched him forward with me; fuck the world, fuck everyone, I would not let her do this, even as another crash came from closer by. I could see the top of the immense dust cloud rising above the distant buildings, rising up towards that hateful Barrier that hung high above everything. We got within a few feet of Maria before she whirled to face us, her palm outstretched to say *stop.*

"Don't," she said. We stopped. "I need you to—*uhh.* Andy, when I was boosted. I saw the country. I saw the lights everywhere. All the Stone Sensitives under the Barrier. You've seen that, haven't you Eric?"

"Yeah, yes I have—"

"*Promise me* you did. Promise me it wasn't just my imagination. All those people. All those children."

"I promise you it was real," Eric said as Maria knelt down over the fallen Stone Man.

She let out a bestial howl that tore and shredded as it came.

"*It's not for me, Andy!*" she said. "*You have to know that, kill* me *a hundred times, take* me, *I'll go gladly, kill* me *but please don't make me*—" Her face came up. I'll never, ever forget what I saw there. That terrible hope against hope, a last, brief moment of belief as she asked an insane question that she knew would not save her child:

"Is there ... any way it can just be me?"

I tried to speak. My throat was a desert. All I could do was shake my head.

"No-one is going to make you do it," Eric said. "I—I'm not even sure we sh—"

"We can run," I said, moving to her now and crouching down. "See how long we survive. Maybe years. Maybe something else will come along and—"

"You know," Maria said, "that we have to stop this now, before there are too many of them. It's now, or never. It has to be." Her hand snapped up and grabbed mine, even though her eyes remained on the Stone Man. She slowly stood. Went to step forward. Hesitated. She leaned in slightly, looking as if she were straining against a rope no-one else could see.

"Help me, Andy," she said. "Now."

...

... Christ. *Christ.*
Oh, God. She.
She wanted me to—

...

Hold on a minute. Hold on.

***

Ok. A little more, then.

...

Maria wanted me to be a part of this. I heard her and recoiled, the coward that I am.

"Are ... are you su—"

Her eyes blazed into mine.

"You need to listen to me," she said. "You put me on there. You hold me there until—until you do what needs to be done. Don't—don't stop—"

"Maria—"

"No matter what I say, no matter what I do, *do not stop*. If you love me, if I am your friend, then you ... help me see this through. Do you understand?" She wiped her eyes, gasping, looking as if she were dreaming. "I am Maria Constance," she said. "This is my choice, but I will then fight you. *You mustn't let me win.* You help me do this first time, *first time*—" She screwed up her eyes again and now I held her trembling body. This couldn't be happening. She mumbled something into my shoulder.

"I can't hear you, darling," I told her.

"*Don't let this be worth nothing,*" she said. "*Promise me.*"

"I promise. I promise."

She nodded, her head still down, and then slowly raised her arms above her head. It took me a second to understand what she wanted before I bent slightly and put my arms behind her legs and upper back. She immediately wrapped her arms around my neck and pulled her face into it, curling against me as I lifted her into the air. She was small, and light, and stronger than I could ever dream of being.

"Oh my God," Eric said, backing up. "Maria." Her hand left my neck but her face didn't come up; she held her violently shaking palm in Eric's direction. He darted in, took it, squeezed it. "Andy," Eric said. "Do you ... do you need me to ..." He didn't know how to complete the sentence. I shook my head. Eric let go of Maria's hand slowly, releasing her index finger last. I knelt, moving Maria down towards the prone Stone Man. Eric watched, his fingernails clawing at his cheeks as he shifted helplessly from foot to foot. He saw me looking his way and slowly nodded. Maria continued to cry against my neck, trembling. I had to say something; for once I had the words. To anyone else they would be childish, not enough, but it was the only way I could put it. "Maria," I said. "You are amazing."

I hesitated. Of course I did. The Stone Man's body lay a foot below Maria's. She needed me to help her. I needed someone to help me.

Maria did. Her voice spoke up inside my head. Inside our circuit.

I need you to help me. So, help me.

She'd said that, if I loved her, I would do this.

I love you, I told her, and moved to lay her on top of the Stone Man.

Maria screeched and came alive in my arms, her fists colliding so hard with the side of my head, my chest, that I nearly dropped her. Her legs kicked uselessly at nothing as she thrashed in the air. She was fighting me, just as she said she would.

"*No—no—no—*" she sobbed, and then her elbow came forward and collided with the bone above my right eye. I nearly fell sideways on my knees but managed to remain upright, and that was when Maria's head darted forward and her teeth closed around my right ear. Her *no no no* became a choked-off grunt right into my ear canal, a hot, wet, desperate sound that will be in my nightmares for a long time. I grunted with the incredible pain of her bite as I continued to move her down towards the Stone Man, hearing Eric idiotically babbling *oh no, oh no, oh no* as he turned uselessly in a circle. Maria's kicking legs had nearly thrashed themselves free of the arm holding them; in a moment she would be loose. Would she run? Would her mother's survival instinct lose control once she was away from the actual moment of her death? Would we then try again?

I said I'd get it done first time—

"Eric," I said, my teeth gritted against the pain. I didn't want Maria to hear me screaming, here at the end. "Her legs. Help me. Help me help her." Eric hurried over, his face corpselike, and wrapped his arms around Maria's kicking legs. Even immobilised she continued to try and buck and writhe in our grasp. The three of us moved down to the Stone Man.

It was hard to lower her onto the Stone Man without touching it ourselves. Oh, of course *we* couldn't touch that thing, oh no. Not the people that stood back and let it happen. No, the people that *made* it happen. The curse of touching the Stone Man was for Maria, the one doing the dirty work and saving *everyone*—

...

I'm sorry, Maria. I'm sorry, even though I know you would make me do it every time.

Maria's body became instantly limp the second it connected with the Stone Man's, her bottom touching first. Now most of her weight was resting on the Stone Man. Her now-sightless eyes flew wide open, her arms falling off my neck and her head falling against my upper right arm, her face turned slightly towards mine. In this way her eyes were gazing right into mine as she began the CTTGATGAGC babbling I'd seen too many times before. This time it was a horror I will take to my grave.

I began to lean her back, her bottom still on the Stone Man's stomach, my grip moving to her shoulders, holding her there with my arms at full stretch. Her babbling head now hung limply backwards on her shoulders. I moved my feet around to the Stone Man's head, bending over it to lean out and lay Maria down backwards. I didn't touch the Stone Man's body. Aren't I lucky? Maria's tiny frame and lime green clothes looked even smaller and brighter next to the immense grey bulk of the Stone Man, and as her back touched down, her hanging back head did too. I could carefully and gently let her torso come to rest, letting her go now, her body completely laid upon the Stone Man's. To my left I heard Eric let out a wail of despair. He began to hammer on the side of the van with his fist and stump.

I wanted to recoil in revulsion from what my friend had already become, but to allow this to go on even a moment longer than necessary would be to fail her utterly. I'd felt the Stone Man respond the second their bodies connected. It knew what lay upon it. I could feel it along our threads, still intact and thrumming with chaos. The monster knew exactly what to do, but without my say so, it couldn't. The Stone Man was like a dog waiting for its master's permission to devour a treat. Once allowed, Maria would be gone.

No. That's not true. Maria was already gone.

I didn't know what form the command should take. As long as it was along the right lines, the Stone Man would surely take over from there. Any word would do. I couldn't look at Eric.

Reset, I thought.

Maria stopped babbling and began to scream.

The temperature dropped violently as that old, distorted brass sound rang off the walls around us. It drowned out the sound of Maria's voice as the process began. I felt it in her thread; Maria was suddenly lucid again, the spell of the Stone Man's touch broken by this new, terribly physical connection of theirs. I reacted quickly. Lightning quick. I will always hold onto that. Her suffering, the actual pain, lasted for perhaps a second. I am very, very glad of that, because as the distant pain rushed and howled in her thread, I took it.

I pulled it towards me, sending peace the other way. I don't know what made me think of Maria's story, told to me as her eyes watched the fire as we camped at Old John Hill. Perhaps it was my desperate intention to try to send her comfort that automatically plucked it from our circuit, her blocks already torn asunder, her memories exposed. I felt my thread drag it out of her and repel it back the other way, amplified a thousandfold. Right before the agony of the Stone Man's absorption filled me, I felt the exchange complete. Maria's fear and doubt and grief, her conflicting self-recrimination for what she considered an unforgivable act waging an impossible battle with her knowledge that *it had to be done* ... all of it fell calm. I know that, in her very last seconds of awareness, Maria knew peace, transported back to the moment when she was safe, content, and loved.

All I knew was hell.

I can only assume I fell onto my back. I don't know. I couldn't see, couldn't feel my body. All I knew was pain. I couldn't even scream. This was beyond anything. I felt the urge to return it, to give it back to Maria but, sweetest of mercies, the worst of it only lasted for a few seconds before my mind felt suddenly *padded*. The pain lessened some; now I could feel my body again, my back against the concrete, and a single hand on my shoulder. Eric. We weren't a circuit; how could he be affecting things?

I wouldn't understand until later, once I was able to logically piece together what had happened. Eric knew how his and Edgwick's energies had connected in a general, unfocused way, same as the energies of Paul and I had before we met a Watchmaker. But what was happening between myself and Eric now was a *circuit*; Paul had put the last of his gift into our circuit as he died, and now the last of Maria's gift was coming into me. I would be no Maria, ever, but *I* was the one connecting myself to Eric. I was a lesser Watchmaker now.

All I knew in the moment was a reduced agony. It went on for several, unending minutes, and as it began to fade I understood that *it* wasn't lessening; I was passing out. The pain was shutting me down, and it was a blessing.

I don't think I was out for long. I was awoken by the much nearer *boom* of another falling building. The distorted brass sound was gone. I sat up, body protesting, and looked to my left. Eric was sitting up against the back of the van, breathing hard and looking as if his soul had been bled out of his ankles. His eyes darted towards me as I moved, his head still.

Then his eyes zipped back to the Stone Man. I didn't want to look.

I looked.

Maria's body was gone.

I began to moan, clawing at my clothes uselessly as I got to my feet on legs made of straw. I needed to stand and look down from above, hoping idiotically that somehow Maria would still be there, that maybe I just hadn't been able to see her from my position on the floor. But she was gone. Pooled on the concrete underneath the Stone Man was a wide expanse of her blood. I looked at Eric again; could he tell me I was wrong somehow?

"Where's Maria—" I whispered, a simpleton's question, but Eric's stunned, ghost-like expression began to twitch back and forth, barely shaking his head *no* as if scared to move, as if his shock might shatter and let reality in. He'd seen the whole thing, then.

I thought the blood might have stained Caementum's body somehow, as the topmost surface of the Stone Man was now crimson. Then I realised every inch of its body was in fact now turning red, intensifying, brightening. The wind around us was picking up too, skittering so much grit that I had to squint.

Before my eyes, the Stone Man's missing leg began to regrow.

***

The Stone Giant walked up Far Gosford Street as if it were high noon.

Its gait was, of course, slow but steady. A default, perhaps. Conserving energy, maybe. It had taken a while for our pursuer to finally come inside visual range. Longer than I expected. Its approach path had been very clear as it had drawn closer. Many buildings had fallen. Eric and I watched them collapse. It was quite the noisy, dust-spewing spectacle, even at a distance. The last one to topple had been the Earl of Mercia pub, all the way at the other end of Gosford Street in a straight line from us. That building was a good few minutes' walk away from our vantage point. We saw the terrible red shape crash through the front wall, blowing debris into the street, and then the pub itself collapsed inwards behind it. We simply watched and waited as the Stone Giant slowly made its way down the middle of the road, the buildings either side of it a funnel carrying it straight to us.

Once it was past the halfway point, Eric quietly spoke up.

"Do you want to wait all the way until it gets here?"

I thought about it.

"No," I said. It was the first thing I'd said since the metamorphosis had completed. "Let's go."

The Stone Man began to walk towards the Stone Giant.

The names didn't match any more. That was okay. The name *the Stone Giant* would live in infamy for the rest of my life, but it would always be the name of *that* creature. The Stone Man had now changed dramatically, but I would not change its name.

It was the Stone Man, and by God, it walked.

Eric and I fell into silent step behind it and off to its side, our faces swollen and sore from crying as we marched along the pavement. The Stone Man crunched its way up the centre of the road, tall and proud, the concrete seeming to burst a little each time one of its enormous feet crashed down. Restarted?

Oh, yes.

Caementum now stood at least the height of its enemy, easily clearing thirteen or fourteen feet tall. Its entire body was a blood red so intense, I could have sworn it was pulsing. Its gait was perfect once more, steady and unshaken. I thought I had control of it before? That had been *nothing* compared to this, but there was no heightened mood now. I looked to the Stone Giant ahead of us, seeing just how right Eric was. The thing was indeed several shades darker than Caementum.

I wasn't worried about it affecting us or using the Prism to do so. The blanketing that had previously been Maria's was now under my control. I had it firmly covering myself, Eric and Caementum for protection from the Prism. I didn't think it was necessary, but there was absolutely no fucking way I was taking risks. It had been difficult to use and yet easy at the same time, like trying to swing an inflatable mattress quickly through the air. All I cared about was destroying the Stone Giant, and then the Prism.

But I wanted the Stone Giant more.

The Stone Giant and Stone Man drew closer, closer, the cracking sounds of the surfaces beneath their feet mingling and forming a sound like that of a marching battalion. As the Giant moved within twenty feet of us—and I can't say this for sure—it might have been speeding up. I held the Stone Man's arms out to its sides. I wanted the Stone Giant to come close. Ten feet.

"*Fuck him up!*" Eric suddenly screamed, and there was hate in it as well as pain. "*Fuck him up good!*"

The Stone Giant moved to within five feet of the Stone Man, already drawing back its right arm. I waited, pausing the Stone Man mid-stride, its left foot planted forward, its stance feeling grounded and firm. As the Stone Giant lunged in, I realised how slow it was. Far too slow.

My circuit's energies thrummed in me, surrounding me with a sense of my friends' essences. It brought a simultaneous sense of comfort and loss. I got the Stone Man's left arm up comfortably without even moving the Stone Man's feet. The swing of Stone Giant's blow was halted before it could gather any steam, landing with a dull, harmless thud.

It immediately began to draw its left arm back to follow up, and now I lifted the Stone Man's back foot and drove it forward, planting the kick right in the centre of the Stone Giant's chest. I pictured the blow busting right out of the Stone Giant's back; the explosive fizzing sound rang through the air as the Giant staggered four or five rapid steps backwards. I advanced the Stone Man as the Giant took a second to right itself, the energies of my circuit swimming in me and urging me forward. I *wanted* the Stone Giant to come at us. It did, moving forward with another obviously telegraphed swing of its right arm. It was attempting a devastating, clubbing blow. Fine, then. I would show it what devastation looked like.

I side-stepped with the Stone Man as the Giant's punch came in, moving Caementum's leading foot forward and slightly to the left, its right leg out behind it. The Giant's blow *whiffed* harmlessly by. I stepped through with the Stone Man's right leg.

The Stone Man's sticking-out right arm collided with a thunderous boom right across the centre of the Stone Giant's face, powered forward by the step-through and a turn of the Stone Man's mighty shoulder. The sheer force of the clothesline lifted the Giant's still-walking feet straight up in the air. I drove the blow forward and down all the way into the ground, slamming the Giant into the concrete head-first. I heard Eric bellowing something, his voice animalistic and raw, but I was already kneeling Caementum down onto the Giant and flattening one red lipstick palm onto its chest to hold it in place. We would see how the Stone Giant liked it. Before it could sit up, I smashed it in the face with the Stone Man's free arm. *Through* its face, as we'd learned. Through its energy. I thought of Maria, saying that she wanted to hurt them. I thought of Paul, wanting to give these monsters some of their damage back. They were both with me then, their energies clear and present as I punched through again and again; I believe that. I could almost hear them saying *yes, yes.* The Stone Giant tried to rise but I didn't ever give it a chance to come fully back online, to get control of its limbs once more. I wasn't going to stop. There was only one result that would satisfy me, and I didn't even know if it would be possible with this monster.

Each time I hit the Giant, its limbs weakly protesting, I could feel less resistance at the end of each strike. I knew I was striking with far more punch-through force and control than I had with the Blues on Old John Hill. Even so, I was still amazed when I saw it: the crack appearing in the side of the Stone Giant's neck.

Just a few more. I turned the process into an automatic and repeated one, Stone muscle memory effortlessly sampled and used to put a new lawnmower principle of motion in place. The force of it would be a little less, but I had to flash out for a moment and talk to Eric.

"Eric," I said, seeing him through my body's eyes. "I don't know what happens when the Stone Giant detonates, *if* it detonates. It might not contain itself if there are no active Blues nearby." I didn't recognise my voice. Flat, lifeless, but calm. To my left, the Stone Man continued to punch down onto the pinned Giant.

"But the Stone Man!" Eric shouted. "If the Giant detonates, the Stone Man'll be overloaded!" He was right. I had to use the Stone Man to kill the Giant, but it needed to be shut down when the Giant detonated. I would need a second after the killing blow to ensure the Stone Man was protected.

And the only way to do that would be temporarily containing the blast.

I flashed back into the Stone Man's eyes, seeing that crack in the Stone Giant's neck continue to open. Three more strikes would do it. Maybe four.

Bang.

Bang.

Bang.

I'd felt it in that last punch; only one more was needed. I moved Maria's blanketing—*my* blanketing—around the Stone Giant. We didn't need to hide anymore, but I had to solidify it, to turn it from concealment to something unbreakable. The idea of such containment was impossible before, possibly fatal to me, but now I was working with the seemingly endless power of the reborn Stone Man. The Giant had to be destroyed, no matter what; we would find out what happened next. My mental shielding of the Stone Giant's energy was now in place. I took full control of the Stone Man's limbs and turned off the autopilot.

I drove its fist down onto the Stone Giant's head.

There was an immense *crack* and a sound like a jack lead being pulled carelessly out of an immense bass amplifier. The Stone Man's punch removed the Stone Giant's head from its shoulders.

I braced the containment around the Giant.

Inside the Stone Man, I felt the first flash of the Giant's Detonation. For a moment, I was aware of the force I was about to try and contain, even if that containment would only be for a second. I knew then that it might kill me. That would be fine. My duty would be fulfilled. All would be well—

I remembered the Prism then. I was still not done.

I screamed in helpless frustration in Stone Space and flashed back into my body, the effort of containment driving my body to my knees as I quickly shut the Stone Man down. I didn't even know if that was necessary; it no longer had chinks in its armour to shore up. It was perfect once more, reborn, but I couldn't take any chances. If the Detonation might overload the Blues, it could possibly even overload a reborn Stone Man.

I told the Stone Man *sleep*, and it did, falling still where it knelt on the Stone Giant's chest, head down. The coast was clear.

"Andy, oh my God, what's—"

"*Brace yourself*," I grunted, and released the Stone Giant.

The unseen force blasted away from the Stone Giant in every direction, passing through myself and Eric and knocking us backwards. Every streetlight on the road came alive for a fraction of a second, then exploded, the force enough to shatter the toughened glass housings over each bulb. Tiny shards fell up and down the road, sounding like the world's most intense hailstorm. Somewhere very far away a car alarm began to sound, and I realised that now, of all times, my fucking headache was gone.

Then all was silent.

I woke the Stone Man. It only required the briefest thought to do so now. The monster stood, its feet planted either side of its vanquished foe.

I got to my feet and turned to Eric, offering him a hand up.

"Come on," I said. "We're not done."

***

The Prism rose before me. Before the Stone Man, I should say.

Edgwick's body no longer lay in front of the disgusting monstrosity. We had moved it to the side and covered his face with some spare clothes from Eric's pack. We'd considered using the Stone Man to smash a hole deep enough in the concrete to bury him, but neither of us wanted to bury him here. Even if the Prism was destroyed this ground would be desecrated. We would move Edgwick once we were done here, and we would erect something permanent in his honour. The survivors—the world—needed to know what he'd done for all of them.

"You're gonna do it now?" Eric asked. "You ready?"

"Yeah."

"What do you think's going to happen?"

"I don't know."

"Do you, you know ... feel anything?"

I looked around with my human eyes, taking in the abandoned streets of the city that was once my home. I tried to remember what I'd been doing the day of the First Arrival; interviewing some act for the local paper? A girl band, was it? I remembered it now; I'd been secretly hoping to pick one of them up, despite being old enough to be their dad. Then I'd maybe gone for a pint in a beer garden? It had been summer, I remember that. I suddenly saw it: Millennium Place, *packed* with humanity, with life, soaking up that beautiful sunlight. But now that sunlight was gone, muted by the ugly dreariness that hung above us, the people swallowed by the greyness that was their city centre, and there was no guarantee that they would ever return. If there were to be any chance of that, I still had one last job to do.

I wanted to try something first.

I walked the Stone Man to the Prism until its feet touched the front edge of the structure's base. I wouldn't let my human body get close; Eric had told me what had happened to the Shufflers when they touched it. I thought the Stone Man would be just fine. I lifted its arms, holding its fingerless hands out flat.

"Watch out for any bubbles," I said, and pressed the Stone Man's hands against the Prism.

The Prism was the only potential node available; there were no bubbles in our surroundings. The Stone Man's touch worked here; the dark sight of the whole country appeared below me, same as it had for Maria, as it had for Eric when he'd touched Aiden's golden bubble. I'd seen something similar once during the First Arrival, standing in a former friend's kitchen and using a roadmap to help my mind's eye see where the Stone Man was going; it had led me to Sheffield. But this was something else. The lights. There were so *many*. There were a handful of larger lights that were clearly the bubbles themselves, seen from above. Eighteen stayed in place; the bubbles hadn't died when we put the Blues down then, but then I could still see the faint light of the twelve fallen Blues at Old John Hill. I could also see the remaining five original Blues still walking towards their bubbles; the children, I now knew, of the Stone Man. Even the Detonation of the Stone Giant hadn't been enough to shut them down. Would they have been rendered dormant had they been closer to the point of eruption?

Here, at the Prism, the connection between the Stone Man and its children was obvious. I could now see the faint, dormant threads between them and Caementum, and knew I could use them. The Stone Man was their lynchpin, after all; we'd been reminded of that the hard way. I sent the same command down all the remaining Blues' threads:

Sleep.

Caementum's children—*our* children now, perhaps—immediately obeyed. I watched them stop walking, standing still and upright. That would do for now. The bubbles next; I tried to reach them but it was as if they were part of a different system. I couldn't connect to them in Stone Space; if they were the work of the Stone Giant, then they remained in place after the Giant's destruction too. If they were the work of the Prism, then I didn't yet know how to access or control them. We might have to travel to them in person, then. Get Eric to take care of them—

You won't have to, I thought, as you're about to reduce the Prism to its constituent parts. Then they're gone.

That brought me to thoughts of the Barrier. Could I turn it off before the Prism was destroyed? I was curious and tried, for a short while, to see if I couldn't access its inner workings. Not too hard; my curiosity wasn't so great that I would risk feeling the gaze of the Caeterus like Carl Baker and poor, heroic Edgwick. I was blanketed more than ever before, though; surely a more than sufficient shield, but risk was still risk. I quickly gave up, all the same. Trying to connect to the Prism's inner workings felt like—at least for now—

trying to connect a mains plug to an HDMI socket. I didn't currently have a way to make them work together. Fine.

I stepped the Stone Man back from the Prism and the vision of the country faded. I paused for a moment, testing the Red Stone Man's—or perhaps Maria's gift's—awareness of Stone Space. While nowhere near as good as the Prism, I was still faintly aware of the echoes of the bubbles's location. There was no need to blanket ourselves, after all—the Stone Giant was gone—and I thought better sight might come in the time ahead. Stone connections always improved over time.

I looked with my human eyes at the strange, scored surface of the Prism and picked a spot at roughly chest height for the Stone Man. That was as good a point to start as any.

The job—

Paul and Maria were gone, and everything else felt like a consolation prize.

I raised the Stone Man's arm, seeing it shake in response to the fresh tears that poured down my human face, thinking of everyone, *everyone*: the Targets, my friends, the tens of millions of people these Bastards had wiped out in an instant. I slammed the Stone Man's hand against the Prism, the movement so hard and fast that my human ears heard the wind *whoop*, rushing and deep.

The Stone Man's hand stopped dead against the Prism's surface with a heavy *clunk.*

Nothing happened.

I immediately swung the left. *Clunk.*

No.

I swung, and swung, and swung, the heavy understanding bleeding into me.

No. Please, no.

I started to hyperventilate, watching from my body as the Stone Man hammered its arms against the Prism, the immense structure impervious to every single strike.

Smash it? I wasn't even making a scratch.

I looked at Eric. He was staring at the Prism, his arms limply by his sides.

"I can't," I said, but that could not *be.*

I flashed fully into Caementum's driving seat, desperate for action rather than thought. I started the Stone Man's arms swinging again, suddenly desperate to be out, to be free, to be *free—*

Chink.

I looked down.

A piece of the Prism about the size of my thumbnail had broken off, bouncing onto the floor.

I flashed back into my human body to talk to Eric, to see if he saw it, but he was already thrusting a finger at it.

"Look, Andy, look, you got a bit—"

He trailed off, slowly straightening up.

His head continued to rise, leaning back on his neck as his gaze travelled all the way to the top of the Prism. His eyes moved side to side, taking in its width. Then they plummeted back to the tiny pebble I had punched out of it.

I gasped. My shoulders jerked up and down. Once. Twice. I watched as Eric's started to do the same, his breath coming in little snorts. Neither of us could believe it … but the shock was turning the despair into something else. I shook my head, my shoulders still heaving. A madman's smile began to creep onto my face. Eric saw it and couldn't help but follow, his mouth twisting up at the corners.

"Heh," he said. "Heh. Heh-heh."

"Mm," I said, grinning. I held the tears back. I'd had enough of them for a lifetime. "Mm."

We'd saved everyone under the Barrier. Saved the fucking *world*; at least for now. If more of them came, I knew, we would be ready. I would use the Stone Man to smash every single fucking one, one by one, if it were needed. I breathed, trying to let the magnitude of it sink in. It didn't. It couldn't. Absent-mindedly, I set the Stone Man to punching. This meant it wouldn't be striking as hard as it would if I was fully at the wheel. But by God, I would surely be here enough in the future. Doing *this* enough.

Eric's staccato chuckles became full-throated laughter, one hand going to his stomach and the other going to the back of his head. He sat down, wincing, and let the giggles take him. I followed suit, walking over to him and sitting down, our eyes on the punching Stone Man and the immensity of the Prism towering over it. I rested my hand on his shoulder as I crouched, and Eric patted it, which just set me off all over again.

The two of us laughed as the Stone Man continued to strike. We sat there for some time, the grey clouds passing over us, the Barrier churning above them all the while.

***

That was two days ago.

Eric's asleep right now. I only got maybe four or five hours myself last night, but the important thing is that I was actually sleepy. Having a real bed certainly helped. I haven't felt that tired today though, or at least not until now.

I didn't start recording this until Eric and I finished our little bubble tour. Before we left the Prism, I'd looked at the bubbles in Stone Space and marked roughly where each of them lay. I didn't think it was hugely necessary; Eric's injuries might have meant he couldn't search mentally until he'd at least healed some, but I figured Caementum's own abilities—or Maria's gift—would find the bubble people just fine. Even so, it didn't hurt to try and memorise a rough map. We figured that, if we took a motorbike, we could get Eric to all of them within twenty four hours. They would be dehydrated and starving, but they would survive. We managed to talk to them long-range before we left the Prism, telling them to hold on, that we were coming, that we would make it to all of them. We left Caementum at the Prism, working away. I wanted to bring it on the road with us but its far more use there. The range of control between myself and it now seems to be endless—the original Giant controlled the Blues all around the country, after all—but it's not the same as when I'm there, *inside* the thing. The punching-through energy works far better when I'm in the driving seat. I still feel it break little pieces of the Prism off, though; I feel the energy crackle and move. It's both satisfying and overwhelming at the same time, seeing just how long it will take to even get a quarter of the way through—

Years. Years.

... I try not to think about how much of it there is to get through.

The last of the three Targets we freed on the first day invited us to stay. She was a very nice old lady called Mavis, and I think she was glad of the company. She took the news about the rest of the country very well—"*I thought something like that had happened, those bastards*"—and even cooked us dinner.

The others we freed didn't take their new reality very well at all.

But at least we could give them hope. If you're trying to make people believe you have Stone knowledge, then opening bubbles is a good way to convince them. They've all asked where to go and I've told them to stay home for now—or to go home if they were bubbled away from home—and await further instructions. I'm realising very quickly that I am the person they will be looking to for answers, and I don't have them yet. Further instructions, you might ask? Yeah ...

... I'll come to that. I'll come to that.

So. Communicating with the bubbles long-range got easier very quickly. I think soon I'll be able to communicate with everyone, and easily, without any bubbles at all. I can already do it a little, even though it's really hard. We experimented with some of the people we freed. Maria's gift and Paul's gift, unblanketed, combined in one place. A fully restored and empowered place at that.

... sorry. I'm okay. I'm just fucked, but I have to finish this. I need it finally *done*.

Finishing. It seems like an alien concept.

...

All the signs point to the Prism needing ... consciousness? Processes? Whatever you want to call it, it seems to need an operator like the Stone Giant to be of use. Maybe I can be that operator in future. I hope so. Another potential way to bring the Barrier down, but hope feels dangerous right now. Early days. Early, early days. The Prism ... there's a quote I once heard you know, or a thought experiment, or whatever. It was a way of trying to comprehend the idea of eternal torment in hell, ironically. I'm not trying to make a comparison to *that,* as it happens, but the metaphor reminds me of chipping at the Prism: imagine a ball of steel the size of the sun. Once every thousand years a butterfly comes and brushes it with its wing. The amount of time it takes for that butterfly's wing to grind that steel down to nothing will be as long as it takes for your suffering to *begin.*

... funny. That actually makes me feel better, because the Prism is infinitely smaller than the fucking sun. My butterfly is far bigger. I have already made teeny, tiny progress. That's *something.*

...

Come on, Andy. Okay, *future plans,* okay. What they will be, I have absolutely no fucking idea. But a lot of people are going to be looking to me for them, and ... man.

Fucking hell. I'm avoiding it, aren't I?

Okay. I'll say it. I'll say it: I don't know what I'll say.

Not now, into this recording. I mean to *them,* when I can talk to *everyone.*

And I try to tell myself: *you just don't know* yet. *You just don't know* yet.

Dispensatori will have to ... *ahhh*. Bollocks.

You know, I think about what the Caeterus will do next. *If* they'll do anything next.

I don't think they're into revenge; they're too methodical for that, and yeah, if they send more Stone Men, I'll be waiting. Then the next question immediately pops up: what if they send something worse? They didn't send the Crawlers—hell I think the Barrier is containment for the crop *and* a defensive wall—but who knows if they have something like the Crawlers on *their* team? I think that, if our tiny corner of the universe is still worthy of their interest, they'd perhaps be curious. I think they'd want to know what happened ... or they'll give it up as a bad deal and they'll wipe us out remotely somehow. They clearly have the power to do it. But I think it'll be the former. If you have an ant farm and one of the ants suddenly got really smart, or really strong, you wouldn't just smash the colony... right?

I guess we'll see.

...

Communications are obviously still screwed under the Barrier, so we don't know what the rest of the world are doing. I can't begin to tell you how much I would like to know. Maybe they're prepping a nuke? Who fucking knows? Now we've freed all the bubble people, we're going back to Scotland, for sure. Back to the Skye Bridge—or rather what's left of it—to talk to Straub. Get an update, give an update. Then we'll go and get Caementum and spend a couple of weeks clearing the motorways. We have to start right, opening up the arteries of the country, making sure it's easy to get up and down; I plan to set up a regular check in with the outside, if we can, at a coastal point closer to Coventry. These are all just ideas, and I'm going to have to have a lot of them. Maybe we can talk Eric's pilot friend Colin into giving us a ride now we have the situation under control; even if he won't, we surely have at least one other pilot under here if there are two thousand or more people left. Maybe they're waiting and seeing. The Prism hasn't sent out any more individual barriers, at least. Like I said: no Stone Giant, no controller.

Recording, reliving all this has just been ... intense. Yes, I slept last night, but it was brief and fitful to say the least. Nightmares about Paul. About Maria. I know I haven't even begun to process what happened to them both. Especially Maria. It's not a luxury I have right now. Maybe it never will be.

I miss my friends very much.

Still. I'm sitting in our new and young friend Jack's kitchen, or rather Jack's parents' kitchen, at their very nice breakfast bar and enjoying—I have to say, I'm really, *really* enjoying—Jack's parents' ice-cold beer. I asked Jack if it was okay, and he said he didn't mind. He was relieved to be alive, but the kid is also dealing with the fact that his parents are dead. Their burst remains are upstairs. Eric found some sleeping pills in Jack's parents' medicine cabinet last night and gave the kid some so he could rest.

Speaking of Eric, he seems to be handling things okay. He insisted, though, that we bury Harry's body as soon as we got back to Coventry. We'd both agreed that the bubble people had to come first; they were dying of thirst, after all. Harry will be honoured, and the others. Eric and I have talked a lot. I like him. I asked him how he seems to be bearing up so well, and all he said was *I don't know; weirdly, it's the first time for a while that I've had choices.* I didn't really understand what he meant, but then we'd been walking into a bubble person's house and I didn't have time to press the issue. Eric wants to go to a lockup in Coventry to get some paintings or something, but that won't be for a while. He says he can't take them anywhere yet anyway; he says they have to go to Europe or something. I'd like to go back to Coventry too, to get those recordings of Sophie that Eric said I could have ... but that has to wait now too. I have enough to worry about. Like Eric's head; in fact; it's very swollen on the back. He has occasional trouble with his vision, but—like he says—there's not a lot we can do about it until we find a doctor. We ice it when we can. He asks me about Paul and Maria sometimes. It's hard to answer questions about the latter. I knew so much about her soul, her essence—you can't be in a circuit so much with someone and *not* know about that—but I know so little of her history. It's a very strange feeling. I'll ask Marcus when I talk to him properly. I'm ashamed to confess I kept my conversation with him very short. He asked about Maria. I ducked the question; saying we had to move on, playing dumb. I'd seen him in Maria's memories; the connection was too painful.

I'll talk to him eventually. I have to. Maria would want me to. But not yet.

So the Prism still stands. In some ways, that might actually turn out to be a good thing.

Hear me out.

Surely, given time, the Stone Man—*we*—will be able to do things with it.

Soon, I'm going to start trying to find out what they are. I think I'm going to have a lot of time to practice. After all, I'm a Watchmaker now, of a kind. I'm connected to the Stone Man. My circuit is now inside me, the energy that was in Paul, the energy that was in Maria. And if I can use that to unlock the secrets of the Prism, maybe we can learn how to protect ourselves from whatever the Caeterus are planning next, if anything. Maybe, in the scope of the war rather than the battle, this time—this access to one of their greatest tools—is a gift.

Or maybe I'm just trying to convince myself of that so I don't go insane.

Soon I'll get back to smashing the Prism in-person, as it were. But I have a feeling that I will have a lot of other things asked of me, too. *Dispensatori* will have a lot of other things asked of him—

There it is. Come on, Andy. Get it on tape. You don't have a therapist to say it to now. Stop dancing around it and fucking say it.

…

I never was him, I now realise. Dispensatori.

That was always just an illusion, but that's okay. My true nature is just too different to what Dispensatori *needs* to be. As long as the Prism stands, I simply have to keep trying. I have to accept that. I think I already have. I don't know. It's still very early days. People like young Jack, here are going to need me. I think the kid's still asleep upstairs—

Heh. I said *the kid.* He's twenty five. I guess I'm at the age now where twenty five is still a kid. When the fuck did that happen? Jack will have a long way to go too, to get his head round all this; another lifelong process. The problem is that accepting that process doesn't *make* me … what I need to … man, I used to write for a living and that's the best I have. Okay: *I'm trying to be something I can never truly be.* I've believed in my own big self-talk too many times, only to discover that, at heart, I'm still a coward. Maybe the big, final, positive transformation of Andy Pointer never comes. Maybe it's always just effort, always trying. And I am so fucking tired.

But trying is the task now. The *job*. And the job was all I ever needed to move forward—

Jesus. Okay. That's enough. I'm signing off.

… hmm. That's strange. I thought that, when I finished recording this, I'd be ready to just pass the fuck out. Instead, I feel like going for a walk. I feel like I could walk and never stop.

The Stone Man walks. It always does, sooner or later. Right now … yeah. I'm going to go for one myself.

Bye for now.

***

Epilogue
The Figures in the Mist
***

The recording ended.

Nathan's seasickness usually bothered him even in the smoothest of sailing conditions, but today he hadn't thought about it at all. He barely remembered, in fact, any of the scenery from the drive from Straub's house to the docks. He'd been lost almost entirely in the words from the device, staring ahead through the windscreen and listening through the headphones Straub had given him. He'd continued listening while Straub had taken care of setting sail. He'd offered help, but had been refused. *You listen,* she'd said. *You're only going to bugger things up. I doubt you know your knots.* Nathan's face felt hot—probably sunburnt after what was now several hours on the open deck—and he realised he needed water.

"Finished?" Straub asked. She was drinking a cup of tea and sitting on the leather bench at the back of the small vessel. They'd dropped anchor some time ago. The sail creaked in the breeze as the rope dinged lightly off the metal mast, the sun beating down. The stormy weather of the day before now seemed like something from an entirely different season. Straub noticed Nathan's skin. "There's some sunscreen in the locker, there. I should have offered you that earlier. Water, too."

"Thanks," Nathan said. He sat up, his back and neck protesting, then moved to the metal floor locker to open it.

"What do you think?" Straub asked, as Nathan pulled out a plastic water bottle and opened it. He considered the question as the warm liquid ran down his throat, the salty version lapping gently at the sides of the boat. Nathan shook his head, looking out across the water.

"It's all just so ..."

"Unfair?"

"*Yes*," Nathan said, leaning on the mast. "How do you even have this?"

"You heard what he said at the end? About coming to see me?"

"Yeah."

"He did it," Straub said. "Eric was there too, of course, and you won't be surprised to hear he tried to open the Barrier again. He couldn't even make a dent. He was right about it hardening, more than he ever suspected." She shrugged. "Then the next time Andy, Eric and I met, we arranged a private meeting, either side of the Barrier. My military escort had to hang back; the whole thing was to be for my ears only. No-one's allowed to do anything like that anymore, as you know. That rule was put in place very shortly after that meeting."

"Why were you the only one allowed?"

"In Andy's words: because you're making the decisions about what's best for the outside world. He said he had enough to worry about in there. Help me, he said. Do with it what you think best. Tell me later. He set the tape playing for me on his side of the Barrier, and then left. We've got a lot to do, he said. I recorded his recording from my side—that's why the audio is so bad—and no-one knew."

"Do-do you still see him?"

He felt stupid asking. Everyone knew the survivors in the United Kingdom didn't—

"I saw him only a few times more," she said. "Before I was removed as his contact."

"You've seen him since? Wait, why were you removed—"

"Stroke," Straub said, patting her chest and scowling, as if disgusted by what she perceived to be her weakness. "Took me out. Everything just collapsed in on me, Nathan. It took a long time to forgive myself for something completely out of my control; stupid. By the time I recovered, Saoirse politely thanked me for my service and retired me." Saoirse. The French-American-Irish coalition who had assumed control of the former British Isles. "I don't know what they told Andy, of course—"

"Wait, so you're confirming that the Sentinel—" He stopped talking as a movement on top of the white cliffs caught his eye. *"Oh my God, look at that."*

Already a commotion was going up from the countless boats floating all around him, an unconnected fleet so vast they looked as if they filled the entire British Channel. Their passengers were all seeing it: the immense red figure, looking huge even when viewed from a distance, striding out of the strange mist that shrouded the entire Cliffs of Dover, indeed, the entire United Kingdom. Ever since that odd, silvery substance had rolled out of seemingly nowhere—the source of it known only to the survivors within—it had filled the inside of the Barrier.

The Barrier. Still intact, even after all these years, that hateful, impossible bubble still clinging to Britain like a cancer.

The mist inside had kept coming, expanding like the densest snow ever seen inside a snow globe, and had stayed there ever since. Did it fill the whole space beneath it, or only the inside edge of the Barrier, some sort of internal cloud bank? No-one knew. Maybe Straub did, but she wasn't telling, although the Barrier—as many, many people claimed—was not as bright as it once was. Perhaps it was degrading, went the theory. Perhaps one day soon it would collapse entirely, the mist departing with it, and the survivors would be free. The UK ex-pats could finally come home, should they wish. Nathan grabbed his binoculars just as the Stone Man strode forward.

It walked all the way to the very edge of the cliff. It stood upright and proud in the small gap between the strange wall of mist and the barrier itself. The boats around Nathan erupted in cheers and applause. The Stone Man just stood there, watching.

"It's ... different seeing it in person," Nathan said. "Every year, on the TV. It doesn't have the same presence."

"Quite," Straub said, standing. He looked at the people standing up on their boats; not one able-bodied person within Nathan's visual range was sitting. The size of the gathering really was remarkable, same as every year. To be in its midst, of all these boats and ships continuing as far as the eye could see—

"You *must* have spoken to him more than that," Nathan said, not taking his eyes off the distant Stone Man. "How was this, all *this*," he said, gesturing at the countless boats, "even arranged in the first place?"

"It was never *arranged*," Straub said. "Someone was in the water—one of the sightseeing vessels—and a sighting was made. People came out the same day the next year just in case, and another sighting was made, and then it became a tradition."

"I *know* the media-friendly version," Nathan said. "But it all seems a little convenient to me." The sightseeing vessels were shut down these days, the entire area around the United Kingdom closed off and patrolled by a dedicated fleet. Saoirse and the rest of Europe saw to that. These waters were only opened one day of the year now. This day. "The Prism is in Coventry; why would the Stone Man come anywhere near the coast?"

Straub smiled.

"You never met Andy Pointer," she said. "As you heard him say; a person's true nature doesn't fully change." The smile became sad. "But I think he's doing his best. Even so: he never shied away from an audience. I think even as Dispensatori, he can't help himself."

"So it *is* him, then?" Nathan said, rushing forward, eager. "The Sentinel?"

"I didn't say that."

"But the Stone Man is with—"

"Doesn't mean the Sentinel is Andy Pointer."

Nathan sighed. There were always more damn *questions*. Straub had tried to tell him this before he even started the damn tape.

"I *will* tell you this," Straub said. "And its big. The reason you're even hearing all this."

Nathan listened.

"The powers that be," Straub said, "heard something from Andy that they didn't like."

"Wait, he talked to them?"

"Yes, but I don't know when he did so. I still have a few contacts that give me the occasional tidbit. Things may be need-to-know, but my duty means *I* need to know. Andy has communicated with them at least once after I was removed."

"*What?*"

The United Kingdom—at least as far as the world had been told—did not communicate with anyone. Every year on this day the survivors came to the Cliffs of Dover to be seen by their families. The most they would ever communicate was with the same symbol: a thumbs-up, held high. *We're okay,* it said. But why never more than that? It was *maddening*. And now Nathan was hearing this?

"Yes," Straub sighed. "I don't know when, or how it was arranged, although it wouldn't be hard from Andy's end. But he did talk to them. Andy—and his people—were planning something, and since that was passed on, there has been no more communication. Or maybe Andy already did what he was going to do, and something happened with *that,*" she said, pointing to the Barrier, "that meant that communication was no longer an option? I don't know. But the top brass don't like anything going on without their approval: *an Arrival hasn't happened in years, why mess around now? Why provoke them?* I thought the same, once; I even said something similar to Andy myself when he told me he was going to experiment with the Prism."

"How—how did he respond?"

"*That's what a lot of people thought last time, Brigadier,*" he said. "*And then nearly everyone in the UK was killed.* Saoirse would love to get in and stop him, if he hasn't yet done whatever he was going to do, but obviously they can't ... which is another element that has forced my hand in going public." She gestured at Nathan and sat back, adjusting herself in her seat. "Saoirse are panicking now, and they're talking about taking control with the nuclear option."

"Which is?"

"The literal nuclear option."

Nathan's mouth fell open.

"Saoirse launch a nuke at the Barrier," Straub said, "there's a possibility that everyone underneath it will be killed; more importantly, in terms of the human race, Andy Pointer might be killed, the man who remains our only asset in terms of being able to actively access Stone technology. He told me that *everything the Stone Men do is all about energy.* We're going to just throw a nuke at that?" She shook her head. "I can't sit back and let that happen. We need an International Kindness Protocol, a database, research, *we need to prepare.*" She jabbed a finger at the Barrier. "Andy and the others are our only bulwark against another Arrival, and they're alone. Power-mad people want to exploit that nation—what would be left after a nuke, anyway, if one were to penetrate the Barrier—and they're taking a big risk while the world is complacent. Maybe if the truth comes out, people know the human side of what happened, it might wake the world up. Restart the conversation. When enough people talk, governments would have to listen."

And then they lie, Nathan thought. Saoirse had long ago 'leaked' that the survivors had managed to commandeer a Stone Man, and that it fought back the invaders. They'd claimed this was the last communication they were able to receive before the former British Isles closed off for good.

"The *survivors,*" Nathan says. "Why wouldn't they write down messages on signs or something? Try and tell the world—"

"Kayfabe, Nathan. Kayfabe. Andy decided—and I agree—that they would keep any plans or progress they're making under wraps; a blanket ban on all communication. The Caeterus cannot know, and the more people that are in on it, the greater the risk from the Caeterus. Yes, I've now told you what was done in the *past* to stop the Fifth Arrival—and it can be told to the world, it has to be now—but I wouldn't tell you anything about what they're doing, or plan to do. That might tip off the Caeterus."

"Do you know what they're planning?"

"*Kayfabe.*"

Nathan looked at the coast of the UK and wondered, yet again, what kind of society they had built under there? Did Straub know?

"Tell *me* something now," Straub said. "Was I right?"

Nathan knew what she meant.

"... about what?"

Straub nodded at the MP3 player. He shook his head, unable to verbalise the truth. There had been no closure from the tape, and now Nathan was realising that perhaps he would never find it. He wondered if, perhaps, what Andy had said about lifelong tasks applied to him, too. He opened his mouth to reply and saw Straub's face light up. She pointed behind Nathan, at the cliff.

"There you are," she said.

The applause grew louder as another figure joined the Stone Man in the distance; many of the people there on the water, Nathan knew, were just there for a novel day out, rich arseholes sipping champagne and thinking the whole thing was just *such a laugh*. But the majority were there because it meant something to them.

It was originally called Survivor's Day, but the name slowly turned into Appreciation Day for a reason.

The second figure was, of course, far smaller than the Red Stone Man; the person that had become known as the Sentinel was human, after all. He always emerged first, ahead of the other survivors. The Sentinel wore his usual get up: a jacket, a blue baseball cap, shades, jeans. All that, along with the thick beard, made it impossible to identify who the Sentinel truly was. There had been many rumours that it was Andy Pointer, even though the public 'knew' that Andy Pointer had died during the Third Arrival. Nathan had never believed that, but he'd always wondered if the Sentinel *could* be Andy. Nathan had been one of the people that thought the Sentinel might not even always be the same person; it could be any white guy with a beard, shades and hat, maybe trying to keep some propaganda going, a figure of hope.

"Just tell me," Nathan said, jabbing a finger in the second figure's direction. "Tell me if that's him. Is that Andy Pointer? It is, right? It has to be!"

"The personal appearances were my idea, you know," Straub said, putting her hands behind her back. "I suggested to Andy, way back then, that someone needed to be seen, regularly. He must have taken my advice. The people out *here* needed to be reminded of the people in *there*. Make it so they couldn't be forgotten, even when everything was *kayfabe*. I don't know what the shades and the baseball cap are all about though. Someone trying to convince themselves, perhaps, that they don't want the spotlight ... but still unable to resist. A compromise with themselves, maybe. One's nature is one's nature, and all that."

"*Whose* nature?" Nathan asked. "Andy's?"

"The Sentinel," Straub said, smiling and ignoring the question, "wears the shades and hat for a reason. And as long as they're wearing them, I confirm nothing. Sorry, Nathan. Andy is running things in there, and the disguise would be his decision, whoever the person wearing them may be. I have far too much respect for Andy to go against his wishes even a little."

"But you're practically *admitting* it, why not just—"

The shapes of other approaching figures became visible in the mist. They were a long way back, as always, far enough that they may be standing on a lower part of the rise; it was difficult to ascertain their true heights. It was only possible to see the ones most visible—which wasn't saying much—because of their size. They were tall. Very tall. They stood motionless, as still as the Stone Man himself.

"Here," Straub said, handing Nathan a pair of powerful binoculars. He snatched them from her and looked to the Sentinel, watching as the person's face turned back and forth slowly. They looked as if they were taking in the view. Nathan scoured the obscured face, gleaning no more than anyone else had from the endless amounts of video footage and photos; there were theories that the Sentinel often stuffed tissue into different points of their cheeks each time. *Doing a Brando,* they called it.

The blue baseball cap nodded up and down briefly in confirmation and the Sentinel raised a hand in greeting. The roar from the ships on the water was suddenly deafening, a wave of respect that would carry all the way to the coastline. There was movement in the Sentinel's heavily obscured face.

That fucking beard and shades, Nathan thought, as the Sentinel finally turned and headed back into the mist. *The shadow from that fucking cap.* The Stone Man turned too, the more visible figures of the obscured figures—enveloped in that silvery-looking cloud—seeming to turn almost in perfect unison with it. *They always make it so hard to tell.*

But Nathan thought he'd caught a glimpse of something through the binoculars, a gentle flicker of meaning seen just before the Sentinel turned away.

Nathan thought that the Sentinel's mouth had turned up in a quiet smile.

***

Author's Afterword

✱✱✱

Phew.

I really, really hope you've enjoyed this book. My life has, in a roundabout way, revolved around it ever since I started work on *The Empty Men*.

Any friends or family members that have heard me talk about future plans will have heard the same refrain, over and over: *once I finish the Stone Man series/I've just got to get the Stone Man series finished.* It was an overwhelming task that just kept going; I didn't start work on *The Empty Men* until I had an entire storyline mapped out for the entire series. There was no way in hell I was going into this without knowing how it ended, what all the major story beats were going to be, and what was driving the whole thing. I'd been thinking about them for years ever since I finished *The Stone Man* and had a good idea, but to get them all to line up and make sense took months. I couldn't drop the ball. *The Stone Man* was the book that brought most of my readers to the dance. I couldn't start the sequels and have them fizzle out because I didn't have a destination in mind. What I didn't realise was that it would take not one, not two, but three new books.

I had several surprisingly angry reviewers saying something along the lines of *I thought the The Stone Giant was going to be the last part of a trilogy, but he's clearly dragging it out.* I'll be honest: that got to me quite a lot, and for two reasons. One, I never said that the Stone Man series was a trilogy. There *is* a trilogy here, but it starts with *The Empty Men* and ends with the book you've just finished. TEM, as it turned out, was the first act of a three-act arc. I thought it would end in two books but there ended up being too much there to cram into two novels. Reason Two: *I would have absolutely fucking* loved *to have this story end in three books.* It has hung over my head for *seven years* like a shadow, a constant cattle prod of anxiety going *you have to get this right, asshole,* every single day. The idea that I would have intentionally dragged this out ... let's put it extremely politely and say it makes me want to *poot my pootles*, and leave it at that.

Before we go any further, to those of you who have been here since The Empty Men, let me thank you sincerely and deeply from the bottom of my heart. Thank you for your time, thank you for your patience in waiting for me to get 'er done, and thank you for your spending your money on my work. I truly hope you consider it well spent.

I just thought about going back to the previous afterwords in the series to see what I wrote, because I know there were a lot of things I wanted to talk about and couldn't because of spoilers. But you know what, I think I'll keep this fresh; it's more genuine that way, and besides, I've cheated: ever since I started work on Book Two, I've been keeping a little file of things I wanted to talk about in this closing (of this arc) novel, so I'm going to work off that. In no particular order:

Just before I started work on what I'll refer to from here on out as The Prism Sequence (books 2-4) I realised I should probably actually jump in the car and pay a visit to Sheffield. I'd never been to the Ladybower Reservoir despite using it in Book One, only working from Google maps and images. I knew that new scenes were going to take place there, so I thought I should probably go and check it out. While standing in the natural basin there I noticed a cluster of white objects on the hillside: plastic tubes placed around freshly planted saplings to help them grow straight, perhaps, or protect them from dog urine. Whatever the reason, this mini-army of white plastic things were sticking up out of the ground in the distance and looked like they were descending the hill. The visual stuck with me. In that moment the Empty Men stopped being dark shadowy figures and became brightly glowing white. I think that works better; as cool as the shadow versions of the Empty Men might have been, that feels too familiar. The white is weirder, and that excites me a lot more.

Many years ago, I'd *just* finished the first draft of the novel that would (over a decade later) become *How to be a Vigilante: a Diary*. It was based around the premise of *what would happen if an actual comic book nerd—one with many issues of his own—tried to become a superhero in the real world?* (This was several years before *Kick Ass*, too, but I digress. Plus, Kick Ass is still intentionally cartoony, and a ton of fun for it. Nigel's world is painfully, brutally immersed in the mundanity of the real world, and the results are... less fun, but interesting in a very different way.) Then I went to the movies to watch a film I knew absolutely nothing about at the time: M. Night

Shyamalan's *Unbreakable* (firmly in my top ten films of all time, Blake Snyder be damned) and discovered to my horror that it was about comic book characters in the real world.

Fast forward around twenty years and I came out of a screening of a film I don't remember to see the poster for a movie called *Arrival*. The poster (featuring a key word from the Stone Man series) featured a large, *stone looking* spaceship in the middle of a field. The air in the lobby of a Los Angeles AMC turned bluer than a Stone child. Then—after I'd described the Crawlers in Book Two and released it—I actually saw the movie and the aliens in it that looked like walking human hands. More silent curses later I changed the name of the *Hands of Stone* to *the Crawlers*.

More tidbits:

—The negotiations for Matt Addis' audiobook narration expenses were even more complicated this time around. Ever since he's been swanning around doing work for smash hit video game franchises and the BBC, he's started referring to himself in the third person. I even thought I was talking to his agent when the man on the other end of the phone call kept repeating *Matt Addis just gots to get the Benjamins, Matt Addis just gots to get the Benjamins*. Eventually I realised I *was talking to* Matt. Three lorry loads of Benjamins and a deed to a platinum mine later, Addis was back in the studio and producing the goods. Thanks as always, Matt. You were excellent and a delight to work with.

—... but some errors still made it into the series and then it was too late to change them. Dead baby Aaron was referred to as a girl in Book One and *not one reader noticed* when he became a boy in Book Two ... and this is with the readers that notice *everything!* I was able to explain this away in this book as being part of Andy's unreliable narration, but not so with Harry's hip flask. How did he have it inside his bubble after he gave it to Eric in Book Two?

—My one (pretty big) regret of the series is a moment I included in *The Stone Giant*, right after Harry is Harvested. The Blue begins to disappear, its task complete, but just before it does, it turns it head to look at Eric.

Shouldn'nadunnit.

This was a case of Overexcited Writer Syndrome, i.e. me thinking how cool that would be in Eric's moment of despair ... and not realising that it totally waters down the moment right at the start of *The Empty Men*. The same turning of the head—in this instance, by Caementum himself—occurs during Maria's prologue on the bus during the First Arrival. That was a moment that was supposed to pay off at the very end of the entire series: Caementum only looks at Maria because of the DIGGS child she was carrying, something that would have been far clearer *if she was the only character a Stone Man turned to look at*. So here is the lesson to any other writers out there: don't ruin your own seven-years-in-the-making setups just because a moment is too creepy to not use.

A few thanks are needed, in no order, thank you to:

The great Sam Boyce.

The wonderful Laura Miller, stepping into the breach in style.

The team in my corner, Kristen Nelson and Ryan Lewis.

Joseph Samaniego for his physics advice; I sincerely hope I didn't butcher it.

Barnett Brettler for the usual input and invaluable career assistance.

Stephen Andrade for his glowing early review that helped put *The Stone Man* on the map.

Mike Godwin for his wonderful cover art; several years ago, Mike emailed me with his fantastic home made alt cover for *The Stone Man* that he'd created just for fun. I loved it so much that I asked if he could design the rest of the series; I came up with some sequel layouts based on his fantastic original design, and Mike absolutely knocked them out of the park as I'm sure you'll agree. This book is the first *Stone Man* novel to only ever feature Mike's work as its first cover, and I think they look amazing.

The good people of Planttalk.com heavy machinery online forum. I'd written the original draft with Andy and co simply driving down the motorways in a stolen bulldozer, clearing a path of dead cars as they went. Then I realised this probably wouldn't be possible. Nine whole pages of forum advice later, I chickened out and went with a lorry, and all the geographical timing nightmares that came with it. Ouch.

A quick request: if you recommend this series to anyone, please tell them to start with *The Stone Man 10th Anniversary Special Edition*. Not only is it a tighter edit of the story, but it comes with *120 pages* of bonus material including deleted scenes across books 1-3 and a brand-new afterword. If you haven't tried it yourself yet, check it out.

The big question: will there be another Stone Man book? If you asked me now, my answer would be an almighty *hell, no.* I just got my life back. Please don't misunderstand: I am *extremely* proud of this series. If I died tomorrow, this would be what I was remembered for, or at least by the people that remember me. The line *a writer hates to write but loves to have written* perfectly sums up my feelings about this series. But the significance of the Stone Man to my life has made working on The Prism Sequence a very stressful and claustrophobic experience because, like I said, they had to be right.

But ...

I'd be lying if I said I didn't know what the next book would be about. I know how it starts, I know what happens in the middle, and I know how it ends. It would be the definitive and final ending to the story, too, and I think it would be great. But rest assured I will be taking a *long* break from anything Stone related for many, many years. If Book Five is never written—and there are very good odds that it never will be—I believe *March of the Stone* Men serves as an ending in the same way Book One did. Open ended, but—in my opinion—resolved enough. Asking me if I'm working on it will be a pointless endeavour because, even if I was, I'd want it to be a surprise and wouldn't tell you ☺ As always, go to lukesmitherd.com and join the Spam-Free Book Release Mailing List to make sure you don't miss any book release news.

So what *is* next? (Seriously: it still hasn't sunk in that this series is complete. That's *mental*.) The good news is that my next book is already written. The bad news is it isn't coming out until October 2025; I'll explain more (and why) in the Spam Free Book Release Newsletter. It's currently late August. *March of the Stone Men* should be coming out in October 2024 (audiobook preparation and processing takes a while) so if you're an early reader of this, you have a year to wait. Hey, the last gap between books was at least two years, so I've doubled my output. I'm going to be releasing shorter novels in the interim; the continuity of a four book series has been one hell of a challenge, and the appeal of writing shorter, contained fiction for a while is extremely appealing. Again, join the SFBR Mailing List at lukesmitherd.com to make sure you catch those. Why not check out my other books in the meantime? If you haven't tried it yet, I recommend *You See the Monster.* People really seem to like that one. Your Second Favourite author also has an interactive radio show on Spotify called *Cracker Juice*, in which we listen to music and try to find out what gets people good and juiced. Come say hello.

If you enjoyed this book, please leave a star rating on Amazon, Goodreads, wherever else you think matters, or tell a friend. I cannot overstate the importance of all that. And anyone that leaves an actual review gets their reviewer name in the acknowledgements of my next book, same as with this one. I'd promise you the usual favours but frankly, my backlog is now immense, and I'm not sure if there's enough Vaseline in the world for me to clear even half of it. But I sure would appreciate the stars. Luke Smitherd gots to get them Benjamins.

Thank you, thank you, thank you for being part of Andy's—and Caementum's—journey for all these years, and don't worry. Andy's doing alright.

The Stone Man walks. It always does.
Stay Hungry, folks.

Luke Smitherd
Los Angeles
August 27th 2024

Insta: @lukesmitherdyall
Twitter @lukesmitherd
Facebook: Luke Smitherd Book Stuff
Join the Spam Free Book Release Newsletter at lukesmitherd.com

READ ON FOR A FREE SAMPLE FROM THE OPENING CHAPTER OF *YOU SEE THE MONSTER*, AVAILABLE ON AMAZON NOW

You See the Monster
Chapter One
2002
***

Sam sits in a café. His coffee is now cold, but the taste was disappointing long before that. He wouldn't have chosen this place to meet. Melissa did.

The clientele says everything Sam needs to know about the establishment, in that there are no other customers present; the only other people there are staff. There's a middle-aged, scruffy-looking gentleman sitting behind the counter reading a paper. There's a woman somewhere, possibly his wife, who wanders in and out occasionally from the back room, saying nothing. There's a large mirror on the wall to the right of the counter, presumably mounted in an attempt to make the place look bigger. It doesn't work, perhaps because the edges of the glass have been plastered over the years with now-faded stickers. The floor is tiled, the walls are tiled, and sounds from a tinny radio echo unpleasantly off both ageing yet impervious surfaces. Sam possesses one out of those two qualities.

Melissa is late—very late—hence the cold coffee, and even though Sam expected that, he's worried that he's already angry. This was always going to be a difficult conversation, but going in with a hot head certainly won't help. He'd told Leslie to stay at home. It took a three-hour argument to get her to listen. Sam has a decades-long history of saying *yes dear* to his wife, but this is one issue on which he is adamant: Melissa has hurt Leslie enough, and she wasn't going to be present for this. Sam realises he's gripping the handle of his cup way too tight. As long as she doesn't bring that piece of shit with her. Even Melissa wouldn't be that difficult, surely? She knows not to wave a red rag like—

The café door pings as it opens. Sam looks up and for a second thinks that Melissa has no-showed and *oh she wouldn't*, sent the piece of shit by himself... but Sam sees he's wrong. The man walking in is long-faced, like the idiot, and unkempt, like the piece of shit, but he's too tall, too stocky, and too well dressed: a full suit and tie job, shoes clean and shiny. In his late thirties, perhaps. Sam notices details like this. He's police, after all. It's 10:27. Sam's brain goes into processes so automatic he doesn't even consciously know they're happening:

Too early for lunch, but anyhow he eats at nice places. A salesman, maybe, needing a coffee to keep him going—

Sam's eyes go back to the door.

"Hello," he hears the man behind the counter say, a slight sigh in his voice as if two customers in the room at once constitutes an early rush. The newcomer mumbles something in response. "Sorry?" the man behind the counter repeats.

"Just a... can of coke please." The suited man is audible this time.

"Right." Again, a slight sigh. Some people are never happy. Sam looks at his watch again. Doesn't Melissa realise this is her last chance? He hears a chair scrape out as the newcomer sits down, followed by a faint rustling of paper. Sam's eyes move in that direction of their own accord; the man has pulled a folded piece of yellow-looking paper out of his pocket and is now staring at it intensely. Even though his mind is elsewhere, some instinct in Sam keeps his eyes on what the man is doing. He fumbles with the outer corner of the paper, eyes dark and serious, fingers lightly playing with it... and then he slowly tears the very corner off.

He keeps the torn-off piece in his hand, looking between it and the paper still held in his opposite grip. The piece he's torn off is tiny, slightly bigger than a postage stamp. It's mildly weird behaviour, but Sam's bad-guy radar isn't going off. In fact, this fellow barely seems to register in his awareness at all, for some reason. It's almost as if the reason Sam keeps looking at him is to remind himself that the man is still even there.

The door pings again and Sam jumps a little in his seat, but quickly comes back to himself as he sees it's Melissa. He mentally winces as he spots two things: she's skinnier than ever, and she's brought the piece of shit with her. Sam's immediate anger switches to a sudden, deep sadness as he sees a faint smile appear on Melissa's face. She saw Sam's expression as the piece of shit walked in. Sam realises this and understands exactly how the conversation will end. He did the right thing not letting Leslie come.

Sam stands up. Melissa reaches the table, her grey jeans, black cardigan and T-shirt creased and unkempt-looking. The POS stands behind her, shifty as ever, gaze darting anywhere around the room except at Sam. Sam still doesn't know how old this man is. Thirty? Thirty-five? Melissa won't tell him and, despite all his contacts and skills, Sam hasn't been able to find out. *Jake's off-grid*, Melissa had proudly parroted, clearly believing that the piece of shit is some kind of shaman, and not a waster from Binley. That said, the off-grid thing may be why Sam can't even get a surname. Leslie wouldn't let him have them tailed. She's always been too soft, too damn *coddling*, and Melissa realised it from the time she was three. Sam knew he was to blame too; if he'd worked less, hadn't always been chasing those promotions, he could have been there to balance it out. By the time he'd realised how bad things had become, so bad that even his weapons-grade denial couldn't curb the truth anymore—when Melissa took the family car for a spin at sixteen, drunk behind the wheel—it was too late. Now she's about to throw her life away with this scumbag.

"Mel," Sam says, trying to keep his voice steady. "I asked for this to be just you and me." He doesn't look at the POS. Melissa makes the face he's seen far too much of in recent years; the one she's *always* ready to pull. She's always waiting for somebody to say something, it seems.

"And I told you, Dad, that Jake is part of my life now and you have to *accept* that," she says, deliberately loudly of course, so the guy behind the counter and the suited man look their way. The latter looks away quickly, eyes back on his folded and yellowed paper—Sam notices he has another torn-off piece between his thumb and forefinger, the previous one now discarded on the table. "I'm eighteen." Melissa lowers her voice, much to Sam's amazement. "I'm an adult now. *You can't tell me what to do.* I don't live under 'your roof' anymore. So if I want to bring Jake, I will. You're the one who wanted this meet-and-greet." Eighteen. And shacked up with a weirdo old enough to be her dad.

It takes everything Sam has not to snatch the ashtray from the table and bludgeon Jake over the head with it until he's a bleeding mess on the floor, but he manages to keep at least *that* instinct in check. Other internal safety measures are falling away with terrible speed, however, and although Sam feels this, he is powerless to stop it.

"Maybe I should, uh, go," Jake mumbles, both his hands in his jacket pockets. "This is a family thing, and—"

"No, she's right," Sam says, suddenly wanting Jake to stay. If that's the way Melissa wants to play, Sam can fucking well play it. "I'd actually like to ask you some questions, Jake. I was going to ask Melissa, but, seeing as you're here—"

Leslie would be losing it at him right now. Another good reason why she wasn't here.

"Don't you fucking dare," Melissa hisses, leaning forward. "You aren't at work. You aren't *questioning* him."

"Didn't say I was, I said I'd like to ask questions, there's a difference—"

"What? What about? What do you suddenly want to know about Jake? You've never asked anything before." Super defensive. Melissa always was a terrible liar, despite a staggering amount of practice.

Sam's heart breaks. He hadn't wanted to believe the worst, the final straw, but Melissa's classic *what, what* told him everything he needed. This was it. He couldn't let her hurt Leslie anymore. They'd failed their daughter in the worst way, but it was Melissa who had banged in the final nails. Like she'd said herself: she was an adult now.

"You know what about," Sam says, and as he sniffs back tears he sees Melissa's screwed-up bulldog expression soften, *just for a moment*, and in there is the little girl he'd delighted with a surprise trip to Center Parcs when she was six. Then the gate falls again and Adult Melissa is fully behind the wheel. The liar. The thief.

"Grandma's necklaces."

"What *about* Grandma's necklaces?"

It's utterly unconvincing. With that sentence Sam feels something profound break off inside him and begin to float away. It leaves a hole that will never fully heal over. Shrink a little—maybe even a lot over the years—but never reconstruct.

"Was it for you?" Sam says, addressing the piece of shit as a flood of sadness automatically switches to anger, as so often with men. "Did you put her up to it? How much did you even *get* for them—"

"Dad!"

"*I'm talking to* him—"

"I'm gonna go," the POS says, face flushed, already abandoning his girlfriend, of course. "You guys, uh, you—"

"*Dad, what the fuck do you think you*—"

"Hey," says the man behind the counter, finally waking up, "can you take this outside, I have customers here!" Sam isn't listening, he's already rounding the table, heading after the piece of shit, flushed now himself, not thinking, but of course he really knows *exactly* what he's doing. Sam's always-on-the-details eye notices that the suited man still hasn't moved, although even more of the paper has now been torn away and . . . is he *crying?*—

Sam's hand grabs the piece of shit's retreating shoulder and Melissa screams. Part of Sam knows this will destroy any remaining hope of a reconciliation with his daughter, but perhaps that's exactly why he's doing it. Rubber-stamping the moment. This was the one thing he'd told himself *must not happen* if Jake turned up, and here he was deciding to—

The POS spins round and slaps Sam's hand off him, shoving Sam away as he does, an action that gives Sam's thick fist the instinctive excuse it's so very hungry for. Sam isn't a big man at 5'9", but he's always had big hands, ones he knew how to use once upon a time. His muscle memory is good, it seems; all the anger, the hurt, and of course the thing that's really behind it all—the knowledge that he let this happen to Melissa and how she's become completely alien to him—shoots down Sam's arm and empties beautifully into Jake's nose. *Smack.*

Jake, Melissa, and the man behind the counter all cry out at the impact—Melissa's is a screech so high Sam almost expects the windows to shatter—and Melissa barges past to get to her boyfriend. Jake's already getting up, a shaking backwards lurch intended to get him as far away from Sam as possible, but the red mist is already leaving Sam's brain and he's realizing just what he's done. It was out of his control, it had just taken him over—

No. He knew what he was doing.

"*Fuck you!*" Melissa yells, bundling Jake towards the door as Sam opens his fists, holding them out to her stupidly. "*Fuck you! You aren't my dad! You aren't my dad!*"

Sam opens his mouth to say *Melissa, wait...* and then doesn't say a word. He just stands there, a storm blowing in his brain that blocks out all thoughts. His pulse beats, hard, and he falls back against the nearest table. His hands are shaking. He watches through the fogged-up windows of the café as Melissa and Jake hurry down the street.

Leslie is going to... Sam thinks. *She'll...*

But how *will* Leslie react? She must have known this was going to happen, or something like it. They both did.

He looks up towards the suited man and now it's Sam's turn to scream.

The suited man is no longer sitting in the chair. There's the detritus he's left on the table, but that isn't what Sam's looking at, even as he hears the man behind the counter make a strangled sound, repeating *ahhk... ahhk... ahhk.* He hears movement as the woman comes out from the back once more.

"What the hell—*OH MY GOD! OH MY GOD!*"

Tables screech as they are flung aside. Sam dives sideways on autopilot, trying to get to a chair that he can swing even as his mind curls up into a ball and gibbers in terror. His big hands grasp two of the nearest chair's legs and he spins round, barely able to hold it, but the attacker has already darted straight to its target: the couple behind the counter.

"*RUN KELLY, RU—*" the man bellows, but it's already too late. The attack is so *fast*, his throat's torn open before he can even finish his sentence. Blood sprays across the room as the man is flung aside and though Sam's legs are telling him to take the man's advice he tries to get to the counter, raising his weapon high, a man wading through water as he attempts to get around the cluster of overturned tables and chairs between him and the woman. She makes a critical mistake, moving out towards Sam—automatically seeking protection, perhaps?—and not towards the back room. Her screams of dismay for her murdered partner—and terror for herself—hit a pitch even higher than Melissa's earlier shriek and Sam knows it's too late. It's a cry of agony as she's torn from crotch to sternum. Bellowing, Sam throws the chair. It misses wildly, shattering the mirror by the counter, and unless Sam can get to another one *right away* he's dead, the speed of the attacker is insane, he probably only has a second or two—

Sam clutches another chair and jerks up with a cry—*AH!*—ready to swing for dear life, thinking only of Leslie now, but he sees he's now alone in the café. The only sound is the tinny, now blood-spattered radio playing away to itself, and Sam's I'm-going-to-start-working-out-this-year breathing. He jumps backwards, eyes frantically sweeping the floor; the attacker's down under the tables!

The attacker is not.

The back room, an exit! While he was looking around for a chair—

He hesitates, light-headed. Spots dance before his eyes. Something shoots down his arm. Wait, is this—

It is. It's really happening. His heart finally rebels after too many steak dinners with a nice red; he drops to one knee as the chair he's holding clatters to the floor. He grunts, trying to stay conscious, fumbling his phone from his pocket. If he doesn't get someone out to him, he's going to die. No one will ever know what the hell happened here. *Leslie* will never know—

"Emergency, which service?"

At that moment, his brain catches up. *Well bloody hell*, it says, like a drunk wandering in after the fight scene. *What on earth did I miss?*

It's not possible. It's just not.

With that, as Sam grunts out the name of the café, holding on—quite literally—for dear life, he's already making a decision, even if he doesn't consciously know it: *all this didn't happen*. He'll give the description of the suited man and how the couple at the counter were butchered, but he'll leave out certain elements. If someone were to know the truth and ask him why he chose this approach, he'd maybe tell them his family had just been shattered, that it was too much to deal with. Or that he had his eyes on promotion and didn't want anything on his record that might jeopardize that. Good, reasonable explanations.

The truth would be that Sam is simply scared out of his mind, and attempting to file the unspeakable away is the only option available to his psyche.

He wouldn't be alone in such thinking. Things have been this way for a very long time after all, and thus mutually beneficial for all parties involved.

Sam will eventually begin to believe his own story, so much so that when the sleepless nights and terrifying dreams come, he and Leslie—and not Melissa, of course—will put it down to job-related stress and get him onto a course of antidepressants. They'll help, a little. Sam will still retire early without ever truly knowing why, and he will never make sergeant.

He will still enjoy his simple pleasures, and a peaceful life.

CONTINUED IN *YOU SEE THE MONSTER*, AVAILABLE ON AMAZON NOW

March of the Stone Men

Current list of Smithereens with Titles

If you'd like one yourself, just drop me a line at lukesmitherd.com, but please try and keep it fairly local. No more entire states, countries or counties! You power-mad swines!! ☺

Emil: King of the Macedonian Smithereens; Neil Novita: Chief Smithereen of Brooklyn; Jay McTyier: Derby City Smithereen; Ashfaq Jilani: Nawab of the South East London Smithereens; Jason Jones: Archduke of lower Alabama; Betty Morgan: President of Massachusetts Smithereens; Malinda Quartel Qoupe: Queen of the Sandbox (Saudi Arabia); Marty Brastow: Grand Poobah of the LA Smithereens; John Osmond: Captain Toronto; Nita Jester Franz: Goddess of the Olympian Smithereens; Angie Hackett: Keeper of Du; Colleen Cassidy: The Tax Queen Smithereen; Jo Cranford: The Cajun Queen Smithereen; Gary Johnayak: Captain of the Yellow Smithereen; Matt Bryant: the High Lord Dominator of South Southeast San Jose; Rich Gill: Chief Executive Smithereen - Plymouth Branch; Sheryl: Shish the Completely Sane Cat Lady of Silver Lake; Charlie Gold: Smithereen In Chief Of Barnet; Gord Parlee: Prime Transcendent Smithereen, Vancouver Island Division; Erik Hundstad: King Smithereen of Norway(a greedy title but I've allowed it this once); Sarah Hirst: Official Smithereen Knitter of Nottingham; Christine Jones: Molehunter Smithereen Extraordinaire, Marcie Carole Spencer: Princess Smithereen of Elmet, Angela Wallis: Chief Smithereen of Strathblanefield, Melissa Weinberger: Cali Girl Smithereen, Maria Batista: Honorable One and Only Marchioness Smithereen of Her House, Bash Badawi: Lead Smithereen of Tampa, Fl, Bully: Chief Smithereen of Special Stone Masonry Projects, Mani: Colonel Smithereen of London, Drewboy of the Millwall Smithereens, Empress Smithereen of Ushaw Moor, Cate1965: Queen Smithereen of her kitchen, Amy Harrison: High Priestess Smithereen of Providence County (RI), and Neil Stephens: Head of the Woolwellian Sheep Herding Smithereens, Chief Retired British Smithereen Living in Canada, L and M Smith - Lord Smithereen of Gray Court, SC, Jude, Lady Smithereen of Wellesbourne, Joan, the Completely Inappropriate Grandma of Spring Hill, Vaughan Harris - Archbishop of Badass, Rebekah Jones Viceroy Smithereen of Weedon Bec, Avon Perry - Duchess of Heartbreak and Woe, Dawnie, Lady cock knocker of whangarei land, Renee - Caffeinated Queen of the Texas Desert, Carly - Desk Speaker Fake Plant Monitor AirPods Glass of Vimto, John Bate - Infringeur Smithereen of Blackpool, Stephen Stewart - Smithereen of Outer Space, DWFG "Abbess of the Craggy Island Smithereen High Order, Dave Carver - Chief Smithereen of Big Orange Country, Drucilla Buckley - Queen Mawmaw Smithereen, Adele - Mistress of her house and all within it (even the cat) Spanish chapter, David Coykendall – Twixton - A Necessary Evil, Tracey Galloway-Lindsey - Joffers the bastard a spaceworm in the Shire Smithereen, Jameson Skaife - Smithereen Caped Captain of Chicago and Pablo Starscraper - Purple Lord of Dorchester, Shara Turley - The Bloody Queen of The Flower Mound Smithereen Scene, and Christy Sawyer - The Most Smithereen Piano Teacher Ever.

Printed in Great Britain
by Amazon